Mob Saint

The O'Rourke Brotherhood

Sabine Barclay

OLIVERHEBERBOOKS

Mob Saint Copyright 2024 © Sabine Barclay

Cover art by Dar Albert at Wicked Smart Designs

Published by Oliver Heber Books

0 9 8 7 6 5 4 3 2 1

"Saints are sinner who kept on going."
~ Robert Louis Stevenson

Find me writing Historical Romance as Celeste Barclay.

Happy reading,
Sabine

Subscribe to Sabine's Newsletter

Subscribe to Sabine's bimonthly newsletter to receive exclusive insider perks.

Have you read *The Syndicate Wars*? This FREE origin story novella is available to all new subscribers to Sabine's monthly newsletter. Subscribe on her website.
www.sabinebarclay.com

The O'Rourke Brotherhood

Mob Boss

Mob Star

Mob Princess

Mob Saint

Mob Bride

Mob Knight

Chapter One

Seamus

I twist my seat to look at my brother as we wait for the prosecution to call their next witness. We've been at this for four days, and the end of this arson case may never come. Cormac—our organization's corporate lawyer—and I—our criminal defense one—rarely sit together in a courtroom. Not in the gallery and not before a judge. It's usually not good press for us to both show up.

But in this case, the DOJ is going after a corporation we just gained in a hostile takeover. They aim to show just how hostile it was. They have a hard-on to prove our family's venture capitalist firm guilty *to discourage business practices that would permit or promote unlawful conduct at the expense of the public interest.* The prosecution would love for this case to be more than just a slap on the wrists since it involves arson.

They think they've found the crack in my family's armor and want to drill a hole to rip it off. Fat fucking chance. Between Cormac and me, we have our family's interests so

1

guarded they're slicker than "Teflon Don" Gotti. That mother-fucker. Humility goes a long way with tax evasion, loanshark-ing, illegal gambling, racketeering, extortion, and obstruction of justice. Never mind the successful murders along with the attempts that put him away. We know our limits and work within them. That's why this case is going nowhere. They're fishing, and their nets keep coming up empty.

"Who's this? I've never heard of Tiernan Furey."

I point to the updated witness list. The prosecution didn't disclose this guy's name during the lead up to the trial. Appar-ently, the prosecution thinks they've found a way to impeach testimony from a witness they called who flipped on them. The guy discovered his twenty-seven-year-old son might need dental implants if he got his answers wrong. But the feds think they have a way to prove our guy lied under oath.

"I don't know. I haven't heard of him either, but he's repre-senting the insurance company, so this ought to be good. They're just as pissed as the DOJ since they can't prove we don't deserve that massive insurance payout they can't force us to return any time soon."

I sit back and watch the judge, but I can see Benedict Hofs-tadter from the corner of my eye. His parents clearly thought he was an ugly arse baby when he was born to stick him with that name. Dict—Dick. Pretty much.

"I would like to call Tiernan Furey to the stand as the pros-ecution's sixth witness, your honor."

To say I'm unprepared for the person who walks between the counsels' tables is a comical understatement. I can sense my brother's surprise since I feel it too. But I don't think Cor's as stunned by the woman as I am. My cock just twitched. Fuck.

From the corner of my mouth, I mutter without my lips moving. "A woman?"

Tiernan is about as good an Irish name as you can get. But

it's a man's name. At least, usually it is. The woman's gorgeous, but the stare she's fixed upon me makes her last name fit. Furey. In English, it might suggest heat or fire. Nope. In Irish Gaelic, it means cold or frosty. It comes from Ó Fuaráin. I took a strong interest in Gaelic history when I was a kid. I wanted to learn all the "real" versions of Irish names. I remember learning that one. I'll definitely remember her.

"Ms. Furey, did your employer assign you to the insurance claim filed for what remained of the RK Capital Group's building?"

"Yes, they did."

RK Capital. I want to grin every time I hear that name. The Kutsenkos merged RK Capital with their venture capital company, Kutsenko Partners, then acquired RK about four years ago when Maksim met his now wife. They planned to tear it apart and divvy it up to make shell corps. But antitrust laws kept them from doing that. Maksim's cousins were involved in fucking over my cousin Dillan's wife while they were dating. Payback's a bitch.

"Can you share with the court why you've been called here today as an expert witness?"

"I'm an actuary for Midlands Grant Insurance. Before this position, I was a fire investigator for the city of Trenton, New Jersey."

If I'd ever let my emotions show, she'd see my left eye twitch. But my face is as stoic as it always is in court—unless I'm charming the jury. Then I'm all smiles when I need to be and near tears when I want to manipulate the fuck out of them. A fresh from the motherland name and from Trenton. Cormac and I know exactly who sent her. Our knees move at the same time and bump beneath the table. Our legs are long enough that no one looking toward us could tell we're acknowledging our shared realization.

3

Gareth O'Brien.

The head of the Trenton mob. Our vassal. Our bitch.

Fucking Welsh name.

No wonder Tiernan is looking at us. She wants us to know who sent her. How convenient she wound up on this case. The real question I wish I could ask during cross examination is what the fuck does that douchebag want?

"Ms. Furey, could you please explain how you gained your expertise?"

"I began as a junior volunteer firefighter when I was fourteen. When I turned eighteen, I became a fully certified firefighter. When I returned to my hometown on breaks and over the summer, I took shifts. I attended John Jay College of Criminal Justice and earned a BS in Fire Science. After college, I worked for Trenton Fire Department for four years. During that time, I gained my certifications to become a fire investigator, and I earned a Master of Science in Applied Mathematics. For the past two years, I've been an insurance actuary specializing in fire damage."

My leg presses harder against Cor's. That's where he went to college, and my guess is she's around our age at thirty-two. I don't expect him to know everyone who went to that college, but we kept a close eye on anyone syndicate affiliated when we were at school. No one wanted to get shanked in their dorm room.

"Can you share with the court the additional credentials you earned?"

"I hold certifications from the International Association of Arson Investigators, the National Association of Fire Investigators, the National Board of Fire Service Professionals, and the Forensics Specialties Accreditation Board. I'm a member of the American Academy of Forensic Science, and I've worked with the Forensics Specialties Accreditation Board."

"So, you've worked in this field for sixteen years?"

"Eighteen."

"Apologies. During your time in the field as an arson investigator and now as an actuary, what is the likelihood of an office building catching fire at night while not even the custodial crew is present?"

"Thirty-one percent of office fires occur between seven p.m. and seven a.m."

"What is the leading cause of these fires?"

"Office kitchen equipment followed by electrical."

"What caused the fire that destroyed the RK Capital Group building?"

"Objection, your honor." I'm out of my chair like a jack-in-the-box. "Calls for speculation. The prosecution has not established Ms. Furey's presence at the scene, let alone her examination."

Here we go. This is where they expect to impeach the witness who flopped around like a beached bass.

"Sustained." The judge is quick to decide.

"Ms. Furey, what did you find at the scene when you examined it?"

"Objection, your honor. Calls for speculation. The prosecution hasn't established when Ms. Furey or at what stage she examined the area in question."

"Sustained." The judge is already looking annoyed, but she's looking at Dickster.

Dickie is staring at me like he's the one who'd commit murder, not me. I watch him clench his jaw then catch himself before he turns back to his witness.

"Ms. Furey, when did you visit the scene?"

"Forty-eight hours after the department extinguished it."

"What measures were already in place by the fire department to analyze the scene?"

"The New York City Fire Department already had their crime scene investigators examine the area for any evidence of human remains. The fire department's inspector had done a cursory and a more extensive search for the cause."

"What were the fire inspector's findings about the fire's cause?"

"It was likely an electrical problem with one of the perimeter fan-coiled units for the central heated and cooled water system."

Likely.

"What evidence led the inspector to that conclusion?"

"There appeared to be unnatural wear on the unit, suggesting someone tampered with it while attempting to make it appear like it was simply an old piece of equipment that had worn out."

"That contradicts the testimony we heard yesterday by a member of the New York Fire Department. That witness claimed it was an issue with a stove in an office kitchen. You're testifying with your expertise that an electrical unit that had been tampered with caused the fire. Is that correct?"

"Objection, your honor. Calls for hearsay."

Dickie spins toward me. "It does not."

I cock an eyebrow. He sounds like the whiney bitch he is. I look at the judge and raise both eyebrows.

"Explain, Mr. O'Rourke."

"The prosecution asked the witness for what the fire inspector led her to believe. He did not establish that she came to the conclusion the prosecution is prompting by her own examination. The prosecution wishes Ms. Furey to make a claim that she's repeating and pass it off as her own sworn statement. Hearsay, your honor."

At the least. Let's plant the seed that the prosecution is inept or trying to dupe the jury.

"Sustained. Let's move this along, Mr. Hofstadter."

"Ms. Furey, did you examine the scene personally and gather evidence?"

"I did."

"What evidence did you find to support the fire inspector's theory?"

It's not a theory, fuck nut. You can't establish a theory until you prove a hypothesis. Basic sixth grade scientific method. You haven't proven shite that Tiernan even came to a conclusion, let alone used evidence to base it.

"The age of the water heating and cooling system didn't match the amount of wear visible on what remained of the fan-coiled unit. It was excessive."

"How could that happen?"

"Abrasive chemicals stored near it. Poor installation. Someone tampering with it."

"Which of those happened?"

"I think it's likely someone tampered with it."

"Thank you, Ms. Furey. That will be all."

The judge shifts her gaze to me, and I stand. Cormac hands me his phone because he must have found something when he looked Tiernan up. I glance down.

"Good afternoon, Ms. Furey. Or perhaps I should say, *tráth-nóna maith.*" I turn to the jury. "That means good afternoon in Irish Gaelic."

Trah-no-na-mah.

It's a tongue twister to figure out if you see it written, but I'm certain Tiernan's heard the phrase plenty of times. She doesn't bat an eyelash at it. She expects this. Good to know. Gareth prepped her. Let the jury think I'm a douche for expecting her to understand Irish because she has an Irish name. That's if they even know it is one.

"You have an extensive list of credentials, Ms. Furey. None

7

are quick to complete. With all the time taken up by school, you haven't had more than a couple years cumulatively in the field, have you?"

"I've been in the industry for eighteen years."

"If the court will bear with me, Ms. Furey, please walk me through this. Four years as a junior firefighter, so not actually fighting fires. Four in college, so not full-time. Two years in grad school, so not full-time. Three years in insurance."

I hold up four fingers, then four more, my two thumbs, and another three fingers from the first hand as I count aloud.

"Thirteen years, so five years in the field. Four of those as a full-time firefighter but not a full-time investigator. So, cumulatively, you've only spent a couple years in the field investigating full-time, haven't you?"

"No. Eighteen years is eighteen years, Mr. O'Rourke."

"In occupations such as yours, isn't experience usually counted in hours?"

"Yes."

"To become a certified fire investigator, it's two years with three-hundred hours of coursework, and one-hundred crime scenes. Of those one-hundred, how many were you the lead investigator?"

Cormac had zoomed in on that when I looked at his phone. He was fast to find the training requirements.

"None."

"Because you weren't yet certified, were you?"

"No."

"Then let's check the math again. Out of five years in the field, you spent two in training. We know you were a full-time firefighter for four of those years. With a two-year program, that means only one to two years investigating without an instructor, isn't that right?"

"That does not negate the more than four-hundred-and-fifty scenes I've investigated between my certification and as a fully qualified, full-time investigator."

"No, it does not. But it means you haven't led that many investigations. The findings from those four-hundred-and-fifty scenes weren't yours alone, were they?"

"No. But—"

"But we're to accept your finding in this case, by your word alone, when you went to a cold scene that was forty-eight hours old. Is that right?"

"The fire inspector went before me, so I wasn't the only person to review the scene or the evidence."

"But an inspector is less qualified than an investigator, correct?"

"Yes, but—"

"So, with your insufficient experience and his even lesser qualifications, we're to accept the accuracy of your expert testimony. Is that correct?"

"Objection, your honor. Badgering the witness."

Tiernan doesn't look remotely badgered. Just the opposite. That last name fits better than ever. She's detached, professional, and likely to shoot me without blinking an eye if she's even remotely connected to Gareth O'Brien.

"One of us needs to establish credibility, your honor." *Or the lack of it.*

No part of me thinks she's truly unqualified to testify. No part of me likes what I'm doing. But if liking myself determined most of my actions, I'd be dead a thousand times over by the ripe old age of thirty-two.

"Overruled, Mr. Hofstadter. Mr. O'Rourke, the ice upon which you skate is cracking. I wouldn't fall through if I were you."

"Yes, your honor. I'm nearly through." I turn back to Tiernan. "Earlier, you answered Mr. Hofstadter's question with 'I think it's likely someone tampered with it.' If it's only likely, then there's at least one, if not an indefinite number of other explanations. Is that correct?"

"Yes."

"And you think, *not know*, correct?"

"One thinks before one knows, Mr. O'Rourke. I've given this plenty of thought, so I know that building did not catch fire on its own."

"But you don't know how, do you?" She hesitates. I risk actually badgering. "Do you, Ms. Furey?"

I cock an eyebrow while I wait. Smug arsehole that I am.

"I'm confident someone who's knowledgeable of electrical wiring, building construction, and fire behavior intentionally started the fire. There are few people with that experience—"

"Just yes or no, Ms. Furey."

I want that last statement dangling in the air, even though I know she didn't intend what she said to support my arguments.

"No, I do not, Mr. O'Rourke."

"No more questions, your honor."

"Redirect, Mr. Hofstadter?"

"The prosecution requests the right to recall the witness."

"Granted. Ms. Furey, the court thanks you for your time. You may step down."

The judge waits for Tiernan to leave the witness box. She walks toward the gallery, keeping her eyes straight ahead as she passes me.

"It is nearly five o'clock. Court shall adjourn until nine tomorrow morning."

Court ends for the day with a heavy rap of the gavel. I want nothing more than to swivel my seat and discover whether Tiernan is still in the courtroom or if she beat a hasty retreat. The next best thing would be to turn to Cormac, but I won't until the jury leaves. Neither of us says a word until there's no one in front of us. We aren't the only people in the world who can read lips, and loose lips sink ships.

"You asking her out?" Cor smirks at me, and I'd throat punch him if he weren't my brother. Tempting, nonetheless.

We have cousins, Sean and Shane, who are identical in every way. Looks, mannerisms, the way they sound, walk, and stand. People outside the family can only tell them apart by the freckle on Sean's throat. Cormac and I look different enough to tell us apart by more than a birthmark. But not by much. When he's smug, it's like looking in a mirror. He's only seven months older than me since I was a preemie. We're closer than Irish twins.

"Can I sleep at your place tonight? She's more likely to gut me than say yes. And I don't date."

"I didn't say you would ask her out on a date. I think you'd asked her out to do something entirely different from dinner and a movie."

"Feck off."

Our parents would skelp our arses if we ever really swore at each other. Not between brothers and not among the cousins. The twins have an older brother, Finn. And we all share our cousin, Dillan. Three sisters married three brothers. Even if we weren't the mob, we'd be a close family.

"You never know. She might be into it."

I glare at my brother. I am not asking a witness I don't know to do anything with me. It's utterly unethical. I'm not asking a woman I don't know to fuck me at a sex club. That's utterly pervy.

"Let's go. We need to brief Dillan."

Chapter Two

Tiera

Fucking asshole.

Gareth can suck a dick. I told him it was a shit idea to get me involved in the arson case, and it was a fucktastrophe getting me on the prosecution's witness list. I would have done better testifying on behalf of the defendant. I just told him that for at least the fifth time in a week as I walk to the soccer pitch.

I looked like a fucking idiot on the stand last week, and I deserved it. But what the fuck am I supposed to do when my third cousin twice removed, who happens to be my uncle's best friend because my family tree is so fucking tangled that all three of us are nearly the same age, tells me to take my fat ass to the U.S. Attorney's office?

That earned him a threatened fist to his dick. It was a douche move, and he knows it. That's why he said it Some really shitty shit's happened to me in the last three years, and I've eaten my feelings. He thinks tormenting me by reminding me of the worst time of my life will make me give in just to make him stop talking. It used to. Now I simply walk away, hang up the phone, or ignore his texts. Let the asshole chase me before I agree to do jack shit for him.

He volunteered me as an expert witness for a case I was only tangentially involved in originally. Volunteered me before I even knew there was a fire clients would file an insurance claim for. That cross examination went better than I expected. Seamus O'Rourke only somewhat humiliated me after backing me into a corner.

If he weren't the hottest man I've ever seen, I'd hold being a douchebag against him. That's probably all the more reason I should since I felt like I ate shit in there in front of the singularly most menacingly attractive man I've ever met.

"Tiernan, are you coming or what?"

"Huh? Let me fasten my shin guard tighter. Give me a sec."

I watch my friend Suze jog onto the field while I screw my head back on straight. I may not be as light on the scale as I was a few years ago, but I'm still light on my feet. I played DIII soccer all four years at John Jay. It's a smaller college, so it's not Division One—the most competitive collegiate division—like Columbia.

Oh, yes. I looked Seamus and Cormac O'Rourke up the moment I got on the subway last week. I know Cormac was at John Jay at the same time as me. Who knew? But Seamus went to Columbia. He and his brother both went to NYU for law school.

I'm no idiot though. I earned my Master of Science in Applied Mathematics at University of Chicago, one of the top programs in the country. Am I overqualified to be an actuary? Yes. Does it come in handy to be able to count to a million? It does when your family's been in the Irish mob for six generations and needs someone clever enough to commit insurance fraud without getting caught.

I pull my sock up and tug on the tongue of my cleat before I jog onto the field. This is my happy place. I was a tomboy. The only girl on the soccer field in elementary school every day before and after school and during lunch. I was the only girl playing indoor soccer during PE in middle school. I was the only girl high school football kicker in my school's league. Football was a fall sport, and girls' soccer was spring. I could kick harder and farther, so they put me on the team. I nearly castrated Gareth when I kicked a football in his nuts for saying I kicked like a girl.

Damn right, motherfucker.

I'm watching my team spread out across our half of the field before kickoff. I'm a left forward, so I take my place on the line. Only then do I look in front of me to scout the team we're scrimmaging against. I nearly miss the whistle.

Pull yer heed out of yer arse, lass.

I had a brawny Scottish Highlander for a coach in college. She played center forward and was a battering ram well into her early sixties. I need to take a lesson from her and focus.

Whether it's moving the ball directly toward the goal or kicking it back to a center midfielder, the objective is clear. I watch our kicker draw his foot back like he's going to take a straight shot forward, but at the last minute before the whistle, his foot moves to look like he's going to do a pass back. That's not our strategy.

The kicker taps it to the player between us, who passes it to me. That gives my team the opportunity to surge forward. In the seconds it takes for me to get the ball, I scan for the openings and where my teammates move. I'm left-footed, which throws people off even more. I see who's barreling toward me, so I put all the force I can muster into the kick, the ball barely whizzing past my opponent's left ear.

I take off forward, swerving around the behemoth who

looks ready to murder me. If we were both trying to gain control of the ball, I'd have no issue shoulder checking the guy who's close to a foot taller than me but likely only forty pounds heavier than me.

"Keep up, O'Rourke."

Seamus was not who I thought I'd stand face-to-face with today. He is not the person I thought I'd pair off with at kickoff. But his position leaves him in a midfield defensive spot as I charge toward his team's goal, since I'm a striker. I keep weaving until I'm even with our center forward, who passes it to me. I dribble around a woman who looks like she's evenly matched with my skill. We tangle as we collide.

Okay, then. Game on, bitches.

She goes for my ankle on purpose, and it hurts like hell. Unlike in men's soccer, I'm not falling on the ground crying like a cranky toddler. This is a coed league with at least three women per team on the field at kickoff. I hip check her, which is usually illegal, but I know where the ref is, and he can't see. I sweep the ball between her feet, and I'm off to the races again. I have this pathological need to score the first goal. I don't need to evaluate my life and take stock. I don't need time for self-reflection.

I want to show Seamus O'Rourke that he seriously under-estimated me if he thinks humiliating me in court will make me shy away. Thinking about the trial might have distracted me as I came onto the field, but not anymore. I have a competitive streak that runs a mile wide and a mile deep. Even if I didn't want to prove something to him, I'd still be just as driven.

"One-two." I call out the signal when I'm forced to pass the ball. I cross the field to switch places with our other flank striker, and it gets me where I really belong, leaving my defender confused since he no longer has an opponent in front of him. I don't need to tell my teammate to switch it—send the ball across the pitch to me—or set it—give me the ball; I'm ready to take the shot.

We know this play. It comes sailing through the air toward me. I've been doing this since I was a kid. The motions are intuitive now. Even with center backs pressing in, I'm ready. No one expects the chunky girl to move with my ease. The guy coming straight at me is about to eat cleat if he doesn't pay attention as I push off my right foot. He lurches away as my left foot makes contact in a scissor kick.

High right corner. The goalie didn't have time to realize where I would aim since there aren't too many left-footed kickers who go airborne to shoot. I land hard when the guy misses my foot, but momentum carries him forward. I was going to fall anyway, but he lands on top of me. I take an elbow to the boob.

Fuck me.

A sports bra is not a boob guard. We wear shin guards, and a lot of guys wear cups. I need one of those steel breast plates like Athena wears in so many paintings. I roll to my right as the guy's weight suddenly disappears. The sun's behind the giant looming over me, making his hair look aflame. Seamus sticks his hand out to me and practically drops the guy beside me. He must have lifted his teammate with one hand. He's shockingly gentle as he pulls me to my feet.

"Are you all right, *cailín?*"

Little girl. Hardly.

I narrow my eyes at him. "I'm fine."

His eyebrows shoot up when I snap at him. He's still holding my hand, so he gives it a tug, making me take a step forward.

"I'm close to ten inches taller than you, and my back is twice as broad. I just pulled a guy who easily weighs two-ten off you. You're little compared to me, *mo cailín.*"

My little girl.

What is he getting at? I stiffen as I pull my hand from his.

"You're not funny." I barely get the words out since I'm still winded. The two I said earlier took all my might because I didn't want him to know I'm the opposite of fine. My ribs hurt like a mother.

I step around him and jog back to the center line. I can't help the instinct to cover my left ribs when the sharp pain shoots around to my kidney. I get back to my team's side and walk to my spot. I truly walk it off. The rest of the game carries on just as it started. I don't make every goal. I'm not a ball hog. But the final score is four-one to us.

The shadow is back as I gingerly raise my arm and my shirt to look at my left side. No wonder it hurts. I don't expect a bottle shoved under my nose. I pull my head back, and it lands against a muscular pec. I look over my shoulder, and I might drool. He was hot across a courtroom. He was gorgeous standing across the line from me at each kickoff. He was drop-dead when he helped me up. But he's Adonis as he stands this close to me. My pussy clenches as his arms wrap around me, his free hand easing my shirt down.

"If I keep looking at those bruises, I might kill him. Arnica." He shakes the small bottle of herbal remedy to rub on injuries.

"Thank you. And it was an accident. He didn't expect that I could do that."

"Then he'd be an idiot. But he wasn't. He did it on purpose."

I hear anger in Seamus's voice, but his expression doesn't show it. He's letting me know he's pissed, but he doesn't want the rest of the world to know. I turn toward him and keep my voice low.

"I promise I'm all right. Yeah, it's bruised, and I'll be sore in the morning. But it's not a big deal, Seamus. Please, let it go."

When a man like Seamus says he'll kill someone, you know he's not exaggerating until he proves otherwise. Our gazes meet, and I've never seen eyes the shade of his. They are truly emerald. It's my birthstone, and I have a ring with one. It's like looking at it right after I've polished it. They're positively brilliant.

"You have the most unique eyes, *cailín*."

The wall goes up, and I spin around. "Thank you for this."

I reach for my gym bag and tuck the bottle of arnica away in the pocket. I won't look a gift horse in the mouth. It'll help with the bruising. I sense him back up more than see him. I swing the bag onto my shoulder as I shift to step around him.

"Wait, Tiernan."

I swallow my aggrieved sigh.

"I'm sorry about court. I didn't enjoy it."

I close my eyes for an extended blink as I shake my head. "You were doing your job. It was embarrassing, and I won't sign up to do it again. But it was what it was."

His brow furrows, and I can tell he's retreating. He's not the mobster he was a moment ago. He's the gentle giant who helped me to my feet and was careful not to touch my ribs when he pulled down my shirt. He was both when he did that —a gentle giant mobster. That's an oxymoron if ever there were one. Right up there with giant shrimp.

"It was presumptuous of me to call you by anything other than your name. I'm sorry for that, too."

"You're being nice to me now, so why do you ruin it by teasing me?"

I didn't mean to say that. I meant to accept his apology and leave. I meant to hide how much it bothers me. I meant to walk away and not look back.

"I never teased you. I don't understand."

He's genuinely baffled. I can't help it. I chuckle. But he

retreats even more. He hasn't moved a muscle, but I can tell. His gaze changes. It's like a curtain just dropped, and I can't tell anything about what he's thinking. I don't explain fast enough because he steps back farther.

"I shouldn't have said anything then or now. Put the arnica on three times a day for a few days. Again, I'm sorry."

"You don't even know what you're apologizing for."

"I might not know exactly what I've done, but it's obvious I've offended you. I didn't intend to, so I'm sorry for that."

He glances around. We're two of the last people on the pitch. It's dusk, and I want to head home to soak in a hot bath. He nods before turning toward the bench with a bag still on it.

"Thank you, Seamus. The arnica and helping me up were kind." Even if you made me feel shitty the rest of the time.

"You're welcome, Tiernan."

I gather my stuff and head toward the gate. I notice he's slow to gather his own gear and put it in his bag. I head out toward the subway stop, and I hear him behind me. I turn the corner to find the woman who kicked me in the ankle and the guy who landed on me talking.

"You know it's just a club sport, not the Olympics." The woman's gaze runs up and down me, and it's obvious she doesn't think I'd make it to the Olympics. That just makes the insult worse since she's implying I'm not as good as I think I am.

I nod and step off the sidewalk, but they turn to follow me. Are we in high school, and they're meeting me behind the bleachers to fight?

"She just got lucky, Emily. You know she was showing off for O'Rourke. Trying to impress him." He looks me up and down with a mocking smile. "You're not his type."

"She doesn't need to try. She impressed me ages ago, Randy."

Seamus's hand is light as he rests it on my hip. It's on my

uninjured side. He's mindful of how he touches me. But his hand tightens when he senses I'm about to step back on the sidewalk. He's practically in the middle of the road.

He did that to protect me.

It dawns on me he isn't just coming to my defense. He's physically shielding me from cars getting too close. He doesn't want me to move because then he can't keep his arm around me. There isn't enough room on the sidewalk for him to step up without bumping into Emily. He doesn't want me closer to them, even though we all know they wouldn't do anything to me. I don't believe they'd do more than insult me if he wasn't there.

"Go home. I'll speak to you in the morning, Randy."

The guy goes ashen in a heartbeat. He gives a jerky nod before he grabs Emily's hand and practically drags her away. I step onto the sidewalk, and he follows me. I look up at him, confused.

"He used to work for me."

"How long ago?"

"Until two minutes ago."

Chapter Three

Seamus

I watch Tiernan's head swing in Randy and Emily's direction before looking back up at me.

"Oh."

She knows what I am. She knows what that means. I keep telling myself that. As a reassurance—I guess. I don't know why it's so important that I reiterate it to no one but me.

"You don't need to speak to him in the morning. I don't want that." She shakes her head.

"I won't whack him. I'm not even going to beat him up. But he is going to tell his grandma what he said."

"His grandma?"

"Yes. She's terrifying."

"What?" Her brow furrows into deep lines that disappear when she relaxes.

"His grandmother is eighty-six and still walks three miles a day no matter the weather. She's also as devout as the Virgin Mary. When she finds out he insulted you, she won't have it.

Nothing I could do would be worse than what Sally MacMillan will come up with, I promise you that. She was my fourth-grade teacher."

"Emily wasn't wrong, though. I was way more competitive than I needed to be. It was a scrimmage, not even an actual game."

"But the point of scrimmages is to practice like it's a game to be prepared for when it is. You did nothing wrong."

"Thank you for the absolution, but I still could have dialed it back a few dozen notches."

"I'm glad you didn't." Fuck me.

I tan well, but with my red hair and freckles, I look like a goddamn fire engine when I blush. I can feel the heat radiating from my cheeks. I need to muzzle myself. I can't seem to shut the fuck up around her. She's already made it clear I irritate her. She wanted to leave, and now I'm keeping her here for what? To tempt me with something I can't have.

"Really? I'm pretty sure your other teammates believe what Randy and Emily did. I was over the top."

"You talk to yourself while you play, don't you?"

"How'd you know?" She shifts nervously. I'm prying too much.

"I could tell from the way you looked around. How you'd adjust course as though you were calling out signals but to yourself. You were predicting what would happen whichever way you would go before deciding where to position yourself." I finish with a shrug.

"You played midfield. How could you see all that?"

"Mrs. MacMillan used to say I had eagle eyes because she was sure I could read the answer keys from across the room."

"Could you?"

"Most of the time. But it was because I was tall, and she kept next to nothing on her desk."

"Or you were already learning to observe everything."

I don't respond. We just stare at each other. She knows what I am. There I go again, but I keep ignoring my own warnings.

"Goodnight, Seamus."

"Goodnight, *cai*—Tiernan."

I don't know why she hates me calling her that so much. I don't think it's because I'm a presumptuous arsehole for doing it. It's the word itself that bothers her. But I catch myself in time for only her lips to flatten. Lips I'd love nothing more than to nip and kiss. It was just as well she stepped away from me when she put the arnica in her bag. If she'd moved a hair backwards, she would have felt my hard on. I have my gym bag positioned in front of me to hide the one I have now.

I was attracted to her last week in court. I was hard for her during most of the game—not a comfortable condition to be in when trying to run. I want to maul her now. I want to pull her against me, holding her arse in my hands as I push my cock against her pussy. I want to discover whether she's wet for me. If she is, is she as wet for me as I am hard for her? I doubt that's possible. I've got a fucking iron pole in my shorts, I'm so hard. I need to go home to an icy shower.

I watch her walk to the subway stop, and I'm tempted to follow her to make sure she gets home safely. But I reassure myself she's been getting around on her own for years. Just because I want her doesn't mean she needs me. That's a kick in the balls.

When she disappears down the steps, I head to my car. Tomorrow is gonna suck so hard. And it won't be the kind I'd look forward to with Tiernan's lips wrapped around my cock. It's gonna blow, and not like it would if she were giving me a BJ. And now I'm back to being hard again.

FML.

We're finally to closing arguments. We've slogged through hours of testimony and a slew of evidence. We've endured Dickie Bird prattling for forty-five minutes while he gives his summation. This should be the final hour of this case, and it couldn't finish soon enough. When it's my turn to speak, I stand and button my suit coat before moving around the table to take my position before the people who decide my professional fate as much as my client's.

Every win makes me more frightening to opposing lawyers. Any loss makes me a mockery—a shitty stereotype of mobsters who can't buy their way out of everything.

"Ladies and gentlemen of the jury, it's been a heated case." I grin and turn on the charm as some laugh at my stupid pun. "We've heard evidence from both sides, but not all of it withstood the line of fire."

A few more chuckles as I sweep my gaze over the twelve men and women. Even though Cor and I aren't the youngest in our massive family—Shane and Sean—in that order—are—my brother and I have the baby faces. We're built like a brick shit house—don't know where the comparison to the crapper comes from, but we hear it often—so our size and our youthful faces disconcert people. We like it that way.

We have the lightest hair, closer to our dad's strawberry blond than our mom's russet, so our beards grow in the fairest. We both shave daily, but from a distance you can't tell. It lends us a youthful innocence, so they say. I flex that strength when I need to—like now. I'm likeable.

Even I can't say that with a straight face.

I continue with my oratory I started practicing the night we heard the prosecution's opening statement. I've been fine tuning it every evening, but I do this to make sure I forget nothing from the beginning of the trial when it could be weeks or months before the case concludes. I remind them of evidence entered for both sides and how it proves my client's innocence. What it really proves is the shite job the NYPD does since we tampered the fuck out of almost every piece. I move through my refutation of each witness the prosecution called, including Tiera's.

Tiera. I've been calling her that in my head since we met. I fucked up, calling her *cailín*. I was more careful not to say that pet name out loud the last time I saw her.

I hate ripping her apart, but she was a key witness the prosecution recalled four days after her initial testimony. I'd feared it would be the morning after the soccer game. That's why I'd dreaded the next day. It didn't get better with time.

My recross of her wasn't any lighter than my first cross examination. I know she's in the gallery. I sensed when she came in. Don't ask me how, but it's the instinct that keeps me alive. I turned my head to whisper something to Cormac so I could check. She's sitting in the middle on the prosecution's side. I'm grateful because she isn't in my peripheral vision as I make her out to be unreliable and easily swayed by less qualified people.

I comb through everything said and shown as I weave a tale that neither RK Capital is guilty of insurance fraud, nor is our client guilty of arson. He's one of our guys we planted as a custodian months ago and is guilty as fuck. I want the part about RK on the record for when Cormac goes next and has to defend them against insurance fraud. It's Donny Mahon I'm responsible for getting off the hook here. He's been sitting like a statue throughout the trial. You'd almost forget he was there if not for the tats his dumb arse has on both sides of his neck.

No one outside my immediate family—since we run the

NY Irish mob—needs to know Donny Mahon was once Albert Hannigan, a fire fighter supposedly killed in the line of duty in some bumfuck town outside of Montgomery, Alabama. Genius that he was when he was twenty years younger, he got into a turf fight with a gang in their territory. His dad was friends with my uncle, so Uncle Donovan got him a new name and a new life. He repays that debt by going wherever the hell we send him. Here, it was to use his experience as a firefighter to burn down the RK Capital building by causing an electrical fire after tampering with an office stove.

We made sure a witness—the NYFD guy we flipped— suggested that, but in a way that sounded too obvious for anyone to take seriously. We ruled out the genuine cause—the stove. Then we tightened the reins around the one my opponent pursued—the supposedly tampered with heating and cooling system—knocking his arguments sideways. We planted evidence near the coils to make them look like someone tampered with them, but no one could ever prove they caused the fire because it was the stove all along.

I go through each of the charges, the judge's instructions to the jury, and my explanations for why the prosecution's burden of proof failed. It takes sixty minutes, and I'm ready for some whiskey with my water. I'm parched.

Numb nuts tries to get one last dig in during his rebuttal, but it's too little too late. The jury's already decided. Cor and I write notes on a shared pad of paper. He's a leftie like Finn and Sean—there's one way he differs from his twin—and I'm right-handed like everyone else. He went to a school for criminal justice even though we knew he wanted to practice corporate law. He wanted it for the courses that helped him learn how criminals tick and a juror's psychology. He wasn't stingy with that knowledge, so I learned alongside him. We know just what to say and do inside and outside a courtroom to keep ourselves out of jail and to put the conveniently wrongfully accused—innocent—behind bars for life. Just as often, it's keeping the inconveniently rightfully accused—guilty as fuck—mobster out of jail.

The judge bangs her gavel one last time before jury deliberations begin. I looked for Tiera as I returned to my seat and spotted her immediately. She wouldn't look at me. My heart sank, and it still aches now as I watch her slip out of her row and turn toward the door without a glance in my direction.

"*D'fhéadfá ceist a chur uirthi amach anois.*" You could ask her out now.

My brother is hardly subtle. I glower at him as I pack up my laptop and papers. The bailiff's already led Donny out of the courtroom in handcuffs. Dickwad and his team are still whispering to each other, and I'm not worried anyone can understand. I just don't want to be pushed. She rejected me once. I'm a glutton for punishment when I work out, but not with a woman I'm inexplicably drawn to when she wants nothing to do with me.

"Fine. You going to your club, then?" Cormac continues in Irish for that question since that's not something anyone needs to hear either.

We're all silent part owners in the best—and worst—BDSM clubs in the tri-state area. It pays—truly—to know where people like to act out their kinks. I don't know of a single syndicate member from the Four Families—the Kutsenkos, the Mancinellis, the Diazes, and us—who isn't kinky when they fuck. It's an outlet that balances what we do all too frequently. We have the control we desire from someone consenting to their submission. It's in a controlled and predictable environment. And sex is fun. We just don't need our names on the letterhead while we collect the membership list and plant informants.

"Maybe after the game."

Yeah. It's not a scrimmage this time. I'm not playing a different position, so I'll be staring at Tiera during every kickoff and trying to block her every time she crosses the center line. Everyone in my family—all the men *and* women play rugby. Some families play badminton at picnics. We drink beer and crash into each other in the mud. But we each have sports we've played independent of the family. Most would assume Cor and I played football or wrestled. Nope. Dillan wrestled, Cor swam and played water polo, and I played soccer. People don't believe Cor's buoyant or that I'm agile. We are.

"Earth to Shay."

"Feck off."

"You didn't hear any of what I said, did you?"

"I tuned out. You were boring."

"Do you have plans with Makayla or not?"

"I do." She's who I might go to the club with.

I'm mooning over a woman who isn't interested in me when I don't even date. I have a sub, and we're in a monogamous arrangement. I wouldn't break that to sleep with Tiera or anyone else. I'd end things with Makayla before that happened. But we aren't romantic partners.

She goes out on dates, but she's found no one she'd rather have sex with than me. I haven't gone out at all. We see each other once during the week and usually most of the weekend if I'm not working. I'm certain she's googled me. After all, we have one of the most intimate relationships two people can have. But she's never questioned me or pointed out when I lie about where I am in the three years we've had a contract.

"I gotta go, or I'll be late to the game. I'll call you in the morning."

"Not too early. I'll be at Deirdre's."

Cormac has the same arrangement with a woman he met at our club the same weekend I met Makayla. They're friends.

Neither he nor I bring women to our places. It's not safe or practical. We also like to shut the door to the outside world and be alone.

We've both considered having an apartment just for the time we spend with our subs, but neither of us wants that kind of permanence despite being with our partners for years. No one would live full-time at these imaginary condos, but it feels too much like we're bringing someone home if we own them. We'd rather the noncommittal arrangement of going to their places and leaving when we want.

It's not like we fuck and run. But they aren't romantic relationships, and they're not quite friendships either. We exchange pleasantries beyond how's the weather, but we don't chat. At least, I don't with Makayla. I doubt Cor does with Deirdre.

I nod to my brother. "Have fun. I'll talk to you tomorrow."

"Later. *Mo ghrá thú*." Love you.

"*Grá agat freisin*." Love you, too.

Our parents and aunts and uncles drilled into all of us to say we love each other when we hang up the phone or say goodbye. No one wants the last thing they said to be something other than an expression of love. We don't always end every call with it or even say it instead of goodbye when we're together. But we say it to each other—our cousins included—at least once a day. If anyone understands the fragility of life, it's a mobster. If anyone understands family before all else, it's a mobster.

I turn on my Albanian language program as I head to Queens for the night game. All of us speak more languages than people realize. Spanish and a healthy dose of Yiddish aren't unusual for native New Yorkers. No one outside our family knows we've studied Russian and Italian. All of us are basically proficient in both, while some of us are closer to fluent in one, the rest of us are closer to the other. With all the shite we've dealt with recently and how the Albanians keep trying to fuck us over, I decided it was time to add that to my dossier.

The app says it takes eleven-hundred hours to learn the language. I'm getting close. I gotta be going on around nine hundred. We have bugs planted in several Albanian leaders' homes and at some of our informants'. I test my skills by listening to them without watching the translation on my computer. If I don't catch something, then I can look it up.

Cormac's working on Japanese since we're doing more business with the *yakuza*. Shane's pretty proficient in Korean, and Sean's studied Mandarin and Cantonese in college and grad school. His grad degree in national security merited at least one foreign language, so he started learning Mandarin in high school, knowing he wanted to pursue that. He picked up French because he loves shitty art-house movies. He wanted to impress a girl in high school. She didn't last, but his crap taste in movies did. Finn's proficient in Polish and German, and Dillan's nearly fluent in Arabic and proficient in Hebrew.

We like people thinking we're ignorant. We like people thinking we're all brawn and no brains. Underestimating us gets us everywhere we want to go with barely anyone noticing. Let them laugh because our name—mob—isn't sophisticated like theirs—bratva, Mafia, cartel. We couldn't give two shites since we're all, individually and as an organization, richer than the rest of them. We take perverse pleasure knowing they don't know.

I pull up to the athletic complex as Tiera's getting out of her car. I gird my loins.

I grab my stuff and hurry to the restroom. I hate changing out of my custom-tailored suits—nothing off the rack is going to fit any of us—in a public restroom. Gross. But I have no choice. I'm back out in a couple minutes and take my clothes back to my car. I'm not wadding up my four-thousand-dollar suit. We might go through them fast because of our line of work, but I take care of my belongings.

"Hi."

I pass where Tiera's standing with a couple teammates as I jog by. She's waiting for me to respond, and I'm being a little bitch because I don't want to get my feelings hurt again.

"Hey." As noncommittal as her greeting. Seems like I have a fear of commitment in my conversations and my relationship with my sub.

Cor and I are the serious introverts in the family. Shocking since our mom and dad are the most extroverted of their sets of siblings. They're not boisterous or gregarious. They're just way more outgoing and enjoy being around people way more than my brother and me. We're not followers by any stretch, but we never feel the need to be ringleaders. It meant we got caught the least out of the seven cousins. We hung back just enough to let our parents and aunts and uncles swoop in and round them up while we stood looking on. No one ever narced on each other, but neither did our cousin Colleen—Dillan's younger sister—ever let us get away with no consequences.

I'm done warming up, and I'm done letting my mind wander. I'll have to re-listen to that Albanian lesson since I don't remember any of what I heard. My mind was all over the place while I drove here. I'm on the field, looking straight at Tiera. My dick would love it if I took off this fucking cup. It doesn't appreciate being confined, but I don't need every person on the field knowing I'm getting a hard on.

"How're your ribs?" I can try to be polite.

We're facing each other at the center line. I see her competitive nature wonder if I'm sincere or if I'm trying to judge whether I can knock her over by hitting her bad side. She smiles, and it's like angels are singing.

"The arnica's really helping. Thank you for sharing. I appreciate it."

"Happy to."

There's no time for more chatting as the ref blares the whistle. It's game on. I watch her, and she's magnificent. She weaves among my teammates; her ball handling clearly comes from years of practice. I looked her up when I got home last time. She played varsity collegiate soccer all four years and captained the team for three. Even after the scrimmage, I see my team's underestimating her athleticism because she doesn't look like she should have the endurance she does, be as strong as she is, or as confident as she deserves. They're fools.

I watch Emily target her again like last time. I don't know what her deal is, but I don't like it. I saw Tiera hip check her when Emily kicked her ankle. As they get close this time, Tiera squares off. She's giving Emily a silent warning to back off. Emily's at least three inches taller than Tiera, but she's out of her league with skill, so her plan to use her height to intimidate Tiera is a waste. Tiera shifts sideways to take one evasive maneuver, but I know she knows Emily isn't giving up. I know she knows where the ref is since I saw her check right before she got close to Emily. She twists just enough so her shoulder rams into Emily's, pushing her backwards.

"Oops."

Tiera's not loud, but I'm no longer in midfield like I'm supposed to be. I'm trailing her like a puppy. My teammate steals the ball mid pass as she kicked it to her own teammate. I nod when mine looks at me. He sends it back across the field to me. I have control of the ball now, and I'm moving it back toward midfield, where I should be. I drive it forward.

"T, take the barge."

I hear someone on the opposing team calling out, but I don't know what it means. I get the take, but other than Tiera, I don't know who on their team has a name that starts with T. I definitely don't know who the barge is, so I'm assuming it's me since I still have possession.

"Seamus, man on!" That's Todd.

Someone's too close to me. I sense the person approaching from behind, but there's no one coming from either side. I push harder, faster than most people. Sometimes you stand and fight, and sometimes you move your arse and run. There's not a slow member of our family, and that's why we've lived through some fucked-up situations.

"No time!" Another teammate warns me my opponent's too close for me to pass.

I shift to shield the ball, using my bigger body to keep whoever's about to attack away. My ball handling's better than most on this field since I walked on to varsity at a Division One —DI—school. I've played since I was four and haven't stopped. Usually, I can keep the ball once I have it. Usually, I'm not playing against Tiera.

She comes around me and pivots. It's too late when I realize she's going for the slide tackle. I can't maneuver away from her. The ball's out from under my foot in an instant, and she's back on her feet with a quick roll and push up straight to standing. I wait for the whistle, but nothing comes. This league's supposed to be no slide tackles, but she executed it perfectly. There's nothing for me to call foul on except for the strike my ego takes. I watch her as she passes the ball across three-quarters of the length of the field. A couple people try to block with their chests or heads, but it's too high. I watch her teammate shoot but miss while she sprints—again. Even I'm breathing hard.

Her cheeks are flushed, and hair sticks to her forehead despite the headband she wears to keep it back. Her ponytail swishes with each step, and it's about the sexiest thing I've ever seen. I want to wrap it around my fist, hold her head in place, and devour her before she sucks me off. That's only after I've made her come on my tongue at least five times. I want to taste all of her.

"You good?" She looks over at me when I catch up to her at midfield. The ref just called half time.

"*Tá mé chun tú a phósadh.*" I'm going to marry you.

I mumble it, and her brow furrows. Thank God. She doesn't speak as much Gaelic as I thought she might.

"I only know a few phrases in Irish."

"Just muttering to myself about needing to be in better shape."

A total and complete bold-face lie. Unless she translates it, she'll never know because I can lie like it's a pathological condition. I do it all the time. But it's to protect other people not my ego, which again is getting way too much attention. If we ever had a future, she'd have to get used to me lying to her. But she would know it's a possibility. She'd know I'd do it to protect her.

"Seamus, if you don't want to tell me, that's fine. Don't lie."

Chapter Four

Tiera

I don't know what Seamus said, but it wasn't about getting in better shape. First, that would be impossible. He's the living embodiment of the perfect physique. Second, his cheeks are already flushed from exertion, but I'm certain they just darkened. He's blushing. He doesn't want me to know the meaning. I didn't hear it well enough to google it later, but I can tell he made something up to deter me.

He gives me a nod. A nod. Not a translation. Not an explanation. Not an apology.

We spend a lot of time staring at each other when he refuses to speak. I'm way too used to this. I've had men do this to me my entire life. I'd already accepted they would until I die. But it extra sucks with Seamus. If he did it to protect me or someone else, then I wouldn't think twice. But he's doing it to protect himself. His ego most likely.

We walk over to the table with bottles of Gatorade that are for both teams. He sees which one I'm looking at and picks it up. He shakes it once, silently asking me if it's what I want. I turn to nod. He twists off the cap before handing it to me. He grabs nothing for himself.

He came over here just to give me a drink?

He came over because he wants to keep talking while saying nothing?

I don't understand. As our gazes meet, I see uncertainty. I caught a hint of it the last time we spoke, but it's in such stark opposition to who he is in the courtroom that it's difficult to fathom they're the same man. But every coin has two sides, and they're meant to be different.

"I'm sorry about court today. I'm sorry about all of it."

"I know. You did your job for your client. We both know I shouldn't have been on the witness stand."

"Why'd Gareth do it?"

It's my turn to stare. I already guessed he knew I'm connected to Gareth O'Brien and the Trenton mob. I didn't guess he would broach it here.

"Tiera, he put you in danger. He did it on purpose. I don't know if he put you in my line of sight because he assumes no one in my family including me would target you. I don't know if he did it because he thought we would. Either way, he put you physically in danger by testifying on behalf of the government when it's obvious you have mob ties. He put you in professional danger by forcing you to testify about something you weren't well-informed on. I don't doubt, given the chance to examine the scene properly, you would have given uncontestable testimony. Why'd he do it? Why'd you say yes?"

I continue to stare. Seamus said nothing I haven't thought a million times since Gareth announced he wanted me on the stand. He thought I could fuck them over. All he did was make me take it up the ass—and not the way I think I'd like it.

Seamus takes a step closer. He could easily intimidate me

with his imposing stature, but I know to my core, he will never hurt me physically. I could see him breaking my heart. I know the O'Rourkes' past, and I know there isn't a man alive in his family who sanctioned their predecessors' shit choices to drag women into the fights that were supposed to be between the men. I know not a one of them would hurt me, order anyone to hurt me, or condone anyone hurting me. I'd feel safe with Cormac, Sean, Shane, Dillan, or Finn. I feel protected when I'm with Seamus.

I don't know if I like it.

"Tiera, you—"

"That's not my name."

I don't think I snapped at him, but he not only leans away from me, he frowns and nods.

"Why do you call me that? It's the second time."

"I shouldn't have. I apologize."

He looks toward his team's bench and where his stuff is. I see a water bottle beside his bag. I don't know what possesses me, but I put my hand on his forearm.

"I accept the apology, but it isn't what I wanted. And it doesn't answer why."

"We have a thing about shortening names in my family. I guess I did it out of habit."

Another lie.

"You should get a drink while there's time." I hold up my bottle. "Thanks again."

He's relieved I gave him an out. I watch him walk away. The muscles in his legs flex with each step. He's definitely not a man who skipped leg day. His shirt pulls tight around his biceps when he lifts the bottle to squirt water into his mouth, then on his face. He checks his laces before walking over to where most of his team's gathered. There's a knockout brunette who just stepped next to him. They know each other well. I can tell from here. I see his smile. It's a gut punch.

I force myself over to my team to join the huddle. I'm only half listening. Who was the woman? Maybe I've misread every cue I thought he gave. Maybe he really is just that nice outside of work. I aim for subtlety as I watch them walk to the field together. She nudges him with her elbow, and he shakes his head while grinning. She bumps her shoulder against his, and he's still shaking his head. Then they split, so she can walk to the goal and her position by it. His smile's more subdued when we're facing each other.

Then I'm in my happy place. I skirt around him as I move to my position parallel the center and right forwards. Our opponents have noticed the plays that'll give me the ball, so I've got at least two people on me at a time. I get it after a sprint to beat one of their defenders. Hours upon hours upon hours upon hours of drills mean I move with the ball without thinking about each step. My feet move independently from the rest of me. I flick up the ball, sending it behind and around my left heel until I can kick up higher enough to lift it with my knee then send it where I want with a header.

That's not banned, just like slide tackles aren't—but are highly discouraged and frowned upon. But plenty of leagues do. Kids aren't supposed to use the move at all in most leagues, but I've already done whatever damage is going to happen after twenty-seven years of playing.

I started when I was four, and I'm thirty-one now. The soccer field is the only time my mind isn't worrying about something, anxious about something, planning something. It's blank besides the plays. I don't know what I would do if I had to give it up. I've watched Seamus, and I think he's the same. He asked if I talk to myself while I play. I do. He knows because he does it too.

We finish the game one-zero. I shot the only goal. Seamus's team clearly learned after we hosed them. I heard some of them talking as I walked by at halftime. They said we tricked them by having a fatty as a ringer. They didn't expect the star player would be an overweight woman in her thirties. It stung, but Gareth's said way worse, and I know his friends have not so subtly done it too. I couldn't give a rat's ass. I'm used to his cruelty.

"You coming out for drinks, Tiernan?" Suze grins at me, and I can't help but smile in return. We're not super close, but we're friends who hang out beyond soccer practice and games. The trial's over, so I planned to drive down to Trenton in the morning. I have to deal with the O'Briens, so I'd rather get it over with. I wanted to set off early, but I don't want to go back to my apartment with nothing to do while I know others are having fun. Normally, I wouldn't care, but tonight, the thought bothers me.

"Yeah. Let me grab my stuff. I'm going to wash my face too. I feel sticky. Where are we going?"

"McGinty's. It's an Irish pub. It's—"

"I know where it is."

"Have you been? It's the best Irish place in the city."

"No, but I've heard about it."

I've heard about it because Seamus's cousin Finn owns it. It's the last place anyone affiliated with the O'Briens should go right now. I need out of this. I'll text her when I get to my car and say something came up. I can't back out now. Fucking hell.

As I approach the restroom, I have to pass Seamus and his teammates. He's speaking to that woman again. I force myself not to bottleneck like it's a crash on the GW Bridge. But she leaves his side to speak to two other women, who do nothing to lower their voices as I walk past. They don't care who hears them, and I don't think they even notice me.

41

"Who knew someone that obese could be so fast?"

Okay. I'm heavy enough to be obese, even if I've only gone up three clothes sizes in the last few years. It's not like I'm being featured on *My 600-lb Life*.

"I say good for her. She's trying to get healthy."

I suck in a breath as I walk past the women who don't see me. I keep looking straight ahead. Besides the weight gain, I am healthy. My resting heart rate is as low as it was in college when I trained four hours a day. My blood pressure is low enough nurses often ask if I'm okay. And I could eat fast food for three weeks straight, and I'd still get a near-perfect cholesterol count. Fuck her.

"I know a guy on the Trenton fire department. I was telling him about her after the last game since I heard about her testifying at Seamus's case. He said her husband left her after a year for her friend after she got fat."

That stops me in my tracks.

"Stella!"

I turn to see Seamus barreling toward the last woman who spoke. The one he was just buddy-buddy with. He's pissed. He doesn't raise his voice again, but we can all hear him.

"She can hear you. You're making yourself look bad and all of us out to be whiney losers."

He looks over at me, and he's not angry when our eyes meet for a flash. But he is when he looks over at this woman. I inhale a deep breath before walking over to the bitch pack.

"My husband did not leave me for another woman. My husband died while driving me to the hospital because I was in labor. I did not leave the hospital with a baby."

They ripped the wound back open. I want to vomit—preferably all over the three of them. I'm struggling not to tremble, and Seamus is by my side. I force another step forward.

"We worked together. That's how we met. We purposely

had the same shifts, knowing anything else would mean we'd never see each other. When we weren't at work, we were homebodies. My husband never had time to cheat on me. Do not trash his name by saying he was an adulterer. Say whatever the fuck mean girl shit you want to about me and my looks. But say shit about my dead husband, and you and I will have trouble."

I spin on my heel and march toward the restroom. I know Seamus is following me, but he's giving me space. I duck inside and lock myself in a stall. I squeeze my eyes shut as I pull my lips in, forcing myself not to cry.

I didn't lie, but I sure as fuck didn't paint a truthful picture except for what happened that day. Aaron never laid a hand on me. He knew I'd fight back. But we had the same shifts because he was controlling as fuck. We were homebodies because he wanted all of my attention. I never, ever gave him reason to think I would cheat. I loved him when we got married. We got married because I believed we loved each other.

Our two-and-a-half-year marriage was hell most of the time, but neither of us had anyone else to fuck, so we fucked each other. We wanted a family, so we tried. Fate fucked us. I wanted to divorce him, but that was a death warrant—one he wouldn't necessarily have signed or followed through with, but one, nonetheless. Fate fucked me.

I'm definitely not going to McGinty's now. I want to shower and go to bed. It's bad enough I have to go to Trenton tomorrow. It's bad enough I'll get little jabs and barbs about the singularly most heinous thing to happen to me. I had that shit laid bare tonight.

I walk out of the stall and nearly scream when I find Seamus inside, leaning against the door. I take a step back and slam into the stall wall.

"Tiera, I'm just here to make sure you're left alone. I wanted to be sure you were okay. I'll wait outside."

"Stay." It comes out as barely more than a whisper. He's protecting me, and I'm not ready to give up that sense of security. It's been decades since I've felt like someone gave a shit about me not being scared. And I don't mean scared because I used to walk through fire—and not metaphorically. I mean safe from the life outside work.

He takes two steps away from the door, and I drop my bag. Then I'm rushing into his arms. He wraps his around me, and I'm hugging a bear. He's even bigger and more muscular than I realized. He does nothing but hold me. I listen to his heart as I fight again not to cry. The longer I listen, the calmer I feel. He makes no move to let go or do more. He just holds me. When I release a shuddering breath, he strokes my hair down my back. I want to take the ponytail out since it's tight enough to give me a headache. But if my hair's down when I walk out, people really will believe we fucked in here. He rests his cheek on the top of my head as we keep hugging.

Can time just stop now?

"Tiera, I'm so sorry that happened. I want to say I can't believe they'd talk about you like that, but I've known Stella since we were kids. I have a past with her sister, Maureen. Truthfully, all the guys my age in my family do. Stella looked down on her sister for—for her many liaisons while trying to convince all of us to do the same thing with her. She was way too young for us, even once she was in high school, and we were in college. By then, none of us saw Maureen. Anyway, the point is, she's always had a mean streak. I don't know the other two women, but neither have struck me as the still waters run deep type."

"But you are." I burrow against his chest more.

"Thank you."

"And I know you apologized because you feel badly that it

happened. But don't apologize for other people being shitty. It wasn't your fault. Don't own their fucked-upness."

I'm not ready for him to hold the outside of my arms as he pushes me away. I want to cling to him.

"I apologized as much for them as for me. I already knew."

"You ran a background check on me as soon as you saw my name on the witness list. Before you even saw me."

"Not quite. We didn't know you were on the witness list until a moment before the prosecutor called you to the stand. Cormac sent Sean a text to have him do it. I knew before the next morning's session. I don't know what to say beyond I feel guilty now that I snooped."

"You didn't snoop, and I don't think you would use that information against me. You did what a responsible attorney would. You found out what you could about a surprise witness. Given you're an O'Rourke, it's no surprise your family dug deeper. I'm not an O'Brien and never have been, never will be. But my family's been tied to them since the O'Malleys kicked them out of Boston generations ago. The moment you heard Trenton, you knew I was connected."

"It still doesn't feel good to know something so intensely private without you telling me. I regret that."

"But I don't believe you'd ever use that against me, Seamus. Never."

I'm adamant about it. My tone makes him narrow his eyes. He practically pulsates with anger.

"Who has, Tiera?"

"I didn't say anyone has."

"You wouldn't be so emphatic about me not doing it if you hadn't already experienced someone hurting you. Who?"

"Shay—"

"Tiera, do not make me ask a third time. You will not like the outcome. Who's hurt you?"

"I'll tell you, but not until you calm down."

He cocks an eyebrow while narrowing his eyes again. How is that even possible?

"You think I'm not calm?"

His tone makes my pussy clench. This is the worst time to be aroused. Or rather, get even more aroused. I loved the feel of his body pressed against mine. I felt him hardening even though he kept his hips away from mine. I want to hear him command me like this in bed—or against a wall—or in a car.

"I think you *appear* deadly calm, which means you're pissed as shit. I don't want you doing anything to anyone. Nothing good can come of you getting involved."

"So, Gareth."

I don't like how he can read me. That's too intense. Too intrusive. I might love it if he could do that during sex—not that that's ever happening—because he might have felt badly that I heard those bitches, but he never disagreed with them or tried to reassure me—but I don't love it while we're talking. I step away from him and cross my arms. The moment I do, hurt flashes in his gaze.

"Seamus?" I can't stop myself from stepping back to him.

"That's a defensive stance, not an angry one. You believe you need to protect yourself from me. I never, ever want that."

He runs his hand through his hair, making it stick up. Even sweating while playing, his hair wasn't out of place. Now it's wild. It tempts me to reach up and flatten it. Instead, I smile. Now he really retreats. I don't want that either. I run my fingers over it, smoothening it.

"It was sticking up."

He offers a jerky nod. It's his turn to move away, reaching for the door behind him.

"I'm crowding you. I'll give you space."

"No, you're not. Wait." My gaze drops because I'm embarrassed. "Please don't leave yet."

I know how needy I sound.

"I won't hurt Gareth any more than I hurt Randy. I will talk to him. I will make sure he understands anything rude he's said in the past—anything his men have said in the past—stays there. No more."

"He'll just say I'm pathetic, and you took pity on me. It'll fuel the fire." There are too many fucking fire cliches and idioms.

"There is nothing pathetic about you, and I do not pity you. If he says a damn thing after I *talk*—talk, Tiera—to him, then he and I will be the ones having trouble."

"He'll want to know why it matters to you. I want to know, too."

"We're at the least acquaintances. I'd like to think we're moving toward being friends. After what I did in court, I think defending you is the very least I can do. I treated you like shite, and I hated every moment. I don't want you to think that's how I see you."

"Seamus, I told you. I get you were doing your job. It sucked, and it's still embarrassing. But you've shown me you aren't that man outside of work. Please, let it go. I appreciate knowing you'd go to bat for me, but I don't want you to do it."

He stares at me for a long time, and I'm not convinced he'll agree.

"One day, Tiera, you *will* tell me who, and you *will* tell me why you're protecting them."

Chapter Five

Seamus

I can't stop thinking about Tiera. She consumes every free moment and crowds into ones that should focus on work and family. I can't help it. I don't like how we left things after the last game. It feels unresolved. Fortunately for her reputation, we weren't touching when a woman walked in on us talking. She was Tiera's teammate and came to check on her. She hadn't seen me slip in and didn't approve, but Tiera reassured her she appreciated both of us checking on her.

I discovered Tiera's team planned to go to McGinty's that night. My team planned the same thing. Even if I hadn't mentioned that, I could tell Tiera wanted to go home. I couldn't blame her then, and I can't blame her now. I can't imagine the pain she felt sharing what I'd learned during the trial. I might have eventually told her I knew. If anything could have come of us, I would have. But there isn't an us, and there won't be.

I know how it felt to lose Dillan's little sister when a mercenary murdered Colleen. I know the pain my entire family still feels when we're reminded of what happened. It's dulled to a persistent ache to just think about her. But what Tiera went through...

I watched Tiera go to her car after she and Suze left the restroom, and I followed a moment later. Then I went to where Stella and our other teammates stood watching it all play out. I lit into Stella. I haven't yelled in a long time. I rarely need to. But it's also been a long time since I've been that pissed at or about someone. I said nothing I couldn't take back or anything that revealed what connects our families. That said, I made sure she knew I wasn't okay with the cruelty. I made sure the two women who were already being catty when Tiera walked by knew I hadn't forgotten about them. They aren't mob connected, but I know they're aware of who my family is.

I left so disgusted it tempted me to quit the team. I find nothing fun about what happened, and I don't want to be around people who think that was okay. No one else said anything to those women. They were silently complacent. It wasn't shock that kept them quiet. None of them thought it worth sticking up for Tiera. I do a lot of shady fucking shite every day. I say things equally cruel to people when I'm interrogating—torturing—them. But I don't do it out of spite. I don't do it for no other reason than to be spiteful. I don't do it to humiliate them in front of people they don't know. To me, that makes what Stella and her friends did worlds apart from what I do.

Maybe I'm just rationalizing it all to myself, but it definitely doesn't feel the same. It's not that I'm absolving myself of my sins, but I feel justified. I wanted to call and check on her, but I don't have her number. I know I could look it up, but contacting her without her offering me a way to is too stalkerish. I have no reason to talk to her as far as the trial is concerned. Not even with the insurance claim.

I won't bring her up to Gareth to get her number or even her email. I don't want to give him any more ammunition against us or her. I suspect he's the one who's hurt her. I wanted to demand she tell me everything about everyone who's ever hurt her. I wanted to ride in with my armor and steed to defend her. It was visceral. But I restrained myself mostly because I didn't want to scare her by letting her see just how angry I was—am. She suspects it, which I didn't love. I thought I hid it better than that, but I guess not.

"Shay?"

I look over at Shane.

"Yeah."

"You're a total space cadet. Could you please pay attention? I've already repeated myself. Twice."

"Sorry. I have a lot on my mind about an upcoming case."

"Sure." Shane doesn't believe me.

I glance at Cormac. He doesn't know the details, but he knows something happened two weeks ago. I cancelled my plans with Makayla because I just wasn't in the mood to socialize. It wasn't that I feared my temper getting the better of me. I just didn't want to be around anyone. The whole thing's bothered me more than I expected. I assume my brother told our cousins I'm into someone.

"I'll pay attention. What's up?"

"Gareth. He can't take a hint. We still don't know why he had a vested interest in fucking us over with the Mahon case. Why get involved?"

I consider that, and I don't have a solid answer. But I suspect a possible explanation.

"I think it was as much about us as it was putting Tiernan in our crosshairs. He wanted her reputation to suffer, and he wanted to embarrass her. I don't know why, but I'm certain he made her testify. Why else would he have someone—even a woman—testify on behalf of the government if she has any mob ties?"

The one thing all syndicates agree on is there are few crimes worse than betraying the organization and helping the government. It's the ultimate sin, really. It's a betrayal next to no one recovers from. They rarely live long enough to try. That's part of the reason I keep thinking about Tiera—I was careful to say her real name just a moment ago. I'm worried about her physical safety. If I'd had the wherewithal, I would have followed her, so I would know where she lives. Then I could have sent guys to watch out for her. The background check returned an address in Trenton in her name and Aaron's. Her social media went dark on the day of the accident. She hasn't posted anything else anywhere. She's not a ghost, but she's definitely more difficult to find than you'd expect nowadays. The only place I know I could find her is at work. I could follow her from there or send guys to do it. I could call her there. But to what avail?

I'd feel better about her safety, so that would be something. But I can't call her. What if she hangs up on me?

"Seamus!"

Fuck me.

"Sorry. I have another case coming up, and it's running circles in my mind."

I don't make a habit of lying to my family. But I also don't tell them everything that crosses my mind. From the looks on the guys' faces, they don't believe me. Cormac must have told them something.

"What do you need from me?" I try not to sound bitchy.

"My company can't start the rebuild without the insurance settlement. It would look too suspicious if we did. We need to know what the hold-up is. I suspect it's Gareth." Shane explains, and I'm guessing it's probably close to the third or fourth time.

I wait for my cousin to continue, but he says nothing. I look around the group again. My chin dips forward as my eyebrows rise as if to say, "well?"

"You know Tiernan now. Find out what's taking so long." Dillan speaks up, and I force myself not to scowl.

"We aren't friends. We play on rival teams."

"You know her better than any of us."

My head whips around to look at my brother. The smile drops from his face, and he knows he's gone too far. I'm not thin-skinned, so it's not me I'm offended for. I don't like what that implied about Tiera.

"I just meant you could ask her if you see her at another game in the next week or so."

"I won't. We've played her team, so I won't see her again."

"If you reached out to her company, could you use her as your point of contact?" Finn's more diplomatic.

"Fine."

I'm never this testy.

I need to think about what I say before I call. Not because I fear giving anything away. I don't want to make an arse of myself. It's been a long arse time since I've called a girl. I feel like the shy seventeen-year-old trying to ask Mercedes Gonzales to the junior prom. I feel awkward all over again.

I've been looking at the phone for the last ten minutes. Really, since yesterday afternoon when I got home from the meeting at Dillan's. I'm hemming and hawing over calling Tiera. I know I have to, but I don't know what to say. I don't want to launch into asking her about

Gareth because I don't want her to think that's all I care about. But what if I chat with her, then ask about Gareth? Will she think I was manipulating her by being nice to warm her up?

I'm not so arrogant as to say I'm so hot I don't have to go after women; they just flock to me. I've been told they like how I play hard to get. I thought only women were supposed to do that. It's not that at all. I'm just not comfortable striking up conversations with people that don't have something to do with work or our family businesses. Work—the unsavory shite. That's what I mean when I think of that word. I can do just about anything if it's for my family. I'll talk to whoever when-ever. But approaching people, in general, just cause isn't enjoy-able. So, this has me wrapped up in nerves as I stare at my phone.

Buck up, buttercup. Stop being a little bitch.

I unlock my phone, pull up her company's website, click on the phone number. I listen to the automated message until it says I can search the company directory. She comes up pretty quickly, so I enter the extension.

"Hello, this is Tiernan."

"Hi, Tiera."

Shite.

"Seamus?"

"Yeah." I didn't catch myself in time to *not* use my nick-name for her.

There's a lull, and I'm certain she's waiting for me to speak up and explain why I called. Find your balls, fecker.

"We have some concerns about the delay in processing our claim. I thought you could point me in the right direction."

"Concerns? What does that mean, Seamus?"

"We expected more progress by now. We can't begin rebuilding without the funds."

Did she just snort?

"You can't start without the funds?" She definitely doesn't believe me.

"Shane allocated the funds based on the award your company accepted during negotiations with Cormac last week."

It didn't go to trial. Once they acquitted Mahon and there were no other suspects, they deemed the fire accidental. The heating and cooling system were still to blame, but the suspicion that someone tampered with it went away. Cormac settled out of court for nine figures. A healthy nine figures.

"I'm aware. But I was called in as an actuary with fire investigation experience." She pauses, and I can practically hear her teeth grinding. "I'm not the adjustor on that claim."

"But you work in the fire loss and prevention department. That's why I hoped you could point me in the right direction."

The pause is even longer this time. I hear a click like a door closing, then she's back.

"Seamus, spit it out. Just say you want to know if Gareth is the reason for the delay."

"If you think that's why I called, it makes me believe he must be. Otherwise, why would you mention him?"

"Because you dislike him, so you assume he's out to screw your family."

"He usually is."

"I haven't spoken to him since before the trial ended."

That's a surprise.

"I expected him to call you two minutes after you stepped out of the courtroom when the jury announced their verdict."

"I was supposed to drive down to Trenton the next day."

The day after the incident.

"But you didn't?"

"I told him I had too much work."

"It's been two weeks. How have you avoided him?"

"I told him I was sick, and that it was contagious. That I was too doped up to stay awake long enough to talk about anything."

"And he bought that?"

"Sure."

"Tiera?"

"Let me look up your claim."

"No, that can wait. What did you mean by sure? What did he do?"

"I really don't want to get into this. It's none of your business."

"Oh, yes, it is. I told you I would find out who hurt you, and I would find out why you're protecting them. Who'd he send?"

"No one."

"I don't believe that or you."

"I don't care if you believe me. It's not your concern."

"You are so very wrong about that." I catch myself before I call her *cailín*.

"Seamus, stop. You'll only make whatever he's planning worse. Please, let me look up your claim. I'll see where things stand. Go to Gareth about that, but don't mention me."

I can't push any harder right now. It's not my place, and it'll only ruin any tenuous friendship we might have.

"Only because you're telling me to. But I'll only relent so many times before I intervene."

"Why?"

Because you're mine.

"Because he's a douche who needs reminding he can't treat everyone like they're one of his men. You don't answer to him, so he doesn't get to mistreat you."

"We both know I do. That's why I was in that courtroom."

"Not like his men. You know that."

"Thank you for coming to my defense and even my rescue. But I can manage Gareth. I have been since we were kids."

"That doesn't make it better."

"It looks like your adjustor needs to send through the last paperwork to the bank. Everything's been approved. I don't know why they haven't since that was four days ago."

"We both know why. What does he have on this adjustor?"

"I don't know. I truly had no idea they were connected at all. I didn't know the woman had anything to blackmail her with."

"It's a woman? What the hell, Tiera? He has no boundaries. This isn't okay if he's targeting women now. It was bad enough when it was you. This is only getting worse."

I don't think I sound as angry as I am. Just the opposite. I think I sound surprisingly calm. But the last time I sounded like this, she told me to calm down. She could tell how I felt.

"Give me a day to look into this and see what I can find. Don't talk to Gareth and don't dig around to find anything about this woman. Let me do it."

I don't like it.

"One day."

"Thank you, Seamus. Your number came up on the caller ID. I'll call you by close of business tomorrow."

"Thank you."

There's a lull, and I don't know if I'm supposed to fill it with small talk. Should I ask her about what happened after the game?

"Well, have a nice day, Seamus."

"Wait. I didn't like how things were the other night. I know you said I shouldn't apologize for other people's fucked-upness. But I still feel badly about what happened. It wasn't right." Something dawns on me. "You said you had too much work to go to Trenton. I know you were avoiding Gareth. Were you avoiding him because it's him or because you didn't feel up to facing him?"

She doesn't answer. I soften my voice.

"Tiera, please tell me."

"It wasn't a great day, so no, I didn't feel like dealing with him."

That breaks my heart. I want to hug her. I never want to hug women outside my family. I don't hug Makayla unless it's part of aftercare. It's not exactly perfunctory because I enjoy the aftercare. But my heart doesn't ache to do it like it does with Tiera.

"I don't want to pour more salt into this, so I'll let it go. I wish I'd known what she was going to say before she started. I would have muzzled her. She's always been a snappy and snarly chihuahua. High-strung and unfriendly unless some-one's spoiling her."

"That paints quite a picture. I can't disagree from what I saw. I'll call you tomorrow. And thanks for looking out for me. I know I'm refusing, but I still appreciate it. It's—it's nice."

That wasn't what she was going to say.

"I'll talk to you later." I want nothing more than to call her *cailín*. It would feel so natural.

"Bye."

"Bye."

I look at my phone when the call ends. That didn't go well, but it didn't go horribly. I suppose that's better than I expected.

I missed Tiera's call because I was at the station. We have an abandoned train station in the Bronx we've taken over. We did some remodeling to accommodate our needs. A bunkroom, a bathroom with four showers, and a kitchen. There're also the meat hooks, acid vat, and various accoutrements for our work. I was there three days, dealing with an O'Malley from Boston. We like to send regular reminders to Ewan O'Malley that he shouldn't have fucked us over, and he shouldn't have put his sister in the middle.

I think that's why I'm extra sensitive about Tiera. It's like recent history repeating itself. Sean's wife, Nicolina, is the Boston mob leader's half-sister. He put his sister in a shite position when the work he made her do didn't stay anonymous. Luckily, she never got caught in the middle of any violence, but it trapped her when Ewan kept trying to manipulate her. Sean's committed to making sure he knows she's not only off limits, but Ewan's still making amends. He will be until Sean says he's done.

In this case, it meant working over one of his guys to tell us who Ewan's hiring to fence some art he recently acquired. The guy held out longer than I expected. It took a day and a half to get the info from him. Then we spent a day and a half getting him ready for Ewan to see when he woke up. Apparently, he screamed like a baby. Our guys didn't stick around once they made sure he saw the corpse. They disposed of his guy, making him ash that's now sediment at the bottom of the Charles River.

All of this meant my phone was off the entire time I was there. I slept in the bunkhouse, so I didn't need to go home. Sean, Cormac, and I were on rotation interrogating the guy. I knew I missed Tiera's call, and I asked Finn to reach out to her. He said she guessed immediately but gave him what she found, which wasn't much. The adjustor was on a planned vacation, and our claim wound up at the bottom of someone else's pile. Tiera said she would see what she could do to push it along. But she warned it wouldn't be much unless she wanted to raise suspicion.

I'm home now, and I don't want to leave for at least a week.

I love how comfortable my place is. We're all homebodies even though we're in our early thirties. The novelty of going out and enjoying our wealth wore off by the time we were legal to drink. We'd rather have a reprieve every night before we face whatever shitstorm that's bound to greet us in the morning. There's always something. Rarely are there no problems. We own so many businesses and manage so many employees there's bound to be something going on.

My phone pings, and I barely want to make the effort to reach for it next to me.

MAKAYLA

> I was wondering if you're coming over tonight. I didn't hear from you that you aren't.

Fuck me.

Shite.

I stare at my phone. I'm fucking tired, but knowing I could spend the night tying up and fucking Makayla usually snaps me back. I completely forgot about her. I didn't think about her once today. I even knew what day of the week it was, but I didn't think about our usual Tuesday night rendezvous. I usually never forget.

I know why I did.

I was thinking about Tiera instead. I have no ties to Tiera; nothing keeping me from being with Makayla. I could fuck Makayla from behind or with a blindfold on, and picture Tiera. That's tempting, but wrong. So tempting. So wrong.

ME

> It's been a long few days. Raincheck.

MAKAYLA

> This weekend?

We usually spend Saturday afternoon through Sunday night together. It's not a sex fest the entire time. But between the things we do, the aftercare, the time for us to rest, and then going back through the cycle, we pass the hours. I never sleep in her bed. I use her guest room. She's suggested and flat out asked me to sleep next to her, and I've refused. She hasn't done it in a long time because I established it wouldn't happen during the first seven months of our contract. It's even in the contract. She gave up asking when I never wavered.

I look toward my bedroom. I can picture Tiera in there. In my bed and not just to fuck. It's fucking disconcerting. I don't know her nearly well enough for those kinds of thoughts. I should push her out of my mind and go see the woman I've been involved with for three years. A woman I know wants me for at least sex.

ME

No but I'll check on you next week.

I do that from time to time. We don't have a 24/7 agreement. She doesn't have to act as though she's a sub—my sub— when we aren't together. It means I don't check on her or monitor her when we're apart. She does her, and I do me. But when I miss several days, I like to let her know I haven't forgotten about her.

Except I did.

MAKAYLA

Okay. Get some rest.

ME

Thx

What the fuck am I doing?

Chapter Six

Tiera

What the fuck am I doing?

I've asked myself that at least a million times since I spoke to Seamus unexpectedly. Talk about a shock. I nearly fell off my chair when I recognized his voice. I hurried to close my office door before anyone could overhear our conversation, but more importantly, so no one could see how he affects me.

He shouldn't matter at all. But he does.

I remember when I met Aaron. He was so cute. I thought he was goofy and sweet. He used to make me laugh all the time. It was a reprieve from the intensity that comes with my family. Gareth and my uncle—a kid from my grandfather's fourth wife—are a few years younger than me. Not enough that I could babysit them, but close. Gareth and Uncle Vince weren't horrible to me when we were kids, but I was the butt of plenty jokes because I was such a tomboy. Aaron liked that I was athletic and didn't mind hanging out with the guys. Because we worked at the same station, we had a lot of mutual friends. And since there were only four other women there, it was mostly guys who we hung out with.

I would get so excited to see him, and I loved how he'd steal kisses. We had a blast on our dates, and we also enjoyed time at each other's places when we watched movies. But I remember finally introducing him to my family. I had to because Gareth came to the station and started bitching at me about missing Sunday dinner. That I was expected to be there when his dad said so. They only invited me that week because I was supposed to falsify a report. I hadn't.

Gareth laid into me. He stopped when he saw Aaron, but it always stuck with me that Aaron did nothing to stand up for me. He didn't even ask how I was when Gareth left. I thought he just didn't want to make a big deal of it while at work. But he never asked how I was doing afterward. I overlooked it. I overlooked it a lot. Hindsight being twenty-twenty, I should have realized how easily Gareth's dad, Darren, sank his hooks in. Aaron was never going to defend me.

But Seamus.

The man is ready to intervene when someone looks at me sideways. I don't want him to know the extent of Gareth's hostility. It'll only sour the already bad blood between the families. But God, it's nice to feel like someone cares. It's been a long fucking time.

And it's too tempting to let Seamus help me. To let him go to battle for me. To hide behind him. That's a disaster brewing, but it just feels so good to feel important to someone. But is it a mirage like Aaron turned out to be? Things seemed so good when we got married. I don't think most people get married, planning for their union to fail. I think some might know they're making a mistake, but I don't think most people plan for it or even expect it to fail. When I look back, though, I know there was next to no chance my marriage wouldn't be a disaster.

It makes me gun shy to get involved with someone new. It's not that I don't want to love and be loved. I don't want the disappointment that could—might—probably will—come along with it.

Oh, but Seamus.

The man is temptation incarnate. If only he were half as attracted to me as I am him. He's a nice guy, and he has honor among thieves. The opposite of what you'd expect. While I hadn't met any O'Rourkes before walking into the courtroom that fateful day—rolling my eyes at myself—I knew of them. Who doesn't?

It's why I know the man is so far out of my league, we're in different universes. And I don't want his pity. I don't know if that's what he feels, but I don't want his attention if he just feels honor bound to give it. And I can't ignore that as nice as he's been to me, how concerned he's been, he's still teased me about my weight. I'm not a little girl. His jabs are more subtle than those bitches. But they were still there. That's probably why he stood up for me. He felt guilty for doing exactly what they had, even if no one else heard him.

Not that it matters. I haven't heard from him since he called five days ago. My guess is he's at their place. The one that's off the grid, that no local police are going to look for, and one the feds can't legally locate to get a warrant. The place where they enforce syndicate laws. An eye for an eye. Very Old Testament. We're all Irish Catholics, after all. Can you roll your eyes so hard they fall out?

It doesn't matter. If I tell myself that, maybe I'll buy my own lies.

SUZE

You ready? I'm downstairs.

ME

Yeah. I'm coming.

I'm over my self-imposed isolation. I needed it to lick my wounds. Now, I'm headed out with Suze. We're going to an Off-Broadway show. I don't know what it's about, and I don't mind. I want to get out of the house. I need the change of scenery now.

I grab my purse and head down the stairs of my duplex condo in East Harlem. It's two stories, and I'm in the bedroom. It's not too big and not too small. It's juuust right. I'm fucking Goldilocks now.

"Hey." I give Suze a loose one-arm hug.

"How're you doing?"

"I'm doing well. I needed a little downtime, but I'm excited for the show."

Suze lives a few blocks from me, so she walked to my place. We slide into the Uber she called. I close my eyes for a moment and sigh. We chat the entire way to the theatre, and I laugh like I haven't in ages. But my laughter dies as we get out of the car. I know that red hair. I know those broad shoulders. I know those eyes.

I don't know who the woman on his arm is.

My gaze locks with Seamus's, and I see the surprise register. I dart my gaze to the woman who's speaking to him. I turn away. I don't want to see him on a date or with his girlfriend. I feel like such a fool. I let myself daydream about something that was entirely a product of my imagination.

"I think it's this way." I point to a sign for our section.

"Yeah. I'm going to the restroom first. You?"

"No. I'm good."

I watch Suze head into the restroom, and I keep my back to

where I last saw Seamus. It means I nearly jump out of my skin when I hear him from behind my right shoulder.

"Tiera?"

I look back at him, but I don't turn around.

"Hi."

His brow furrows at my brusque greeting.

"I'm sorry I missed your call. I didn't mean to."

"I know. I figured out what was going on when you didn't call back, but I spoke to your cousin."

"You look beautiful."

Is he blushing? I don't think he meant to say that.

"Thank you."

I'm in an A-line dress that I love. I feel good in it, and I get compliments on it. But they're about the dress. They're rarely about how I look in it. I think I'm blushing now, too. I can remember my manners.

"That shirt suits you."

Suits you? FML. But it does. It's a deep cobalt blue, and it makes his eyes even greener. It's snug in all the right places and is pretty much guy lingerie for how little it leaves to the imagination.

"Seamus?"

It's the beautiful woman who was with him a moment ago. She's even more gorgeous up close. She's tall with the smoothest complexion I've ever seen, eyes that are riveting, and braids that hang down half her back.

"Hey, Ally. This is Tiernan. Tiernan, this is my cousin Finn's wife, Ally."

She sticks her hand out, and I almost don't recover from my surprise fast enough. I shake and smile.

"It's nice to meet you."

"Shay, we're going to go in. Here's your ticket."

I watch her hand him a slip of paper. We?

She heads back to where I spotted them when I came in. A man who's almost too good looking to be real slides his arm around her and pulls her in for a quick kiss. I look back at Seamus. I prefer his looks. He has a baby face, but there's nothing childish about him. I love how broad his shoulders are and how imposing his build is. His cousin is clearly muscular but leaner than Seamus—and Cormac, now that I think about it.

"Was that Suze I saw you come in with?"

I turn back to him. "Yeah. She just ran to the restroom."

"Um, we know some of the cast. There's a party afterward. Would you and Suze like to come?"

"I can ask her."

"Ask me what?"

Suze walks up and smiles at Seamus. It didn't thrill her to find us alone in the restroom because how long I was in there worried her. But she soon realized Seamus was no threat. Just the opposite. My knight in shining armor.

Seamus answers, but he's watching me. "There's an after party for the cast. My family knows some of them. I wondered if you would like to come."

Suze glances at me. She must hear my prayers that she'll say yes.

"That would be cool. Thanks."

Seamus flashes her a smile, but his attention is back on me. It nails me to the spot.

"Wait for me here. I'll come and get you. You can ride with us if you want. Or I can give you the address once I get it from Ally."

"Sounds good. Thanks."

The announcement comes through the speaker to find our seats since the curtain rises in five minutes. As I turn away, Seamus puts his hand at my lower back.

"You really are so beautiful."

I turn my head, and we could practically kiss. I smile, then he's gone, and I'm left staring. I could catch flies with how my mouth hangs open.

"You ready?"

I shift my focus to Suze, who's watching me with a smirk. She says nothing else, but I can tell she has plenty she'd like to share. I respond with a jerky nod, and we make our way to our seats.

I spotted the O'Rourke men, Seamus and three other men with women I assume are their wives. Seamus seems like the odd one out. Not just because he's alone, but because he doesn't seem to watch much of the play. I'm trying to remain focused on the performers, but my gaze keeps drifting to him. He's observing the crowd more than he's paying attention to what's happening on stage. He's alert, like a guard dog patrolling a property. Except he never leaves his seat until intermission.

I make my way to the restroom while Suze stays behind. I spot the O'Rourkes outside the one I planned to go to, but I don't want to make small talk, and I don't want to look out of place among seven of the best-looking people I've ever seen. The woman with the braids is stunning, but there's a woman with platinum blonde hair that I'm certain is natural. She's the definition of willowy elegance. The third woman can only be defined as voluptuous, like a forties pinup girl. I feel dowdy

I turn in the opposite direction and weave through the crowd to the bathroom farther down the hallway. By the time I get to my turn, then wash my hands, the bells are chiming to let people know intermission is nearly over. I'm still drying my hands as I rush to the door. I use the paper towels to pull on the handle before tossing them. I nearly slam into a man's back. He's not standing directly in front of the door, but he pretty much is because he's so big.

"Seamus?"

He moves aside for me, but he doesn't look at me. Odd.

"Tiera, let me walk you back to your seat."

It's not a casual offer. It's not quite a command. But it's certainly not a suggestion.

"What's wrong?"

"The Mancinellis are here."

"Who?" I scan the remaining people, but there's next to no one loitering. A few people rush to their seats.

"*Cosa Nostra.*"

I know plenty about the various mob branches across the country. But I've purposely remained ignorant about the other syndicates outside of Trenton. I didn't want to know as a kid because it scared me. I didn't want to know when I was married because it pissed me off Aaron was involved.

"Do I need to worry?"

"Carmine and his best friend, Gabriele Scotto, are here with their wives. I know they won't do anything while Serafina and Sinead are with them, and they wouldn't do anything with Mair, Ally, and Nikki here. But we're still being cautious."

"Okay." What does that have to do with me?

"Tiera, Gabriele saw you talking to me. He saw how close we stood. I noticed him as soon as I turned around. I don't want any of them approaching you."

"Would they?"

"The men? No. The women? Maybe."

"Do you think they'd threaten me?" I look down the hall, but we're the only ones standing out here.

"Definitely not. But they might want to know how you're connected to my family. That could lead to them learning you're connected to the O'Briens. There's no love lost between them. I don't want you caught in the middle."

His hand goes to my lower back like before, and it's sexy as fuck. He doesn't quite touch me, but I can practically feel its warmth through my dress. He ushers me back to my row, and Suze sits back. She looks like she was about to get up and come looking for me. When she sees me with Seamus, she grins. No!

My face flushes since I can guess what she assumes. Seamus's hand presses dangerously close to my ass, but only for a second. I might have even imagined it. Then he's heading back to his family, and I'm slipping into my seat.

"What was that about?"

I don't look at Suze, but I lean toward her. "He saw some people that he didn't want approaching me."

"His teammates?"

"I don't think so. I didn't ask. I just headed back here with him."

I don't like lying, but it comes easily to me. Too many years of hiding my family ties and hiding my emotions. I'm too good at it. Suze nods and shrugs before focusing on the play that's just begun its second act. I glance at Seamus a few times, but I force myself to concentrate. I planned to enjoy this play before I spotted him. I still want to enjoy it. I might have missed half the first act, but I'm determined not to let anyone distract me from the rest.

"That was amazing." Suze claps as the cast comes out for a second bow.

"It really was. Thanks for inviting me. I needed to get out of the house, and I'm glad I came."

"I bet you are with Mr. Delicious watching you the entire time."

"What?"

"Come on, Tiernan. Seamus O'Rourke probably can't remember a single line of the second half. He watched you the entire time."

"Hardly."

"I was curious about whether he would look over here after he escorted you to your seat, which was after asking you to a party. He did more than look. He stared. He wants you."

"Suze, stop." I don't mean to snap at her. "He's a nice guy, but he's not interested."

"You've been out of the game way too long if you can't tell he wants to get between your goal posts."

She waggles her eyebrows, and I can't help but laugh. I cover my mouth to smother it, but I can't keep from giggling as she puts her arms up, bent at ninety degrees, like a football ref when he makes the field goal sign. As if that weren't enough, she wiggles her fingers.

"Stop. You're horrible."

"Just sayin'. Do you still want to go to that party with them?"

"If you're game. I wouldn't mind sharing a cocktail with the blond guy who played the roommate."

I nearly jump out of my skin when a voice comes from behind my left shoulder this time. How the fuck does he do that? How can someone as sturdy as him tiptoe around?

"You're still planning on joining us."

It almost sounds like an accusation. I spin around, but I wish I hadn't when my gaze meets Seamus's. My brow furrows at his closed off expression. I glance around, wondering if the Mancinellis are close. Is that what has him so guarded?

"We'd like to, if that's okay."

I look over at Suze, and she's trying not to laugh. She nods. What's funny now? We follow Seamus to a waiting limo. The back door is open, and I can see people already inside. I nearly step on Suze's heel as she maneuvers herself in front of me as we reach the vehicle. Seamus stands beside the door after nodding to the driver. Suze slips in, and I can hear her introducing herself before I can put one foot inside. I climb in and quickly realize there's only the back seat open. Just two spots. One for me. One for Seamus.

Suze, not exactly subtle.

Seamus settles beside me and closes the door. Since my friend has already introduced herself, I suppose it's my turn. I'm certain the three other men know who I am, but I assume the women have no idea.

"Hi, I'm Tiernan."

The voluptuous woman's brow crinkles for a moment before she smiles. "I'm Mairghráid."

Fuck me. She's Irish. Like real Irish. She knows I have as Irish a name as she does, except mine's for a man.

"I'm Ally, and this is my sister-in-law, Nikki."

The blonde woman waves.

Ally—the one with the braids—keeps speaking as she leans against the almost too handsome to be real guy.

"This is my husband, Finn. That's his brother Sean. Mair is next to her husband Dillan."

That catches my attention. I try not to squirm. I'm sitting across a limo from the NYC mob boss. Why did Seamus do this to me? He has to know how uncomfortable it is for me to be in the same car as a man who's actively trying to dick my extended family over because they're rivals. I've heard about how he's the mastermind.

Seamus's thigh presses against mine. He's not man spreading. He just has long legs. I move mine to stay out of his way.

I'm taking up too much room even though I thought I was only on my seat. His shoulder nudges me then remains touching mine. I don't want to acknowledge what he's doing because I don't want to draw attention to us.

It's embarrassing to think he doesn't have enough room because of me. Rationally, I know that's not the case. His shoulders are twice as broad as mine, and he's nearly ten inches taller than me. All that height seems to be in his legs from how much longer he is from knee to hip than I am. I try to give him space, so I shift. He does nothing else. I think he even leans away. I don't know what to make of any of this.

I join in the conversation on the way to the party, and it's lively. The guys tease each other, but the women are merciless when they pick on their husbands. It's hilarious. It's sweet. It's completely foreign to me. I don't know any syndicate family that laughs this much, let alone during one car ride that lasts fifteen minutes.

The driver opens the door on Seamus's side since it's closer to the curb. When he's standing, I see him fasten his suit coat button. Then he sticks his hand out to help me. I put my hand in his, and he wraps his fingers around my palm. The warmth travels up my arm and into my shoulder and directly down to my pussy. He could let go, but he doesn't. Instead, he wraps my arm around his. When Suze gets out, he doesn't hesitate to offer his free arm to her. He calls over his shoulder to his cousins.

"Who's the boring one now?"

Did they tease him earlier because he didn't have a date?

The party's in an art studio loft. It has to be three or four thousand square feet, so there's plenty of space for people to mill around.

"Tiernan, look. It's Jimmy and Hilary. I'm going to say hi." Suze doesn't wait for my response before she waves and walks over to our teammates.

Seamus still has my arm wrapped around his as we walk to the bar.

"What would you like, Tiera?"

"Just a ginger ale, please." I rarely drink anymore.

"Two, please."

He pulls out a bill that's folded, so I can't tell how much it's worth before he tucks it into the tip jar. He hands me mine after he intercepts it from the bartender. He's glowering at the guy. He might have been looking at my tits, but that's just because the dress accentuates them. Not in a trashy way, but they are definitely on display.

He steers us away from the bar and towards a quieter corner. There's a DJ, so we're standing at the opposite end of the loft.

"Thank you for inviting us. I didn't think we'd run into people we know here."

"Small world." His eyes keep scanning the crowd.

I'm not sure if he's looking for a way out now that he's trapped himself with me or if—

"Tiernan, there are a lot of people here I don't know. Same as at the theatre. I'm working tonight."

"You mean, you're the women's extra bodyguard." Their husbands are their primary ones.

"Yes. I'm not ignoring you, and no, I don't want to be anywhere else. But I am being diligent."

"I can tell."

He focuses on me, and I feel like I'm the only person in the room with him. A moment ago, I thought he regretted walking over here with me. Now I feel like I have his undivided attention. His gaze is intense. He slides his hand around my waist and pulls me closer, leaning forward to whisper.

"Will you go up to the roof deck with me? I'd like to talk,

but it's loud in here. I need to let the guys know if you're cool with it."

"Sure."

I expect him to let go, but he doesn't. His arm doesn't stay wrapped around me, but his hand is definitely touching my lower back—finally—as we walk across the open space. He leans in to speak to Finn, who nods. We make our way to a spiral staircase that has a bouncer of sorts standing at the bottom.

Seamus cocks an eyebrow, and the guy moves aside. He's not eager to do it, but nothing about Seamus encourages the guy to argue with him. He takes my hand and leads the way up until we get to a door. He holds it open, and we step outside. A gust of wind lifts the hair off my back. It's not cold right now, but it will get that way after a while. Seamus realizes that before he slips his suit coat off and wraps it around me.

"Tiera, I spoke to Gareth this morning. I didn't bring you up. He did. I didn't like what he said, and I pointed out that he set you up for failure. His response didn't make me loathe him any less. Why is he like this to you?"

"Seamus, I don't want to talk about this. Not here. Not at all."

It's been a great night so far, and now it's all going to crash and burn. My gaze locks with Seamus's, and I know he won't relent. We're going to have this out now, or we'll keep dancing around the subject, neither satisfied. His gaze softens when he realizes I relent. I don't think he wants to browbeat me, but he also won't let me keep brushing this off. He confirms that when he speaks again.

"And I've told you more than once that I will find out who's hurt you, and you will explain why you're protecting them. After the way he spoke today, I can't fathom why you'd protect him when it's obvious he's one of the people who's mistreated you."

I look away, unable to speak while seeing his intense eyes on me.

"Our families have a tangled past. His best friend is my uncle. Gareth and I are like third cousins a few times removed. I don't consider him family because it's not like we spent holidays with his. He's the boss, and my dad still works for him. I won't do anything that could make my dad's life harder. I have a thick skin."

His gaze sweeps over my face, down my throat, to my chest. He nods, but I can tell the momentary distraction isn't enough to change his course. He's pissed I won't explain more.

"So, you're protecting him for your dad's sake? I can appreciate that. But it feels like there's more you aren't telling me. I want to know, Tiera. Don't skirt my questions anymore. I'm not that patient."

"There's nothing more to say. Gareth is an asshole, and we both know it. He has been since we were all kids. He says what he wants."

And now I want to swallow what I said. Seamus's gaze hardens to the point of emerald shards. That did *not* diffuse the situation. I just lit a match and tossed it on a powder keg. I just hope it doesn't explode while I'm still standing here.

"Calm down, Seamus. I told you before, I don't want you getting involved."

"I am involved, and I am calm."

"Yeah, deadly. I already know you won't back down just because I ask you to. Don't shove me in the line of fire in your attempt to shove me out of the way."

Chapter Seven

Seamus

I'm walking a fine line of not bullying her. She reads me too well, knowing I'm angrier than I want my expression to tell her. I wanted her to know I'm not okay with whatever's going on, but she knows my level of anger is to the point of what most would call menacing. I don't like Gareth—fucking Welsh name for a wannabe mob boss—because he's young and impetuous. He doesn't think enough steps forward. He thinks he can bully his way into everything, and that's exactly why I don't want to come across like him.

At the same time, the thought that anyone intimidates Tiera makes me stark raving mad. It makes me want to wrap my hands around their throat and shake them until they're blue. Then I want to kick them in the balls, so they puke. Then I'll consider how I want to kill them.

I'm irrationally protective of her, and I know that. She's right that I need to calm down. Not my anger. My possessiveness. I have no hold on her. I know the accident happened three years ago. But her grief was plain as day when she told Stella and the others the truth. She's pissed I spoke to Gareth, even if I didn't bring her up. She doesn't want me or any overtures I might make.

"Gareth does say whatever he likes, and I know that means his guys think they can do the same thing. You don't want me involved, and I get why. But the other men won't stop if Gareth doesn't. Why are you willing to put up with that if I can help? Why are you protecting these other guys? Who are they?"

She watches me, then shakes her head. What she says next does the opposite of what she intends.

"Seamus, I don't want to say who because it'll only make everything worse. Please trust me. I know you know Gareth. But I've been around him our entire lives. He's younger than you and your cousins and Cormac, so he has a chip on his shoulder. He wants to prove himself. I don't want it at my expense. I'm the one who has to go to Trenton tomorrow and deal with him."

The fuck you are.

"No."

She blinks at me. "What do you mean 'no'?"

"Don't go to Trenton tomorrow, or at least don't go alone. You've waited this long, and it's pissed him off even more. He knows what happened in the courtroom, and I don't want him near you. Nothing you've said—or not said—each time we've talked convinces me he won't attack you. If he already says shite to hurt you, so he can control you, then I can imagine what he'll say to ridicule you as he manipulates you even more. Maybe you can withstand his theatrics and his machinations, but I don't want you facing this alone."

Her shoulders droop as she turns her head to look at the skyline before looking at me, her head still turned away.

"You're not wrong, but you're not right either."

"Then let me take you." What am I doing?

She shakes her head, and I feel her sadness as strongly as she must have felt my anger. I study her before I brush hair from her cheek. She closes her eyes as her cheek turns into my hand. She leans into me, her body pressing against mine. It's seductive as fuck. When her eyes open, there's no annoyance left. Not even sadness like there was a moment ago. Her lips part as our gazes lock. Her hand slides up my stomach to my chest while pressing her cheek harder into my hand.

Does she just want to fuck? Or could it be more? From how upset she was after the game, I don't think she's over her husband's death. If she's still grieving him, I don't want her picturing him or wishing it were him instead of me. I don't want to be a hit it and quit it. I want way more.

There. I admit it.

"Wait to go back a couple more days. Tell him the U.S. Attorney's office still has some stuff for you to do or that you still have too much work to get away. I pissed him off because of how my cross examination went. But he couldn't vent his spleen at me, so he blamed you. He's going to be a dick to you. Give him a couple more days to settle down again, then let me take you."

"I—"

"Tiera, I'm going to be there. I'd rather we not be adversaries when what I want is to shield you."

"It's not your duty. I'm not your responsibility."

But you will be my woman.

Fucking hell. These thoughts.

"You are the furthest thing from either of those. I want to do this. I want—"

Fuck. I barely catch myself.

"What do you want, Shay?"

I knew she wouldn't let it go. And now she calls me by a nickname no one outside my family uses. Oh, hell.

"I'm not asking you to stay in the city for this reason, but I'd like to take you out."

Do I sound as rusty to her as I do to myself?

I don't expect the tears that well in her eyes. This isn't what I want.

"*Cailín?*"

She jerks away, and the tears are gone. It's loathing I see now. I know she doesn't like me calling her that, and it honestly slipped out. But I don't understand her visceral reaction to it. She glares at me, then reaches past me for the doorknob, yanking it open. I barely move in time for it not to slam into my back and head. I'm not surprised at how fast she moves, but I'm surprised she's running from me.

"Tiera, wait... Wait."

I catch her arm, but I'm careful not to squeeze. I pull her back against me. I know her arse feels how hard I am. Her hips tilt back on their own. I slide my hand down her arm and slip it from her waist to her belly. God, I love how every inch of her feels.

She pushes my hand away as though I scalded her.

"Don't do that. Don't touch me there. Don't call me that. You're a liar and a hypocrite."

"I am those things. All the fecking time. Way too many times. But what have I done today to make you think that?"

She whirls around on me. Tears are back in her eyes, but these are angry ones. I draw her away from the door. How did all of this flip on a dime? She's hurt again like she was after the game. Except this time, it's my fault. And she's pissed on top of it.

"You make me think you want to protect me. You make me

think you'll take care of me. Instead, you try to manipulate me to get me to agree to you coming to Trenton with me. You asked me out to really make sure the pathetic, fat widow is on the hook. Then you taunt me."

I look around, spotting a potted plant a few feet away that will hide us if anyone else comes up here. There's a table that I didn't notice until we get closer. I tug her along with me before I pull my suit coat from her shoulders and toss it onto the table. I pull her purse off her shoulder and fling it halfway across the table. Then I back her against it.

"I don't know what you're talking about. I haven't figured out why you dislike that word so much. But you know I'm hard for you. You knew I have been before. If I were manipulating you—if I were pitying you—do you think my body would react this way?"

I wrap her sleek ponytail around my hand, just like I've dreamed about—the way I've pictured her when I jack off. My free hand fists the front of her dress and pulls her tits to my chest before I let go to grab her arse instead. My mouth crashes down on hers. I'll stop the moment she objects, but she doesn't. She's surprised, but then she's sucking my tongue into her mouth as her hands travel up my pecs before her fingers weave into my hair. I press forward until she's leaning back against the table.

I let go of her to grab her wrists, pinning them over her head with one hand. I rest my right hand on her throat, not squeezing but pressing. My thumb pushes her chin toward me when I pull back to look at her. I make her look at me. I rub my cock against her pussy before I thrust as though we're really fucking. Her knees bracket my outer thighs.

"I don't know what you think I mean when I call you *cailín*, but I told you what I mean during the scrimmage when I said it the first time. You are shorter than me, and my frame is twice as broad as yours. You are smaller than me. You are someone I will protect. Someone I will take care of. I will because you're mine."

Everything between us changed in a matter of seconds. I don't know what shifted in us both. My kiss is even more demanding than the last one. What am I doing? None of this is right, yet it feels sublime. I shouldn't trap her beneath me, dictating what's happening. I shouldn't have her pinned to a table where anyone could see us. I shouldn't be kissing her when I still have an arrangement with Makayla. I sure as shite shouldn't be thinking about where we can go, so I can get her off on my cock. I have no right to claim her as anything, let alone as mine.

But she's not pushing me away. She isn't trying to get away. Just the opposite. Her body strains to meet mine, her hips trying to match my movements. Her arms are lax as I hold them above her head. She even nips at my lip when I pull away.

"But I'm not little."

I tilt my head as I study her.

"I never thought you were a Little."

Her eyes widen before she shakes her head.

"Are you a Daddy?"

"No."

She peers into my eyes, and I have never felt more exposed.

"But you are a Dom. Like as in regularly."

"I am. But I am not a Daddy Dom, and nothing about you makes me think you're a Little."

"I'm not, and that's not what I meant. I'm not little in size. I'm fa—"

"Finish that word, and you will learn what kind of Dom I am."

"Yes, sir."

"Is that who you want me to be to you?"

"I—" She shakes her head, and the sadness returns. I hate this. I hate that she's ever sad, and I hate that I keep causing it.

"Talk to me, Tiera. Explain what's going on. I don't understand. You know now, without a doubt that I want you. For this and for more. I've told you as much."

"And to what avail? You know I can't say yes to a date."

"I do not know that."

"You're an O'Rourke. My uncle is Gareth's best friend. My family has worked for the O'Briens for four generations. Gareth's dad turned my husband."

"Turned? You make it sound like they were vampires."

"Blood-sucking leeches they both were. They may as well have been. No. I met my husband my senior year of college at the fire academy. He and I were doing some additional training. He was so charming and kind. He laughed a lot, and he treated me with respect and as an equal. When I moved to Chicago for grad school, he came with me and worked there. We dated for three years before we got married. The week we came back from our honeymoon—not even a month after the wedding— Darren knocked on our door. We'd just gotten home after twenty-four hours on every other day for five days. I went to shower and get changed. By the time I came back down, Aaron was totally different. I knew Darren recruited him. I thought I'd found a way out. Darren found a way to bring another man in."

I didn't expect her to start telling me about her husband, but I won't stop her. I want to know everything about her, even if I have to listen to her tell me stories about being with the men she loved—loves—I don't fucking know.

"Aaron was nearly as tall as you, but nowhere near as

muscular. But he was strong, and he'd grown up hunting. We'd dated six months before I started hinting about my family. We were together a year before I finally admitted my family was in the mob. We were married three weeks when Darren made him a mobster. He fell right into the role. He became possessive and controlling. Demanding. He never hurt me, and he didn't even say hurtful things. But he monopolized my time and all my energy when we weren't at work. I wanted a divorce. Darren wouldn't allow it. He didn't make empty threats."

Fuck. What am I doing? I shouldn't have pushed her. I pull back, wanting to give her space, but she whimpers. I release her wrists, and she wraps her arms and legs around me. I lift her off the table and move to a bench along the wall that keeps anyone from walking into thin air.

"Seamus, seriously. I am not a little girl. I am fat. I know you're strong, but I'm too heavy."

"Let us be clear about this before you tell me whatever else you want to share. My brother weighs two pounds more or less than me on any given day. We are both close to two-fifty. I can carry his dead weight when he's passed out. I've gone up and down stairs. I've done it for blocks. My cousins are lighter than us, but they still weigh more than you. I can carry all of them with ease. I'm not volunteering to, but I can. I will never tell you what to think or feel about your body. But you will not convince me anything about your body is less than the most desirable one I've ever touched. You could weigh fifty—a hundred—pounds more or less than you do now, and I'd still think you're the most desirable woman I have ever seen. Do you know why? Because it's you."

I didn't give her a chance to answer that question.

She inhales so deeply our chests press harder against each other. The tip of her index right finger traces a scar near my eyebrow before it glides down to my jaw. She runs the pads of her fingers over my stubble.

"You know firefighters have weight and fitness standards. I used to meet them with ease. I left the department three years ago. I hadn't planned to be an actuary when I started grad school. I wanted to work for the New Jersey Bureau of Fire Department Services as an analyst and statistician. I wanted to use what I knew from investigations and my knowledge of numbers and stats to work on fire prevention. After the accident, I swore I wouldn't step foot in another fire department. I wanted nothing that would remind me of Aaron. Not the people I worked with. Not the lingo. Not the smells, sounds, tastes. Nothing. It took me months to physically heal, too. My grief was over what I lost, but I spared none of it for Aaron. I ate my feelings because food was the only thing I felt I had control over. I couldn't control other things about my body, like why it took me so long to recover from—"

She can't say whatever she was thinking. I ease her head against my shoulder.

"You don't have to tell me more. I think I understand."

"I haven't talked about this with anyone but my psychiatrist and psychologist. I shut everyone else out. My mom's tried, but I don't want to rehash what we both already know since she wouldn't leave my hospital room until they discharged me. My dad's tried, but it would put him in a shitty position because he worked for Darren and now works for Gareth. I trust no one else."

"I never want to break your trust, *cailín*. I won't call you that anymore if you truly don't like it. But to me, it's a way to let you know how special you are to me. I've called no woman that. Ever."

"I get it now. It's sweet. You're sweet. Seamus, I want to say yes to a date. But you know your family will hate that. It'll trap my family in the middle, and Gareth will lose his fucking mind."

"First of all, my family will not hate it. Thanks to my brother's propensity to gossip, my cousins won't leave me the hell alone about asking you out. My cousins are going to have plenty to say on the way home. I swear if one of them tells me what I already know—that until today, I was too chicken shite to ask—I will throat punch them. Cormac knew I was into you the moment we both saw you. Gareth can think whatever the feck he wants. If he says a goddamn thing or gives you or anyone in your family shite, he will never shite again. Darren and now Gareth exist because we let them. I mean the O'Briens as an organization. Darren fecked up one too many times."

I won't say anything more specific than that. If she's as close to the O'Brien leaders as she says, then she knows what happened to Darren and how it happened. She knows I'm not doling out empty threats. That's why she didn't want me involved earlier.

She laughs, and it eases some of the tightness in my chest. I don't expect her to cup my cheeks and kiss the tip of my nose.

"You won't say fuck in front of me. At least, not in a non-sexual connotation. I heard that about your family. I didn't believe it, but now I do. I told you, you're a sweet man."

"Sweet or not, my mom and aunts terrify me. I'd rather my dad and uncles didn't send me to stand before any of them. God help me if it's all three. Cor and I learned faster than the others to fly under their radar. I'm not fecking around because I already found out. My mom and aunts know we swear like sailors around each other, but if we swear at each other or in front of women and children—truly, I don't know what they'd do to me at my age and size. I have no wish to spark their creativity."

She grins. "I don't think you're exaggerating."

"I'm not. Auntie Breda comes up with the ideas. Auntie Saoirse organizes everything. And Mom carries it out. You must have met Donovan at least once. My uncle was a piece of shite to everyone except them. If I didn't know them myself, his fear of his sisters would have been enough to convince me to never meet them. At least, not in a dark alley."

"Your mom and aunts sound marvelous."

It's my turn to grin. "They totally are."

I look around. We're not somewhere I'm worried about people spotting us, but it's way too unprotected. It's reckless of me to be out here with Tiera when I don't have my gun, and we're exposed from all directions.

"We need to go, don't we?"

"Yes. But—"

"I don't want to finish talking either. I don't want to clam up again, but I don't know if I'll feel this comfortable talking about all this shit again any time soon."

I'm praying she likes this suggestion. "There's a coffee shop down the block that's open for another hour or so. Do you want to go there? Would your friend be okay with it?"

She bites her bottom lip before she nods. Did she want something else? To come to my place? For me to go to hers?

I help her to her feet before I grab her purse and my suit coat. She puts her hand out for her bag, but she snatches it back when my expression says no without me making a sound. I hold the coat out for her to slip on. I pull it snug around her as the breeze picks up, and I know she tries to hide her shiver. Then I hand her purse back to her, though I'm secure enough in my manhood to carry it for her. We walk to the door, and I stand where I can see more of our surroundings while she stands beside the door.

"I understand now—and appreciate now—why you call me *cailín*. Thank you for explaining and for having the patience you do. We've talked about a lot of heavy stuff tonight and the last time we were alone, and I think more will come out. But I want to know something before we're close to anyone who could overhear. You said you're a Dom. I get the distinct impression you have plenty of practice, and it wasn't from a long time ago. Is this about me becoming your sub?"

Chapter Eight

Tiera

I need to know this. I don't know what I'll do with the answer either way. We glossed over it earlier, but I haven't forgotten.

"No."

Seamus's answer is fast and emphatic. I know he's paying keen attention to our surroundings now, and I know he regretted being distracted earlier. We should leave, but I don't want this part of our conversation overheard any more than I did the parts we've already discussed. I wait for him to explain.

"You knew what I meant when I said I don't think you're a Little. You knew to ask if I'm a Daddy. Are you familiar with the lifestyle?"

"I am." I suddenly am *not* feeling as chatty as I want him to be.

He runs his hand through his hair again, flattening it when he realizes what he's done.

"Then you understand there's a deep connection between a Dom and a sub. There's trust and sometimes even affection.

There's desire to give and take that feeds emotions for both partners that goes beyond merely the physical. But sex is at the heart of plenty BDSM D/s arrangements. It's not inherently romantic, even if it becomes that way for some people. I desire you more than I ever have another woman. Yes, I want to touch every part of you, show you how much I want you. I also want way more. The way I want you, the reasons I want you are more than just physical attraction, Tiera. I want things with you I've never wanted with any other woman."

"Like what?" I speak barely louder than a whisper. I think he reads my lips more than hears me.

"I want companionship. I want other kinds of intimacy than what just sex or even BDSM can offer. I want time on the soccer field with you."

That makes me laugh. I reach out and place my hand on his heart. I don't want him to think I'm mocking his admission. Just the opposite. I step closer.

"I've already said it twice, but you are a sweet man. You're being open with me, and I appreciate it. But I see the way you retreat when you're not sure what I mean. You're guarded about everything because of who you have to be. I think you're also really shy. I don't think people see it because you command every space you enter. Because you exude dominance. You have to, to stay alive. I don't think you're usually as forward as you have been while we talked out here."

"You understand more about me than most people who've known me most of my life."

"Because you've let me see the real you."

"That's why the answer to your question is no. I don't want you to be my sub. If that's what I wanted, you wouldn't have a clue how I truly feel about anything beyond sex and the dominance and submission that can go with that."

"I think you have a sub right now."

I say that, but I really don't want to know the truth. I can't take it back. He doesn't look thrilled to answer, but I can tell he'll be honest.

"I do. We are free to date if we want, but our agreement is to be sexually monogamous. That's been fine for me because there's been no one I've wanted to date since I graduated high school. That arrangement no longer works for me. Even if you say no when I ask you out again, things have changed for me. I don't want—can't—be with her if I'm thinking about someone else. I won't do that to her because that's what will happen if I try."

"You want to end your arrangement—your relationship—because of me?"

"Because it no longer works for me. You may never want what I do. You may never agree to go on a date with me. But it wouldn't be fair to her if I'm picturing you when I'm with her."

That's a lot to take in. I understand it though.

"Have you been with your partner long?"

"Yes. Three years."

I didn't expect that.

"Three years, and it's remained only sexual? Never romantic?"

"No. She knows I can't—" His shoulders drop. "I couldn't give her that. I didn't—don't—want to. I didn't think I was capable of giving anyone more."

"But you think you are now?" This is flattering and scary.

"I want to try, Tiera. But only with you."

I lowered my hand at some point, but I don't remember when. Now I look down at them. My head pops up the moment he backs away from me.

"This isn't what you want. I shouldn't have said all of this. You don't have to say anything, Tiernan. I get it. I still don't want you to go to Trenton without me. I don't trust Gareth, but I don't want to make you more uncomfortable."

I think my jaw just hit the ground. "I never said what I do or don't want. You've read me with uncanny accuracy until now. Do not call me Tiernan. I don't want distance between us. Just the opposite. Shay, I have a 24/7 with my Dom. I shouldn't be here with you because of that alone, never mind our families."

"Do you live with him?"

"No. It's not romantic either. I'm not cheating on him by being here with you right now and kissing you. But I'm definitely not acting acceptably. Whenever I'm near you or think about you, I want to walk away from that relationship. But you and I barely know each other. Two times in a courtroom during a trial and two soccer games plus a phone call, yet I feel like I've known you for ages. I left Trenton and moved to the city six months after the accident. Aaron was controlling to the hilt, and it left me angry and resentful. I needed to let that go. To let go of a lot of shit. I wanted to feel appreciated and supported in a way I thought I was going to when I got married. My arrangement fulfills a lot of my needs, and I've been happy with it. At least, that's what I've told myself."

I look down at my body, and the void I've felt since Darren walked into my home that night threatens to swallow me whole.

"The way my body's changed over the past three years hasn't altered the relationship. We don't care about each other beyond our D/s dynamic. I've known all along, though, that it wasn't and couldn't be everything I need. I just haven't wanted to say it aloud. He doesn't know about my family. He doesn't know why I still feel so out of control about so much of my life. Why my relationship with food isn't what it should be. I can give up control about a lot of things voluntarily. But there's so much more I feel like I can never control. I won't give away control of what I eat, and no one's taking it from me. So, it's a comfort."

What the ever-loving fuck possesses me to share this shit with a man I barely know? A man who feels like he knows me better than any living—or dead—soul ever has.

I plow on.

"You said your relationship isn't working for you anymore. I'm afraid you and I won't work. I'm afraid to walk away from a relationship that helped me put my world back together. But it will never be what it was before I met you. Seamus, this is confusing and scary. Yet, you're who I want to turn to because I'm afraid."

"You're in a 24/7, but you said it isn't romantic. Are you open to dating? Putting aside our families, is dating an option?"

"We agreed it was for either of us, but we haven't revisited it since we got together three years ago. Neither of us has dated anyone."

"Are you sure he doesn't see your relationship differently now?"

"I don't think so. Neither of us has suggested we see each other outside of our agreed upon time together. He calls to check on me, and I check in with him. We chat, and we tell each other things about our day. We talk about what we have coming up and things like that. But we don't talk about our past or our families beyond things we might do with them. Nothing substantive. I can't. We don't plan for a future together. We don't talk about something more binding or permanent."

"But would he if he thought you'd be receptive?"

"I don't think so. I don't know, Shay. I haven't thought about it."

"How I feel about my commitment is separate from how you feel about yours. Don't change anything, Tiera. Continue with how things are if that's what makes you comfortable. If you want to date, then I'd like that. If you want to be friends who compete against each other, then that's fine too. I don't want you to feel adrift."

Fucking easy for him to say. I'm fucking holding onto a plank from the Titanic right now. I read a romance a while ago called *The Red Drifter of the Sea*. The pirate captain would set people adrift once he'd pillaged their ship. He even threatened to do that to the heroine who becomes his love interest. Seems rather apropos considering Seamus has come into my life and turned everything upside down, stealing what I'd insisted was harmony in my life. Maybe I should go back and read it again. It's kinda kinky, and the pirate had red hair, too. Actually, now that I remember, the hero had a twin. Could be fucking Seamus and Cormac since they look so damn alike you could confuse them from a distance.

I nod. I haven't felt this conflicted in a long ass time. I wish I was sitting on his lap again. I wish he was hugging me again. Safe and protected. Those words reverberate in my mind when I think about being near Seamus. Horny as hell, too. But that's neither here nor there right now.

"Let me talk to him and see how he'd feel if I say I want to go out with someone."

"Is that what you want?"

"It's the first hurdle. If I get past it, then we'll see about our families." My brow furrows. "If he has a problem with it, then I need to reevaluate the relationship, anyway. I don't know if it will still work for me if he says no. I need to think before I do anything."

"I'm not going anywhere, *cailín*. Whatever you decide, I'll respect it. It will not change my promise to protect you, and I will make sure Gareth never mistreats you again."

I chew on my upper lip before I say something I pray I

won't regret. "Please come to Trenton with me tomorrow. I can't put it off any longer. I don't want to make things blow up in my face even worse than they're already going to. But I don't want to face Gareth alone."

Seamus kisses the corner of my forehead. "Of course."

I nod and sigh. "Do we need to go to the coffee shop at this point? I think it's closing soon."

"No. I suppose not. I'm glad we shared all of this. If there's a path to walk along together, then at least we know what's paving it for now. We can't stand outside like this again. At least not somewhere so open. It's a risk I shouldn't have taken when I've said over and over that I'll protect you. But I don't think we would have shared all that we have if we'd had to pause to drive somewhere else."

"I don't think we would have either. I'm glad we did."

Nothing about any relationship involving the mob—directly or indirectly—is easy. Rarely are they this open, though. I like it. That's why I shared what I did. But I'll be happy to not have another intense conversation for at least a day or two. I don't know how Zack's going to take it.

We head back downstairs, and I point to Suze. He walks with me until we're standing beside her and some guy she's chatting with.

"Hey. I saw you headed up to the roof."

"Yeah. The stars are gorgeous, even if the city lights get in the way of seeing them clearly. I'm going to call it a night because I'm driving down to Trenton in the morning."

She shifts her gaze between Seamus and me. He speaks up before I do.

"I'll walk you out before I find my family."

Suze and I hug while Seamus fires off a text. By the time we're on the street, a town car is parked behind the O'Rourkes' limo. Seamus walks me over to it.

"I'd prefer you not take a rideshare or taxi, and definitely not the subway. Pauly will take you home. Give him the address, and he'll walk you to your door."

I wish he wasn't on bodyguard duty tonight. He's already let that slip by walking away with me. His cousins probably wouldn't appreciate him totally ditching them. He stands beside the open door as I give the driver my address. He hands me his phone, and I program my number into it. He shoots me a quick text, so we have each other's number.

"Where should I meet you in the morning?" I don't know if he wants us to drive down separately. I don't want to get my hopes up.

"I'll pick you up. How's eight-thirty?"

"Sounds good. I'll be ready."

"Goodnight, little one." Seamus looks at my mouth, but he doesn't kiss me. It's for the best, even if it leaves me aching for him.

"Goodnight, big one." I stretch onto my toes and kiss high on his cheek.

He closes the car door for me. He waits until the car's pulling away before he steps back from the curb. He watches me as the distance grows, but the driver takes a sharp left turn a few blocks from the art studio. Seems rather symbolic.

I passed out hard last night when I got home. It was a great night out, but as is usually the case with Seamus, our conversation got heavy fast. It's draining in one sense but invigorating in another. I have hope for the first time in a long time. I have something to really look forward to. Someone to look forward to. My arrangement with Zack gives me a consistency I've needed, and I like our time together. It's usually the highlight of my week, but it's become routine. Predictable. Whatever this is with Seamus is new and exciting. I feel like myself from before I got married. I feel young again. My marriage, the accident, and the fallout aged me.

My phone dings with a text alert.

GARETH

Can't meet with you today. You're not off the hook but something came up. I'll be away. I expect you here the day after I get back.

ME

How long will that be?

GARETH

Don't know and none of your business.

But I'm supposed to wait around for the summons as though I have nothing else to do until he deems me worthy of his time.

ME

Text me when you're back.

GARETH

Try not to fuck anything up like you usually do. Your life might be miserable but you don't need to make everyone else's too.

ME

I could also punch you in the dick but I don't think you want that either. Fuck all the way off. I'll come when I feel like it.

That's not true, and we both know it. If I didn't show up until I wanted to, I'd never go. If I punched him in the dick, my hand would have to touch his junk. Neither of us wants that—I don't want to touch him, and he doesn't want the pain.

GARETH

Testy testy. You already know how fast things can be taken from you. Do you want to lose more? By the way, your dad's here for a meeting.

ME

The threats are getting old. So are the insults.

But they still work. I know he's manipulating me. I know he's a douche. But I believe his threats. I've seen what he does to people who don't believe him. I don't want that for my dad.

GARETH

The only thing old--and fat--is you

I don't respond. There's no point. I've heard it all before. Whether he means the specific insults, he means the manipulation. I'm not so stupid or naïve not to recognize it. But he owns me just like his dad did.

If Seamus knew...

Fuck. He's going to be here soon.

I hurry to finish getting ready. I tug down my top and twist to see my ass in the mirror. I think these are flattering jeans, and they're comfy too. That counts more than anything these days.

The doorbell rings, and I jog downstairs.

"Coming!"

I wish I was. I suspect it's Seamus, and that's exactly what I want to do when I'm with him. I want him to say the same thing—that he's coming—and I did that for him.

I open the door and step aside. "Hey."

"Hi." He offers me a bright smile that turns rueful. "Did Gareth text you already?

"How'd you know?" I didn't expect—nor want—that to be his greeting.

"I know lots of things about him."

An informant or bug told him Gareth's traveling.

"I'm sorry you wasted your time coming all the way over here."

"I live five minutes away. And it's never a waste to be around you."

His voice drops like twenty decibels when he admits the second part. He had me pinned to a table with my hands above my head as he ground his cock into me. I think we're beyond shyness. He makes my heart flutter to see how—mmm—not quite self-conscious and not exactly reserved—unsure?—of himself he gets when he doesn't know how I might react. It's endearing. It makes me feel like I'm something or someone unique to him, so he's not sure how to proceed. That I'm not like everyone else in his life.

"I'm sure you moved things around to make time for this. I'm sure you have bet—'

"Do not finish that sentence, Tiera."

There's that warning that filled his words last night when I called myself fat. He told me I'd learn just what kind of Dom he is. I sorta want to test that, but he'll know I'm baiting him if I do.

"Do you want to come in?" I realize we're still standing in my entry way.

"Thank you. Are you shoes on or shoes off?"

I notice him looking around and spotting my shoe rack. I keep them there because they're convenient, but I prefer shoes off.

"You can keep them on. That's thoughtful of you to ask." No one else ever does.

"My mom loathes shoes on in the house, so I've learned to pay attention and ask."

I want to say good to know, but that implies I'll go to his

parents' place one day. Fat chance of that. I wonder if I could get away with saying that.

"Can I get you something to drink?" It would disappoint my mom if I didn't offer.

"I try not to turn down a chance for water, so yes, please."

I stare at him for a moment. He's serious. There's a reason he looks the way he does. Healthy living. His manners are also impeccable. I move around the kitchen to get us both a glass of water. He nods when I hold the glass near the fridge's ice maker. I lead us to the living room, though I don't know why. He notices the coasters immediately and sets out two—next to each other—in front of the loveseat. I have a sofa and a recliner. He waits until I sit before he does.

Someone drilled this etiquette into him, but it was his choice where he sat. Again, it makes me feel unique because I don't think he's like this with other women. Then again, he has a sub, so maybe he is. He said it's not romantic, and I believe him. But there's usually a level of affection during aftercare regardless of other emotions that are or aren't there. Maybe this is just how he is with all women who aren't his cousins' wives.

"What would you be doing if you weren't going to Trenton? It's a Saturday, so I assume not going into the office."

He angles himself, so he can see me as he speaks. His arms rest casually on the armrest and back of the loveseat, putting his back in the corner. I twist to see him, and it brings our knees together. He doesn't move his.

How do I say I'd usually be with Zack?

I hesitate a moment too long. He nods and glances away. It threatens to embarrass me, but I refuse to suddenly turn timid.

"I suspect you'd be doing the same thing."

Okay. That felt like a gut punch to point out he'd probably be having sex with another woman. His gaze locks with mine, and it pierces straight through me. I don't know what to do. I'm ensnared and can't look away, but I don't know what to say. Technically, isn't it his turn to say something next?

"It's a good way to spend a Saturday afternoon." His eyes shift as he looks from the top of my head down to my knees. It's as though I'm sitting in front of Superman, and he has x-ray vision. I feel naked. I wish I were naked.

"Not a bad way to spend a Sunday, either." This isn't about one upmanship. Why did I say that? I didn't intend for him to know how I spend my Saturdays, but he guessed. Then I point out how he spends his. I didn't leave well enough alone and doubled down.

Shut up, Tiera.

Tiera. I've never thought of myself as that. He's rubbing off.

Fuck. The thing I want to rub off is his cock.

If you don't get your mind out of the gutter, he's going to know just what you're thinking.

When my gaze meets his again, he knows exactly what's on my mind. From his focus on my lips, maybe he's got the same thing on his.

"It's a nice day out. Would you like to go for a walk?"

I didn't expect that. "Uh, sure. That sounds really nice."

It does.

It only takes me a moment to slip my shoes on, then we're headed out my door. He guides me to the right when we get down my front steps. We point out favorite places in our neighborhood and laugh that we go to the same bodega but have never met.

There's no way I'd forget you, Tiera.

We were standing at a stoplight, waiting to cross, when he said that. It made my toes curl in my shoes.

We spend an hour and a half walking around. He's just invited me to lunch, but his phone rings. Or rather it vibrates in his pocket because he pulls it out, and I see Finn's name on the screen. I turn away as though I'm looking around some more. I know every building on this street, but I don't want to appear nosey.

When he speaks Gaelic, I know what's coming. No one in my family or the O'Briens' speaks it fluently. I know some phrases like how he greeted me in court, and I knew the word for little girl. It's obvious he's fluent and must use it regularly.

When he hangs up, he turns a regretful expression to me.

"It's okay, Seamus. I know it's work." He'll never tell me what kind of work.

"It is. I'm sorry. I don't want to run away when we're having such a nice time."

"You aren't running. It's family work."

He doesn't appear thrilled when I put it that way, but he nods. "I'll walk you back."

"It's okay. I'm going to stop by the deli and get some bagels." It's the best place in the neighborhood since they're baked fresh daily.

He hesitates before he nods. He doesn't like my suggestion.

"Is there a reason I shouldn't walk back to my place alone? Has someone seen us together?"

"I don't know, but you know I'm cautious.

We walk to the corner where the deli is. He slides his hand down my forearm and takes my hand. He leans in and kisses right beside my mouth. I turn and our lips brush. He kisses me properly, but it's over way too soon.

"Tiera, will you go on a proper date with me tomorrow?"

"I'd like that."

I watch him walk away, and it's like a chilly wind just whipped between the buildings and blasted me in my face.

Chapter Nine

Tiera

Gareth's been gone for seven weeks. He's had two trips back-to-back and three more spaced out, but with little time in between, which means he's left me the fuck alone. Uncle Vince has texted me a few times with complaints about me not doing this or that for them. I'm supposed to lose an insurance claim, deny another, and report a third for fraud. The only fraud to be committed would be me if I did any of those. I've talked my way out of it, but I know my reprieve is running out.

He summoned me—fucking douche bag—down to Trenton to sneak onto a house fire site to examine the wreckage. He wanted to be sure it wouldn't blow back on them. He sent two of his men up to escort me. I could have refused, and they wouldn't have manhandled me or anything, but it was just easier to give in. Especially once he started bringing up how if I'd done what I was supposed to and met Aaron at the hospital like Darren insisted if I went into labor while Aaron was "working", then nothing would have happened that night. I hate him so much. I know I shouldn't wish a relative dead, but I do. All the time.

It was challenging dodging Seamus that night when we've seen each other nearly every single day since our walk. I know he suspected something when I said I needed to make it an early night because I had a lot of work and wanted to go into the office early. He didn't question me, he just nodded.

I've dodged Zack too. I've canceled every weekend, telling him I had family or work events or games. It's happened before where I've had long stretches of weekends in a row with commitments. I haven't seen him during the week like I usually do, either. We have a 24/7, so I talk to him nearly every day. I consider Seamus a friend—though I want a shit ton more—so I can rationalize that I'm not lying to my Dom when I say I'm trying to get out more and make more friends. I had my period twice, so that was an excuse, though not one I've used often.

Seamus has gone dark four times since that walk. He could warn me the second time, but I had to guess the third time. His brother called to explain the other two. By explain, it was "Seamus didn't plan it, but he has to be away." Away usually means at the syndicate's *place*—some hideaway where they do things I shouldn't even try to guess—or an unexpected trip out of town. Each time he was back, he volunteered nothing, and I didn't ask.

Besides that, we've been inseparable, basically. We meet for coffee or lunch or dinner. We've been to the movies a couple times. We saw another off-Broadway show, and I only barely remember it a little better than the one we saw the night we kissed for the first time. We've texted for two months, and I feel like I know him pretty damn well for a mobster who probably reveals nothing to anyone who doesn't share his DNA.

I've told him the things I can about work and what my job

is like. He's told me about his legit businesses, of which there are way more than I expected. Way more than any of the men in my family or branch—I hate thinking I'm a part of a syndicate, but I am—have. We've talked about our childhoods and families in person and through text on the days we can't meet. We've talked about where we'd like to travel and even what we hope to do in retirement.

By mutual silent agreement because of our individual arrangements, Seamus and I haven't done anything more than hold hands then kiss goodnight. He'll rest his hand at the small of my back sometimes, and it's about the sexiest thing ever. But we take it no further than that. It's rather innocent and sweet. I'm getting to know him without sex complicating things.

We also haven't defined our relationship. In a normal situation, I'd consider him my boyfriend. What else do you call someone with whom you share—at least I think we share—romantic feelings that you see every day? But, between our D/s relationships with other people and family ties, we haven't brought it up. I want to, but I'm too chicken shit.

"You ready?"

"Yeah. Let me grab my bag." We're going to the park to kick the ball around. We do a few times each week. We're honestly equally matched in skill, so it's challenging, which makes it fun

I lock my front door, and he takes my bag from me. He looks ridiculous carrying both when I'm dressed to work out and can obviously do it myself. But he refuses to let me. When elderly couples see us like this and holding hands, they smile. The men usually nod to Seamus. One woman who had to be nearly ninety winked at me!

We get to the park, and we strap our shin guards on. We chatted about dinner after this on the way here. If we were anyone else, we'd sound like a normal couple.

"Shay, I can't avoid it any longer. Gareth's been home three days, and he's demanding I go to Trenton." I pass the ball to him, but rather than pass it back, he stops it with the inside of his foot.

"I'm going with you."

Here we go.

"You don't have to. I'm fine on my own." And I am. A break from Gareth always helps me deal with him the next time I have to see him.

"Great. I'm still going with you."

We haven't argued yet, but I think we're about to.

"Seamus, it'll only complicate things. It's better if I just see him and leave."

"You won't just see him. He's going to lay into you, and that pisses me off."

"We've known each other three months. I've known him since he was born. I can handle this."

Seamus walks over to me and drops his voice. "I don't doubt you can handle it. That's not what bothers me. It's that you have to. You may have known him longer than me or longer than you've known me, but I know him in a way you never will. I don't trust him, *cailín*. I'll never trust him."

It soaks my panties when he calls me that. Despite us not progressing our physical relationship or defining our emotional one, he's never stopped calling me that. Hearing him call me Tiera is as natural as everyone else calling me Tiernan.

"I don't want you there." I hate saying that, and it sounds horrible.

"I know that, but it doesn't change my mind."

I step back and shake my head. "So, I'm the one who's supposed to back down."

"I don't want there to be a standoff where either of us has to back down." Seamus sounds like we aren't having a disagreement, and it pisses me off. It feels dismissive.

"You assume you'll give me a mandate, and I'll obey. I'm not doing that again."

He knows what I mean from the little I've told him about my marriage. He steps forward, so we're back to standing how we started. If he were any other man, I'd say he was looming over me. But Seamus doesn't intimidate me. If he wasn't pissing me off, I'd think it was sexy as fuck because he makes me feel small when nothing else and no one else does.

"This is about your safety, so yes, it is a mandate. And Tiera, you will obey."

"No."

"Then you aren't going."

"Seamus, you do not decide that. I appreciate you being protective, but you don't dictate who I can and can't see."

"You're right, except with Gareth and his little toadies. Tiera, I can't tell you why I'm more concerned than usual. But he knows we've been spending time together. I'm more worried than usual about him in general. I'm frightened about how he'll treat you. I'm being heavy-handed, and I know it. But I will never back down about protecting you. I should have led with that. I'm sorry."

He takes the wind out of my sails when he puts it that way.

"I'm not one of your men for you to order around, Shay. You know how things were with Aaron, and why I don't want anything like that again."

"And I don't want you to think I don't see you as my equal in all things. You are. I don't want it any other way. But your wellbeing is one thing you will never sway me on if I think you're at risk. You just can't convince me otherwise."

I'm falling in love with this man.

I put my hands on the outsides of his biceps and lean in. He wraps his arms around my waist. I nod, and we smile.

"Thank you. Thanks for hearing my objections and

listening to me. Thanks for explaining your position. And thanks for looking out for me."

"Always."

As a friend or as someone more?

I want to ask that, but I'm scared I won't like the answer.

I'm slipping on my shoes when someone knocks. I hobble to the door as I try to get my shoe on all the way. When I peek through the spyhole, I recognize Seamus immediately. He's close enough that I can only see the division between his pecs beneath the open top two buttons of his shirt. I don't need to see anything else to know it's him. I run my hands down the dress I'm wearing. I hope he likes it.

"Hi." I open the door and step aside.

He stares at me, not coming in, even though the invitation is clear. My brow furrows. I try to retreat, but then he's on me. He encircles my waist and tugs me toward him. Even though I've pressed my body against his before, I'm unprepared for the brick wall I slam into. His pecs flex, but otherwise, he doesn't move. Our gazes meet.

Then he pounces again. His lips meet mine as I step backwards when he passes through the doorway. He reaches behind him to push it closed. He keeps backing me up until we reach a wall, and we can go no farther. I can't keep up. I've never had a kiss like this before. Not from any man. Never have I felt like someone wants to consume me whole.

I'm caught between two immovable objects, and I have no wish to escape. I open to him and relish the feel of his tongue sweeping through my mouth before I capture it and suck. The sound he makes is feral as his cock rubs my pussy. My entire body feels like it's humming at a frequency only he and I can hear. We're in a private lust bubble with space only for the two of us.

His stubble abrades the skin around my mouth and chin even though he's freshly shaven. His fair complexion makes it look like he wouldn't have a thick beard. Up close, I can tell that's not the case. I wonder what he'd look like with facial hair. A rugged lumberjack. I don't know why that idea pops into my head, but I like it. It arouses me even more.

He isn't restraining my wrists like when he had me pressed against the table. I seize the chance for my hands to roam over his body, exploring every inch I can reach. He nips at me, but he doesn't stop me. I relish every moment of my exploration. There's nothing I don't want more of. His kisses trail along my jaw, then down my neck before the tip of his tongue glides up to the spot just behind my ear.

"I told you once before that you're mine. Wear dresses like this, and I'll prove it. I won't let you leave the bedroom until you're too spent to want to go anywhere."

"What?" My lust-filled mind can't understand.

"I never imagined I was a possessive man, but apparently, I am."

"Huh? I don't get what you mean."

"I mean, I'm on the edge of demanding you change into something that covers you from head to toe. I mean, I don't want any other man seeing what I want to be mine and mine alone. I mean, I'm about two seconds from ripping that dress off you and having my way with you."

"Yes, please."

We both freeze. What did I just agree to? Whatever it is, I'm certain I meant it. I have to stop and think, though. The words flew out of my mouth before I knew I was going to say anything.

"*Cailín*, I know I have no right to demand anything because we haven't discussed this part of our relationship, and I'm serious about not usually being possessive, even if I'm protective. But I admit I don't like the idea of other men seeing you in something so revealing."

Revealing? Is he out of his mind? I'm in a knee length, wrap around dress with a tank top on to make sure I'm not showing too much cleavage. If anything, I'd call it boring.

He hooks a finger down my tank top and tugs. It doesn't take much, but he has a clear view between my tits. I feel his cock twitch against me. I'm focused on his hungry expression as he looks down my dress, so I don't realize his other hand is sliding up the back of my dress until I feel his bare hand on my bare ass. My thong covers next to nothing. He kneads the flesh, and it feels amazing. I'm still sore from soccer practice three days ago. I pushed myself harder than usual because I had a shitty day and wanted to forget about it.

"This dress hugs all your curves and does nothing to hide how hot you are. Any person with one working eye can see how sexy you are. I might gouge out any that are looking in your direction."

"Seamus, you're exaggerating so much it's not funny."

I don't like this. It makes me feel the opposite when he blows things out of proportion to the point where I feel like a caricature of what he describes.

He releases my dress and wraps his hand in my hair, tugging my ponytail until I have to look up at him. I can't move my head without feeling like he'll scalp me. I like it. He presses his lips to my ear.

"I am not. I know more about the private lives of the men we're about to meet than you will ever want to know. Suffice it to say, I know all their predilections and proclivities. I do not want them ogling you. We'll accomplish nothing because there won't be a man left living to talk to. I never dreamed I would dictate what a woman wore, and I never thought I'd do it to you. But I'm asking you, please change, Tiera. Not just because you're a distraction to me. My dick won't go down if I keep looking at you in this dress. The men will stare and make you uncomfortable. I don't think you've understood why those douches have said what they have. Until now, I didn't understand what Gareth or the guys I could overhear meant the last time I spoke to him, and he brought you up. Their comments are grossly inappropriate, but they were never about disliking what they see when you're around. Just the opposite."

"You cannot possibly mean Gareth sees anything sexually appealing about me. I'm like a sister to him."

"I don't mean that. But he sees what I see, and he knows his men like it. He taunts you not because you're unattractive. He'd whore you out to them if he thought he could force you."

"Shay—"

"Tiera, I know what I heard, and it all makes sense now. Please believe me. At least for today. Find something less form fitting."

"Like a muumuu?"

"Preferably."

He's not joking.

I cup his dick and stroke my hand over the length. He groans and grabs my wrist.

"Unlike you, I don't have a spare change of clothes here."

I rub my palm as much as the little freedom I have allows. He pushes my hand aside and slides his iron thigh between mine as he pins me to the wall again. I'm so damn curious about what he'll do next. I want to keep pushing him, keep getting him to react to me.

"Tiera, I will text my sub and break it off right now. I won't fuck you while I still have an arrangement with her, but I will end it now. But once I'm inside you, it changes everything. I will not share you. You need to decide whether that's what you want. Because there's no going back once I make you mine."

"I thought I already was yours." I barely speak louder than a whisper, and it's not because I can't take a deep inhale. I'm too entranced.

He lets go off my ass then slides his hand down my tank top and under my bra. He pinches my nipple hard enough to make me come onto my toes. He moves to the other and twists before pulling his hand loose.

"Those are mine."

The same hand goes back up my dress, and this time his hold on my ass is painful. Almost more than I can take. His fingertips dip between my ass cheeks.

"This is mine too."

He thrusts his hips against my pussy. His hand on my ass guides me to ride his thigh. I clutch his shirt as the friction pushes my arousal to the point of a sharp ache.

"That is definitely mine. I'm going to make you come. When that happens, it'll prove your pussy belongs to me. If you don't want me and only me, then stop me now, Tiera. Because once it happens, there's no one else for either of us. I won't claim you and not give you all of me in return."

"Let me get my phone."

His brow furrows.

"I'm going to text Zack. I won't come for another man while I'm his sub. But I will come before we leave, and it won't be me doing it to myself."

"Do you think a text is fair?"

"You're going to do the same thing to your sub."

That makes us both pause...and sigh. We both know that isn't the right way to end our arrangements. I don't know if what we're doing or about to do would constitute cheating or unfaithfulness when neither of us is in a romantic relationship, but we've both agreed to monogamy with someone else Neither my Dom nor his sub deserve to be deceived.

"*Cailin*, I meant every word I said. I take back none of it Perhaps we have to pause, but I'm not walking away from you or this unless you tell me no."

"I don't think I'll ever be able to tell you no."

It's true.

I don't know if I should have admitted that. I don't know that I should feel that way. I don't know a lot of shit right now but I know a rightness has settled over me that's never been there before. I don't want to say I had doubts with Aaron, but I was nervous about whether I made the right decision when I accepted his proposal. It's not like Seamus is asking me to marry him, but I feel right about being with him. It's the only thing that feels right.

"I'll call Makayla right now. I'm not saying we have to have sex immediately afterwards. Not even today or tomorrow. I want to take you out on a date without either of us having something looming over us. I want to show you I want you even if we can act on our physical attraction. But I also know the thought of being with someone else makes me feel ill. And the thought of you being with someone else—I don't know if I want to cry or tear him apart.'

I slide my hands over his chest, around his neck, and into his hair. I kiss up his neck until I reach the spot behind his ear and make him shiver. I can only do this because I'm wearing heels. Otherwise, I'd be way too short.

"Shay, I'm yours. My body belongs to you and has since the first time you touched me. But I want more too. I want that date with nothing to stop us. Then some more after that and more after that. I don't know how this will work with our families and everything that comes with them, but I don't care anymore I only care about what's between us."

I let go of him, and he gives me room to move away from the wall. He watches me as I grab my phone from my kitchen counter. He pulls his from his back pocket. I walk back to him, and I rest my free hand on his waist.

"I'll call while I change."

Chapter Ten

Seamus

I watch Tiera head into her bedroom. She doesn't close the door the entire way. I can see her move to her closet. Does she want me to watch her change? Does she want me to know she's really making the call?

I look at my phone before I unlock it. I suppose I always knew my relationship with Makayla would end. I always thought there was a greater likelihood she'd meet someone else and want a romantic relationship with them over our physical one. I always thought I'd eventually get bored or no longer find fulfillment with her and move on to someone else.

Never did I imagine I'd be the one to want a romantic relationship, and that's why I don't feel fulfilled. Never did I imagine I would call it off over the phone. It's shitty of me. But I don't know that doing it face to face is all that much better. Neither will feel good for either of us, but I know I can't keep seeing Makayla if I have feelings for Tiera. I've cancelled on Makayla every time I was supposed to see her since I met Tiera.

I've blown her off for two months with lies piled on top of lies. We've gone this long before, and I've lied about that too. But there was always some glimmer of truth when I said I had a family commitment or work.

I don't want to know whether Tiera's been with her Dom since she met me.

That's not true. I desperately want to know, but I have no right to ask. And I have no right to expect that she hasn't just because I didn't want to be with Makayla.

I unlock my phone and hit her speed dial. I don't know whether I'll get her since she might be at work already. I won't end it over voicemail. I can be a little less shitty than that.

"Sir?"

"Good morning, Makayla."

"Hello, Sir. I wasn't expecting you to call."

I never call her during the day. Usually we text more than call, but I do sometimes.

"Are you at work? Do you have a moment to talk?"

There's a pregnant pause.

"I can talk."

"I don't enjoy doing this over the phone, but I don't know that in person is all that much better."

"You're ending things."

"Yes. I've met someone."

"I figured."

I wince. She doesn't sound hurt or pissed. Just resigned.

"I've kept to our agreement, but it's time for me to end it."

"I knew it wasn't just work that was keeping you away. You've been canceling further in advance than when you get called away. I saw this coming."

"Makayla, you don't sound okay with this."

"How can I be? Seamus, there's a reason my dates went nowhere."

Oh, hell.

"You told me you couldn't be emotionally involved, so I accepted that. I tried to find that elsewhere, but I always came back to you. Didn't you ever figure out why?"

"Makayla, if I'd realized that, I would have ended this sooner. I didn't mean to lead you on."

"You didn't. You were clear from the beginning and all along. It's not your fault I feel more. I guess I just hoped…"

I'm watching Tiera as I speak to Makayla. I shouldn't spy on Tiera, and it's wrong to watch one woman while I break things off with another. It's wrong to have a raging hard on for one woman while speaking with the one I promised to only get hard for. I'm an arsehole.

"I'm sorry I never felt the same thing. You deserve to have someone who can reciprocate your feelings. You deserve a Dom who can give you all that you need without reservation."

"I suppose I should be glad you haven't been with her yet. That you kept your part of the arrangement. I—"

She didn't sound sad. She sounded like she was about to confess something.

"You what?" I infuse command into my voice.

"I wasn't always so honorable."

What the fuck?

"You were with other men when you told me you wanted us to be monogamous."

"I wanted to see if I could be with someone else. If I could be happy with someone else."

"How many someone elses did you try out?"

"Seamus, I don't want to say. I shouldn't have said anything at all."

"But you did. I called, feeling guilty to be doing this over the phone and to do this while I know you're not dating anyone else. Now I find out you were the one who didn't keep their end of the deal."

"Are you angry?"

"No. Disappointed in you but not hurt."

Maybe that was harsh. But it's true. She's sworn over and over for three years that she didn't want a physical relationship with anyone else, and that if she did, she would end ours. She played upon knowing I wasn't with anyone else because I didn't date. I don't feel so bad now.

"I'm sorry, Sir."

"I'm not your Dom, Makayla."

I hear her suck in a breath. It just got real for her. It feels freeing to me.

"I wish you well with her."

"Thank you. I hope you find someone to make you happy."

That sounds so trite, but what else do I say?

"Goodbye, Seamus."

"Bye."

I look at the phone as I hang up. I can honestly say that did not go how I thought it would. Truth be told, I always suspected she'd fucked at least one other guy during the past three years. But she'd also made herself out to be someone who took making promises seriously. That she took being a sub seriously. At least, it's done now.

Tiera's had her back to me while she's gotten dressed. She has the finest arse I've ever seen. I want to run my hands over all of it. I want the handfuls that I can grasp anywhere I touch. I don't know how I concentrated on that call because all I can think about now is bending Tiera over that bed and fucking her from behind. Fucking her arse.

But those thoughts evaporate the moment she turns around. She's crying.

I don't hesitate to barge into her room and over to her.

Before she knows what I'm going to do, I pull her against me and press her head to my chest. I also take the phone from her.

"What did you say to make Tiera cry?"

"Who the hell is this?"

"Believe me. You want to answer my question first and not make me wait."

"Put *Tiernan* back on the phone."

"No. You are done talking to her. You're talking to me now."

"I don't owe you shit. Obviously, she lied about yet another thing. She's not dating someone. You're her new Dom. She just told me that to get out of our arrangement. If I'd thought she could find someone else, I would have left her ages ago."

My ears are ringing.

"What did you just say about my girlfriend?"

"Girlfriend? Bullshit."

"I don't need to know what you said to make her cry. I can guess. That was a mistake. That's the only mistake you get to make. Do not call her. Do not text her. Do nothing to contact her again. I promise you, that would be a mistake you don't want to make. She's been faithful to your relationship and ended things with you rather than disobey you. You have no right to make her feel badly about moving on. You're a fool to talk about her with anything but the highest praise. Besides the physical pain she's agreed to, have you made her cry before?"

Tiera pulls back and tries to grab the phone from me. I straighten and hold it out of her reach. I shoot her a warning glare. Her response tells me everything. I was displeased a moment ago. Now I'm pissed.

"That's none of your business."

"It is when you've made my girlfriend cry. Stay away from Tiera. You do *not* want to discover just how defensive I can get when it comes to her. You will never make her cry again."

"But I will make her scream when she comes. Just like I have for years. You won't last. You talk a big game now. But she's broken. That's why she's found no one else who could want her. That's why she likes to be degraded. She knows what she is."

My head may explode.

"Come near Tiera, and you won't get your dick up ever again."

I hang up before I can say something I can't take back. Something that could be held against me in a court of law. I hang up before he says something that'll make me kill him. I toss the phone on the bed and pick Tiera up. She squeaks and wraps her legs around my waist.

"Seamus, put me down. I'm too big to be hefting around. I know you said you can carry Cormac, but that's not the same."

"You're right. It isn't. Cormac's heavy arse is annoying. Your arse is the finest I've ever seen."

Her eyes dart to the door before looking at me.

"You didn't leave the door open on purpose? To let me watch you?" I sound disbelieving.

"I didn't think about whether it closed all the way. I live alone. I rarely close it. I thought I'd shut it enough because I knew you were out there. I didn't check."

"I'm glad you didn't. I enjoyed watching every inch of you I could see. I look forward to seeing the front of you too. In fact, I feel a little robbed that I didn't. Tiera, I don't have a type. I'm not making some exception for you. I've wanted to fuck you since the moment I saw you walk past me in that courtroom. My cock's never had that much of a mind of its own. I buttoned my suit coat *before* I stood when I cross-examined you because I knew if I stood first, you and the judge would see how hard I was for you."

I rub her against my dick.

"I was just like this. *You* do this to me. Tiera, I haven't been with anyone since I met you. But I have jerked off. A lot. More than I have since I was like fourteen. I'm always thinking about you. Picturing you."

"Wonderful. You have an idea of what I look like. I doubt it matches what you'll find."

"I saw more than you think, and I like all of it. Do you think I got hard arguing with him? I was hard when I came in here, and I'm hard now."

"You do things to me, too."

She smiles, and it's like the sun came out after days of darkness. I perch on the bed, and I wipe the last of her tears. It rips at my heart to think anyone—especially someone like her Dom, who is supposed to make her feel good about herself—makes her doubt how special she is.

"Seamus, what he said about what I like. I—"

She snaps her mouth shut and looks away.

"Do you want vanilla or more between us?"

"Definitely not vanilla. But you told me you don't want me as your sub. What do you want between us?"

"I'd like to explore what we both enjoy and what we want to share. Are there things that are off limits?"

"Not really. Just the really hard-core taboo."

"What are your hard limits?"

"Anything that will make me too sore to play soccer."

I grin. I can't help it.

"I wouldn't do anything to keep you from being magnificent on the field."

"You don't strike me as a man prone to exaggeration, even if you put on a good show in front of a jury. But you sure are full of it when it comes to describing me."

The more Tiera shares with me, the more I realize she's had very little support in her emotional life. It makes me wonder what her parents are like with her. But it's obvious the men in her life haven't treated her how they should have. They've disappointed her, even if she doesn't realize it.

"*Cailín*, I'm not someone who exaggerates. What I say about you is what I see and feel. I don't have to."

"Thank you." She cups my cheeks and offers me a soft peck on my lips. "What about you, Seamus? What do you want or need?"

"I'm not sure. Some things I've done in the past don't appeal to me now."

"Such as?"

"I can't imagine marring you with bruises like I've left before."

"Did your subs agree to those? Did they want them?"

"Yes to both. Do you want that? I won't ask to birch you or paddle hard enough to leave lasting marks, but if that's what you need..."

"It's not. At least, not all the time. You said I'm not your sub, so I don't really know what I want in this kind of romantic relationship."

"He said you like to be degraded. What did he mean?"

I won't say that areselick's name. Just thinking it makes me want to beat his head into a brick wall.

"It's not so much that I enjoyed being degraded as it was how it fit with the way I felt about myself. But you don't let me question my worth, so I don't think I'd like to be called those things if we're not in the middle of having sex."

"Such as?"

"Slut, whore. I'd like to hear it while we're having sex, but not while we're doing other intimate things."

"I can live with that. I couldn't call you either of those at any other time. Did he?"

"Yes. But not like in regular conversation. Only when he gave commands or while I was restrained."

"Were there rules you want now?"

"No. There was nothing that wouldn't make me feel like a sub rather than a—"

"Girlfriend. I meant it when I said it both times. I know we haven't discussed it yet, but I've also told you I won't share you. I won't make you share me. I only want something that is exclusive."

"Casually exclusive?"

"Do you mean do I see this going somewhere serious or long term?"

"Yes."

"That's the only way I'd draw you deeper into my life. I don't know what you know, but I doubt your husband was as senior as I am. I doubt his schedule could be as unpredictable as mine or came with the same dangers mine does. I wouldn't expose you to any of that if this were just about fucking or a fling."

She nods as I speak. We've skirted this, even though I've had to be gone more than once. She's hearing me out, and I think she gets a lot of the things I'm not saying. She's reading between the lines, knowing an unpredictable schedule means I could be away far longer than I have been the four times I couldn't see her. That being away usually means I'm doing some seriously illegal shite. That I'm being a man I hope she never sees up close and personal.

"I wouldn't bring you near the O'Briens and put you in danger with them if I didn't want something serious with you, too. I know how things are, and I wouldn't risk making you Gareth's personal target if I just wanted to fuck and walk away."

"Because of the danger that's already around me and

because of the way things are between my family and the O'Briens, I will have some rules, Tiera. Ones that are non-negotiable. They're for your safety and my family's. These aren't about any type of Dom/sub dynamic. I—"

"What about your safety? I don't want to do things that might get you hurt." She cuts in, and she's emphatic. It makes me smile, and it melts my ice and steel heart.

"All right. Yours, mine, and my family's. If you break the rules I put in place to protect you, I will punish you. I will spank you. I will edge you."

"I can live with that. There's a lot of shit in my life that makes me question my decisions, makes me think I don't know what I'm doing. I feel like I'm in over my head all the time. I usually am thanks to my family ties. I got into BDSM because of that. I enjoyed handing over control for a while and not having to think about what's coming next. It was an escape from real life. I like the idea of continuing that with you. But I —I—need—I—"

She stumbles over her words, and her cheeks flush. She looks monumentally uncomfortable telling me whatever is on her mind.

"Are you embarrassed to admit what you need? Or are you that unused to asking? Or do you expect me to reject you?"

"Yes." She offers me a timid smile.

I know we should have already left for Trenton, but I don't care. Whatever she wants to talk about is important to her—to us. There are few times when I've put anyone ahead of work and duty. I will put Tiera ahead of everything whenever I can. I help her off my lap, and she looks like I kicked her puppy.

"Strip."

"What?"

"Strip, Tiera. All of it. I want you naked. Now."

I'm not commanding her like I could, like I did when I was

on the phone with Makayla. She can tell we're equals, that she can say no.

"Seamus, I'm not sure I can do that. I don't feel confident about you seeing me like that."

"Which is exactly why I want you naked. I want you to see how much I appreciate you just as you are."

I reach behind her and unzip the loose flowing skirt she put on after I already told her to change. I've never been so demanding about any woman's clothes. She pushes it down over her hips. I push up the top she's wearing, and she pulls it over her head. I unfasten her bra and ease the straps down her arms.

"I never want to see panties on you again. When I undress you, I expect to see your pussy immediately. When I slide my hands down your pants or up your skirt, I expect to find your pussy with nothing in the way."

I slip my hand down the waistband of her thong and cup her cunt.

"Take them off before I shred them."

She hurries to obey.

I can feel the heat coming from her. I can feel how wet she is without sticking a finger inside her. I rub the heel of my hand over her clit.

"Get on the bed, *cailín*."

She does as I say, and I kick off my shoes before climbing on beside her. Never have I appreciated having long arms like I do now. My hand trails from her mid-thigh up and over her arse. I squeeze, then bring my hand down in a ringing slap. I do it four more times. I dip my fingers into her pussy before my thumb presses against her arsehole.

"When I want to touch you, I will. If you don't want me to, you tell me no. I'll always respect that."

I massage up her back until I get to her shoulders. I rub the knots I feel, and she relaxes. I sweep my hand over her tits, settling on the one she isn't lying against. I knead it as I lean to whisper to her.

"I can't wait to taste your nipples and make them hard."

Then I ease my hand to her belly. She sucks in. I pull my hand away, and she shuts her eyes. I land a spank far harder than the ones I did before. I put my hand back on her belly. She sucks in again. I spank her even harder. When I put my hand on her belly a third time, she does nothing. She has the softest skin I've ever felt. I trail my hand over her before running my fingertips from just below her breast to her clit. I grasp her thigh and draw it over mine. I love that there's plenty to touch and hold.

"Tell me what you need, little one." I soften my voice as I continue to run my hand over every inch of her I can touch.

She hesitates, and I wonder if I've pushed way too hard.

"I need you to—to help me when—" She licks her lips and looks completely lost.

"You need me to help you when real life feels out of control, and we're not roleplaying. You need me to take control when things with Gareth and his men are too much."

"Yes." She speaks so softly I have to read her lips.

"Thank you for telling me that, but it was already a given. I will always take care of you, Tiera. I will try to anticipate what those needs are and to protect you. But you may need to tell me if I'm not there the way you need me."

"I don't want you to think I can't take care of myself or that I don't want to."

"Tiera, I know that. You're highly capable, and I don't think you're suddenly going to turn helpless. Let me share the burden, so you don't have to face all of this on your own."

"Thank you. What do you need?"

It's rare anyone asks me that. At least, anyone who isn't my parents or my brother or my immediate family. Anyone who isn't asking about more than what I want to do with a "guest" at the station.

"I need to know you're safe. I need to know you're happy. Seeing you smile makes the weight of the world disappear. Hearing your voice allows me to forget about my responsibilities for a while. Taking care of you makes me feel useful as Seamus, not an O'Rourke mobster."

She reaches out and unbuttons my shirt. She pushes it open as her hands run over my chest and belly. She scoots closer and kisses my neck.

"And if I want to take care of you?"

I gaze down at her upturned face. I feel a surge of emotion that makes me want to promise I'll be beside her for the rest of time. But I can't even promise tomorrow, let alone a long life. I could get stabbed or shot tomorrow, and that ever-present danger makes me an arsehole for wanting Tiera to be my girlfriend.

"You already do, *cailín*."

"You're bigger than me, stronger than me. You're protective, you want to take care of me, and you're just the right kind of possessive. You sound pretty fucking perfect. You call me little one. I called you big one once, but that was in jest. If I'm your *cailín*, then what are you to me? What do you want me to call you?"

A word comes to me in a flash. It shocks the shite out of me, though it shouldn't because I've heard my cousins' wives whisper it before. Tiera will completely misunderstand if I suggest it.

"Whatever you want. I'll answer to just about anything."

"That is *not* what you want, and we both know it. I think

129

there is something you want me to call you, but you think I won't agree or that it'll freak me out. Say it, Seamus. Say what you want me to call you."

Chapter Eleven

Tiera

Seamus watches me for what feels like an eternity, but it's probably just a few seconds.

"No woman has ever called me this. I've never suggested it before. And it'll sound exactly the opposite of what I told you the first time we talked about anything like this."

"I already know the last bit. I'm happy to know the first two things. I don't believe you suddenly want something different from what you told me. But I believe we'd both be happy with it. Tell me what you want me to call you."

"*Cailín*, you're going to call me Daddy."

It makes my pussy clench. Fuck, that's hot. I grip his shoulder and pull him as I roll onto my back. He follows me, his right arm reaching across me, so he can prop himself up on his right hand and left forearm. The way he gazes at me as I speak is everything I could ever dream of.

"Daddy. I like the sound of that. I don't want age play, and I don't think you do either But I think you need to feel useful and like you can shield me from some of the things that surround our life. I think you want me to know you take your promise to take care of me seriously. I think you need to feel control, and I'm happy to give that to you."

"All of that."

"Seamus, I tested after Aaron died. Zack never went without a condom, but I still tested anyway. I think he was with other women even though he swore he wasn't. I wanted to be careful, so I not only use birth control but also insisted he wear protection. I haven't been with anyone but him since Aaron died."

"I haven't been with anyone other than Makayla for three years, who I just found out didn't live by the agreement we had."

"Oh, Daddy. I'm sorry." I love how easily that rolls off my tongue.

"It doesn't surprise me, but it is disappointing to discover someone isn't who you thought. I tested regularly with her even though I thought we were monogamous. I think I always knew in the back of my mind that she fucked at least one of the guys she dated while we were together. I always wore a condom with her. I've never had sex without one."

"Never?"

"No. The first girl I had sex with—she will never know the meaning of monogamy. She was someone who—I'm not the only person in my family who was with her. I'm pretty sure she was a couple of my cousins' first, but none of us were even close to being her first. Knowing that, I never went bareback with her because I didn't know who outside my family she was sleeping with. All of us practically double bagged it with her."

Saying this aloud makes him wince. I don't think he realized how bad it would sound until he started speaking.

"Anyway, I always wore them when I was at my clubs with

the few women I scened with before I got together with Makayla."

"Clubs?"

"I belong to two BDSM clubs, Tiera."

That interests me, and he can tell. He places his thigh between my legs and presses it against my cunt. I flex my hips, rubbing against him.

"Does that intrigue you?"

"Yes."

"Do you want me to take you?"

"Yes. Very much."

If I were his sub, I'd answer with Sir, or I guess in our case, Daddy. But I'm not. Daddy is a term of endearment, not a sign of submission.

He rests on both forearms, and his right hand strokes hair back from my forehead. He cups my jaw and turns my head even more toward him. He presses the softest kiss to my lips. It's quick, so I have no chance to open to him.

"I don't think you can guess all the fantasies I have about you and with you, *cailín*. All the ways I wish to pleasure you."

"You've really given it that much thought?"

"Practically every moment I'm not focused on work. I want to take you to a World Cup game and watch you watch the match."

I stare at him for a moment before I laugh so hard I snort. I cover my mouth with both hands. Then it's my turn to cup his cheeks when they flush. I lift my head and give him a smacking kiss on his lips.

"You sweet, sweet man."

My next kiss isn't quick. My tongue flicks against his lips before I press it into his mouth as he opens to me. He lets me initiate the kiss, but he soon takes control. He rolls onto his left hip, moving his leg from between mine as his body hovers over mine. He squeezes my tits before his hand rubs circles over my belly three times. Then his hand is where I've wanted it since the first moment I saw him. His fingers run between my pussy lips before three dip into me.

"You're so wet for me, little one."

"I'm always like this when you're nearby. Or I think about you."

He strokes the inside of my cunt, pressing against my g spot. He soon has me writhing beneath him. I tilt my hips, wanting to take more of him, telling him I need more. I open my legs wider for him. As he rubs my clit, I can't keep my eyes open despite how I try. I can feel myself getting closer.

"Daddy."

"Yes, *cailín*."

"Can I touch you too?"

"This is for you, Tiera. I'm not pleasuring you to get something in return."

"I know that. I want to touch you while you touch me. Together. Seamus, this is important to me."

And it is. I don't know why I need to watch him come as badly as I want him to make me come. It's not just that I want the satisfaction of knowing I'm the one to pleasure him. I know there's a bit of that, but there's also more. It's not just to see him pleasured.

I want it to be equal between us. I don't want him to only give. He's already doing that in so many other ways. For me, for his family, for everyone in his life. I don't want to just take. I want him to know he means as much to me as I seem to mean to him.

"Take me out. But I'm warning you, if my cock gets anywhere near your cunt, I will fuck you. I will come in you. And you will keep that cum in you until it drips down your thighs while we deal with Gareth."

"Don't say his name when we're together like this. That asshole doesn't get to be a part of our relationship. Not any of it, not even in passing."

"Once I come in you, there's no going back, Tiera. I won't end this. If it's over, it's because you don't want it anymore. Once I come in you, nothing will keep me from you. This isn't something I take lightly. I told you I've always worn a condom. There is no woman who'll be able to claim what you have. You will have all of me."

There's significance in that, and I don't miss it. He wants me to know he's not holding back. But how much of his heart could I have at this point? He's inching into every crevice of mine. I don't know if it's possible for him to reciprocate. I don't know if he can give that much. Not just because of his family and how important they obviously are to him. I don't know if he will open his heart that much to me.

He's told me more than once that he didn't have a romantic relationship with *that* woman—bitch. How could anyone cheat on Seamus? — and he told her he couldn't with anyone. What makes me different? What makes this anything more or other than infatuation? I don't want to give my love to a man who can't return it.

"I know how significant that is, Daddy. I don't want you to think I don't. It means the world to me that you want to share this with me."

"I want to make you happy, little one, because you make me happy. I know some of the time we've spent together has had a pall cast over it. But that doesn't mean I don't find happiness in just being near you."

"I know that. I feel the same way. There have been some challenges, but I'm happier with you than without.

He lowers his body to mine, careful not to squash me. His lips brush over mine before he presses them to me. It's as demanding a kiss as earlier. One that lets me know he wants me. One that lets me know I matter. I haven't felt like I matter to anyone but my parents in years. Even before Aaron died.

I reach between us to finish unbuttoning his shirt. I push one sleeve down, then the other as he shifts his weight to shake the sleeves free. Then I'm pushing his pants down. He has to break the kiss long enough to get them and his socks off. Thank God. No guy has ever had sex with me while his socks were on. It's too cliché, and I'm glad Seamus didn't break that streak.

I stroke him when he moves back to hover over me again. He shifts to be between my legs, but I grab at him when he scoots down the bed. He settles between my legs and looks up at me. Wolfish is the only way to describe his expression. He's the Big Bad Wolf, and he's going to gobble me up. Who am I to stop him?

He smatters kisses all over my belly. I want to suck it in again, surprised and nervous. But he didn't like it when I did that before. His massive hand slides along my left ribs before sweeping over my tummy and up my right ribs. Then his hand slips back to my waist, gripping it. I don't like it at first when he has a handful of my rolls. But he sighs. Fucking sighs.

The sexy heat in his eyes is gone and replaced with—I don't know—relief? Contentment? He just looks at ease for the first time ever. There's always been an edge of wariness. I've never felt it toward me, but more about our surroundings. Like he's never relaxed around me, and it's been more situational aware-ness than anything else. Now he's just Seamus. I truly have the man, not the mobster, and he's between my thighs.

That tempts me to giggle, but it would be the most inopportune time for that. He's shy, and I realize he puts on a bigger persona than is his genuine personality. He is who he has to be when he's around everyone else. He was who he believed he had to be around me. I'm seeing him with his guard down, and it makes me feel like a million bucks. Not just because he likes what he sees and feels. It makes my heart near bursting to know he can have this with me—have this reprieve. I don't think he has it often. Maybe around his family. I don't know. But I cherish it.

He lowers his head to my pussy and licks. Fucking hell. That feels beyond amazing. What is the next level? Divine? He slips his tongue into me and flicks my clit from beneath it. Then he swirls his tongue over it as his lips close around it. He sucks, and my hips nearly come off the mattress. His hand is tracing lazy circles over my belly, and I don't think he notices because he appears fully interested with my pussy. He's looking at it now like he's planning his attack.

"*Cailín*, I don't know what I want short of devouring you. If there's something you like or don't like, tell me. I want to make you scream my name over and over. I want to feel you come on my fingers and dick and tongue. Tell me whatever you want me to do. I'll do anything."

I believe him.

"Just keep doing what you're doing. I like it. Love it."

He returns his mouth to my pussy, sliding two fingers in. Then three. I want him to move faster. I want him to move slower. I want him to hurry up and get me off. I want him to prolong my excitement and need. I just want him.

He strokes my g spot, his hand now pressing down on his fingers from on top of my stomach. It feels incredible. Is that higher praise than amazing? I want to close my eyes and revel in the moment, but I also don't want to miss a moment of how Seamus looks at me. He concentrates as though nothing else is going on in the world. Nothing else exists.

My need is building to a point where I don't think I can stop my body even if my mind tells me to slow down.

"Seamus, I'm close."

"Who am I?"

"Daddy. My Daddy."

He sucks so hard on my clit that it hurts. He grazes his teeth over it, and I shake. He rubs his thumb in hard, fast circles until I know I'm going to come if he keeps going for another three or four seconds.

"May I come, Daddy?"

"Don't ask unless I tell you that's how we are."

I squeeze my eyes shut as it starts. I concentrate on the sensations as the wave moves toward the shore. Then I need to see him. I need to know what he's doing. Not the fingers that are working my clit. I need to know if he's staring off into space when he thinks I'm not watching. I've had plenty of men do that. I had a past before I was with Aaron, and it wasn't one of abstinence.

No. Seamus isn't like any other man I know, and I should have given him more credit. He's watching what he's doing, and he appears fully immersed in the task. His gaze shifts to my face, perhaps sensing I'm watching him. The hunger is back in his eyes, and I come when I see it. I've never felt so desired in my life.

"Daddy!"

I suck in a lungful of air after I scream. Thank God my neighbors are probably at work. I hope they are as he pushes up onto his hands and moves back toward my head. He kisses me, thrusting his tongue into my mouth. I want to recoil, never enjoying tasting myself.

"You will taste what I do."

He reads my mind before he sticks his tongue back into my mouth, swirling it around to touch practically every inch of mine. I'm stroking him, and he's a fucking iron pipe in my hands. He's big. Long and thick. I've been with men nearly like him. Maybe they were, but I can't remember that clearly. I just know no one is going to feel like him. I guide the tip of his cock to my pussy. I barely get my hand out of the way as his hips draw back. I know what's coming, and I don't want to stop him.

He enters me so hard I scream around his tongue. My thighs grip his hips as my fingers claw his back.

"Fuck, Seamus."

I tear my mouth from his, panting. He freezes.

"I'm sorry."

I stare at him for a second. "What?"

"I hurt you. I should have thought about you being smaller than me. That you haven't felt me before. I'm sorry."

"That's what you think just happened? Shut up, Daddy, before you ruin the mood. And keep doing what you just did. I told you. I don't want vanilla. I want a good hard fucking. Now."

"Are you commanding me?"

"This time, I am. We're equals, remember?"

I waggle my eyebrows. He growls! Fucking growls like a feral animal as he draws back his hips and slams into me even harder.

"Is this what you want? Is this how you want me to fuck you? Fuck you hard enough you'll not just have my cum dripping down your thighs for the rest of the day, but you'll be sore with every step? It'll remind you that you belong to me."

"I do. All of me belongs to you."

Does he get the significance of that? That I'm admitting what I think he admitted earlier.

"Yes, you are. You are mine to pleasure. You are mine to make come whenever I decide you should. You are mine to deny whenever I decide I should. You are mine to take care of. Mine to protect. Mine to keep for as long as you want me, Tiera."

He's said that before. That it's up to me to end this. That he won't go anywhere. That he wants this to be long term.

"I'm not letting you walk away from me, Seamus. I'm not walking away. You are mine. You are mine to pleasure. Mine to take care of. Mine to protect. If you're giving me control of when this ends, you better settle in because it won't be over for a long ass time."

He thrusts harder and harder. I don't know how he does it. Every time I think he can't give me more, he does. Every time I think I can't take more, he makes me. Every time. Over and over. I can't get enough. They say it only takes one hit of heroin to be addicted. It only takes one time with Seamus to be addicted.

His hand comes to rest on my throat. He doesn't squeeze, but it's heavy.

"I will lead, and you will follow in our sex life. I will dominate, and you will submit when we are like this. But that is not how we are anywhere else. You get today to command me. In everything, you have the final say. If you don't want something or don't like it, then you tell me, and it stops. What's your safe word?"

I have to think for a moment, then I know.

"Midfield."

He freezes, then laughs. His cock twitches inside me.

"*Tá mé chun tú a phósadh.*"

He said that at the first game. This time, I repeat it over and over until I think I remember it well enough to look it up later.

"Okay, *cailín*. Midfield it is."

His hand tightens around my throat as he thrusts over and over. He was holding himself up on one hand a moment ago, but he settles back onto his forearm. He leans to whisper in my ear, and the warm air tickles, making me shiver. Fuck. My pussy clenches around him as my fingers dig into his back again.

"My little slut is so tight for her daddy. Does she need his cock?"

"Yes." I answer on an exhale.

"Whose slut are you?"

"Yours, Daddy."

"Why?"

"Because I'm a whore for you."

"Who am I?"

"Daddy."

"That's right. Your tight little cunt is going to take me whenever I want. You won't keep me from it because you're my little whore."

I relish every word. I love it. I needed the degradation when I was with Zack. It's fucked-up to say it. But it validated some of the shitty feelings I had about myself. My doubts. In its twisted way, it made me feel confident that I knew who I was. I don't just come with suitcases as baggage. I come with trunks. I know that.

But with Seamus, it just feels sexy. It doesn't feel like he thinks I'm those things. He just knows I like hearing it. He knows it gives him that dominance without being domineering.

He keeps tightening until it's breath play, but his thumb strokes the side of my neck. It's getting hard to breathe, and I normally would have a flash of panic at this moment. A fear Zack wouldn't let go in time. I know he liked me to feel that way. It was his sadistic side. But Seamus doesn't make me experience that. The soft movement of his thumb lets me know he's being careful, that he's doing this for me.

As our gazes remain locked, I can tell I'm more into this than he is. That this is something he's tolerating for me. I don't think he likes it.

My ears are beginning to ring, and I want to suck in a breath, but I can't. You'd think now would be when I claw at his back. Now would be when I want him to know it's too much. I don't. Just the opposite. I relax. I'm still moving to meet his thrusts. I'm still tilting my hips to take him as deep as he can go. But I'm not fighting his control. Not that I ever really was. I guess the right word is surrender. I surrender to him.

His expression changes when he feels it. There's a flash of panic. I think he fears I'm going to pass out, but I haven't stopped watching him. I try to smile, but it's too hard. But I think he sees what I'm trying to say in my eyes. He squeezes extra hard for a second before he lets go.

I gulp air. My chest rises and falls faster than it was and now is when I have a moment of light-headedness. But it's gone in an instant. I slide my hands to his ass and squeeze. I push, so his hips grind against mine.

"Was that too much?" His whisper is beside my ear before he kisses just behind and below it.

"No. It was just right. I want more. Again, please."

He lifts his body and looks skeptical.

"I trust you, Daddy."

His kiss isn't like any other we've had. I love the soft ones. The bare brushing of our lips. I love the gentle ones when I feel precious to him. I love the hungry ones where I've never felt more alluring and provocative. But this one is desperate. Like he needs something, and he's scared he's about to lose it. I stroke his hair and his back as he continues to kiss me. His thrusts are different, too. They're not softer or slower, but they last a little longer somehow. I pull my mouth free of his.

"Daddy, I'm not going anywhere. I'm yours. Seamus, I swear. I trust you, and I'm not going anywhere."

Then I'm the one leading the kiss. I want to infuse all the reassurance into it I can. The entire jumble of my feelings.

Tenderness. Lust. Happiness. And the beginning of falling in love.

He pulls back and kisses my neck on both sides. Then his hand is back around my throat. His fingers don't dig into me, careful not to leave marks. He just presses harder with his fingers and squeezes between his thumb and forefinger.

"You're my little whore who'll beg for my cock because you can't get enough. You like to fuck. You like to fuck my cock even more."

I squeeze around him, including my pussy. His hold on my throat is tighter than it was. I can feel the world closing in. The black dots start in my peripheral vision. I feel the light-headed-ness from before, but it's while he still has hold of me. I relax into it. My trust in him absolute. I know he'll stop. The moment my eyes droop, he lets go. He's kissing my neck again, and these are soft. His thrusts slow. He circles his hips, rubbing my clit with his pubic bone each time he tilts his hips to get as deep as he can. Giving me every inch.

"I'm close, Daddy... I really need to come...I'm so close...I want you to come too...I want to be your good girl...I want to—Daddy, I'm going to come. I want your cum."

"You're going to get it. You are my good girl. Come for me."

I strain, and then I feel it.

"Daddy, don't stop. I'm close. I'm close...I'm coming, Shay. Don't stop... Fuck...Seamus!"

"Tiera!"

He shudders, and I'm sure he's coming hard. We keep moving, and I know we're both trying to draw out each other's orgasm and our own. When mine subsides, he gives one more thrust and stops. But only for a moment. He rolls us, and I grip his shoulders.

"Ride me."

I follow his order and grind my pussy against him. I rock as

I get off again. I shift my hands to the pillow beneath his head, afraid my nails will break the skin if I dig as deep as I need to. This is one of the best orgasms I've ever had. In fact, I don't remember another like it. I feel it all the way into my teeth. Fuck.

I sit back and look at him. His hands have been moving all over me, and I didn't even notice. I shift to rise and fall on his cock, swinging my tits with every move. I press my hands into his chest to balance for a moment. His fingers are definitely going to leave marks now. I can't wait to see them in the mirror.

"Ride me, Tiera. I'm going to come again."

He's panting, and he sounds surprised. I do as he says. I put my hands on my hips, so he can see my tits bounce without any trouble. He tweaks my nipples hard enough for me to yelp. He rubs them between his thumb and forefinger before doing it again. I moan. He pinches harder. I whimper. He eases off. He waits a moment, then pinches again. He gets another moan for his efforts. He does it harder, and I whimper.

"Daddy."

"Too much?"

"No. I like it. More."

It hurts almost too much. But I love it. I love the pain. I love knowing I'm doing something he enjoys, and that he's giving me something I enjoy. We're doing this for and to and with each other. That's an aphrodisiac without eating a damn oyster. That just makes me think about sucking his dick later. I'm definitely doing that. I enjoy giving blow jobs. I don't enjoy swallowing, but I'll do it for him.

"Fuck, Tiera. Keep doing that."

His hands are back on my hips to help me balance as I move faster.

"You have the finest tits ever made."

"And I grew them myself."

"That's what makes them so fucking fine. Fuck, I want to suck them."

I push them together as I lean forward. He accepts my right one. Sucking hard then biting the nipple. I scream because I can. I really hope my neighbors are at work.

He moves to the other side, his tongue toying with my nipple this time. Then he's sucking hard. Over and over. Shifting between them as his eyes close. He squeezes sometimes, his fingers sliding over them at others. But throughout, he holds them to his face.

But he lets go abruptly, and he spanks me over and over as he shifts my movements to rock on his dick.

"You feel amazing, baby girl. Keep doing this."

"You feel amazing too, Daddy. Don't stop. I like the spankings."

They make me want to move faster and harder.

"I'm coming, Shay... Fucking hell... Goddamn, this feels good."

It does. He thrusts into me, pinning me, then moving my hips forward and back just enough to keep rubbing my clit.

He thrusts once more, then I know he's coming again. I watch his abs contract. I love seeing his muscles move while we fuck. It's the hottest shit I've ever seen. His body is a temple to worship. He's built unlike any man I've ever seen in real life. I've worked with firefighters who are in shape since it's a physical job. I've worked with ones who are cut. But none have had a body like the one I'm getting to play with today.

He pulls me down against his chest and kisses my forehead. His touch is so light as he strokes my back. He keeps kissing the top of my head as his other hand rests on my ass. I close my eyes and sigh. I've never had orgasms like those before, but I've also never had this kind of post coital bliss. Even with Aaron at the best of times when he was affectionate, and I felt the same in return, it wasn't like this. I never ever want to get up. I want to close my eyes and live in this fairytale world.

"Tiera, you okay?"

"Can't you tell I'm in heaven?"

"I just want to be sure. I was rough."

"Just the way I needed and wanted and just at the right moments. You were also gentle when I needed it. I've never—"

I find myself biting my tongue a lot. I keep wanting to admit my deepest, darkest secrets because it's so easy to talk to Seamus. But it often feels like I'm admitting too much too soon. It scares me to be that vulnerable in case I'm wrong. I don't think I am. But it would destroy me to confess so much just to realize he doesn't feel even an ounce of what I do.

After all the time we've spent together over the past two months, I'm still apprehensive that his feelings aren't as strong as mine. It makes me wish we'd defined our relationship sooner. Cut ties with our subs sooner. I don't really know why we haven't. Maybe he's as uncertain about me as I am about him.

"What, T? You have this habit of stopping mid-sentence like you regret what you're going to say. I never want you to feel you can't tell me everything. No matter what it is, I will listen. I won't judge you, but I think you're scared that's exactly what I'll do. Would it help to know I've never experienced anything so earth-shattering as that? I've never come twice. I've never felt so completely in tune with someone else. I've never felt like anyone else has understood exactly what I needed at the exact moment I needed it. I didn't have to ask you for a thing or tell you. You knew. I can't believe it."

I push up on my forearm on his chest, careful not to dig my elbow into him. I move, so I can put my arm next to his head, but his hand covers my arm. He wants me to keep touching him.

"Seamus, you have no idea what that admission means to

me. That you feel this way and that you're telling me. You said what I was thinking. When I told you I wanted the breath play, it wasn't because I didn't think you knew that or that you wouldn't give me something else I'd enjoy. I did it to surrender to you."

"I know, little one. That's what I meant about knowing what I wanted and needed. You get me."

"And you get me."

"You didn't mind the stuff I said?"

"I loved it. It was just right. Just enough to get the message without feeling like it was over the top or mean."

"Good. That was my goal."

I don't know what to make of the look that just flashed in his eyes.

"Didn't you like it?"

"I was nervous I went too far. That I squeezed too tightly, or that I demeaned you too much. I didn't enjoy worrying about that. I'm not sure how I feel about calling you those things again, but I will if you enjoy it."

"I won't enjoy it if I know it bothers you."

He's quiet for a moment while he thinks.

"I'll do it sometimes, and like you said before, only when we're having sex. I won't do it during foreplay. I can't."

I stroke the back of my fingers along his temple, and he turns into my fingers a little. His eyes slide shut, and he releases a deep sigh. His face is completely at rest, and he looks even more boyish than usual. It's about the sweetest thing I've ever seen. It makes me wonder what our kids would look like. A baby girl sleeping in my arms or a toddler boy sleeping in a little bed. I'm certain he was the most adorable kid ever.

"*Cailín?*"

"Yes, Daddy."

"If this isn't real—if this isn't going anywhere, and it's just been dirty talk—tell me now. You'll break my heart otherwise."

"Seamus, look at me."

He opens his eyes, and there's the shyness I see hints of. A vulnerability I doubt any sub ever saw.

"It was not just sex or dirty talk. It wasn't roleplaying either. What we talked about earlier was probably the best start to a relationship I've ever had. Even with my Dom, we didn't define things before the very first time we had sex. I like that we did. It's a relief that we did. I know where we stand, and it's exactly where I want to be. I'll say the same thing to you. If this was just all roleplaying or sex talk, then tell me. If I think it's something more, and it's not, it'll break my heart."

"I've never felt any of this before. I don't know what it is to be in love. You do. I don't know if that's what we're moving toward. But I don't think this is infatuation. That I can recognize."

I kiss his left cheek as I cup his right. I rub our noses together.

"I have been in love before. But it was never the kind meant to last because it wasn't with the right person. Perhaps some of it was being in love with the idea of being in love. Or it was being in love with the idea of love in general. Maybe it was being in love because it gave me—or at least, I thought it gave me—the chance for the future I wanted. I don't know. But this is different. All of it, and I don't think it's infatuation. Just the opposite. It makes me wonder if what I felt the past three times I thought I was in love was just infatuation."

"I don't want you to question how you felt about people in your past. About how you felt about your husband."

"I'm not. I'm understanding it more. I don't know where you and I are going or where we'll wind up. But I like the path we're on. I like where I think it's headed. You've said more than once this won't end unless I want it to. I appreciate that, but I don't like it. I don't want you to feel you made some pledge you can't take back. I know what your honor means to you. I never want you to feel trapped with me because of something you said this early in our relationship."

"Thank you, Tiera."

"Now, let me rest for a few minutes. I was extremely comfortable. You're the best pillow I've ever had."

I settle back onto his chest, and he goes back to stroking my back and holding my ass. I kiss his chest. I could fall asleep like this. His body no longer cooperates, so he isn't inside me like he was earlier. But this is peaceful, and soul restoring. I close my eyes and listen to his heartbeat. It's a steady cadence that is lulling me to sleep.

"Rest, *cailín*. Let yourself let go for a bit. I'll hold you, so nothing can bother you. You're mine to have and to hold."

I remember that line from my marriage vows. It was just a series of words in what felt like a reverent occasion. Never did they mean what they do now.

"Thank you, Daddy." I wrap my arms around him. "You're mine to have and to hold, too."

"*Tá mé chun tú a phósadh.*"

Chapter Twelve

Seamus

I've told Tiera three times now that I'm going to marry her. She's never reacted like she knows what I mean. But one of these times, she's going to remember and look it up. That possibility doesn't make me mean it any less. But I don't want to freak her out. We've gone from zero to five thousand in two hours. Things were building gradually over the past eight weeks, but they skyrocketed today.

While I've never felt this way about anyone or been in a relationship like this before, I'm used to things escalating at an astounding pace. Things flipping on a dime. I can live with it. It's normal to me. Life would be frighteningly dull if it didn't. Too much quiet—things being too easy—scares me. It's usually the sign something is about to go extremely wrong. But it would be bliss if things were uneventful with Tiera.

Having sex with her was a spiritual experience. I stopped going to church regularly when I was sixteen. I lasted longer than anyone else in my family. I knew I was a hypocrite for doing the things I did and thinking a few confessions with veiled meaning and saying the rosary a bunch of times would be enough. But I wanted to believe forgiveness and salvation were possible even for the worst of sinners. Now I don't know. Maybe for other people, but I'm not convinced it is for me.

Being with Tiera is a glimpse into heaven. It's a glimpse at the redemption I prayed for. The peace that used to come when I was much younger and prayed. It's not like I'm going to anoint her as a saint or even hold her up on a pedestal from which she can only fall. I won't set her up for failure like that. But I know this is a chance for me to have a different life.

At least part of it can be different. I can finally have some balance. I can finally have a reprieve. I don't want to put too much of my hopes and needs on her shoulders since that's a weight that would crush her. I just know she makes me happy, and I want nothing more than for her to feel that, too.

I glance down at her. I know she's not sleeping. We're both just resting and enjoying the calm before the inevitable storm that is life in the mob. I haven't forgotten about Trenton and Gareth. We'll still go. But this is more important. Tiera will always be more important even if I can't always put her first. For now, I can, so I am.

"Seamus?"

"Yes, *cailín*."

"We have to get going. We can't stay here much longer. It's going to take us at least two hours to get down there, and that's assuming there's only a little traffic getting out of the city."

"We get there when we get there. You owe Gareth nothing after he tried to feck you over."

She giggles, and it goes straight to my cock. I love hearing her happy, or at least amused after seeing her cry. I can't think about that, or I'll lose my shite and go on a rampage. I'll find that fuckwad and rip him apart. And this time, it wouldn't be with just my words. I'd take him to the station and make sure nothing but ash remains of him. Better yet, the tub of acid would ensure there's nothing left. Maybe a little sludge that couldn't be chemically or physically separated from the acid. Nothing that could identify him.

"Daddy, what are you thinking about? You just tensed, but it was after you finished talking. What did you just think of?"

"Nothing important, little one. I just thought about how much I prefer hearing you laugh to seeing your tears."

She rolls off me despite how I tighten my hold. She sits up to look at me.

"Are you going to do something to Zack?"

"No, despite the temptation. You wouldn't want that. You would know if I had even if I lied or just didn't tell you. I don't want you caught in the middle, and I don't want to upset you."

"I don't want you to think he did it regularly. We were together as long as you and Makayla. It only happened a few times, and they were misunderstandings more than anything."

"I don't care what they were. He was your Dom. Even with degradation kink, you should feel fulfilled and good about yourself because you got what you needed physically and emotionally. Even when the roleplaying ends, a Dom should make you feel safe and appreciated. If Zack made you cry, and it wasn't from consensual pain, then that's a problem. I won't do anything, and I trust your judgement about why you stayed with him. But that doesn't mean I have to like what I heard him say or that he upset you in the past. I know we may argue in the future, and I know my words might hurt you, but I will always regret that. I will always wish I hadn't no matter my feelings about whatever's making us argue. He didn't sound an ounce repentant. I don't like that."

"Shay, please let it go. I appreciate how you're always ready to come to my defense. I appreciate that you care, even though I think you'd do it for any woman."

"You're right that I would defend any woman. Anyone in a position to not defend themselves or needs an ally. But I haven't defended you just because you're a woman. You're my woman. You have been since the moment I laid eyes on you. Neither of us may have known that, but the universe did."

"I know I wanted it. I remember seeing the back of you and Cormac. You're both impressive and intimidating without seeing your faces. You're huge, and even from the back you both look like Armani models in the custom-tailored clothes. Then I saw your face. I know how similar you and Cormac are, and I can't say you're attractive without admitting your brother is too. But you've been a magnet since the moment I saw your face. It's not just that you're the handsomer of the two of you, but your everything. Your aura, I suppose. I'm a moth to your flame, and I prayed I wouldn't get singed."

"Then I treated you like shite."

She leans forward, so I can't help but look directly in her eyes. But she's not satisfied. She takes my hand that's resting on her thigh and tugs. I sit up, and she moves to straddle my lap. I was semi-aroused just being near her because she was lying on me, and now I'm looking at her.

The second her pussy touches my cock, it's alive with a mind of its own. She glances down and strokes. Then she kneels, and her cunt slides onto it. She moans, and I think I did too. It wasn't the manliest sound I've ever made. But she does nothing to make this sex, and I don't think she's just warming my cock. When she wraps her arms around my neck and begins talking, I know she understands the very thing I need when we're having serious conversations. I need to be inside her.

"Seamus, you did *not* treat me like shite. I don't like you thinking you did. Even if we weren't together, I wouldn't want you to think that. You did your job as a stellar attorney. You did exactly what your client needed you to do. I do not fault you for that. What you said only confirmed what you and I both knew. I shouldn't have been involved. It does nothing to negate my eighteen years of experience. It does nothing to negate my time as a firefighter, fire investigator, or actuary. It just proved I wasn't an expert meant to testify during *that* case. You didn't paint me as incompetent like I think you believe you did. You just pointed out I didn't know enough to give testimony."

"But I made it sound like you weren't qualified to give any testimony when I said you hadn't led that many investigations. I made it sound like you're a novice."

"I'm not, and I know that. But you didn't say anything untrue, even if you framed it in a context to serve your point. I didn't lead those investigations while I was in training. Or at least, I didn't work them solo. The ones I led still had my work checked by a more experienced investigator. But no scene is supposed to be solely determined by one person. That's why a firefighter alone isn't enough to assess cause. It's why we gather evidence. You're being way harder on yourself than you need to be. I wish you'd cut yourself some slack. I don't enjoy knowing you feel guilty over something I've been over since it happened."

"I worry that it'll affect your future work."

"I know you do. And I'll cross that bridge *if* and when I get to it."

"There'd be no bridge if it weren't for me."

"Seamus, don't beg trouble where there is none. Let it go."

She's told me that too many times. She shouldn't have to. I watch her, and I know if I keep pushing this, it'll only drive a wedge between us. That's the opposite of what I want. I nod and give her a peck on the lips. She leans against me, and I pull her hips toward me.

"What do you think Gareth is going to say to you since you've waited so long to go down there? Have you spoken to him today?"

"He won't say shit with you there. I talked to him the day the verdict came in and the day your brother got the settlement. I told him what I knew about each. He told me both outcomes were my fault. I told him to screw off both times. Beyond that, it's only been texts about him being too busy or me not having time to make the drive."

"And if I wasn't with you?"

"He'd have some shit to say about me being a disappointment to him just like I was as a wife. He'd say I failed just like I did at becoming a—"

This time, when she cuts herself off, I know without a doubt what she was going to say.

"He fecking says that to you?"

My heart is racing. I'm more pissed than when I spoke to Zack. I'm more pissed than when I heard Stella insult Tiera. I remind myself I don't want Tiera to see the side of me threatening to come out. I don't want her to know what I'm capable of. That whatever she imagines is a fraction of reality.

My grandfather was a fucking tyrant when training my brother, cousins, and me. He insisted we practice until we could master every move to get out of a hold or put someone in one. Uncle Donovan insisted we practice on each other. It was my mom's cousin Declan who punished us when we got it wrong. Granddad and Uncle Don would walk out of the room and leave Declan to it.

That fucking sick bastard. None of us are quite right in the head after what our families train us to do, what we see, and what we carry out. But that motherfucker loved to see our pain.

He was thirty years older than us and got a kick out of making boys want to cry.

To this day, Finn and Dillan won't speak about our training. I don't know that they even let themselves think about it. It was worse for them because they're the oldest of the six of us. Sean and Shane came as a package deal, and Cormac and I basically did, since I came two months early. Finn and Dillan only had each other while the rest of us came in sets of two. Finn and Dillan had already been doing jobs and started training two years before the rest of us. They knew shite, and Declan used to make them demonstrate on each other and on us. Granddad just encouraged him because we might have been his grandsons, but Declan was also his nephew.

Uncle Donovan actually stepped in a few times when we were really young. He had to remind Declan that if he broke any of our growth plates, we'd be no use to them in the long run. The worst was when we had to go up against Uncle Don's best friend, Colin. He'd been a golden glove boxer until Maksim Kutsenko rang his bell one too many times.

He was a bitter old shite because he couldn't fight for money anymore. He'd pick bar fights and roughed people up for money—usually Granddad's. We had to box against him to learn to hold our own in a fight. Really, it was more about learning how to take a punch. The five concussions I've had in my life were all from punches I took to the head from Colin. A fucking wrecking ball to the temple is what it felt like.

But all of this made me into the enforcer I became and the enforcer I remain. We all have our roles beyond the obvious jobs we do for the family. Dillan's the boss, and Finn's the accountant and second-in-command. Sean's the intelligence gatherer, and Shane's the PR guy. That leaves Cormac and me as the enforcers. Part of it is because we're the biggest and automatically the most intimidating. But a lot of it is because we've made people believe we have the shortest fuse. All of us have the patience of a saint—though Sean's stubbornness makes him more patient than the rest of us. It just serves Cormac and me to have a reputation for flying off the handlebars faster than anyone else—in our family or the other syndicates.

Besides being an attorney too, Gabriele Scotto is the biggest in the Mancinelli family and their head enforcer. Sergei Andreyev and Anton Kutsenko are the Ivankov bratva's best hackers, and Anton is the head enforcer. Alejandro Diaz is probably the most emotionally fucked-up of all of us, even though Pablo is probably the most emotionally dead. Alejandro's their strategist because he gives no fucks about anyone who isn't related to him. Even his own men know not to cross him because he won't wait for an explanation, but he will fillet them the same as he would anyone outside his organization.

We're all roughly the same size, which is bigger than the other guys in our families but not so much that we can't all wear our brothers' and cousins' clothes. There aren't too many other people in our world who rival the six of us. In rugby, we would make up three-quarters of a tight scrum—the guys who huddle, push, and run together. All six of us could play any position because we're all fast despite our size. We're all as tall as each other and the other members of our family—though the bratva guys have us by about two inches—and we're all stronger than anyone else we encounter except for each other. Too bad we aren't friends.

"Daddy?"

"Sorry, little one. My mind wandered for a moment."

"You weren't plotting his demise, were you?"

I don't like the fear I hear.

"No. My mind leapfrogged from him to rugby."

"What?" She leans back.

"You don't want to know how I got to that, but I was

thinking about how some of the other syndicate men are the same size as Cormac and me, and we could make up six out of eight guys in the tight scrum."

"Okay." She sounds hesitant and as though I'm nuts.

I am.

I'm certain at this point all the men in our families are.

"Daddy, I think it's time you filled me with some more cum."

I look at her face, and I know she's worried, so she's trying to distract me. Not so I won't think about Zack and what I could do to him, but so I'll relax. I know she can feel I'm tense despite the silence.

"Is that so, *cailín*? Do you think it's time I got you off again?"

"That would be nice. But I really want to feel your cum in me and how it'll drip down my legs."

"You want me to mark you."

"Yes."

"Will that make you more confident facing Gareth and his men?"

"Yes."

"Tiera, you know you don't need that for me to be by your side, right? You know I won't abandon you to them. You know I'll make it clear how things are between us."

"I know all that, but it would still make me feel better. I think some of it is a perverse pleasure in knowing I have a secret Gareth can't get out of me and that he can't ruin."

That makes me pause.

"Tiera, there's shite Gareth could and probably will say to hurt you, and it involves me. His sister was my sub for about three months. She was my first one, and it was over the summer of my junior year in college. It didn't last long because I didn't trust her not to repeat everything to her brother and dad—even the most intimate things. She has a mouth like a truck driver, so nothing is off limits. If she could gain information for her family, her dad and brother didn't care if it meant she discussed her sex life."

"Oh, I know Hillary just fine. The bitch tried to get Aaron to slip away with her at our reception. I found them arguing outside the restroom. I thought he was going to break her arm when she tried to touch him. He didn't manhandle women, but the things he said about her afterwards told me he thought of her as one of the guys since she treated men the way plenty of guys treat women—like whores."

"She did that?"

"Yeah, well, they had a past, too. Before he and I became exclusive, he was dating a few other girls off and on. She was one of them. He and I met while we were doing a training at his firehouse. She'd come round to see him. Once he and I started to get to know each other, he stopped seeing the other women. Hillary wasn't so easily deterred. When she saw us kissing one day, she threw a monumental fit that made the chief ban her from the firehouse. She tried to get him to dump me, but Aaron and I were glued at the hip once we got together. Back then, it was because we loved each other's company. After we got married, it was to control me because he couldn't control anything else in his life once Darren got involved."

She pauses and bites her bottom lip. She turns her head to look over her shoulder and stares at a photo on the dresser. It's a wedding picture. You'd think that would dry up my arousal to see the woman sitting on my cock looking blissfully happy with another man. It doesn't. It makes me want to replace him.

She returns her attention to me.

"I was so angry with Darren and felt so betrayed by Aaron that I didn't stop to think being so controlling was probably Aaron's way of protecting me. As I think about it now, I suspect he was too proud to ever admit he couldn't make Darren or Gareth leave me alone. So, his solution was to never let me be anywhere without him. Or at least, that's what it seemed like. He didn't keep me from my friends or family, but he didn't encourage me to go out very often. It felt suffocating, and he used to nitpick about every little thing. Maybe he did it because he was trying to make sure there was nothing that would bait Darren and Gareth. I don't know. But a lot of the shit from back then suddenly makes sense in a way it couldn't when I was in the thick of it and during my grief after losing my baby. Even though it wasn't a happy marriage, and I wanted out, I keep the photo up because it reminds me there's hope."

"That makes sense. I'm sorry to bring up a bad memory. I don't want Gareth blindsiding you or humiliating you by bringing up something you didn't know about."

"I appreciate it. You should know I broke up with Keith O'Brien a week before I started seeing Aaron. I did it because I had feelings for Aaron even though I didn't know if anything would come of them. I told Keith the truth. I told him my feelings weren't the same as they were when he and I started dating, so I didn't think it was right to lead him to think there was more between us than there was. We'd only dated a couple months."

Her jaw clenches, and I don't know if it's because of what she just told me or what she's about to tell me.

"No one but Hillary really knew Aaron at the firehouse because they met while he was at some party her best friend's brother threw. She never told him her family ties because they were casual. Keith stayed quiet until I started bringing Aaron to family events and introducing him to more people. It was right after I told him what my family is connected to. That was a year and some change after we started dating. It was when we came home from Chicago for a few weeks over the summer after my first year of grad school. Keith cornered him one night and unloaded. He told him pretty much everything about my sex life with Keith. Where we'd done it. How many times we'd done it. What I liked. Aaron beat the shit out of him. It was the one and only time he ever defended me because he just couldn't ignore what Keith said. It wasn't like the time he heard Gareth laying into me. It was way worse. I found out later that fight made Darren take notice of Aaron."

That motherfucker. Keith O'Brien. He's gotta be at least ten years older than Tiera since he's close to that much older than me. She told me she started seeing Aaron her senior year of college, so she was probably twenty-one or twenty-two. What the fuck does a thirty-something-year-old want with a twenty-something-year-old college girl? He wants to bang. He fucking used her. No wonder Tiera's fears and insecurities made her Gareth's easy target.

"*Cailín*, did you date anyone else from within the organization?"

"No. Keith was the one and only. I didn't date much in high school because who were my options? Gareth, who's younger than me and like a little brother. His best friend, Vince, is close to my age but my uncle. Keith is Gareth's oldest cousin and seemed so mature compared to the guys I'd see when I came home from college. I hadn't gone near any O'Briens—the ones with that last name or the ones in the organization—during high school, and I was too scared to date anyone who might find out my family's in the mob. I dated while I was away at school, but it's not like the city is that far from Trenton. There were other guys during high school and college, but I wouldn't call any of them relationships since they never lasted more than a month or two. I was too scared to get serious in case they found out about my family or the O'Briens found out about them. I gained experience, but I never gained a boyfriend. Then I met Aaron, and I was with him for nearly six years."

"So far, I've presumed you want the O'Briens to know we're together. I haven't asked. Do you want me there as a bodyguard, a friend, someone you're seeing, or—"

"My boyfriend. And not just because you're bigger than all of them."

I chuckle. Her answer was adamant, then the words tumbled out as she explained. She must feel my cock twitch as my abs contract because she moans and shifts. I cup her soft, pliable arse. I pull the cheeks apart as I picture fucking her there.

"Daddy, you can have all of me whenever you want."

"Do you want me to come in your arse?"

"And down my throat and across my tits and in my pussy."

I gather her hair and wrap it around my fist, tugging it. Her head tilts back, and I graze my teeth up the side of her throat before nipping her earlobe. I squeeze her arse until it has to be painful. She rocks her hips, trying to get the friction she needs.

"Is that what you think's going to happen, little girl?"

"That's what I hope will happen."

"Right now, I'm going to fill your cunt with more of my cum. Tonight, I'm going to fill your arse with it. I think you're going to go to sleep like that every night for the next week."

Her eyes widen before there's a flash of nervousness. I don't like that. I never want her scared or timid around me. I never want her to be uncertain about where we stand or whether she can express her thoughts.

"You and I are going to share a bed. You are going to fall asleep in my arms and wake in my arms. If, after a week, you want to go back to sleeping alone, then we'll do that. If you want to continue to share a bed, we will. If you only want me to come and fuck you to sleep, I will. Or I will leave you alone all together. But you are going to know what it feels like to be desired above any and everything else. You are going to know what it feels like to be cherished. You are going to know what it feels like to be with someone who wants to put your needs ahead of his own. I want you to have that, Tiera. I want you to know you can keep having that."

"And if you change your mind?"

"Then we talk about it. Same if you change yours. I'm presuming a feck ton again. I want to be sure you understand you can always say no to any of these things. I might speak in absolutes because I'm used to giving orders, and I like that dynamic between us. But unlike anyone else outside my family, you can tell me no. You can tell me to stop. You can tell me you don't like something. You can tell me what you'd prefer. You can tell me absolutely anything. I will always respect your wishes."

"I like how you speak in absolutes. I like the commands you give because you always make me feel desirable and cherished. But thank you for reminding me I can say no if ever I want to."

"Always, *cailín*."

She kisses me, and I'm the one who feels desired and cherished. So much has passed between us this morning. I planned none of it. All because she wore a dress that made me want to fuck her and beat the shite out of any other man who looks in her direction. I don't think my possessiveness would suffocate her, but I've paid attention to how she described her relationship with Aaron, especially her realization that maybe—in his fucked-up way—he was protecting her.

"After we get back, where do we stand? I mean, I know where you want us to lay. But are you just my boyfriend when you're defending me? God, that sounds pathetic."

She pulls back and ducks her chin.

"Look at me, T."

She raises her gaze, but she keeps her head down. I put my finger under her chin and try to nudge it up, but she resists. I grasp her chin between my thumb and forefinger, not fighting her to raise it, but to hold her in place as I whisper in her ear.

"Never call yourself pathetic or the things you say pathetic ever again. Just like your comments about your body will earn you a spanking, so will insulting yourself. I don't live inside your head. I can't hear your silent thoughts. They're yours to have. But I will not ignore the things you say. To ignore them is the same as silence means consent. You will not convince me of those things, and I will not let you think—even for a moment—ever—that I agree with them. The only rules I want to have with you are about your safety because they are about your wellbeing. But I will extend them to how you treat yourself because that's part of your wellbeing too. You've seen how I react to other people speaking badly about you. I have no tolerance for it. I know you're not perfect, and I won't set you up for failure by believing or saying you are. But you are perfect for me. I have shirts from high school that I still wear because I take care of what's mine."

"Am I like an old t-shirt, then?" She grins as she lifts her head.

"I'm comfortable around you, and you're comfy to wear." I lean back, so she's draped over me. "I'm inside you like I would be a shirt."

"Seamus, you're ridiculous. And that makes you perfect for me, too."

I roll us, so I'm back on top. I draw back my hips and surge into her. I'm not rough like I was earlier. I'm worried that if she isn't already sore, she will be in the morning. I know I told her I wanted her that way, and I do. But there's a difference between being sore and being harmed. I won't cross that line.

We move together as we look at each other. We're much

slower this time, even though we know we need to get going. Neither of us is in a rush to end this. Our hands move over each other, our touch soft and meandering. I know I'm savoring this, and I think she is, too. This isn't lust. This is the beginning of love.

God help anyone who tries to fuck this up.

Chapter Thirteen

Tiera

I wore a dress I like this morning because I think it's flattering, even if I still get a bit self-conscious that it shows too many lumps and bumps. I never expected Seamus to flip out about it. I hoped he'd think I look nice. I even wished for a compliment. I didn't imagine he'd practically rip the dress from me or tell me to change because I looked too good in it.

I think he exaggerates. A lot. But I believe he believes every word he says. And that is worth its weight in gold. No one else might appreciate my looks like he does, but I don't give a flying fuck about anyone else—well, that's not true. If I didn't care, I wouldn't get self-conscious. But their opinions—if they even exist—don't matter nearly as much as Seamus's.

I didn't expect to end a three-year relationship either. It lasted longer than my marriage, even though I was with Aaron for six years altogether. I couldn't hear what Zack said to Seamus about me, but it pissed him off. I didn't volunteer that whatever he said to Seamus probably wasn't as bad as what he said to me. I didn't know he had that spiteful side. I was on the receiving end of the dominance, but never the emotional hostility.

He threw things back in my face I'd confided about my loneliness. He *never* said anything like that to me before today. He always made me feel confident, despite my changing body. There were only a few times I got a taste of it when we argued, but that was rare. What was there to argue about when it wasn't a romantic relationship?

For a while, he wanted more of my time because we were sexually compatible, but I didn't have it to give because of work. We argued over that, and he was unkind about me not prioritizing him. I didn't back down, and he eventually relented. He got angry once about me cancelling at the last minute because my mom was sick. He accused me of lying and being with someone else. I sent him photos from urgent care even though the place said they weren't allowed.

There were a few times after particularly nasty encounters with Gareth or his men that I was distracted. That really pissed him off. Not because I could have gotten hurt by being inattentive. No. It was because he wasn't the center of my world. I'd gone to him each time, telling him I'd had a bad day but never gave him specifics. Not names. Not things said. He just knew I was upset and wanted distracting. When I couldn't get my mind off the earlier arguments, he tried to shame me and remind me I was lucky to still have him.

I hope I never have to share these with Seamus because he won't be as forgiving, or at least as tolerant, as I was. I don't want him seeing Zack. Not just because I don't want him to hurt Zack—more for Seamus's sake than Zack's—but because I don't want those two parts of my life to splatter together. I want Zack in the past, and Seamus in the present and future.

"*Cailín*, you're deep in thought. Are you all right?"

I shift my focus from out my window to Seamus, who's sitting beside me in the backseat of a town car. He drove to my place because he wanted us to have time alone on the drive down to Trenton, and he wasn't sure how long it might take to strategize before we left. He didn't want to make one of his drivers wait around until we were ready to leave. That was a blessing in disguise. But he changed his mind once we got dressed. He said he wanted the privacy of the backseat with the glass divider up, so he could keep his arm around me.

He's had it around my shoulders and his free hand covering both of mine on my lap. It's like having a giant bear wrapped around me like a shield. I've had my head on his shoulder for most of the time. He's left me to my thoughts, but I'm being rude ignoring him. If nothing else, I'm worrying him.

"Yes, Daddy. I'm fine. My mind's wandering like yours did earlier, but I'm not thinking about rugby." I turn my head to kiss his neck.

"I'd gladly hold you up in the air if it meant I could look up your shorts." He waggles his eyebrows.

"You're incorrigible, you know that?"

"You're a bad influence."

"Me?"

"Yes. You're far too enticing."

There he goes again. The exaggeration. But when I gaze into his eyes, he means all of it. To him it's not hyperbole. It's gospel.

I twist to kiss him properly, and his arm drops so his hand can rest on my hip. It's deliciously possessive. It's sexy as fuck.

"I could strip you, *cailín*, and no one would know but me, even though we aren't alone. No one would see you but me, even though we're practically in a public place."

"I could kneel and suck you off." I cup his cock, which hardens under my hand.

"*Teampaill.*"

"What does that mean?"

"Temptress."

"How do you even know that word in Irish? That's random."

"I'm fluent. My entire family is."

"Oh. I suspected but wasn't sure since I only heard you speak it that first time we went for a walk." Though that explains why that sentence he's said a few times flows off his tongue so smoothly.

"I greeted you in Gaelic in the courtroom. Did you know the phrase?"

"Yeah. I know some simple ones. Mostly what you'd say in passing or might need as a tourist in a village. I can't think of when else I would use it. Really, it's just a smattering of Gaelic. When did you learn?"

"The same time as I did English. Everyone grows up mixing the two together until they get to school and can only use English. My parents and aunts and uncles insist we use it when we're around them as though we might somehow forget without the practice. All of us use it regularly. If not every day, then close to. There's usually something that comes up that makes speaking a foreign language useful. Or we just lapse into it because we're as comfortable reading, writing, and speaking it as we are English."

"Wow. I can't imagine there are that many people in America who speak Irish."

"Probably half a percent, and they're probably all in my family. Our men speak a little for when we absolutely have to give commands. We keep the phrases simple for them."

Probably because they don't want even their men to understand most of their conversations.

"That explains why Gareth announced he wants to learn it. He wants to know what you're up to."

"We know he's hacked our emails, and that's fine. They aren't the accounts with anything important in them, and we purposely send nonsense to each other in Irish just to piss him off."

I laugh. "It doesn't take much to set him off these days."

Seamus's smile falls, and his gaze bores into me.

"No, it's not always directed at me. Shay, I don't want you to think every word out of his mouth to me is fucked-up. It isn't. Most of the time he's fine. It's just when he isn't, he really isn't."

"I don't care if the fecked-up stuff he says is once a year. That's too many times."

I sigh. "I'd rather give you a blow job, but we never discussed what's going to happen when we get there. That was the entire point of you coming up to my place."

"It's what we thought was the point. If they try to separate us, will you have somewhere to go where no one can bother you? Or will there be some of his guys around?"

"I don't know. Since it's going to be nearly two by the time we get there, there probably will be some of his men coming in and out. They'll be his inner echelon, though. He doesn't like his lackeys or the low-level guys going to his house."

"Would any of the bonesmen say shite to you?"

"No. They're all really nice to me. They remember Aaron, and they feel badly for me about what happened. If they're around, they usually try to keep Gareth's docksmen from bugging me. I can't think of any button men who have given me shit."

Docksmen, bonesmen, button men. I don't know who came up with these names and when. For some dumbass reason, someone generations back thought nautical sounding names would be good for the *very* loose mob structure. Dillan and

Gareth are Skippers or Captains. Godfather, *jefe*, and *pakhan* all sound a shit ton better than either of those. Most heads of mob families or clans just go by boss.

The warlord is pretty much the mob's equivalent to an underboss. That's Uncle Vince. Keith is his caddy. That's an extra stupid name for a chief advisor. I get what caddies do, and it's more than just carry golf clubs. But it sounds ridiculous when the Italians call their guys *consigliere*.

Below them are the docksmen. They handle logistical shit for the illegal businesses and are usually collectors. There are clean and dirty ones. The clean ones are low-key and just do some laundering and maybe even directing some drug trafficking, but usually they handle the legal enterprises. The dirty ones head up operations for the bigger transactions and operations.

Every clan or family has a fixer. That's my dad. Shocking that my dad, who has a pretty senior fucking job, can't get Gareth to leave me alone. But my dad works for Gareth, not the other way around. Gareth also keeps his mouth shut when my dad's around. Dad's almost as big as Seamus. I've seen photos of my dad, and when he was younger, he was as big as Seamus. He's in his late fifties now so not as bulky. But his reputation precedes him. No one wants my dad to make a house call.

And the rank and file are called button men or bonesmen. They're higher than a lackey who does shitty odd jobs here and there. The button men have been initiated and are full members. They carry out most of the day-to-day operations when it comes to fencing, illegal gambling, theft, shake downs, and that sorta stuff. Aaron probably would have risen through the ranks because of my dad's position and on his own merit. But he was only in long enough to be a button man.

"Should I expect Vince and Keith to be there? What about your dad?"

"I don't know. I don't think my dad'll be there, but I can text him and ask."

"That's probably a good idea. While I might want to surprise Gareth, Keith, and Vince, I don't think it'd make a good impression at the start of our relationship if I arrive as the muscle when I'd be facing off against your dad."

That makes my blood run cold. I stare up at Seamus, frozen.

"Little one?"

"Are any of those scars from my dad?" I saw and felt them, and there are plenty.

"No. And I haven't given your dad any of his."

Both men have healed wounds that clearly come from knives and bullets. Seamus has a few nasty ones, and there are several faint white lines from lesser knife cuts.

"Have you fought my dad?"

Seamus looks at me for a moment before he nods. I don't expect to see shame, but I do. I recognize that expression far too well.

"Did you know your dad had a broken nose and two fractured ribs about five years ago?"

"Yeah. I thought some guy didn't want to pay up and thought he could take on my dad."

"I did take him on, and I won. Darren wanted us to pay for some product that never arrived. He swore it did. We swore it didn't. Turns out we were right, but we didn't get to prove it until after your dad and I got into a fight."

"What happened?"

"He said something about Colleen."

My brow furrows. The name is familiar. Then it comes to me. My mouth drops open, my eyebrows shoot up, and my eyes almost fall out of my head. Holy fucking shit.

"That must have been right around when it happened."

"It was. It was like four months later, and he suggested we were weak because we couldn't protect her. He suggested she got what she deserved for being in such a weak family. Tiera, your dad is only alive because I got to him before Dillan. I broke his ribs, and when I broke his nose, it knocked him out. If my cousin had gotten a hold of him—" He shakes his head. "There wouldn't have even been a funeral."

Fucking hell in a hand basket. Colleen was Dillan's younger sister. From what I remember, they were super, super close. Like they were the twins in the family. Colleen was in the wrong place at the wrong time, and the shooter confused her for someone else. She died because Seamus's mom's cousin put a hit on his mom and aunts to ensure his control when he took over as boss. I guess that wasn't the line of succession that was supposed to happen. Dillan was supposed to take over when Donovan died.

"Tiera, Dillan was there when Colleen was murdered. They'd just gotten her a puppy, and the dog was in her arms. She was shot in the forehead, and Dillan caught her as she collapsed. He had to sit there, holding his baby sister in her pool of blood, while he called my aunt and uncle."

"And you still want me anywhere near your family? Seamus, I told you this was a bad idea. I told you our families wouldn't accept this. What—"

"Tiera, stop. My family already knows I'm into you. One thing I can promise you with my family is that we know we don't get to pick who we're related to. If we did, none of us would be in the mob. You are not your dad any more than you are Vince since he's your uncle or Gareth since he's whatever kind of cousin he is. His actions one day five years ago aren't being held against you. You are your own person, and my family knows you're important to me. That's what matters."

"But how can they possibly trust me?"

"Because I trust you."

"Now that I know what happened, how can you trust me? That's probably one of the more fucked-up things that's happened, but our families do *not* like each other."

"I just told you. We know you aren't your dad, uncle, or cousin. I trust you because you've given me no reason not to. Just the opposite. And I could make the same argument. How can you trust me? Especially now that you know I beat up your dad. Why aren't you telling the driver to stop and let you out?"

"Because you are the most trustworthy person I know. You've proven it over and over."

"See. We're the same."

"Bullshit. I haven't done anything, and all you've done is protect me." My stomach cramps acknowledging that.

"You make me happy."

The way he says that. There's no arguing against it. It's too absolute.

"Do I make you happy because you get to rescue me?"

He stares at me. I think he's at a loss for words for a moment.

"No. I don't have some savior complex. I love watching you play soccer, and I love playing against you. I love the moments when you laugh, and your whole face lights up. I love the little bits of humor you let slip out when you know I'm getting upset. You know when I'm getting upset. You bring me a sense of calm I rarely feel when I'm not with you."

"And I also upset you more often than not." My stomach's in some complicated Boy Scout knot.

"No. You do not upset me. The shite that's happened to you upsets me. Those are not the same thing."

"I'll text my dad to see where he is. Regardless, should I tell him you're coming with me?"

"That's up to you. By the end of the day, he'll know we're

together one way or another. It would probably be better coming from you. But if you think he'll confront me before we finish with Gareth, then maybe wait until we're back in the car. If he's at Gareth's, then he'll know right away."

"Okay."

ME

Hey. I'm almost in Trenton. I have to see Gareth. I can't put it off any longer so I'm going to his house. Are you there?

I watch my phone, but nothing pops up. I put it on my lap rather than back into the pocket I pulled it from. I'm still sitting twisted toward Seamus, so he squeezes my hip before patting it. I put my head back on his shoulder and close my eyes. But I don't get to rest long before my phone vibrates.

DAD

No but I can head over there. I don't want you to face him alone. He's being a jerk about you not coming down sooner. I told him I don't want to hear about it since you did him a favor. I don't want him to light into you.

I look up at Seamus since he could see my screen when I typed my message and as I read this one.

"It's up to you, Tiera. I'll follow your lead."

"This equality blows." I grumble it, and he laughs. I'm only half joking. I appreciate he isn't dictating to me how things are going to happen, but I'm scared.

I stare at my screen. Maybe my dad'll think I'm driving, and that's why I don't respond right away. Maybe he'll think I dictated the first message. I'm unprepared for Seamus to reach across me and unfasten my seatbelt. Instinct has me scrambling to fasten it again, a streak of fear exploding from the top of my head to the tips of my toes.

But he scoops me up and nestles me against him. Will I ever get used to that? Zack couldn't pick me up, which I always saw as a reflection on me being fat, not him being weak. Compared to Seamus, he was built like a boy not a man.

I feel safer now than I have in a vehicle in three years. I know how ridiculous that is, but it's true.

"I'm here, and I'll be beside you no matter what happens today."

"Beside? I kinda like you under me."

"I kinda like you sitting on my dick." He grins, and I can't not return the smile.

I don't want him to think I can't handle something as simple as sending my dad a text. But I'm getting more and more anxious that all of this is going to explode in our faces.

"I think I better tell him, Daddy."

He nods before he presses my head to his chest, then rests both hands on my hip. I listen to his heart, and I instantly settle. It's a metronome for my breathing. His heart rate is so slow that it's comfortable to inhale and exhale with every two beats. I stare at my phone, wondering if I should just blurt it all out.

ME

You can if you want. Seamus is coming with me.

The response is immediate.

DAD

What???

ME

Seamus is coming with me. He said he needs to speak to Gareth anyway and he doesn't want him talking to me without him.

177

DAD

And why does that matter to him?

ME

He's my boyfriend.

And it takes five seconds for my dad to hit the call button. "Hi, Dad."

"What do you mean Seamus O'Rourke is your boyfriend? What have you done?"

I lean forward and watch Seamus, but his expression is impassive. However, he pulls the phone from my ear and hits speakerphone. He puts his hands back on my hips.

"I met Seamus while I testified. Turns out our soccer teams are rivals. I met him a couple more times at games. We hit it off. We started dating."

"You can start undating. You said he's coming with you. Can you talk now? Will he know what we're talking about?"

"Dad, he can hear all of this. He's the one who pointed out it would be better not to show up and surprise you. Gareth, sure. He didn't want to do that to you."

"I suppose I should be grateful for small mercies. O'Rourke, leave my daughter alone."

"Brant, I'd have the same reaction if the situation were reversed. But my feelings for Tiernan have nothing to do with you or your family. I may not care for the O'Briens, but I can still see Tiernan's intelligent, brave, kind, forgiving, under-standing, witty, gorgeous, independent, determined, resilient, and a lot of other things that make her remarkable. I know she's no more you than I am my grandfather, Uncle Don, or Declan. I also know Gareth isn't going anywhere near her without you or me with her."

Seamus watches me the entire time he's speaking. He's waiting to see if I object to anything he says. I don't. Instead, I feel like the most important person in the world with the way he speaks about me. He's so matter of fact whenever he describes me, and I love that. It's as though he simply can't believe I'm anything other than what he says. Like it isn't possible for me to be less than what he thinks. No one has ever made me feel like this.

"My daughter is all those things, and that's why she's far too good for you. But you're right that Gareth isn't going anywhere near Tiernan without me there. You can drop her off. I'll take her back to the city."

"No." I speak up not liking that idea at all.

"Tiernan." I know that warning tone.

"Dad, Seamus is staying with me. If you want to be there too, then great. But I am not going near Gareth or anyone else without him. And you're not separating us. Not for this meeting and not in the future."

"You are making a mistake, nugget."

Seamus looks at the phone in confusion. I cover it and whisper.

"A nugget of gold. He says no one and nothing is more precious than me."

Seamus's eyes narrow, and I can tell he thinks my dad should have tried harder to protect me if he thinks I'm so special. But I can't fault my dad. I haven't told him everything that's happened, and I can't run to him every time someone hurts my feelings. I won't tell Seamus every time it happens. I can't. It would be a never-ending battle with him not to defend me.

"Dad, I don't think I am. For once, I think I've really gotten it right. Shay doesn't hold me at fault for my family and is getting to know me for me. Please do the same. Or at least give it an honest try. I know who and what he is, but that's not the man he is with me. You're not the same with Mom and me as you are with other people. Can't you believe Seamus can be the same?"

"I won't until he proves otherwise." There's a pregnant pause. "But I'll let him try."

"Thanks, Dad. He knows Gareth says things to me to manipulate me. He has an idea of what he's said, but I haven't told him the specifics."

"You haven't told me the specifics either. Even when I've demanded them, you've kept mum."

"Exactly. I haven't told him things I refuse to tell you or Mom. I don't ask questions he can't answer, and he doesn't ask me things I can't answer. I didn't know you and he have history until like two minutes before I texted you."

"Seamus." There's that warning again.

"Brant, what you said was wrong. You're still lucky I was standing in front of Dillan and got to you first. I won't back down on that."

"Dad, I don't know the exact words you used, but I know the gist of it. You called them weak and said Colleen deserved what happened to her. Do you deny that?"

"No. I said it to bait them."

"It worked." Seamus's wry tone belies the anger I feel pulsating from him.

I only brought it up, so my dad knows Seamus isn't filling my head with lies and that Seamus doesn't hold my dad's actions against me.

"How far away are you, Dad?"

"I can leave now. I'm at the house."

Fifteen minutes. Good.

"We're ten minutes out." I look up at Seamus because I don't know what he wants to do.

"We'll wait for you, Brant. Do not go in without us. I do not want Gareth knowing I'm with Tiernan, so he doesn't have time to come up with things to hurt her. I won't leave her side. If there are things he wants to discuss that she can't hear, it'll have to wait until another time. I don't trust him or any of his men if Tiernan's out of my reach. I want to know why he has an extra sharp burr up his arse with us, but if I can't ask him that today, then I'll do it later. You will not convince me to let Tiernan go anywhere without me."

"Good."

Seamus and I both wait for my dad to say something more, but he remains silent.

"Tiernan, I'm taking—"

"Don't call me that, Shay. You know I don't like it. I don't want to walk in there upset."

"Wait. Why doesn't Seamus use your name? What's wrong with it?"

"Calm down, Brant. Nothing is wrong with Tiera's name, though I'd like to know why you gave her a man's name. But I call her Tiera because that's just who she is to me."

"Do you want to go by Tiera, nugget?"

"No. Only Seamus can call me that." My answer is fast and resolute.

I won't share that with anyone but my boyfriend. I don't need the nickname to be a secret, but I also don't want anyone else to have something I share only with him. It's special, and I want to keep it that way.

"Okay."

"Tiera, I'm taking your dad off speaker for a moment. I need to ask him some things, and because I don't know what the answers will be, I'd feel better if you didn't hear them."

I nod. I'm desperate to know what Seamus is going to ask, and I really want to know my dad's answers. But if Seamus doesn't think I should, I'll live with it.

"Did you know it was going to happen?"

What is he talking about?

"What the fuck, O'Rourke?! How...ask...that's...fuck you... my daughter...kill you...fuck you."

My dad's yelling, but I can only catch parts of what he says. I don't know what he means, but it obviously involves me. He obviously knew what Seamus meant, despite how vague he was.

"Did he do it?"

"Yes."

I can hear that. Whatever that means is worse than anything that's happened so far. Seamus just tensed so hard he could be a marble statue. I'm not sure he's taken a breath yet. His free hand is curled in a fist, and the rage is pulsating off him. I'm surprised I'm not vibrating from it.

"Did you know then?"

"No...found out...too late...years...can't do...hate...dead."

Not being able to hear the complete answers might drive me crazy.

"Does he know?"

"Yes."

If it's possible, Seamus is even angrier. His heart rate hasn't changed, and his breathing is still even. But he's still stone under me. If I didn't know beyond a shadow of a doubt he'd never hurt me, I'd be terrified being in such a small, enclosed space on a highway.

"If I tell you to take Tiera and leave, do it."

"Shay—"

His stare tells me not to ask and not to argue. I snap my mouth shut and nod. I drop my gaze and stare at my hands in my lap. He immediately relaxes. His entire body just melts, basically. He's extra gentle when he cups my cheek and turns my head to face him. His thumb sweeps over my cheekbone.

"Whatever happens, Brant, the only thing that matters is

Tiera's safety. If I feel like anything said or done could be a threat, I want her out of there. I will deal with it. I don't want her leaving alone. I need your word you'll do that. You'll let me deal with it, and you'll get her out of there."

"Of course." I heard him clearly. This is the first time he sounds fully in agreement with Seamus and not pissed about answering.

"We're getting off on Highway 29. We'll wait around the block for you." Seamus drops the privacy glass an inch. "Todd, pull off two blocks before we get there."

I don't know what my dad says when Seamus finishes speaking because I can't hear it at all.

"One last thing. I get why you can't stop Gareth. But if I find out you condoned even one damn word said against Tiera, you and I are going to have serious problems. You'll live for Tiera's sake, but that's all I'll promise."

Chapter Fourteen

Seamus

I hang up and drop the phone on the seat next to me before Tiera can scramble off my lap.

"I won't hurt your father, Tiera. But he needs to know I would. Not just that I can, but I would. Not only do I not exempt him from being held responsible for the shitty way you've been treated, I hold him more culpable than anyone else if he let it happen. There's a big difference between being unable to stop his boss and letting his boss hurt his daughter. I can forgive one, but not the other. He needs to understand that, so I never have to do anything. I don't want to, T. But if your wellbeing is in question then I'll do whatever I have to, to protect you."

"You make it sound like the things Gareth says are worse than they are. They make me feel shitty, but they aren't life threatening."

"I one thousand percent disagree. If Gareth's men think you don't matter, or worse, think Gareth doesn't want you around, I don't put it past someone to think he'd be doing Gareth a favor."

"Gareth would never, ever let someone physically hurt me. That's one thing I'm sure about."

I run my hand through my hair and consider what I'm going to say.

"*Cailín*, he doesn't have as tight a hold on the reins as he thinks. He has men who only obey him right now because it works to their advantage. He has men who would kill their own mother to impress him. If he keeps letting people think you're more trouble than value, then I'm worried about what will happen."

"Seamus, what did those cryptic questions mean? Why did my dad blow up when you asked if he knew about whatever it was?"

"I hope I can tell you at some point, but I don't know yet if I can. I had to know, but I wish I hadn't had to ask in front of you. If your dad spoke more than a smattering of Irish, I would have spoken to him in that."

My chest tightens because I think Tiera just figured out what I was talking about. I wait for her to call me out on it. But she remains silent, and that scares me even more.

"T?"

"Later, Shay. Knowing one way or another won't do me any good if I get too worked up to go in there."

She knows.

I look into her eyes, and they well with tears. She's swallowing over and over. When she closes her eyes, tears leak from beneath her lashes. She appears to shrink as her entire body curls into a defensive ball. She pulls her legs up and tucks her head into her lap.

I fumble with my belt and pants. She doesn't look in my

direction. I get them open and push down my boxer briefs before I gather her skirt up to her waist.

"Come here, little one."

I lift and turn her. Her eyes are still closed, but as she sinks onto my cock, she sobs. I monumentally fucked up. Like possibly worse than I ever have because I'm the reason she's crying. I shouldn't have asked. I should have known she'd figure it out. I hold her against me, cooing in her ear.

"I'm here, *cailín*. I won't let go. It's all right. I'm here."

"Daddy."

The single word rips at my heart because it's filled with such despair.

"I'm so sorry I hurt you. I promised to protect you, then I'm the one to cause you pain. Shh. I'll hold you. Shh. It's okay. I'm sorry. I'll hold you."

I kiss her forehead over and over as I rub her back. I feel the deep inhale before she speaks.

"Daddy, it's not your fault. Don't say it is. I should have known years ago."

A fresh wave of sobs escapes after she speaks. I don't know what to do to console her. I did this even if she doesn't blame me. She will later. I so royally fucked up.

"I can hear your thoughts, Daddy. I won't hold this against you because you did nothing wrong. You asked, so you could be prepared. You asked because it's an important truth that should have come out years ago. I should have realized Darren caused the accident. I should have figured out my dad knew Darren did it and that Gareth knows what his father did. I'm glad to hear my dad didn't know beforehand, but I'd never think he did. I know how distraught he was when I came round in the hospital. He couldn't speak for the first two days I was awake. He'd just silently cry. My mom was the one who held it together for all three of us those first few days. Then the dam broke for all of us."

"This was a fecked-up time and place to learn all this, though. I should have thought better of this."

"It's not ideal, but I'm glad we're alone. I'm glad I know before seeing Gareth again. I'm glad to know part of the why behind the way he is toward me. I need to be with you like this, and we couldn't do that if we found out somewhere else."

I hold her tight against me. I was hard the instant she sat on my lap. I was very aware of her arse so close to my dick while we were on that call. But when she started to cry, I got hard for a reason besides pleasure. This is how we connect. It might be through our bodies, but it goes a lot deeper. This isn't about getting either of us off. This is about there being no end and no beginning to us. We're one. We're a unified force. She's a part of me when I'm inside her.

"Daddy, I don't know how you knew this is what I needed, but it is. Being one with you makes me feel safer than I've ever felt before. When we are like this, I feel like I can talk to you about anything and everything. I feel strong enough to tell you the things that scare me and the things I need. When we're like this, I don't feel alone anymore. I hope one day I can make you feel the same way. Not because I want something bad to happen, but so you know I want to give and not just take."

"Baby girl, nothing about you makes me think all you do is take. I need this too, and you letting me inside you has a lot of significance to me. You're a part of me now."

I thought that to myself, but it feels weightier—has more gravity—when I say it aloud. It feels even truer when I tell her.

"Seamus, I don't understand any of what's happening between us. I don't want to question it because I don't really care what the answer is. I just know I'm grateful you came into my life. And you make me happy too."

Our kiss is everything to me. She told me she keeps her wedding photo on her dresser because it reminds her to have hope. Having Tiera in my life reminds me to have hope. This kiss is pure tenderness and affection. Even though my cock's buried deep inside her cunt, there's nothing sexual about what we're doing. It's wonderful.

She rests her head against my shoulder again until someone taps on the window. Fucking real life just rudely interrupted. Tiera scrambles to get off me, but I hold her in place. We can see it's her dad, but he can't see in.

"Little girl, no one rushes us. What do you need?"

"Another kiss and hug, then I'll be ready."

I'm happy to do that, but it's over too soon. I help her off my lap before I look down at my glistening cock. Just like I've filled her with my cum to mark her as mine, she's left part of her on me to remind me I'm hers. I close my eyes for a moment and sigh. Then I'm tucking myself back into my pants. My dick's not thrilled it didn't get off, but it'll survive. The rest of me doesn't feel like I missed out on something.

I drop the privacy glass again when I'm certain Tiera's decent. "Todd, once we're inside, pull up to a couple houses before Gareth's. Stay out of sight, but stay close."

"Got it, boss."

I open my door and step out. I nod to Brant but turn back to help Tiera. She squeezes my hand as she slides out. She hugs her dad, and he kisses her on the cheek. Then she's standing beside me again, her hand in mine. A bit of me wants to gloat.

We walk toward the house together, Brant leading the way, shielding Tiera from the front. My right shoulder is just behind her left. I don't want her walking next to the street. It's too dangerous. But I don't love that this makes her easier to spot from the house. Either way, I can block her back with one step sideways, and I can wrap myself around her while pushing her to the ground if I need to.

"Brant?"

Fucking Vince. He's young enough to be his nephew, not his brother. Their dad's still alive and just as much a dirty old man as he was twenty-eight years ago when he knocked up some girl from Patterson—NJ has some shitty parts, and Patterson is one of the shittier—who was after his money. She blew through a stack during the first sixteen years they were married, and he still controlled his finances.

Brant is the executor of his dad's estate now that the guy is ninety something and senile. Brant has a tight hold on the purse strings. His stepmom is on a strict allowance that barely covers her weekly Botox and collagen. I'm shocked so many needles in her face haven't made it pop like a balloon. If only she'd fly away like one or deflate and shut up. She has the voice of a fucking goose.

"Yeah. Is Gareth home?"

"Yeah. What the fuck's he doing here with her?"

I grit my teeth.

Don't say anything. Don't say anything. Don't say anything.

"My daughter has a name. Use it."

"A man's name. I know you always wished she was a son. You made sure she has some brass ones on her. She wearing the pants, O'Rourke?"

I wait for Brant to react to Vince saying his daughter has balls. I'm waiting for him to deny Tiera has a man's name because he wished she'd been a boy. The man says nothing. And I don't think he's just biting his tongue. I glance at Tiera, and she appears unfazed. Does she have that much of a poker face? Or is she just that used to hearing shite like this?

"She can wear whatever the hell she wants, Vince. She's beautiful in everything."

He laughs. The motherfucker laughs. Tiera squeezes my hand so hard it hurts. I nearly wince. What the fuck kind of death grip does she have? If we have kids, and she holds my hand when she's in labor, she'll fucking crush every bone.

That was a thought I never planned to have. It's not the right time to have it. And I probably shouldn't have it at all since I don't know what the future holds, and I sure as shite don't know if she ever wants to have children after what happened. I don't know if she can have kids.

I curl my fingers around hers and tap them. She eases her hold when I say nothing else.

The four of us walk up the driveway together. The guys outside the house step forward when they recognize me. Or rather, they recognize the red hair and green eyes. I don't know these guys, and I doubt they know which one I am. But they definitely know I'm an O'Rourke.

I put my gun in a small drawer under my seat when we got into the car. I hold out my suit jacket and twist so they can see my lower back. I lift each pant leg. When one of them takes a step toward me, I push back my shoulders. I don't even need to inhale. He freezes and thinks twice about frisking me. He and the other guard know I have at least one knife. They also know the guns they have don't scare me, so I will fight back if they try to take my knives.

"Tiernan, I need to see inside your purse, please."

The guy on the left takes a step toward Tiera, and I step in front. I don't believe he's a threat, but I will make sure they know they go through me to get to her. I stick my hand out behind me, and she hands it to me. She already showed me the contents, so I know she has a pocketknife in her cosmetic bag hidden under some tampons. I pass it to the guard who scowls at me. I cock an eyebrow. He pushes shite around and gives it back to me. Good. He's learning. I pass it back to Tiera.

As we follow Vince to the door, I keep my voice low and keep looking straight ahead. "Do they usually search your stuff?"

"No."

Did Vince signal them somehow I couldn't see? Did they get suspicious the moment they saw her holding an O'Rourke's hand? Has Gareth already ordered them to search her? Would they have frisked her?

Plenty of questions and no answers. We enter the house behind Vince and Brant. We immediately hear raised voices coming from the living room. I recognize Gareth's and Keith's. Marvelous. Tiera recognizes them too because her nails dig into my hand. I try to ease my hand free, but she's back to her death grip.

"Shh, *cailín*. Let go."

She whimpers but does as I say. I wrap my arm around her waist and pull her tight against me. I feel her sigh since she's silent now.

"You do not go farther than my reach."

"Yes, D—"

I glance down at her as she catches herself, and she's looking up at me. She nods. I slide my hand a little lower to her hip. She smiles and knows it's a subtle, possessive gesture. She tilts her head against my chest for a moment before straightening. The voices go silent when Vince calls out to Gareth.

"Tiernan's turned traitor."

I steel myself against reacting, but I tighten my hold on Tiera until I'm the one with the death grip. It's instinctual. But I also want her to see the marks I leave when she gets undressed later. I want her to remember I won't let go, that she's mine to touch however I want.

"Vince, I'd think twice about how you speak about my girlfriend."

192

I want to say whether I hear it or not doesn't matter since I'll know. Everyone will assume I mean Tiera will tell me. There's no need to assume anything. We already have spies, and I'm going to plant more specifically to watch out for her.

"Girlfriend?" Keith snorts before shooting Tiera and me a mocking grin.

Brant steps in front of Tiera and crosses his arms. He's still impressive even if he isn't as muscular as me anymore. He definitely doesn't have a dad bod, and his reputation was earned, not given. Gareth promoted him to the position he's in now as his fixer. Before that, Brant didn't hold a title, but he's been the O'Briens' most feared enforcer for decades. He did lesser jobs most of the time, except for when Darren demanded he do more. It's why I didn't know about Tiera. He was only on our radar when he stepped in front of it. I never took interest in his family before I met Tiera and learned of her connections.

"Gareth, don't waste my time. You wanted me here to discuss my testimony. I came. Either we get on with it, or Seamus and I leave. The three of us have better things to do than wait on you. Keith, you're just pissed I dumped you before you ever got to call me that."

Tiera's tone belies any fear she has. Is she always this direct? Or does she feel more confident because she isn't alone? Is it me, her dad, or both?

"Don't be a—"

"Finish that sentence, Keith, and you know there's no way on God's green earth I can stop Seamus. I wouldn't if I were you." It's her turn to smirk.

I flex my fist, and I know Gareth and Keith can see me. When I narrow my eyes, Keith shifts his gaze to Gareth. At least, he has an ounce of sense.

"My office, Tiernan. Brant, Seamus, wait for me."

"No."

Gareth took a step forward, but he freezes when I speak. He glares at me, and I notch up my chin. Tiera was right. Nobody is stopping me from doing whatever I want. There aren't guards nearby, and even if there were, they know it'll take at least five O'Briens to restrain me. It took seven the time I knocked out Brant.

"This is my house, Seamus."

"And?"

I can be purposely obtuse. Even people who know my record in the courtroom forget I'm more than just muscle. They see the man who could snap them in half, but they rarely think I'm intelligent. That's totally fine by me.

"You don't decide what goes on here."

I laugh.

I know where his office is since I've been in it before. I turn Tiera and face the hallway it's down. Gareth owns a large home in a nice neighborhood, but it's nowhere near the size of my parents' home or either set of my aunts and uncles. It's not as big as Enrique Diaz's in north New Jersey, or Salvatore Mancinelli's or Maksim Kutsenko's in Queens. He can't afford that. In my family, my generation's opted for more discreet abodes anywhere but Queens. Though Dillan, Finn, and Sean have moved into mansions twice the size of this place now they're each married.

Basically, Gareth has no wealth to impress or intimidate me. This is a dollhouse compared to the other, far more important bosses'.

"There's not a chance in hell you're listening to this conversation, Seamus. You were opposing counsel."

"Were. Now I *am* Tiernan's boyfriend. My girlfriend goes nowhere in this house without me. You get nowhere close to her without me. Period."

"Tiernan, I thought you swore you were done with possessive men. Your taste hasn't improved."

"Since your dad never did shit to protect you, I don't blame you for not knowing the difference." Tiera's gaze could pierce ice.

"I'm plenty protected." He stares at me.

"Because you pay them." I guess Tiera wasn't done.

"How much are you paying Seamus to pretend to be your boyfriend? We all know it's in cash."

I let go of Tiera's waist and slide her hand into mine as I take a menacing step forward.

"You may have gotten away with insulting her in the past, but there's nothing stopping me from stopping you. Do not underestimate how protective I am."

Yeah, that was a dig at Brant, and we all know it. Let it be an announcement that things change as of now. I don't retreat but wrap my arm around Tiera again to bring her back to my side. I take a step toward his office, moving Tiera and me from behind Brant. We're closer to the hallway than Gareth, so we lead the way. I know he doesn't lock the door because he's that arrogant in his home. I push open the door and let Tiera in first after I scan the room.

I lead her to the sofa in front of Gareth's desk. I glance down at Tiera and dip my chin. She sits, then I take my place beside her. I cross my right ankle over my left thigh. It lets me press my knee against Tiera's leg without being obvious. I stretch my arms over the back of the sofa, my right hand around Tiera's shoulders. It would be bravado if I didn't know I control this meeting now.

"Sit, Gareth." I speak when his cologne wafts to me, and I hear footsteps behind us. He could put a bullet through the back of my head since my back is to the door. I hate that part. It makes me hyper aware. But he knows the weight of the entire

O'Rourke organization would descend on him and annihilate his entire organization. As much as he hates me right now, he's not so shortsighted as to act on it.

"Make yourself comfortable, Seamus. You've never had manners."

That's laughable. Cormac and I are known for having the best manners in the family, and that's saying something since my parents and aunts and uncles drilled etiquette into all of us. Cormac and I were just the ones who never had to be told to write thank you cards after Christmas and our birthdays. We were the last to call adults by their first name rather than their honorific and last name. The last bit is because we're also the shyest of the cousins. We've always preferred to be seen and not heard. When we were young kids, it was because we hated standing out as the tallest and biggest. By the time we became teenagers, we realized it was useful.

"What did you want to see me about, Gareth?" Tiera's not interested in our posturing.

Gareth remains silent as he sits at his desk, staring at us. Tiera leans forward as though she'll stand.

"If you won't talk, then I'm not wasting more of my time on you."

He narrows his eyes at her, but he continues his silence.

"You won't insult Tiernan in front of me, so that tells me you're quiet because you have nothing else to say to her. It's not good for your health that I figured that out."

"Or I'm not discussing my family's business in front of you."

"Either way, this was a wasted trip, then." Tiera starts to stand again, and I don't stop her. My knee is still touching her leg. She's not out of my reach. She's thinking the same thing I am because she presses her thigh against me.

"Calm your ass down. Fine."

I lean forward as Tiera eases back onto the couch. "I don't like your tone or your words. That's your only warning in here."

I heard the door close, and it's just the three of us. I don't doubt someone summoned guards to stand outside, ready if they hear any kind of scuffle. The thing is, no one will hear me get to Gareth before he can do anything to sound the alarm. I'll be over the desk in three steps. Two if they're really wide.

"Calm *your* ass down, Seamus."

I crack my knuckles. My mother detests the habit, but Cormac and I developed it as teens because we thought it was the intimidating mobster thing to do. Now people know it's a sign our patience is wearing thin.

Gareth's left hand twitches before he leans back in his seat, trying to appear casual. The fucker wants even six more inches space between us because he's a little bitch.

"Get on with it, Gareth. Seamus and I have plans this evening."

We do. Her arse and my cock have a date.

Gareth opens his mouth, then snaps it shut. At least he's trying to keep his head on his shoulders. He looks at Tiera, and I know he's weighing his words.

"I arranged for you to testify because you had all the information you needed."

"You forced me down there, but you can't force what comes out of my mouth."

There's something in those words that sets me on edge.

"What do you mean he forced you? How?"

Tiera tenses. She knows I want the full truth, and she knows I'm certain she didn't mean figuratively.

"Two of his men escorted me to a town car, then drove me into the city. They made sure I walked into court."

She lives in East Harlem like me, but in a more modest

home. My place doesn't look as large as it is or that it'd be decorated as nicely as it is. I'm a few blocks from where Sean used to live before he and Nikki got married. We've all preferred understated places as bachelors, and only Finn lived in the city —the part people really think of as Manhattan, even though Harlem is technically part of it. He lived in SoHo, so he was in the heart of "the city."

That means she was being strong-armed just a few blocks from me, and I had no way of knowing. I didn't know her, and I didn't know it was happening. It makes my stomach clench.

"What else has Gareth made you do?"

"I've testified in a few other cases, but I was qualified to do it, and I told the truth. But someone better qualified should have done it. He just couldn't guarantee they'd say what he wanted."

"And he had men escort you then, too?"

"Yes, after Aaron died. He made sure Aaron knew he was responsible for getting me wherever Gareth wanted. His dad did the same."

"Anything else?" I direct this at Gareth, giving him a chance to confess.

He taps his fingers on the desk before he catches himself and tries to look nonchalant as he curls his fingers into a loose fist. But he speaks, nonetheless.

"There have been some falsified reports and some planted evidence. Some evidence that went missing or was never found."

"You made a woman do that?"

The rules are simple because they've been the same since all our families were still in the old country. Women don't get involved. They don't work for their family's bosses, and they aren't collateral. My family—fucking Uncle Don and Declan—

broke the second part, and we've been paying for it ever since. But we don't have women work for us.

At least, not like this. Our strippers report back anything they hear, but it isn't their job to do that. Theirs is to entertain. That's no different from the women who work in our restaurants, casinos, bars and nightclubs, stores, gas stations. Any business we own. If people hear shite, they tell us. They don't go looking for it. Unless, of course, you're Mair. But that's entirely different, and it worked out for Dillan and her. And now she's married to the mob boss.

"It's not like I plucked some woman off the street. It was just Tiernan."

"What did you just say?" My voice is low, and that scares most men more than if I yell.

"It was just—" Gareth realizes his fuck up. "Sorry."

"Why Tiernan?" The name doesn't quite feel right after only calling her Tiera, but I've gotten used to it. I want to discuss her parents' reason for picking the name, but I'll do that with her dad later.

"Because I can." Once again, he realizes what he said. "Could."

"And why's that?"

It's a cross examination, except I'm the only one asking the questions today.

"My dad used to threaten her by telling her he'd put a hit on her dad. He wasn't full of shit."

No, Darren wasn't. When he said he'd have someone killed, it usually meant he'd already done it. No wonder Tiera did what she was told.

"And you? One of the lessons your daddy taught you?" I feel Tiera's leg tense when I say daddy. It certainly has a different meaning for us now.

"Yeah, but I didn't threaten Brant. I did it because she was useful, and I knew she was broken."

That pisses me off. The way he says it, and its meaning.

"You took advantage of a widow who'd just lost a child. Do you know what a piece of shite that makes you? Do you know what a worthless and pathetic piece of shite you are that you had to use someone so vulnerable because you couldn't do it yourself? Because none of your minions could do it. Because it made you feel like your dick wasn't micro. Because you could only feel powerful by using her during the worst time of her life. You're lucky I don't kill you right now. Say thank you to Tiernan because she's the only reason you're breathing."

He knows I'm serious. He mutters, but I'll take it.

"Thank you."

"Why have you kept doing it?"

He does a double blink. It's fast, but it's his tell. He's about to lie.

"Because she's good at what she does."

That's not the lie. It's whatever he's not telling me.

"And you think insulting her about her loss and how she looks is the only way to convince her?"

"No. That's just—"

He looks like he wants to swallow his tongue. His gaze darts to Tiera before he looks at my chest. He can't meet my gaze. Weak fucker.

"You can attack a woman, but you can't look me in the eye. You are pathetic."

His fist clenches on the desk, and he doesn't stop himself. He's getting tired of my insults. Oh, well.

"Your father manipulated Tiernan by threatening her father, then bringing her husband in. He arranged what happened, and you know that. You picked up where your father left off by using her grief to manipulate her. You

200

continue to use that grief to torment her. All of this because neither you nor your father had the balls to ask a woman a favor. Did your dick grow whenever you thought you were such hot shite attacking her?"

"I didn't fucking attack her. Get off your high horse, Seamus."

"If I get off anything, it'll be to wrap my hands around your throat. Are you inviting me? And you know damn well you attacked her with your words. I'd even call it civil assault."

"Come on, Seamus. That's ridiculous."

"In the State of New Jersey, 'a person is subject to liability for an assault if (a) she or he acts intending to cause a harmful or offensive contact with the person of the plaintiff, or an imminent apprehension of such a contact, and (b) the plaintiff is thereby put in such imminent apprehension.' I paid attention when I studied for the bar. You had her manhandled into cars, so why wouldn't Tiera be afraid you'd do something worse? You threatened to hurt her dad just like your father did, so why wouldn't Tiera be afraid you'd do something worse? Since you did it in this house, and you reside in the State of New Jersey, you're liable. You're lucky I'm only in the mood to be your judge and jury, not your executioner. You can thank Tiernan for that again."

I'm kicking myself because I let my pet name for her slip. It gives too much away about my affection for her. It's one thing to know I like her and care about her. But the nickname is too much because they'll weaponize it. I just made her an even bigger target. Fuck me.

Chapter Fifteen

Tiera

I'm content to let Seamus do the talking. I'm worried about what's happening to my dad. Is he just waiting around? Or are Vince and Keith doing something to him? Vince may be my dad's youngest brother, but he doesn't like my dad. He's so fucking jealous he's greener than fucking Kermit the Frog. If anyone's a manipulative little fuck, it's him. He might not lay a hand on Dad because he's weaker than his big brother, but he'll find some other way to pay Dad back for what's going on in here.

Seamus sat back once I settled into my seat again. His arm is back around my shoulders, and it grounds me. It keeps me from letting my anxiousness show. It lets me focus rather than expecting the worst. Expecting everything to blow up.

My second cousin three times removed—or some shit like that—is sweating. I can see it beading on his forehead. It's not hot in here. I'd say a pleasant seventy, seventy-two. He doesn't enjoy being under Seamus's spotlight. I can't blame him. But he put himself there. He just didn't know it would be Seamus shining the light.

"What's the next job you plan for Tiernan?"

I felt his pinky move against my shoulder when he let Tiera slip a moment ago. I know he didn't intend to do that. He's already called me that in front of Dad a few times, so it's not that he intends it to be a secret we take to our graves. But he knows he just gave Gareth leverage if he caught it.

"*Tiera's* going to process a claim for a small residential fire in Manhattan. She's going to make sure her company's client doesn't get a penny."

"That is not my name to you, *Garry*. Call me that again—tell anyone to call me that—and an anonymous informant will turn everything over to the U.S. Attorney's office."

I modulate my tone, so it's a threat without me sounding bitchy or scared. He needs to know I'm deadass serious. I've found those balls Vince claimed I had now that Seamus is in my corner.

He glowers at me, and I grin. He *hates* being called Garry. Like passionately hates it. He thinks it makes him sound like some fat, bald, middle-aged, used car salesman. He's not fat or middle-aged yet, but his maternal grandfather was bald, so there's hope for him yet. He's as smarmy and skeezy as a stereotypical used car salesman.

"Fine."

"Tone."

Gareth snapped at me, and Seamus doesn't like it. I lean against Seamus and smile demurely at my distant cousin. Seamus's thumb noticeably rubs the outside of my shoulder, and I know Gareth sees it. I don't think Seamus is doing it for effect, but I suppose in for a penny, in for a pound. If Gareth knows Seamus has a nickname for me, then he may as well see I really matter to my boyfriend. It's also super soothing for both of us. I know it is for me, and he feels more relaxed than he did.

The mob boss doesn't enjoy taking orders from an enforcer. Gareth grimaces when he catches himself glaring at me. He turns his focus to Seamus.

"I need Tiernan to get the case assigned to her, and I need her to expedite it. The homeowner owes me money, and he's way behind on his payments. I could let him file the claim and get the money, then pay me back. But I want him even more screwed because he'll have to borrow even more from me."

Loan sharking. It's one of Gareth's best skills. Extortion, coercion, and loan sharking. He excels at all three since they're so closely related. He talks people into a corner, then pounces.

"No."

That surprises me. Gareth and I both look at Seamus, but I'm quick to snap my gaze forward again. I won't let Gareth know I'm unprepared for anything Seamus says or let him think I'm not on board with everything Seamus says.

"What do you mean 'no'?"

"Tiernan doesn't work for you anymore."

"Seamus, you're pushing me too far. You don't tell me how to run my family."

"You really believe that, don't you? My family's owned yours since your dad's unfortunate and untimely accident. My family allows you to live in a quaint home, have plenty of money, and think you're in charge. You exist at our largesse, but our benevolence is about to run dry. Don't push me, Gareth. I push back."

When I feel Seamus's chest move, I look down to see him Terry Crewes his pecs. He flexes one side, then the other five times. I swallow my laugh, and it nearly kills me. If the knuckle cracking earlier didn't remind Gareth that Seamus doesn't joke, then seeing those muscles move ought to. I see fear flash in Gareth's eyes before his smirk is back.

"You should be on a pole, Seamus. Banana hammock and all."

"Would you like to see how much bigger my dick is than yours? I heard you enjoy looking at them. I draw the line at touching, though."

I nearly choke. There's been a rumor going around for years that Gareth and Vince are more than besties. It's not true, but it's definitely been inconvenient for both of them.

"Fuck you, O'Rourke."

"Language. Don't swear in front of my girlfriend. I don't like it."

"I don't give a shit—"

Seamus is out of his seat with a knife flicked open faster than I can understand what's happening.

"If I trusted Tiernan was safe to leave this office without me, you'd already be dead. I have more reasons than the ocean has sand. *You're* the one pushing too far, Gareth. I didn't like you before I met Tiernan. Now I can't stand you. So, let's try again. Swear in front of my girlfriend again, and I will take off a finger for every letter."

I don't dare stand up. I don't dare get in the middle of this. I'd only intervene for Seamus's sake. We're in O'Brien territory now, and we only came with one other man who isn't in shouting distance. I can't be sure my father would come to Seamus's aid. I don't want to do anything to distract Seamus, but I wish there was a way to distract Gareth.

Fucking think.

"Let me off the hook, and maybe I can convince Seamus to only take your pinkies."

Weak, but something.

"Stay out of it, Tiernan. This is between me and O'Rourke."

"Until it isn't. Don't fight him, and there's a chance the rest of his family won't descend upon you like a horde of locusts. We went to Sunday School together. You know the Bible story and what's supposed to happen and what little is left. Don't make some ancient prophecy come true because of your ego. It'll be your fault when nothing's left."

Seamus doesn't take his eyes off his nemesis—my nemesis—and I can tell he thinks I'm trying to protect Gareth. I'm not. I'm so not. I'm scared for Seamus, and I wish I could tell him that. I wish I could send him some message by telepathy. I wish he had ESP and could tell what I want him to know. But he doesn't.

"If he lets you live but cuts off your thumbs because you have a potty mouth, how are you going to explain that for the rest of your life? Rather than wash your mouth out with soap for swearing, Seamus O'Rourke cut off your thumbs. Shay, go for the thumbs, not the pinkies. Way more inconvenient."

Seamus moves the knife that was at Gareth's throat after he grabs Gareth's left hand, which is his dominant one. He slams Gareth's wrist on the edge of the desk, and the hand flies open Seamus's knife points straight down at the thumb.

"All right, all right. I'm sorry, Tiernan. I won't swear in front of you or at you."

Seamus lets go, but not before he grabs the thumb and twists it until I hear the pop. Gareth opens his mouth to scream, and Seamus's hand goes around his throat.

"I wouldn't."

Please let that be a piece of Seamus's advice Gareth takes. The latter snaps his teeth shut and nods. Seamus releases him, but not before he moves around the desk and pulls open the center drawer.

He pulls a gun out, and terror bursts through me. He leans over and puts it on the ground before kicking it away. He does the same to the other drawers and pulls out two more guns, kicking them away, while Gareth cradles his hand. Then he takes the gun from under Gareth's elbow and walks back around to the sofa. He switches the gun from his right hand to his left and sits with his right arm over the back of it. I don't look away from Gareth as I lean into Seamus.

"Let's finish this conversation, *Garry*. There was something you didn't say earlier. Who's been forcing your hand to keep using Tiernan?"

That shocks me.

There's a knock on the door before Gareth can answer.

"Baby?"

Fucking hell.

I bolt from the sofa and run around it to the door. I turn the lock just as the doorknob turns.

"Gareth? What the hell? Let me in."

I look over my shoulder at Gareth, then at the gun Seamus is still pointing at him. No one says anything. The knock turns into pounding.

"Gareth, open the damn door. What are you doing in there? Keith said you're in there with Tiernan. You better not be fucking her. I heard what you said the other day about her and her ass."

Is my jaw on the ground? What the ever-loving fuck?

"Told you, Tiera."

I shift my gaze to Seamus who's looking over his shoulder at me. I don't think he could look smugger if he tried.

"Gretchen, it's Seamus O'Rourke. I'm chatting with your boyfriend. Go wait for him somewhere else."

"Seamus? It's been a long time. I wouldn't mind talking to you, too. I've missed you."

Bitch.

208

"I'm busy." Seamus couldn't sound more disinterested. It makes me smile.

"Come on, Shay. You, me, and Gareth could chat."

Gross.

"I wasn't interested the last five times you've offered. I'm not interested now. And I'd stop talking before my girlfriend rips you apart. She doesn't share."

"Girlfriend? You don't date, Shay."

"You said you knew Tiernan's in here. Who do you think's my girlfriend? Maybe you didn't believe whoever told you, but you already knew I was in here with my girlfriend. By the way, don't call me Shay. We're not friends."

But do they have some sort of past together? Why does she think she can be so brazen?

"Gareth, I know you didn't text anyone since you came in here. Do you still have a standing order to whore your girlfriend out to me any chance she gets? I've never accepted and never will."

That allays any fear I have, but it shocks me to hear Seamus speak about a woman that way. But the disgust oozes from every word. He truly can't stand her.

"Tiernan, how much are you paying Seamus to claim he's your boyfriend? You could have just said you hired him as your bodyguard."

"Gretchen, shut up. Go away." Gareth looks ready to shit himself.

He knows Seamus won't hurt her—physically—but he can't say the same for me. She pulled my hair one time when she was sixteen and I was nineteen. I slapped her so hard it left a mark for a week. It fucking hurt, and she didn't let go the three times I told her to.

"No. I want to see the happy couple for myself."

I look at Seamus and shrug. He nods. I unlock the door and

open it, stepping out of the way. Once she's inside, I slam the door shut and lock it again. I put my hand between her shoulder blades and shove. She nearly falls.

Oops.

I shove her again. I have to go around the sofa the other way to get to my seat next to Seamus. As I try to step by, he pulls me onto his lap.

His lips go to my ear. "The gun's loaded. Never step in front." He kisses my temple, never lowering his arm. He speaks louder for the assholes to hear. "I missed you, *mo stóirín*."

Mu-store-een. My little darling. He knows they understand that. He won't call me *cailín* or little one or little girl in front of them. It's too private, and he knows they'll assume the same thing I did the first few times he called me *cailín*.

"Come off it, Seamus. You haven't been touching her for all of ten minutes. You're laying it on a bit thick." Gareth rolls his eyes.

"What part of our conversation so far makes you think I don't want my girlfriend next to me? What part makes you doubt my feelings?"

"Tiernan, how much are you paying him? I didn't know Seamus could be on Broadway." Gretchen sneers at me, and I want to slap her all over again.

Before I can say anything, Seamus does. "Insult her again, and there's a first time for everything. I will beat you until no one recognizes you, Gretchen. Leave Tiernan alone."

She goes chalk white. I laugh. Nothing about Seamus right now would make anyone think he's joking. He hasn't lowered the gun a millimeter since he pointed it at Gareth. The look on his face right now—the one directed at Gretchen—would make the devil run for cover. Unlike other times when something has bothered him, he's not tense beneath me. He's as relaxed as he was when we were lying together in my bed this morning. Dare I say he's in his element?

"Gareth, don't think I forgot my question from before we were so rudely interrupted. Who's been forcing you to keep using Tiernan?"

My distant cousin's gaze darts to Gretchen, shocked Seamus would bring this up in front of her. I lean back against Seamus, wanting to watch how this plays out. His free hand is once again resting on my hip, and Gretchen's staring at it. I can't see him very well from this angle, but I'm certain Seamus looks completely at ease with me on his lap. To be honest, I'm not entirely sure he realizes where his hand is. He must because he does nothing without a reason, so he must be proving a point. But maybe he realized he could make a point after he'd already put it there.

I'm waiting for an answer because I've wondered for ages if there was another reason besides Gareth being a douche that's made him torment me. He wasn't like this when we were younger. He could be a jerk, and he'd like to show off for his friends, but he wasn't cruel like he's been in the past three years. Just when he opens his mouth to say something—anything—someone pounds on the door. This is definitely a guy knock.

What the fuck? Who's interrupting now? It's gonna be wall to wall in here soon.

Okay, maybe not quite that full. But it shocks me anyone—let alone two—is dumb enough to interrupt a meeting between Seamus and Gareth. They must really be scared for him.

"Who is it?" Gareth sounds less than thrilled. There's definitely no hope for someone coming to his rescue.

"It's Jimmy. It's time, boss."

"Time for what?" I ask the obvious question.

"I have a meeting, so this one is going to have to wrap up."

Seamus had the gun pointed at Gareth's heart. He raises it to point right between his eyes. He cocks his left eyebrow. It's so fucking hot when he does that. There's a wealth of meaning in that one gesture. He shakes his head.

"Jimmy, I still got some stuff to finish up in here. Can you take Gretchen home? I should be done by the time you're back."

I stand, and Seamus tilts the gun up to the ceiling, so I can walk past. Once I'm not in the line of fire, he aims it at Gareth's forehead again. I walk over to Gretchen. I gesture to the door with my right arm as I get in her face.

"Come near my boyfriend again, and you will find out what a real woman raised by the mob can do. I'll fuck you up so bad even God won't know it's you. Fuck off."

I let her go ahead of me, but I'm at the door the moment her hand touches the knob. I let her open it wide enough to slip out, but when a hand tries to reach around it, I slam my weight against it. The howl of pain is satisfying. Jimmy's taken Gareth, Keith, and Vince's disdain for me and run with it. He's made me cry plenty of times, but I've never let him see me.

I ease back a little, bringing the door with me before I lean into it again. This time, I bend all his fingers back since his hand is caught in midair. He's swearing up a storm, and I just keep twisting and bending.

"Boss, what the hell? Make the bitch stop."

Seamus is out of his seat in an instant. I barely get out of the way as he throws the door open, grabs Jimmy by the front of his shirt, yanks him into the room, and slams him against the door frame. He puts the gun under Jimmy's chin as he reaches around to take his gun. Before Seamus can do anything, I wrap my hand around it. He lets me have it, and I turn toward Gareth.

"You keep getting spared, but no more. Who's been forcing your hand to keep me in line?"

Gareth looks at me, then Seamus's back. He was standing, but he slumps into his seat.

"Seamus, send Jimmy out. He doesn't need to know this."

"Boss—"

"Do as I say." Gareth may look defeated, but he can still sound like he's in control.

I don't know that he'll ever live down the humiliation of Seamus coming into his house and holding him hostage in his own office. That's what Seamus is really about. I know he won't hurt anyone in front of me unless it's to save me. But he's making a point so big he may as well have it plastered across most of the billboards in Times Square.

Seamus shoves Jimmy out of the office. Before the bonesman can say shit, Seamus drives his fist into Jimmy's temple. He crumples like a cliché from a TV show. I close the door and hand the gun back to Seamus. He looks like some cowboy gunslinger with two weapons in his hands.

"I don't give a fuck who the next person is to knock on that door. I'll shoot your fucking mother if we get interrupted before you answer my question. Who, Gareth?" Seamus stalks forward until he's directly in front of the desk.

"I don't know."

Seamus's long reach allows him to put one barrel to Gareth's forehead and one to his heart. "Try again."

"Seriously. I don't know. If I didn't know my dad was dead because I saw his body, I'd think he'd risen from the dead to fuck me over. It wouldn't surprise me if he could. But someone's been threatening Tiernan and extorting me since just before the accident."

"Threatening me?"

"Yeah." He runs his hand through his hair before he

remembers there are two guns touching him. It's a nervous habit.

"I might not kill you in front of Tiernan, but you're sorely tempting me to shoot you in the dick in front of her. Explain."

I may think Seamus is prone to exaggeration about my looks, but nothing about anything that's happened since we walked in here makes me think he's exaggerating.

"Four months before the accident, Dad demanded I get a detail on you, Tiernan. He wanted you followed everywhere. He knew you were mostly with Aaron or at work, but he wanted someone watching you at every call and any time you weren't at home. He tapped your landline, but you never used it."

"It was only there in case of emergency and our cells weren't working."

"I know. I told him that, but he insisted. He tapped your cell, and Aaron found out. It was two-and-a-half months into Dad's surveillance. He lost his shit on me, assuming I ordered it. I didn't, even though I made it happen. Aaron suspected something was going on, but he didn't know what."

"I was six months pregnant. That's when Aaron became almost unbearable to live with. He was so demanding of my time I thought I would suffocate in that house."

"He was protecting you."

"No, he wasn't. Not really. He never shared any of his suspicions with me. He let me—his pregnant wife—leave the house not knowing people were watching me, listening to me. He left me alone in the house when I was least able to defend myself. He might have had good intentions, but he wasn't protecting me."

"I disagree." Gareth shakes his head. "But, anyway, he lost his shit with me. Then he lost his shit with Dad about three weeks before the accident. He threatened to move away with you and make you both disappear. He knew people outside our organization that could make it happen. Dad knew he wasn't faking. Aaron was a liability."

"What about me? What the hell did I do wrong? What did my baby do?"

I'm the one being pushed too far hearing this story. I don't think I can do it. I'm shaking and wishing Seamus didn't have both hands full. I need him.

He must sense it because he shoots Gareth a look more menacing than any I've seen yet. One more threatening than I thought possible. He puts the safety back on both guns and tucks them down the back of his pants. He steps back from the desk and reaches out his left hand to me. I rush forward, and he engulfs me.

"Shh, *cailín*. I'm here, and I'm not letting go. You're safe with me. Shh."

I nod my head against his chest, but I feel—I don't know how to describe it. It's a jumble of rage, agonizing grief, fear, and whatever else. I feel like I want to vomit, but I also want to tear this room apart. I want to throw anything in my reach while I cry. It's too much. It's all too fucking much.

Chapter Sixteen

Seamus

Tiera's trembling so much it's frightening me. I glance at Gareth, who's gone even whiter than Gretchen when I told her the truth. It wasn't a threat. It was a promise.

It's clear Tiera's behavior shocks Gareth. He's never seen her this way, and I'm certain he was around her for the funeral — funerals? —I won't ask Tiera. I scoop her into my arms, and Gareth's eyes widen.

Motherfucker. Does he think I've been faking my feelings for Tiera so far? Is he shocked I can lift her? He knows how strong I am, so it would only reflect what he thinks about her. I walk to the sofa and am careful as I sit. I cradle her in my arms and keep cooing to her. Today's been emotionally tough on me. I can't imagine how Tiera's managing not to fall apart. She's stronger than anyone gives her credit for. She's calming in my arms, which calms me.

"Should I get her some water? Some whiskey?"

Gareth doesn't know what to do. He sounds as genuinely

shaken as he looks. Tiera shakes her head and curls into me as though even a drink would take her away from me. That it would threaten her. He moves around his desk but gets no closer than that.

"Tiernan?"

"Leave me alone, Gareth."

He nods as he reaches into his pocket. Silently, he pulls out his keyring and holds one up. He points toward the door. I can lock or unlock it from the inside, so he won't trap us. He's offering to give us privacy. Maybe there's still a humane bone in his body—at least toward Tiera. He slips from the room, and we hear the door lock. There's the soft murmur of voices in the hallway, but nothing loud enough for me to understand.

"*Cailín*, what do you need right now?"

"You."

I tilt her head back, then cup her jaw. "You know I'll hold you for as long as you want. You're where you belong, anyway."

"On your lap?" She offers me a watery smile.

"And in my arms. When you're ready, we'll leave. We don't have to talk to anyone you don't want to. We'll get in the car and go wherever you want."

"Can we go to my place?"

"Of course."

"Would—would—you stay with me?"

I don't like the timid whisper. She's scared to ask. She's scared I'll say no. Why wouldn't she be after what she's learned in the past hour?

"Not 'would' as though it's hypothetical. Not 'will' either. There's no question, *mo stóirín*. I didn't say that for their sake. You are my little darling when I can't call you *cailín* in public. You're my little darling in private, too. But I won't hide my affection for you from anyone. My feelings for you aren't a secret."

She sighs and closes her eyes for a moment. Then she smiles again, and it's not as weak as before.

"You have such a big heart, Daddy." She places her hand on my chest, and I wonder if she can feel it beating. She rests it there briefly before sliding it until her fingers are in my hair. She lifts her chin, and I gladly accept the invitation.

Nothing compares to kissing Tiera. Nothing compares to being inside her. Her pussy is so tight it nearly squeezes the cum from me each time I enter her, but it's as though it were made for me. Being with her is unlike being with any other woman. I've enjoyed sex in the past. It's felt good, and I've gone back to the same women more than once. Hell, I enjoyed being with Makayla so much we were involved for three years.

But Tiera will wipe my past from my memory. She could consume all of me if I let her. It's fucking tempting to. I can keep some of my mind and heart for my family. I can keep some of my mind for work. But she'll have my soul if we keep going like we are.

"Daddy, I believe everything you said, but I know it was posturing. It reminded Gareth that the O'Briens answer to you."

"It may have done that, but that wasn't why I said and reacted the way I did. I will do anything to keep you safe. I will defend you until my last breath, and you've seen I have no patience at all for anyone who disparages you—no one who looks sideways at you. People are going to understand my woman is off limits to them."

"Your woman?" She grins, and it's like the sun came out from behind rain clouds.

"Yes. You're my girlfriend now. I don't know where things are going, but whatever you are to me—friend—girlfriend—lover—whatever—you are mine, and you're a woman. Therefore, you're my woman." I return her grin.

She sits up and wraps both arms around my neck. She leans in, but she doesn't kiss me. I fist her hair and tug. She sighs. I run my free hand from her right collar bone down to her tits and squeeze both. I slip my hand beneath her shirt and bra, finding her nipple. I tweak it before I pull my hand free and slide it up her leg under her skirt.

I push her legs open and cup her pussy. I dip my ring finger into her and flick it. I pull my hand free and lick my finger before gliding it up the outside of her thigh until I get to her arse. I know she feels me harden even more. My fingers dip into the divide between her arse cheeks, and my ring finger presses against the hole. The one I plan to fuck tonight.

Maybe I should wait until at least the second day we're having sex before I take her there. But I won't. I will claim every part of her by morning. I've had her cunt. I'll let her jack me off. I'll let her suck me off. I'll titty fuck her and give her a pearl necklace. Then I'll fuck her arse. It might take me all night and all day tomorrow, but I will do it.

The waistband of her skirt is too tight for me to get my hand under it and up her shirt, so I give up going that way. I squeeze her arse again and the back of her thigh as I slide it free of the skirt. Then I pull her blouse up. I touch every part of her back and belly I can. I feel when she sucks in. I yank my hand free and land a spank hard enough that she yelps.

"You will never hide any of you from me. Every inch of you is mine. If I didn't like it—if I didn't want it—I wouldn't touch you. I wouldn't hunger to touch you and see you. Devour you. Never change who you are for me. I won't be happy if you do."

I give her another hard spank for good measure before I return my hand under her shirt and continue to enjoy the silky skin and all her body offers. I didn't lie when I told her I've never had a type. I don't. I've been attracted to all types, and all types have been unattractive. But no woman makes me react like I do with Tiera. I love that she's more than just Rubenesque. It's not that I'm a big guy, so I don't want a skinny woman. It's not that I'm a big guy, so I want a big woman. I just want Tiera.

"Seamus, I've heard how your family is together. I know there are two sides to all the men in your family. The one who does what he must, and the one who chooses to be with his family. Don't hide the part of you, you think I'll fear any more than you amplify the part you think I want. You are both, and I've known that since the beginning. I don't want one without the other. And not because I can't manage without the one who will do what he needs to, to protect me. The man I've fallen for is both. Never change who you are with me. I won't be happy if you do."

Her tone is soft, but her gaze is pure steel. Completely unbendable. I've fallen in love with this woman. I've known that from the start. She gets me in a way no one outside my family ever has. I don't have to explain myself, justify myself, or hide myself from her. I still never want her to see what I can become, but she knows about it, and she accepts me despite—for—it.

"I've fallen for you too, T. Hard." My voice is barely loud enough for her to hear. I want her to know that, but I still feel exposed admitting it. Even after she just said what she did, it's hard to admit my vulnerability. She has the power to crush me.

As she gazes into my eyes, I think she gets that. She cups my cheeks and rubs her nose against mine. Then she presses her lips to mine and opens. But she does nothing more. She's surrendering to me again. I'd lightened my hold on her hair, but I clench my fist around it again. I hold her head in place as I kiss her, forcing her to open wider for me. I invade her mouth with my tongue. Just like her body, I refuse to let there be a single inch of her mouth I don't claim. She moans and presses her lips to me even harder.

When we pull apart, it's only because we need to breathe more than we can with our faces locked together. I wrap her hair around my wrist and rest my other hand on her throat.

"We are going to your place, then we are getting in my car. We're going to a store where we will buy everything that even remotely interests us. You are spending that week in bed with me. You are calling in sick to work. I will tell my family I am unavailable. Then I am going to have my way with you. I'm going to tie you up. I'm going to spank you. I'm going to clip your nipples and clit. I'm going to stick vibrators in your pussy, and I'm going to plug your arse. I'm going to spread your legs as wide as they'll go. I will edge you, and I will fuck you. I will be rough, and I will be gentle. You will tell me how you want it, but I will decide how we do it. You will be naked the entire time. Try to keep me from seeing you, and you will need an entirely new wardrobe because I'll burn it all. Do you understand me, baby girl?"

"Yes, Daddy."

Her pupils dilated as I spoke. I suspect what I discover before my hand gets to her pussy. She's soaked. She's not wearing panties, so I can feel how wet she is before my fingers touch her cunt.

"Daddy, I want to leave right now. I want to get in the car where it's private and suck you off. I need to."

"Because you want to submit?"

"Yes. God, yes."

"But you know how much I'll enjoy it. You'll know you're the one making me come. That you have the power to do that."

"Well, yes. But your hand on my head, pushing me to take you deeper, is what I need right now."

I stand and lower her to her feet. I wrap my arms around

her waist and bring my head down, so our foreheads rest together.

"Thank you for telling me what you need, *cailín*. Knowing you're comfortable speaking aloud what you need makes me feel ten feet tall. Please know I value your trust and your faith in me more than anything else. I'm not exaggerating, Tiera. I know you believe I do when I talk to and about you, but I don't. Nothing matters more to me than you, and your trust is more valuable than anything else in the world."

"Have I told you you're a sweet man? You truly are the sweetest. I pray you never question whether your feelings are one-sided. They're not. My relationship with my family differs from the one you have with yours. We're close, but not like yours. I don't know that any family is. I don't want you to think the depth of my feelings and putting you first is because I don't have anyone to care about, or at least not that much, so it's easy to put you first. I do because I want to."

"I never would have thought that, but thank you for telling me. Our situations *are* different, but I don't think that changes the significance of what either of us feels or says right now. Not ever."

I press a quick and gentle kiss to her lips, then peck her nose before I straighten.

"It's time to go, *cailín*. No matter what happens, you do not let go of my hand. You do exactly what I say if I tell you to get behind me or to run. I don't know what's been going on out there since we came in. I trust no one, Tiera. *No. One.* Decide now whether you'll go with your dad if he asks or tells you to."

"No. Only you. Once upon a time, I would have chosen Aaron because I trusted him but also because I believed it was the right thing to do. But I would have thought about it first. I choose you because I don't have a second of doubt. I'll do whatever you say, but I have one caveat."

I look down at her, and I know what's coming. I'm already shaking my head.

"Don't shake your head at me, Seamus. You can disagree, but you will not change my mind. I am not leaving you behind. I'm not saving my own ass at your expense. I won't stay and distract you, but if I can defend you, I will. If I can protect you, I will. You cannot change my mind."

I believe her. I can't change it. I want to. But I know there's not a chance I will. It makes me feel special, even if I hate the danger it invites.

"It'd better be I'm on death's doorstep for you to do that. Anything less, I will spank you so hard, you won't sit for a month. I'm serious, Tiera."

"So am I."

"I know. But you and I are not trained the same way. You and I are not matched in strength. And you and I definitely don't have the same experience. If I tell you to run, you do it. Even if it's my last breath, you do it. I won't punish you if you stay with me because you care and can protect me. How could I? But if it's an unnecessary risk or stubbornness, I will make your arse match those firetrucks you love."

"I can live with that."

I grit my teeth and shoot her a warning look. She smirks, then grins. She bounces onto her toes to kiss my cheek before she slides her hand into mine.

"Ready to face the world, *cailín*?"

"Ready, Daddy."

We walk to the door, and I hold up my left index finger. I press my ear to it. I hear nothing. I pull out one of the guns I tucked into my waistband at my lower back. I let go of Tiera's hand and step in front of her. I put my hand on the doorknob and count to ten. I won't underestimate the O'Briens, and I doubly won't underestimate them when Tiera's nearby. I open the door, the barrel already pointing out. There's no one in sight. I wait.

I'm certain Tiera would like to peer around me to see if I see anything, but she remains tucked behind me. I know she's getting more nervous because she tucks her hand into my waist-band near my hip. It isn't there to grab the gun if she thinks she needs it. It's inches away from the weapon. She's doing it to hold on, so we can't get separated.

Once I've counted to fifty, I step out, but I keep Tiera still shielded by the door. When nothing happens, I hold out my left hand and let the gun rest beside my right thigh. She pulls the office door closed behind her. We make our way down the hallway to the foyer. There's no one there, but we can hear voices in the living room. I glance back at Tiera since her dad's is one of them. She shakes her head as she shrugs. She's letting me decide.

I steer us to the front door and open it. Two guards turn toward me, but they decide it's better to lower their weapons. I nod. I signal for Todd to come over since he's resting back against the hood of the car. When he reaches the walkway up to the house, I lead Tiera down the steps to meet Todd.

"Take Tiera to the car. *Mo stóirín*, wait for me there. I'll be back in a few minutes."

Her gaze jumps over my shoulder to the house, and she's livid. She thinks I'm betraying what we just talked about. I'm not.

I lean in to whisper to her. "They will talk if it's just me. They'll think I'm less threatening alone. They'll say more without you being there because you're a woman and because it'll be about you. I need you to go with Todd. Please."

"I don't like this, Shay. It doesn't feel right."

"I know. But there's something else I need to talk to Gareth about. I was going to come down here before I knew you needed to. I wasn't sure if I'd get the chance, and I was willing to make another trip here if I needed to. But this is the right time. Please, little one."

"I will. Please be careful, Daddy." She leans far enough forward for her lips to brush my ear. It's erotic as hell. Unfortunately, I can't stay to enjoy it.

I wait outside until I see Tiera get in the car. Todd holds up the fob, and I hear the car lock. I turn back and glower at the guards. They do nothing to stop me going back inside. I follow the voices to the living room. As I step in, I'm tempted to shoot a photo or something on the mantle to make my point.

Gareth only allows upper-level men to carry guns in his house. If he's alone, he allows one guard. Otherwise, everyone checks their guns at the door. There are men besides Keith, Brant, and Vince here, but I know they don't have guns. I didn't want anyone confiscating mine, so I didn't bring it in. I took two while in the office, so I'm even more armed than when I arrived.

But my silence is menacing enough. It actually makes more of a statement than if I came in guns ablaze. It shows them I don't believe I need a weapon to intimidate them. I look around at the lower-level guys who must be here to give a daily or weekly report. I jerk my chin toward the front door. All of them dash their gazes to Gareth. Now I raise my gun. It's the one I took from Jimmy. He's who I'm aiming at. None of them look at Gareth this time. They file out in a hurry.

Once I'm alone with Gareth, Brant, Vince, and Keith, I step all the way in. I sit on the sofa in here, my legs crossed the same way as in the office. Except now I have both guns resting on my lap. I'm as good a shot lefthanded as I am righthanded. They all know because they've all seen me in action. Not at a range. Nope. They've seen me shoot to kill. They've seen my accuracy.

"Keith, who're you paying to extort Gareth, so he intimidates Tiernan?"

"What? Fuck you, dude."

"I know some unnamed fucker is intimidating Gareth, which includes forcing Tiernan to do things she doesn't want to at work. I know you're involved. You've tried to have Gareth killed at least five times since he turned eighteen and posed a threat to you. It's always pissed you off that he's smarter than you, so Darren never questioned handing the mantle over to him. But you are pettier, which makes you more deceptive. So, who're you paying?"

"I'm not paying anyone, you piece of shit."

"Really?"

I let go of the gun resting on my left thigh to reach into the inside right breast pocket of my suit jacket and pull out papers folded in half. I put down the other gun and quickly fold them into an airplane. I launch it at Gareth. It flies smoothly to him, hitting him in the chest. I was always good at making them.

I rest my hands on the guns as he opens and skims what I just gave him. His brow furrows, and I can see the anger building in him. We all can. Mount Gareth is ready to blow. He has a bit of a temper. My family might have the red hair, and he might have the Welsh name, but his temper is legendary. Tantrums most of the time, but this should be good.

"What the fuck, Keith?"

He must have been practicing sounding like my cousin Finn. It's way more intimidating than he used to sound.

"He's lying." Keith sounds like a little bitch. Boo-hoo-hoo, fuck nut.

Gareth holds up the papers and flaps them in the air. "Bullshit. These bank statements and phone bills don't lie."

I hadn't lied to Tiera either when I said Gareth doesn't have as tight a hold on the reins as he thinks. This proves it like a slap across the face. I genuinely don't know who's pulling the strings. That's why I asked Gareth. I gave him a chance to confess, in case he set Keith up or tasked him with this. Now, I'm certain he didn't know. We've suspected for a while that someone's been forcing Gareth's hand, but we hadn't known until just after the trial concluded. When I found out Tiera needed to come down here, I decided it was a good time to confront him.

But that was weeks ago. I could have come down here without her, and I could have come back with her. I'm kicking myself that I didn't. It would have spared her, but as agonizing as it must be for her—it's agonizing watching—she needs to learn all of this. I'm glad I'm here to support her. I hate thinking what it would have been like for her to discover all of this alone. Even a regular friend would be better than nobody. The juries out on whether her father would be useful.

Keith pointing a finger at me pulls my attention back.

"You're going to believe this pathological liar over me? What the fuck, Gareth? How do you know he didn't forge all this? Fabricate these lies out of nothing? He's doing this to fuck with us, and you're buying into it."

"Nope."

I don't need to defend myself. I don't need to convince Gareth to believe me. Through our spies, we know Gareth's had his doubts about Keith for a while. That's why we decided to bring it to his attention. Of course, we're sowing the seeds of doubt. Of course, we're butting in. Of course, we're doing it to fuck them over. They're still on probation for getting involved with shite that hurt Finn's wife and her family. This started as just a test, but now it's my personal retribution for what they've done and are still doing to Tiera.

"What the fuck do you mean 'nope'?" Vince can't stay out

of shite. He always has to be up to his brown eyes in it. The only part not in the shite is his blond hair.

I shoot him a dismissive glance and focus back on Keith and Gareth. That makes Vince livid. He's the one to listen to, but not yet.

"Vince, shut up. You're pissing me off, and you remember the last time you did that."

We all do. Vince's still limping even with the knee replacement.

I have the temerity to laugh. With a grin on my face, I shake my head. "Aren't you still in physical therapy?"

"Fuck off, O'Rourke."

I ignore Vince flicking me off and keep my gaze on Keith as I speak.

"Gladly, as soon as you tell me who you're paying to fuck with my girlfriend. I, frankly, couldn't give two shites about your family right now. You're doing a good job of fucking each other over. I want to know who thinks they can fuck with my girlfriend because they are not long for this world if they don't stop. As I see it, Keith, you're suspect number one, with no one behind you in line. So, you can fess up, or I'll bust your kneecaps too. Then I'll cut off your thumbs and shove them up your arse. And I might be done when I cut off your dick and make you suck it. But the longer you make me wait for an answer, the pissier I'm going to get. The pissier I get, the more you'll suffer."

"I don't know what the fuck you're talking about. You made this shit up, O'Rourke."

"You're really going with that. All right."

I pull the safety off the gun in my left hand and point it toward his right knee. I slide my finger around the trigger, and I know Keith can see it bending.

"Fucking, all right. Stop." He waves his hands in front of him as though he could ward me off.

I keep the gun pointing at him.

"You've got it backwards. I'm laundering money, but I didn't hire anyone. Some guys approached me right after Aaron died. I don't know why Darren arranged the accident, but I don't think he knew Tiernan was going to be in the car. None of us knew she was in labor when he suddenly left a meeting." Keith raises an eyebrow, and I roll my eyes.

A meeting. A motherfucking shakedown. Aaron was there probably as muscle or a gunman while Keith and whoever else forced some schlub to pay for breathing. The idiot likely borrowed money or had a business where the O'Briens wanted to store shite they fenced.

"Vince followed him back to his house but waited around the block. He's sworn up and down from heaven to hell that he didn't see Tiernan get in the car, or that she was in the passenger seat when they drove past."

I glance at Vince, and he nods. He's looking at the floor, and for the first time in all the years I've known the piece of shite, he looks ashamed.

"Vince called Darren to tell him Aaron bailed on the meeting and went home instead. Aaron was only there for like five minutes before he pulled out of the garage again."

"The winter sun was at that fucked-up angle that practically blinds you, so I couldn't see anyone in the passenger seat when Aaron drove by." Vince takes over telling the story, and he looks like he might cry. "I never would have called Darren back and told him Aaron left the house if I'd known Tiernan was in the car and in labor. If I'd known, I'd have told him she was there—in labor or not."

Vince swallows three times then shakes his head. He can't

keep going. I might actually believe the guilt plastered across his face. Keith picks up the story again.

"Vince followed them out of their neighborhood, and by then, I was done with the meeting and was around the corner. Vince and I planned to box Aaron in and confront him. Rough him up a bit. He was at the top of a hill, and I was at the bottom. I'm certain he saw my car, but it was just after twilight, so I have no idea if he recognized it. I kept thinking he needed to slow down, but the car just came at me faster and faster."

"I was following, and I never saw brake lights. I heard his horn as he kept honking and honking. He lowered his window and gestured for Keith to move his car." Vince sounds as though he's a million miles away as he stares blankly forward. "He drove over something, and I watched his tire blow. The car swerved left before it jerked to the right. It careened over the edge and—"

Vince shakes his head again and looks up at Brant. Tiera's father's eyes are watering. He has his right arm wrapped across his chest with his left elbow on his wrist. His left hand covers his mouth. When their gazes meet, fury blazes across Brant's face. He turns away and runs his hand through his hair. I think he did it to keep from wrapping his hands around Vince's throat.

"It rolled four times before slamming into a tree. Vince and I ran down there, and we could hear Tiernan screaming. Aaron was already gone. And Tiernan—God there was so much blood." Keith looks like he's reliving the event. Good. Let the fucker remember.

Brant turns back and inhales so deeply I watch his chest rise. "There was nothing the doctors could do for Tiernan. They barely kept her alive. I'm the one who told her about Aaron and the baby. After that, I don't think I spoke for two more days. I never wanted to hear my voice again after telling my daughter what happened. The pain in her voice when she screamed..."

I see the hair on his arms stick straight up. He can't fake that.

"What was your role in all this Gareth?"

He shakes his head. "I was in a massive fight with Gretchen that night. I had no idea what was going on. It pissed her off because I didn't take her when I went to Atlantic City the night before to scope out that casino Finn had just bought. She wouldn't listen that it was purely for work. I didn't know what happened until Vince called me from the hospital. Tiernan was still in surgery."

"Explain to me how the three of you went from ignorant or innocent bystanders to tormenting a widow who lost her child. Help me understand how you went from the supposed grief you're pretending now to making Tiernan feel like shite every day for the past three years."

I look at Brant, wondering if he's ever demanded answers. He feels me watching him, so he turns his attention to me. I study his face, then his posture. What does he know?

I don't look at Gareth when he continues the fucked-up tale, but I listen with ears like a dog.

"Dad called me the next morning. He told me he'd arranged the accident, but he hadn't planned for Tiernan to get hurt. Since he was tapping their phones, he knew Tiernan called her doctor's office to see if they thought she should go in. He knew she'd texted Aaron that she was in labor. He might not have planned for her to get hurt, but he didn't stop it from happening. He'd had someone cut Aaron's brakes in the five minutes he was inside. Vince couldn't have seen anyone slip in and out of the garage from where he parked. The day Dad died, so did the man who did that job. I found out he knew Aaron was taking her to the hospital, and he went through with it, anyway."

"You still haven't explained why you've treated her like shite, played on her grief, her insecurities, her goddamn trauma. Why the fuck would you do that to someone who's one of you?" I yell the last sentence. It's the first time I've raised my voice since I arrived, and they know it's rare that I do.

"I don't know what put Tiernan and Aaron on Dad's radar. I've never figured it out. I started getting cryptic calls about her, saying she'd better do what Dad asked without argument. Dad dismissed them as some guy in Chicago putting pressure on a deal we had going. He said the guy got Tiernan's number and thought he could force our hand."

Gareth's face flushes as he darts his gaze to Brant. Whatever's next is something he'd rather take to the grave than have Tiera's father hear.

"But three weeks after the funerals, I got a call from a burner we couldn't trace. The guy told me exactly what Tiernan was wearing the night before and what we ate when I went to her place for dinner. She'd already cooked everything before I got there. He fucking knew what color her socks were. I told my dad, and he shrugged. Said he'd look into it. A week later, I got a text with a photo that showed Tiernan walking out of her bathroom naked. I told Dad about the text, but I didn't tell him I assigned a detail to watch Tiernan's place. It took three weeks of getting fucked-up calls and texts about Tiernan before my guys caught someone operating a drone. It was a high school geek who was jacking off, watching Tiernan take a bath. He got paid two hundred bucks every time he filmed or photographed her."

"Filmed?" The kid better be dead.

Gareth nods before shifting uncomfortably and looking at Brant. "The first time I got a video text, I didn't know what it was. I made the mistake of opening it with some of my men around. I recognized Tiernan's voice as she ended a call with someone, but the video was aimed at a door I didn't realize was inside her bedroom. I didn't think much of it because it went quiet. I put my phone on my desk, the video still playing, because Jimmy handed me something to sign. He's the one who pointed out Tiernan was naked in the video. She was getting into bed—naked—with a—the video—"

Gareth can't say it with Brant glaring at him. I get his drift.

"Move along with the story. Tiernan's waiting for me."

"Jimmy grabbed the phone and passed it around to three guys before I got it back. They thought it was hilarious. I knocked three of Jimmy's teeth out for not giving me the phone back the first time I told him to do it."

"More videos came to Gareth, and I received some, too." Vince looks away for a moment before he continues. "No one besides Gareth, Darren, Keith, and I knew about the ones after that first time. But the guys wouldn't stop talking about it. Three months after this shit started—and yes, we searched for who was doing this—the threats started. It was make Tiernan falsify reports or plant evidence or make shit disappear, or this mystery fucker would kill her and ruin us. We thought it was an inside job since the guys suspected more videos and photos came in, but they never got to see any. Some of them started sniffing around Tiernan, but she wasn't interested. A few got the message, but others thought she was playing hard to get."

"From all of this, you felt the need to tell her she was fat and disgusting, that it was her fault the accident happened, that she deserved all of it. Get from where you are in this meandering story to the part where you explain your fucked-up rationale."

Gareth steps forward, finally finding his balls after taking it up the arse from me all day. He's pissed when he speaks. He thinks he can justify being a fucking shitbag to Tiera.

"It was the faceless, nameless person who insisted." He practically spits the words at me. "It worked and fucked with her mind. When she ate to console herself and started gaining weight, the guys didn't ease off on the comments, but they stopped being sexual in a way that made us nervous someone would get too handsy and not believe no means no. Eventually, the comments became taunts and insults. But we figured she was safer with that. We were protecting her."

"Why didn't you just tell her the truth?" Brant cuts in.

"That's what I'd like to know, too. Just how fucking stupid and incapable do you believe I am that you had to fucking wreck my life to *claim* you were protecting me?"

Chapter Seventeen

Tiera

It felt like forever, and Seamus still hadn't come outside. I rolled down the window to ask Todd if he knew what was going on. I believed him when he shook his head. I could see him through the window the entire time, and he never took out his phone. It didn't look like he spoke to anyone, and none of the guards spoke to him. The minutes dragged, and I got nervous. I tried to be patient. But I know those men better than Seamus does. At least that's what I thought until I just heard what I heard.

I lied to Todd and said I had to go to the bathroom too badly to wait. It was against his better judgement, but he let me out of the car and walked me inside. I heard Gareth's tone and knew he was about five seconds from his fuse igniting. I hurried forward, but stopped dead when I heard him explain.

My dad may want an explanation, but I guarantee I want it more. Seamus is out of his seat the moment he hears my voice. I walk over to him, and he doesn't hesitate to wrap his arm around me and draw me to his side. I encircle his waist, but I don't lean against him. I want the others to see Seamus and I may be unified, but I can still stand on my own. I want his support, but I don't need it. Not the way I thought I did while we were in Gareth's study. Seamus told me I was stronger than anyone realized. I remind myself he's right. I won't let anyone ever believe I'm weak again.

"Answer the question. Any of you. Why the hell did you ruin my life when I'd already lost everything?"

I keep my tone even. I refuse to sound like a hysterical female. I refuse to sound like a demanding bitch. I won't give any of them an excuse to ignore me or diminish my right to know. Seamus wouldn't let them. I want to do this on my own, but with him at my side.

Gareth glances at my dad, who looks as curious as me. I don't think he knows any of this. Good. I don't want Seamus to beat the shit out of my father, but I think he would if he believes Dad hasn't protected me. Gareth looks at Seamus when he speaks rather than at me.

"This person swore he'd know if we told you anything— even hinted at anything. He'd be the one to torment you. Tiernan, Edie didn't die of old age. Your dog was slowly poisoned. Someone was getting into your home because you never kept food or water outside for Edie. You always made sure she could come back in if it was hot enough for her to need water or too cold to stay out. When I discovered that, I knew the threats weren't just talk. I knew he could get to you."

"I still don't understand how blaming me for the accident and what happened was the right way to protect me. Unless we were outside, how would they know what the fu—hell—you said to me?" I catch myself before I swear in front of my father.

"I've swept this house for bugs nearly daily for three years. I've had your office and home and car swept too. My vehicles and any you've ridden in are swept before and after. I've had your place searched with a fine-tooth comb to see if there are any cameras anywhere."

"You invaded my privacy? My home? Rather than whisper something in my fucking ear somewhere like the damn grocery store, you ransacked my home. I'll give you that your men are good. I've never suspected anything."

So much for not swearing in front of Dad.

He takes a menacing step forward, and Gareth, Keith, and Vince look like they want to jump back at least thirty feet. But they stand their ground. Barely. "And you couldn't have told me somehow? You couldn't let me know some whack job is out for my daughter?"

"How is this person contacting you?" I want to know how this fucker has so much control.

"Email, texts, calls, couriered notes. And they always track back to nothing." Keith shrugs. I want to slap the pathetic expression off his face.

"What were the threats? You tell me and what? I die? You lose money? You die? What was so horrible that you asked how high every time this person told you to jump?"

Vince cracks his knuckles. It's a nervous habit he's had since he was in fourth grade. "This person sent me videos of faceless people being tortured. When I say faceless, I mean it. Their faces had already been peeled off. We could never see who the torturer was, but it was always something different. We had no reason *not* to believe this person would act on it, especially after Edie."

"Tiernan—Brant—" Gareth looks at me, then my dad, then back to me. "—I kept a detail on you around the clock. The men rotated, so no one got too close to you. No one became too predictable. I switched guys out for months at a time. But somehow this person kept getting audio and video of you in your office and at home. I don't know how they slipped by, and you didn't know about my men, so you never invited them in. The more violent the videos became, the more demanding this person became about what we said to you."

I shift my focus and gaze to Seamus. He's already watching me. Our gazes meet, and I want to know what he's thinking. Can he tell what I'm thinking? I don't know what to believe, but I know I want someone from his family going through my home, office, and car. I know I'll let Seamus see any and everything in all those places.

"Explain the bank statements and phone records, Keith." I don't know what Seamus is talking about. "You said they are forcing you to launder for them. If that's the case, why did this come as a shock to Gareth?"

Keith shifts nervously. Seamus's hand tightens around my waist, and I know he's ready to push me behind him. He doesn't trust Keith, and neither do I.

"Keith, don't keep us waiting. It sounds like you're getting some kickback. What's Seamus talking about?" I want to know who's benefiting from this.

"Because they have shit on me, too."

"It'd better be some horrific shit, Keith. What do they know?"

"That I'd been trying to break you and Aaron up since the beginning. I sent Hillary to start the fight at the firehouse. I encouraged her to approach him at your wedding. I thought between the two, it would make you doubt him. I got him so drunk he passed out after playing poker a few times when you guys came back to visit while you were in grad school. I'd do it to piss you off since he didn't come home those nights. The one time I did it after you were married, I made sure he couldn't remember whether he fell asleep on my couch or somewhere else. I parked his car outside Hillary's. I told him she called me to take him home, but I took him to my place. He knew that was a lie. I have never been more scared for my life than that day because I'd already hinted to you he was with her. That's the closest to death I've ever come."

"I remember that. He came home so pissed he couldn't speak to me for an hour. His knuckles were busted, and there was blood splattered on his shirt. I burned it because I didn't know whose it was. I bleached the entire bathroom, which I shouldn't have done because I was four months pregnant. But I didn't want to risk any evidence, and Aaron was too angry and too hung over to do it."

"I recorded the guys talking about you, but he never heard the parts where I instigated it. I spliced parts that made it sound like you were into the attention, that you were considering being unfaithful."

"He never once confronted me about that. He never even hinted at questioning me."

"Because he knew you wouldn't. I'd hoped he would think it, but it just made him suspicious of everyone else. Of me. It's why he wouldn't let you out of his sight unless he knew who you were going to be with and where you were going unless you were with your parents. He didn't trust you were safe."

"He didn't tell me any of that. None of you told me any of this. None of you even considered I might have my own thoughts on my protection. You never thought I deserved to know because you all believed I was too—what—stupid? Incapable? Weak? Talkative? What?! Why the fuck didn't you tell me someone wants to skin me alive?!"

I let go of Seamus, and he reaches for me, but I shake him off. I walk to stand in front of Gareth, Vince, and Keith. I don't understand Keith's motivation at all.

"Not one of you is fit to lead. You pathetic, weak, little men. You couldn't figure out who this was. You couldn't make it stop.

You couldn't trust me because you'd have to admit you're too weak and pathetic to find out who's doing this or to make it stop. Did it make you feel like your dicks were bigger to know you were supposedly protecting me? Did it make you feel like you're men to be respected because you believed you were protecting me from something so dangerous? Did you feel like real leaders because you made me depend upon you, even though I didn't know it? Did you feel funny and clever when you came up with different insults to make me feel like my life was worthless? I don't think the three of you combined could count as high as the number of times I was ready to end it. If it weren't for my parents and the shame and guilt I felt for what it would do to them, I would have. Believe me when I say I want nothing more in life than to put a bullet in each of your heads. Sleep with one eye open because one day, I will kill each of you."

I pull the gun from the back of my skirt. I took it out of the small drawer under the backseat where I saw Seamus put it. I know he felt it when he put his arm around me. It's why he tried to hold me back.

I aim it at Vince. "I lied to Darren for you when you couldn't shoot Billy Wilkinson, so I did it for you. I took the blame for it grazing his ribs rather than going through his heart because I said I distracted you. Did you know he beat me for that? It was winter, and I wasn't dating anyone at the time, so no one saw the bruises. I just said I was sore from training."

I aim at Keith. "I never told anyone until today that you couldn't get it up. That I wasn't the reason either. That it only twitched when we watched gay porn and that you've been taking the little blue pill for years to fake it with women, so no one would guess."

I couldn't give two shits who gets him off. Once I knew neither of us would have a fulfilling sex life together, my feelings for him waned. I broke up with him when I realized—I thought—I would find what I needed with Aaron. But that's why I don't get why he wanted to break Aaron and me up.

Finally, Gareth. He puts his hands up as I put the barrel to his chest and press hard enough it'll leave a mark. "You. I've covered for you since we were kids, and you broke your grandmother's little Hummel figurine." I point to my dad. "My parents grounded me for three weeks from soccer because of that. I missed the league tournament, and my teammates wouldn't talk to me until nearly midway through the next season. I covered for you when you were failing geometry and did your homework for two months to get you caught up, then tutored you till the end of the semester. I covered for you with Gretchen when Darren made you go out with Sarah O'Malley for three months. I told her you never went out with Sarah let alone touched her when I knew your dad was practically watching you fuck Sarah. Every time you went to Boston, I told Gretchen you were off training with my dad. I covered for you when your dad died because you were too busy fucking Gretchen to answer your phone. I said you were helping me with some plastering, and your phone died. I covered for you when my dad suspected you were treating me like shit and wanted to confront you. I told him I started an argument, and I got nasty first. I have done nothing but cover for you since you were five. You worthless sack of shit."

Gareth opens his mouth, and I'm quick to point the gun between his lips.

"If you even, for one second, think to claim your way of protecting me was how you returned the favors, I'll blow your fucking head open."

I lower the gun and look at my dad before I turn around to Seamus. I hand the weapon to him and wrap my arms around his waist. I turn my head to look at the three stunned faces.

"You are relieved of protecting me. I'll take my chances. You are fuck out of luck having someone work at the insurance company. I'm quitting today. You are fuck out of luck using me to falsify reports submitted to and by fire departments. You are just plain ole fuck out of luck because I don't care enough to hate you. I wish you were dead, and I'll dance a jig on all of your graves. But I refuse to give you any more of my emotions or thoughts. Find some other patsy. Come near me again, and I'll put that bullet through your head."

I look at Seamus's face for the first time. His expression screams not to test him. His hand slides up and down my back. I wonder what he's going to say once we're in the car. I doubt he's going to say 'attagirl.'

"From now on, you are relieved of anything to do with Tiernan. She's under the O'Rourkes' protection. Contact her, and I will take that as a threat. You talk to me, my brother, or my cousins if you have a message for her. Do anything to speak to or see Tiernan, and I will take you to the one place you never want to go. I promise with good food and long naps, I'll last longer than you do."

Their place. Every syndicate family has one. It's the one place they completely control. It's an environment where shit can't go wrong. They can handle the messy shit without anyone seeing. No one outside the senior members and a few selected button men know where it is. No one leaves alive. I'm not supposed to know where it is, but I was eight months pregnant when Keith showed me a photo of Aaron tucking a hundred-dollar bill into a woman's g string at one of the strip clubs Vince owns. The next photo was her giving Aaron a lap dance.

I tracked his phone until the location services turned off. It was an area of town where no one lives. I knew he hadn't gone to the woman's place, and I doubted it was some place he'd want to fuck, even if they stayed in the car. His location flicked back on four hours later when he headed toward home. I pulled up an aerial map and figured out roughly where he must have been.

I did a little searching through fire records I could access thanks to my position and found a building that was supposed to be condemned after a fire. I watched Aaron's locations and saw he stopped at Gareth's, so I drove by and noticed it was still in good shape. I knew what I'd found.

I confronted him when he got home. I showed him the photos and told him I found the building. He was livid that I risked going anywhere near the place. He called Keith and put him on speakerphone. He made me stay quiet while he walked through everything that happened at the strip club, and Keith confirmed it all. Yes, he'd put the money in her g string, and yes, she'd straddled his lap. But no, he hadn't gotten a lap dance. Aaron slipped her a note to take to her boyfriend. Some guy who was running drugs for them. Then he acted like he changed his mind.

He worded it so Keith admitted Aaron refused the lap dance idea before they even got to the club and that Keith threatened to record himself fucking the woman and send it to me, saying it was Aaron. They had a similar build, but I'd know Aaron's body from anyone else's even if I were blind. We were together for six years. He had a light birthmark just below his left shoulder blade, so I would have known from that alone.

Aaron took a baseball bat to Keith's vintage Coupe de Ville. Smashed the headlights, taillights, front windshield, rear windshield, and both side view mirrors. After the beating to his body and the beating to his car, Keith never claimed Aaron cheated again. For all his faults, unfaithfulness wasn't something Aaron would ever commit.

"Come, *mo stóirín*. Let's go home."

Seamus takes my hand and leads me to the front door. The

guns I saw on his lap when I walked in are back in his waist-band, and he's carrying his own gun. My dad follows us out. No one says anything until we get to the car. Then my dad engulfs me in a hug that leaves me struggling to breathe. But it's the second-best hug in the world. Only Seamus has ever surpassed my dad's hugs when it comes to feeling safe. Even Aaron's didn't reassure me the way Seamus's and Dad's do.

"I am so sorry all of this happened. I could never get any of them to tell me why they gave you a hard time. I never guessed the extent of what they said to you. Why didn't you tell me?"

"What could you do? You work for Gareth, not the other way around. You've been like an uncle to him, and you're Vince's brother, but I never trusted your life with either of them. I was scared if I told you anything, they'd take it out on you. I know you can protect yourself in a fight, but there were other ways they could punish you. I didn't think I could risk it. I love you."

"Aw, nugget. I love you, too. I pray you never think you have to protect me. It will always be the other way around. Come to me the moment you think you might need me. We'll sort whatever it is out together. No one and nothing mean more to me than you. You're my one and only."

"Thanks, Dad."

I know he means this shit, but he also means Seamus. If things don't work out with him, my dad thinks I might need him to keep me safe. I don't want him to question my relation-ship with Seamus.

I pull back.

"I know you'll always put me first. It's why I didn't go to you. But I know I'm where I belong now. I know I've never been safer than I am now."

I look up at the bear of a man who's been my champion since I was born. He and my mom haven't always been perfect parents, but they've tried their hardest. I know they both love me more than anything. It's what kept me from acting on the darkest days of my life. I know this must be excruciating for him to discover.

"If that ever changes…" He looks past me at Seamus. I don't know what Seamus does, but my dad nods.

"Dad, whatever you're thinking, don't do it. Please, just leave this alone, at least for now. Don't stir things up with them. We have enough to deal with right now. I don't want Gareth's ego to lead him. He'll do something to you if you test him."

"I know. I won't. But he and I are going to talk somewhere I'm certain no one will hear."

I don't know if that means the place or somewhere else. I won't ask. I don't want to know what he'll say. I give him another squeeze, then step back to Seamus's open arms. His solid wall of muscle presses against my back as his arms wrap around my waist. I rest my hands on his forearm. It's like a force field just went up around me. I feel untouchable. I lean back into him, my head resting against his chest. I close my eyes for a moment and exhale. He tightens his hold, and I just want to curl up on his lap again.

We watch my dad walk to his car. Todd's already in the vehicle since it wasn't a conversation he needed to overhear. A light breeze blows, and it feels refreshing. Revitalizing.

"Can we go home now, Daddy?"

Chapter Eighteen

Seamus

I wish home meant our place. But she already told me she wants to go to hers.

"Of course, *cailín*. Anything you want."

I hold the car door open for her and slide in once she's on her side. I drop the privacy glass just low enough to tell Todd where to take us. Then I shut it again. I lean forward and press the latch to open the drawer beneath the seat. You'd never know it was there if you didn't already know where to look. I put the three guns in it and snap it shut. Tiera's watching me, and I'm not sure what she needs. I know what I need. I put my hands on her waist, but I don't move her. Not until she nods.

Then she's on my lap, and I can finally breathe easier.

"Shay, are you angry with me?"

"What? No. Why would I be?"

"Because I pulled a gun on three mobsters."

"It didn't thrill me since I thought you'd shoot at least one of them. But once I knew you weren't acting impetuously, I was more concerned about how they'd react."

"None of them would have done shit with you and my dad there."

"And if we hadn't been? What would they have done?"

"I never would have found out. I'd never have done that if you weren't there."

I don't want her to tempt fate and think she can take risks because I'm there to protect her. I always will, but I can't guarantee I always can.

"Shay, I won't go around doing stupid shit just because you're bigger than everyone else. I'd say today was extenuating circumstances."

"You could say that."

"I know I should be in my seat with my belt on, but I really don't want to move. Can I stay like this for a while?"

"Yes. You're where you belong, Tiera."

Our lips meet, and her hand slides up my chest to cup my neck. We take our time, savoring every moment. I hope she knows how much this means to me. I hope it means as much to her. There's so much I want to say about my feelings, but it's too soon. I don't think I'm confusing lust for love because I've never felt this depth of emotion before. I know my future is with Tiera. I've known it since the very beginning. I wouldn't have asked her out—pursued her—if I didn't know it.

I've prayed more in the weeks I've known her than I have in years. I've prayed I'm right about her being my future. I've prayed I'm not making a mistake and risking her life. I've prayed she'll feel the same way about me as I do her. I've prayed I can make her happy. I've prayed I can keep her safe. I've prayed to be forgiven for whatever I end up doing to the men in her life. But I won't pray for forgiveness for what I'll do when I find the motherfucker terrorizing my girlfriend.

By the time the kiss ends, I have a hand up the back of her skirt and one up the back of her shirt. It tempts me to strip her naked and feast upon her since we have at least two hours until we get to her place. Maybe I will in a little while. Right now, I just want to touch skin to skin, even if it's only my palms.

"Thank you for standing by me throughout that. You could have been on my side purely for appearance's sake, while silently disagreeing with me or not caring about what you heard. But you supported me, and I never felt alone. Thank you."

"*Cailín*, even if I disagree with something you do, it won't change that I'll always support you. I never want you to feel alone again. I don't want you to think you have to go through any of this on your own. I'll be on your side."

And I want nothing more than to always be *at* her side.

"You're more to me than just this, but you're also a good friend."

Thank God for the first part, or I would have my hand on her arse while getting friend zoned. That would be awkward.

"No matter what happens, I always want at least that."

As we gaze at each other, something clicks into place for both of us. We aren't looking at each other with lust, even though there's never been a moment without some amount of desire. This is soul deep. It's like we understand the inevitable.

"Seamus, are you my future?"

Her question is barely more than a whisper. She isn't timid. It feels a bit more like she doesn't want to tempt fate.

"You are undoubtedly mine. I want to be yours."

"What does that mean to you?"

"It means I want an us that has *our* place. It means waking up to you and going to bed with you for more than just a week. It means knowing I'm always coming home to you. It means cooking together, doing each other's laundry, knowing each other's favorite foods to make for dinner, and understanding when we need space and when we need comfort. It means no one matters more to me than you."

She appears thoughtful for a moment before she nods. There's something she's holding back. Not a secret. Something she's still uncertain she can share.

"Tiera, what's the matter? Was that too much too soon?"

"No. Could you ever see marriage in your future?"

"To you, yes."

"So, not to anyone else."

"No. Have I wished I could have what my parents have? Yeah, but I didn't assume I would."

"What does that mean? I mean, what is it your parents have?"

"An unwavering partnership that's been tested and never failed. Someone who makes them happy and understands them in a way even the rest of the family doesn't. Someone they can each confide in, laugh with, cry with, and grow old with."

Growing old is all relative in my—our—world. My parents are in their mid-fifties, so my father is practically ancient by some standards. I often feel like I live on borrowed time. On any day, at any moment, I could die. That's not me catastrophizing or being melodramatic. It's simply the truth.

"Do you see anything else? Do you want something else?"

I hope I don't misinterpret that when I answer.

"I do, but it doesn't change what I've already said I want. What I've said isn't contingent upon anything."

Does she get what I mean?

"I nearly died in the accident. It's nothing short of a miracle that I didn't. While I was in the hospital, I didn't know if I could have children. Once I knew I could, I didn't think I'd want to. When you put your hand on my belly, there's still an instinct to suck in and hide. I know you don't like that, and that makes me feel beautiful. But when I get past that moment of fear you won't like what you find, I like how—"

Whatever she was about to say makes her think twice.

"Tell me the truth, Tiera. What were you going to say?"

"I think I've misunderstood. Never mind."

"Little one." I infuse some command into my voice.

I don't want her to feel bullied into sharing her thoughts if it makes her uncomfortable. But if it's something she likes or needs, then I want to give it to her whenever I can.

"After what Gareth said, it'll sound stupid."

"What part of the shite Gareth spewed do you mean?" The guy said a lot of bullshite.

"About being into—or rather supposedly being over being into possessive men. When I get over the moment of self-consciousness, I like how possessive it feels. I really liked it when we stood with my dad, and your hand was on my belly. It was like you were protecting what will be ours one day."

Her cheeks flush.

"I was. You are mine. All of you. And I want that future with you. I wasn't going to broach the subject until you did. I didn't know what you wanted or whether you could. I never want to hurt you by bringing up what happened and being insensitive."

"You are the furthest thing from insensitive, Daddy. Will you always get things right in the future? Probably not. Will you maybe say or do something insensitive from time to time? Yeah. I'll make the same mistake too. But you are not an insensitive man."

"Could you picture that?" I see the hope in her eyes.

"Yes. Do you want that?" I hold my breath.

"Definitely. You?"

"Absolutely." And I exhale.

Did we just discuss marriage and having children together?

253

I think so. Is that nuts? Probably. Am I excited by the possibility? Absolutely. Does it scare the shite out of me? One hundred percent.

What if she gets tired of the lies? What if she gets tired of me disappearing? What if she gets tired of me? Just because she's used to this life doesn't mean she'll be happy with it after all.

"Shay, I can practically see your thoughts written across your face. I know what I'm getting myself into, and I don't think our marriage would be like my past. You and Aaron couldn't be more different than chalk and cheese. What I had with Aaron wasn't what I signed up for. It was the exact opposite. That's why it was so hard. It was a life I was familiar with and had purposely tried to abandon. I resented Darren and Aaron for sucking me back into it. I'm in a different position than I was back then. I'd like to think I'm wiser, but you are exactly how I want you. And I don't think that will change."

"But I will lie to you."

"And it will keep you, your brother, your cousins, your father, your uncles, your mom, your aunts, your men, and me safe. What kind of person would I be to hold that against you? Especially since I know you will, and more importantly, why you will. I might not know where you're going when you disappear for days, but I'll know why. Daddy, you've already had to do that four times since we started dating. I knew then. You were born into this life. You've never had a choice. It's not a choice you can make now. I can live with all of that. I can live with not coming first because I know that going into this."

"You and any children we have will always come first when you can. I will always *want and wish* you could."

"You've shown me that since the first soccer game. I haven't doubted it." She cups my cheek and gazes into my eyes with an intensity that wasn't there a moment ago. "What did the Gaelic you said at the game mean? You've said it again since then."

Am I blushing? Heat radiates from my cheeks. Fucking curse of being a redhead. Fortunately, next to nothing makes me blush. But this does.

"It means I'm going to marry you."

"Tay my hen—"

I laugh. She tries, and I know it's an honest effort.

"Tay-may-hun-to-ah-fahsu." *Tá mé chun tú a phósadh.*

"Tay-may-hune-to-aw-fatoo."

I don't want to laugh at her because I don't want to insult her. But it's adorable. She's concentrating so hard.

"Close."

"I hope—Am I going to practice that?" She stumbles over her words at first, but she grows more confident.

"Tá." I give her a peck. "Yes."

We sit in silence before she curls against me, and I hold her tighter. What more is there to say? I'm not proposing yet, and certainly not in the back of a town car. We haven't even said we love each other. I don't know if she does. She says she sees herself as my wife and us having children. But can she love me? Will she let herself love me? Maybe a deep affection. Can I live with that? I might have to. But that doesn't necessarily mean I can. If ever there were a reason to pump the brakes, that would be it.

We'll leave the topic alone for a while. I think we've said everything we should and all we want to at this point.

I hold my girlfriend while I close my eyes. I know she isn't asleep, but we enjoy the silence. At least for a few minutes, then my phone vibrates in my back pocket.

"Hold on, *cailín*." I shift and pull it out. Fortunately, it's in the pocket that's on the opposite side from where she's looking. I can read the text without her seeing the screen.

CORMAC

You on your way back yet?

ME

Yeah we left about twenty mins ago

CORMAC

How long do you think it'll take you?

ME

1.5 hrs maybe two what's up?

CORMAC

Kutsenkos called the cops on Mitchell for scalping tickets for the concert last night we just got his call he's still in lock up

ME

You need me to go down there?

CORMAC

Yeah

ME

I need to take Tiera home. I want guys outside her place. Things didn't go well.

CORMAC

How not well?

ME

They're lucky neither of us shot any of them. It got close

CORMAC

Marvelous

ME

I know that tone. Don't.

I can hear my brother's voice in my head. I know what that word means. He's been using it since we learned it in third grade. It was around the time we learned sarcasm.

CORMAC

Fine. It's that serious?

ME

Very

CORMAC

Good you deserve it

ME

Thanks I'll let you know when I get there

CORMAC

Let me know if you need anything

ME

Will do thanks

I pull up Dillan's number.

ME

I need a detail for Tiera. Things didn't go well. They're all in one piece but barely.

I wait for a response, but it doesn't come immediately. He could be busy, or he could be arranging things before he confirms. I don't know. I have to be patient. But that's the last thing I am with getting protection in place for Tiera.

I don't want to shift too much since Tiera's still resting against me. But she knows I was texting someone while holding her. I hope she doesn't think I'm being rude.

"*Cailín*, I have to go out for a bit." Whatever a bit means.

"I'll be okay, Daddy. Call me, text me, or come by whenever you get a chance."

"I know you're being understanding, and I appreciate it. But you are not giving me wiggle room to back out of what I said earlier or because I don't want to be with you. I told you, I'll put you first whenever I can. When I'm done with this, you'll go back to being first. I was serious about the days together. I still want that if you're okay with it."

"I hope this doesn't take long. The five days don't start until our first night together." She leans back enough to look up at me.

"They definitely don't count until we're together. I just texted Dillan because I want a safety detail for you. I'd arrange for one anyway because you're my girlfriend, but after today, I won't consider going without."

"Your men are the best chance I have for being safe after what we learned today. I'm not as worried about Gareth and his twats, but whoever this is has targeted me for years."

"It won't be one of our men. It will be a man from my family. I won't agree to anything less. Dillan knows that without me saying it."

"That's inconvenient for them. They probably have stuff to do already. You might scrape up some men."

"Scrape up some men? There's not even remotely a chance that's happening. I trust no one as much as I do the men and women in my immediate family. My brother and cousins are the only ones I'll allow on your detail until we know what's going on."

"Seamus—"

"It's non-negotiable. Even if we weren't involved romantically, now that I know what's been going on, there's not a chance in hell I'm ignoring the risk. And there's not a flying feck I'm letting anyone else near you if my brother or cousins aren't with you, too."

She stares at me before she nods. She tucks her head back against my chest and sighs. It's not a beleaguered one. I think it's a content one. I run my hand up and down her back as I kiss the crown of her head. I close my eyes for a moment, but my phone vibrates.

DILLAN

Everyone's busy today. But I can get
something together for tomorrow.

ME

Then I don't deal with Mitchell. I'm not leaving
Tiera unprotected.

DILLAN

Cormac's got a client meeting. Finn's running
payroll. Shane's got a city inspector visiting
the mini mall project. Sean's with Nikki
because Ewan just announced he's in town.
And I'm heading into a meeting with the
tequila distributor.

Ewan O'Malley. My cousin's wife's shitbag half-brother
heads up the Boston Irish. He's no better to Nikki than Gareth
has been to Tiera. He didn't hide shite from her, but he was
willing to risk her life and get her involved in mob business.

ME

Then I deal with Mitchell tomorrow.

DILLAN

You can't leave him in lock up.

ME

You're still admitted to bar you go

DILLAN

Don't be testy

ME

Don't leave my girlfriend in danger

A response isn't immediate. That's rarely good when you're
talking to Dillan. I don't want to shift restlessly, but as the
seconds tick by, I'm getting anxious and irritated.

DILLAN

Is it really that bad?

ME

Worse. I won't say over text but I don't want Tiera alone for even a minute. Someone in our family is always with her. I'll take her to Mom and Da's if I have to.

DILLAN

Are you okay with Sean and Nikki?

ME

It's not safe for Nikki. It has to be someone else or I don't go.

DILLAN

Let me work on it

ME

I'll ask my dad.

That is going to make Tiera monumentally uncomfortable, but I don't have any other choice if no one else can deal with Mitchell's situation. I trust my father without any reservations. My dad and uncles usually guard my mom and aunts, so it's not like he's sitting around doing nothing. He and my uncles still serve our family, but they aren't in the thick of things like they were when they were my age. Instead, they're what I'd call semi-retired mobsters. They go on missions when they're needed, but rarely.

They've always had regular jobs, but they've always been at businesses they own. Now they work full-time without their senior execs or managers having to cover for when they'd disappear unexpectedly or couldn't come in for a few days because of injuries. If my mom and aunts are going about their day-to-day routine, and it's predictable, they have a rotation of our most trusted guards. But if anything deviates, and they're going places where they don't already have men positioned, then my dad and uncles go with them.

DILLAN
If you think he'll be okay with it.

ME
If he's available he will be.

My dad will understand if I ask him to do this. He knows about Tiera. He's the only one who does. Cormac's guessed but hasn't pushed me too hard on how serious I am. The other guys are probably getting the abridged version of next to nothing from Cormac. I've talked to my dad about what a relationship might be like. My mom and aunts are the daughters and sisters of former mob bosses. One is the mother of and two are the aunts of the current mob boss. They're like Tiera. They've never known a life without the mob. My dad and my uncles come from a mob affiliated family.

DILLAN
I'll leave it up to you.

ME
Thanks if he can't I'll try your dad and Uncle Ronan.

I'm an O'Rourke from both sides. The two branches haven't been closely related for like ten generations, but each generation keeps having sons. It's kept the name alive, but it's also meant our family can never leave. Three brothers married three sisters, so my dad and my uncles understand the overpowering need to protect the women we care about. They understood when Dillan, Finn, and Sean started dating their wives. They'll understand about me too.

My dad's been really encouraging since I first talked to him.

It was on the way home from the scrimmage against Tiera and her team. He told me to go slowly. She's known the mob, but it's been from a few tiers removed from the top. Even though her father has a senior position, he's not one of the senior leaders. I am in my family.

DILLAN

My dad's headed to the Shore with Mom for the night.

The Jersey Shore is the only time any of us enjoy going to New Jersey. It's the closest set of beaches, so it's not a horrible place for a night or even a weekend. But if we have more than a weekend off, we'd rather not spend it in New Joyzey because we're not Guidos. But for all the shite everyone who isn't from New Jersey gives the state, the Shore is pretty nice. I'll take the Caribbean and the Med over it anytime, but for a night, it'll be okay enough for my aunt and uncle.

ME

I forgot. I'll ask Uncle Ronan if my dad can't.

DILLAN

Okay keep me posted

ME

We still need to talk about Tiera's security after today. I don't want her alone at all. There's shite I can only explain in person. Let's just say it's like when Declan ran things.

Our moms' cousin swooped in and took over during the one time Dillan went on a vacation without the family. Uncle Donovan fucked around and found out the bratva will punish anyone who goes near their women. They aren't any different from us. Dillan was so pissed we lost a shite ton of money because Uncle Don refused to listen to Dillan's warnings.

We felt bad for our moms—mine, his, and our Aunt Breda —because he was their brother, but no one liked him by the end. Only a few respected him. Dillan was always the presumptive heir since Uncle Don had no children. Declan thought otherwise.

To secure his position, he put a hit out on our moms. It only took him a heartbeat to fuck shite up even more than Uncle Don. We made sure he was too injured to run. Then the bratva —rightly—took care of him for us. But not before he could call off the hit.

Dillan was with his sister when a mercenary mistook her for my mom. The woman shot Colleen in the forehead while she held her brand new puppy that she'd helped rescue. Dillan was standing beside her when it happened. I know he still pictures it.

I don't doubt for a second whoever is terrorizing Tiera and extorting Gareth would do something like that to Tiera. You don't stalk someone for three years with no intention of harming them when the family you're after is in a syndicate.

DILLAN

Then we need to talk tonight

ME

Fine but only if I get everything set up. If I don't then you have to wait or you have to come to me

There's a long pause that pisses me off. He shouldn't need to think about it.

DILLAN

I just called Mair. She'll go to Uncle Ronan and Aunt Breda tonight. I'll come to you. Text the others.

It's not like Dillan's wife, Márgrég—Mairghráid to those who can come close to reading and pronouncing it, and Margaret to the useless—can't stay on her own. But I've made Dillan sufficiently nervous. Good, but I hate it.

ME

> Finn and Sean should take Ally and Nikki to their parents too. I don't think it's wise any of the women are alone right now.

DILLAN

> Truly that bad?

ME

> You can't guess the half of it. I'm with Tiera now. I need to go since I need to text my dad.

DILLAN

> All right. I'll check back later to confirm time and place.

ME

Thanks

I rest my phone on the seat next to me as I gaze down at Tiera. She's asleep. I don't know if today exhausted her, or she understandably got bored while I texted. That took longer than I wanted. I'll text my dad in a moment. I want to enjoy having my girlfriend close and not fearing for her. I want to know that for now I can protect her. I want to feel her body pressed against me and enjoy running my hand over her when I know she won't be self-conscious.

I hope with time and affection, she'll appreciate her body as much as I do. I know what other people think about women Tiera's size. They can fuck all the way off. No other woman has ever had a more perfect body for me to enjoy. I've been hard since she sat on my lap but thinking about what I want us to do tonight's making it fucking uncomfortable in these damn boxer briefs. I need to adjust myself. Or preferably shoot my load into my girlfriend's cunt.

That shouldn't be my last thought before I text my dad, but it is.

ME

Hey. Answer when you get this. It's important.

I know my dad's with my mom today because they're having lunch with a couple they've been friends with since college. It's the woman's birthday. I hate interrupting, but my parents will understand.

DA

We're in the middle of lunch. Can it wait?

ME

No

DA

Hang on. Should I call?

ME

Text would be better. I can't talk right now.

There's a pause in his responses, so he's probably getting up from the table. I want him to hurry, but maybe he is. I don't know. But I'm getting anxious worrying that neither my dad nor Uncle Ronan will be available. I'm not leaving Tiera alone, and I can't take her with me. I don't want to ask my brother because he's got a trial coming up, but I will if I have to.

DA

What's going on?

ME

It's Tiera. We found out why the O'Briens have been treating her the way they have. Someone's stalking her. They've been doing it for 3 years. They've gotten into her house and office. They're extorting the O'Briens by threatening her. I don't want her anywhere near them. I refuse to leave her without someone in our family. The others are busy. Can you do it while I deal with Mitchell?

I really don't want to say more via text. But I have to give my dad something of an explanation, so he knows why I'm asking.

DA

Bring her to the house. When will you get there? We can be there in thirty.

ME

It'll be at least an hour since we're coming up from Trenton. Let me ask Tiera what she prefers. I don't know if going to a stranger's house will be more uncomfortable than having a stranger in her home.

DA

Text me when you're close. I'll be wherever she decides.

ME

Thanks I appreciate it. You should take mom to Aunt Breda's if Uncle Ronan's there. If he's not, you need to get him there.

DAD

She's as good as my daughter, isn't she?

ME

Yeah I think so.

DA

I'm happy for you. So's Mom. She's one of
us now.

I know what that means. No one is more protective of
Cormac and me than my parents. There's truly nothing under
the sun they won't do to protect us. That extends to Tiera now.
My dad's stronger and can inflict more pain physically. But my
mom—hell, my aunts too—anyone who comes too close to their
sons and nephews and their wives—they'll wish it were my dad
and uncles. They'll beg for my dad and uncles. All of them
have always been that way, but since losing Colleen—cross the
six of them, and you're better off offing yourself.

ME

I think you'll really like her.

DA

We don't doubt that.

ME

Thanks love you

DA

Love you, too.

I'll never get too old to see or hear those words from my
parents. It's food for the soul.

Tiera's phone rings in her purse.

"Daddy, whatever's about to go wrong, we'll figure it out
together."

"What makes you say that?"

"Only one person has that ringtone in my phone. It was
Aaron."

Chapter Nineteen

Tiera

I was awake the entire time Seamus was texting. I know he thought I fell asleep, and I was close many times. But I didn't let myself doze off. I was scared something would happen, and I'd be unprepared. I didn't expect to hear my dead husband's ringtone after finding out someone's been threatening—probably plotting—to kill me for three years.

I sit up and reach for my phone. I don't expect to see a number, so it's no surprise when the screen says unknown. I glance up at Seamus, and he shakes his head. I'll let it go to voicemail. If it's a threat, I refuse to hear it until Seamus can do something about it. Whoever it is can leave a message. I don't want to hear them say something directly to me. I can't handle that.

"You never assigned it to another contact?"

"No. I never wanted to hear it again. It hurts too much. He called me when he turned on our street to let me know he was almost there. It was the last sound I heard that wasn't from either of us. If I knew how to delete a pre-installed ringtone, I would have. I just haven't used it for anyone else."

"I'll see if Finn or Sean can figure that out."

I assume that means they're the O'Rourkes' hackers or intel gatherers.

"I know we planned to go to your place. I have to deal with one of our guys who got arrested. I can't get out of it, so I have to leave. My dad's going to guard you. Would you prefer he comes to your place, or would you rather go to my parents'? My mom'll be at my aunt and uncle's."

"You take this so seriously you don't want your mom near me." That doesn't freak me out or anything.

"I don't want my mom near a threat. I feel the same way about you. That's why my dad's going to guard you until I can get back. I know this has to be uncomfortable since you don't know him yet. But my dad's already guessed what you mean to me. He gets why I need him. Where do you want to go?"

"I don't want to inconvenience either of your parents. It would be easier if we went to him, but then that means your mom won't be able to come home when she wants."

"T, if my mom found out I asked my dad for help, and he thought it was any kind of inconvenience, she probably wouldn't speak to him for a month. Neither of them will ever consider taking care of family as an inconvenience."

"But I'm not fam—"

"I told you from the beginning I'm going to marry you. Whether or not you understood is irrelevant. My parents have known the same thing since the start. I've talked to my dad about you. Asked for his advice. He doesn't keep secrets from my mom, except for the ones he has to. I know she knows about you. You wouldn't be part of my life if this weren't something special, something I want to share with no one but you. My dad was the same way with my mom. If we don't work out, they'll understand, but they know what I want without me saying it."

"And that's the same things as earlier?"

"Yes. My future is with you. When we're ready, we move to the next step, then the next, and the one after that."

"What are those steps?"

"We move in together, or we get engaged. We get married one day. And when we decide it's right, I get to watch you carry our children and know we made them together."

My heart is near bursting when he says things like that. It took months for me to fall in love with Aaron, and it took weeks after that for me to feel certain about my feelings. I don't know exactly when it happened with Seamus, but I don't think it took me the full two months we've been dating. It's not just that I want to be in love. I don't want to make the same mistakes I did before. But I feel it with a certainty that's bone deep—I love Seamus. That's my future too. I'm glad we talked about it earlier and hearing him say it again makes it real.

"I want the same thing. I know you thought I was sleeping, but I was awake. I felt you stroking your hand up and down my back, then when you slid it over me. I was too at ease to feel self-conscious about any of it. Your gentleness makes me feel cherished. I want to feel your hand on my stomach knowing one day we'll have children we created together inside me. That you'll be able to feel them and know how incredible it is. I've told you before, I love how the protectiveness and posses- siveness make me feel. I know it's a sign of affection. I know I belong to you just like you belong with me."

"I heard the difference, Tiera. I belong *to* you just the same way you belong to me. I want to know you claim me as yours. I don't think either of us has an unhealthy sort of possessiveness, but don't underestimate how special it makes me feel to know you want me in the same ways I want you."

I shift to straddle him, so it's easier to look into his eyes. Our gazes lock, then we're kissing. I don't know how we both wind up naked since we don't stop kissing. Then I'm sliding down his cock while I hold the headrest. We revel in the moment and enjoy just being connected. Then need takes over. The gentleness evaporates, and in its place, carnal desire and need drive us. Seamus controls my movement, and he wants it rough just like I do.

"I'm going to fill you with my cum again today. I'm going to fuck you until you can't think about anything but the feel of me inside you. You'll think about it when each step reminds you you're sore from riding me. When you're sitting and feel empty without me inside you. You will see where my fingers held you because you're mine to fuck however I want and to mark you because you told me you belong to me."

"Yes, Daddy. Do you want me to be your little slut?" I don't know if he's in the mood for dirty talk.

"You already are. My little whore's going to take my cock whenever I want. Isn't that right, *cailín?*"

"Yes, Daddy."

He fists my hair and pulls my head back as his tongue glides up the side of my neck. He pushes me back so he can suck my tits. He bites my nipple until I have to stifle my scream. Then they throb when he lets go. He holds them together as he goes back and forth, sucking and teasing my nipples.

"Daddy, I'm close."

"You come when I give you permission. Not yet."

"I don't think I can stop." I want to swallow the words.

He presses down on my hips, and neither of us moves. I whimper, and he presses harder.

"Do as I say, or I will get off, and you won't. I decide how you get fucked."

"Yes, Daddy. I'm your little slut. You decide."

"Good girl. Ride me but don't come."

We just talked about each of us having the right amount of possessiveness. Anyone hearing us would think I'm submitting, and he's controlling me for his own desires. That couldn't be further from the truth. Yes, I am submitting sexually right now, but it's because I know he likes it as much as I do. He's mine to pleasure physically *and* emotionally. I'm the only one who gets this side of him. Only I satisfy his need for control. This is the give and take we've talked about. We're showing it the best way we can. Words are significant, but our actions mean just as much.

We go around and around; me getting close and him stopping. Sometimes we don't move because he's the one who's too close to coming. When the pauses get too close together, he grinds my clit against his pubic bone.

"Come."

Within seconds, my entire body tenses as I squeeze his cock from deep inside me. He groans as he tenses, too.

"Fuck, Tiera."

He bites my shoulder as he grinds me twice more before he groans once more, then moves me faster and harder than before.

"Come again."

He demands it, and I'm happy to obey. I throw my head back and dig my fingers into his shoulders as I hold on. When it finally subsides, I flop forward, my head resting on his shoulder where my nails just bit into him.

"Thank you, Daddy."

"Thank you, *cailín*."

It's more than just good sex we're thankful for. It's being an "us" that matters the most.

"Hello, Mr. O'Rourke. Thank you for coming here."

"It's Kieran, and it's nice to meet you too, Ms. Furey."

"It's Tiernan."

Kieran and Tiernan. I used to hate having a man's name once I discovered it was one. It's not great that my name is going to rhyme with my potential future father-in-law. It makes my parents' choice stick out even more. It hardly makes it subtle marrying into a family even more Irish than my own when people will expect a man, and they'll get a—it would *not* please Seamus to hear how I'd describe myself, so we'll go with —more than pleasantly plump woman.

I haven't told Seamus why my parents picked a man's name. Gareth just wanted to twist the knife by saying my parents picked it because they wished they'd had a son. That's not entirely the truth.

"Tiera, I need to talk to my dad for a moment." Seamus kisses me on the cheek, and I'm pretty certain his dad can tell his hand is precariously close to my ass.

I watch them walk into the kitchen while I head to my office. I was serious about quitting my job. I don't know what the fuck I'm going to do now, but I have a healthy nest egg saved. Aaron and I saved for the baby. Then there was the life insurance payment. I don't know what the hospital bills came to. My parents made them disappear while I was drowning in my grief. Maybe Darren did something, or maybe Gareth. I don't know. I asked, but the answers were always vague.

I used the life insurance and the proceeds from selling my New Jersey house to pay for most of my place here in New York. Now that I live alone, I have very few expenses. My grad school loans will probably go to the grave with me, but beyond that, I live modestly. Truly, I'm not extravagant about anything. In fact, Gareth says I'm miserly. I say life taught me to save for a rainy day. It's not a flood like it was three years ago, but it's a steady downpour right now.

I sit at my computer and start typing my resignation letter when I hear Seamus walk toward the door. He comes in and smiles. It lights up his face like it's a piece of art. He truly is the most gorgeous man I've ever seen. His face, his body, and his heart. All of it. He's remarkable, and I'm extremely fortunate.

I push back my chair, but he shakes his head.

"It's all right. You don't have to get up. I told my dad an abridged version of what we learned. I didn't go into everything that happened. If you don't want others to know, then it'll stay with the O'Briens. If you want others to, we'll explain it together. I don't want to speak for you and say the wrong thing."

"That's thoughtful. I don't mind you speaking for me. I have nothing to hide from you or your family. I'd rather it all be out in the open."

"I'll still be circumspect about how I say it. I'll have to say more than I'd like to because I need to give them as much information as I can, so we can figure this out. My dad'll be here until I get back. It shouldn't take me too long. I just need to post the guy's bail and find out when the arraignment will be. I'll probably have to take him home. A few hours, but not more than three-and-a-half, probably."

"We'll be here."

"My dad'll keep himself occupied, so work or do whatever you need. I just ask that you stay away from all windows. Don't go near any doors, and if anyone does come, you go to your bedroom and lock yourself in the bathroom until my dad comes to get you. I want you to do that regardless of whether you recognize the person. You do it before Da opens the door. I don't want anyone coming in, Tiera, unless he's related to me within two degrees—my generation or my dad's. Absolutely no one from your family or any O'Briens."

I push my chair back and walk around the desk. I slide my arms around his waist, and I feel the gun at his lower back. I want to ask why since he's headed to a police station. But my guess is that's the place he most needs it, and the least likely place for anyone to take it from him.

"It's okay, Daddy. I know you don't like this, but we'll be okay. Your dad is as big as you, and honestly, I think I'd probably put my money on him. He doesn't scare me, but I'm certain he terrifies most people."

It takes one glance to see who Seamus inherited his build from. His dad has blue eyes, but Seamus's hair is pretty close to his dad's. The man could pass for Seamus and Cormac's brother rather than their father. Seamus and Cormac look youthful for their age, and it's clear where they get it. I'm sure I don't want to know about Seamus's experiences in the mob, but nothing I guess about him can possibly touch what I'm certain Kieran knows or has done. He has at least twenty more years' experience as a mobster.

"He does, and that's what I want. If you get another call from that ring tone, leave it like you did before. I'll give the phone to Sean tonight. I'll be back here as soon as I can. Then I need to speak to the guys. They can come here if you don't want to leave, or we can go to my place."

"Six of you here? Seven if your dad stays. You'll be overflowing out to the yard. We can go to your place."

"They can sit on each other's laps for all I care. Where will you be more comfortable?"

"Wherever you feel most comfortable. I don't want you on edge because you're worried there isn't sufficient security."

"Here is all right. My dad is the only one who comes near

you, but Dillan texted me a few minutes ago. He has men positioned around the block, and there's a guy outside your back gate. He's tucked behind the elm tree, so your neighbors won't question why there's a man skulking around."

It doesn't surprise me. The week Aaron and I found out I was pregnant, he insisted we have the same security at our home. I thought it was excessive, and so did Darren. Aaron wanted it permanently, but Darren refused. He said I wasn't the first pregnant woman, and every other one made do with nothing. I want to think no one would've tampered with Aaron's car if we'd had the guards. But they would've been Darren's men, so they wouldn't have stopped the guy who fucked around with the brakes.

"Thank you. That makes me feel even better."

"Do you want to come back here tonight after the meeting?"

"Should we?" If he feels like we need that many men surrounding my place, then maybe we shouldn't.

"It's up to you. I normally have that many men at my place, but I'll have more wherever we are once it's dark."

"I don't want to impose on you."

"Impose?"

He looks insulted before he turns to shut the office door. Then he's on me in an instant. He presses me back around the desk until there's nowhere for me to go short of climbing on it.

"Let's get this clear this one time. You are not an imposition. You are my girlfriend. You are entitled to all the security in the world regardless of your status because it's the right thing to do. But your status as my girlfriend damn well means you'll have all the protection I deem necessary. No one argues with that. If you *even imply* you aren't worthy of that, I will spank you with whatever I can reach. It will not be foreplay. It will be the worst punishment you've ever had. You are more important to me than anyone else in the world. It's not up for debate or discussion. You know why I can't always put you first, but that doesn't make you less important than the fecking mob. *No one* comes near you unless I say they can. Anyone stupid enough to try will learn just how possessive I am of what's mine. There's nothing I won't do to keep you safe, and there isn't a fecking person alive who can stop me, including you. We go wherever you want to stay, but we do things my way."

I fist his shirt and yank. He only leans forward because he lets me pull him. I kiss him as hard as I can. I nip at his tongue before sucking him into my mouth. I slide my hand between us and run my hand up and down his cock through his trousers. I rip my mouth from him.

"When we're alone, you will strip. Slowly. I want to enjoy every moment. Then I am going to suck you off. You are going to toy with me and edge me until I think I'm going to lose my mind. Then you're going to fuck me in the ass like you said you would."

His hand wraps around my throat and squeezes until I think I'm going to pass out. He stops just short of that.

"Is that what my little girl thinks?"

I try to nod.

"You think you can issue me orders?"

I try again.

"You want Daddy's cock down your throat and up your arse without asking?"

I try a third time. It's getting seriously hard to breathe.

"You think I should obey *you* rather than you obey *me*?"

"Yes." I can only mouth the word.

His lips crash down onto mine, but he releases me a moment before. I suck in a lungful of air, then I'm ready. His kisses drug me. There are so many different kinds, and all of them wipe my mind clear of anything but him.

"I will never compromise about your safety. But we're equals in everything else. If that's what you want your daddy to do—if that's what *mo cailín* wants Daddy to do—then that's exactly what I'll do."

I know *mo* means my. My little girl. He tucks hair behind my ear, and it's so contrary to the way he just touched me. He made me feel desired, and now he makes me feel cherished. Together, they make me feel loved. He's looking at me as though he wants to say something, but he remains quiet.

"I liked that, Daddy."

My voice is soft, not because I'm scared to voice my opinion after his dominance. Not because I can't speak louder after he squeezed so hard. I barely speak louder than a whisper because I want him to know how special this feels. It's as though it would lose some of its meaning if I spoke louder. Like I'd just be stating a fact rather than sharing something deeply meaningful. I guess I'm trying for reverent.

"It wasn't too much? I didn't scare you?"

"Seamus, even if we got to a point where I needed to say my safe word or snap, it wouldn't be because I'm scared. We might meet my limits, but it won't be because I fear you. I remember when I was seven, I was in the front yard playing. Our neighbors had a dog that was practically feral. It only liked the dad, so even the wife and kids barely touched it. It got loose and came racing toward me. I screamed, but I was frozen in fear. My dad burst out of the house and scooped me up just before the dog got to me. I mean like a second before. He yelled in his deep voice, and the dog ran away. I was terrified and burst into tears. I wouldn't let go of my dad for five minutes. I sobbed harder when he tried to put me down. He undoubtedly saved me from getting bitten. I knew I was safe with him. I only felt safe with him. You give me that sense of relief multiplied by at least a thousand. I have never felt like I do with you. Not even with my dad. Not even like that day. The only time I'm not frightened of anything is when I'm with you."

This is one of his kisses that makes me feel precious. It's so tender, it makes my heart feel like it'll burst.

"I'll be home before dinner. We'll go to my place. Pack a bag with at least a week's worth of clothes. No panties. I'm having my five days with you. Feck the world."

Chapter Twenty

Seamus

I'm pissed, but what can I do? This isn't a great time to prove the mob comes first, but when would it be easy to show that? When we're sitting around watching some old show on a streaming platform? No. When we're out at the grocery store? No. It's only a test because it's hard. This day is just harder than others.

I'm pissed at the world. I'm not pissed at Dillan—though I am annoyed—because this is the role I play. I'm not pissed at my brother or cousins because I know they would help if they could, but they have their roles to play. I'm not pissed at Mitchell because he's a damn good scalper, and he didn't ask to get arrested. I'm certain the Kutsenkos had this in the works for weeks—that's how long they take to plan anything. I'm pissed because this is just another reminder I can never leave this behind.

But being pissed changes nothing. I force myself to get over it by the time I get to the police station in Manhattan. I head inside, and people take one look at me and find other things to do. It's not like officers haven't brought me here in cuffs before, but it's been fifteen years since they forced me through the doors. They've questioned me since then, but no one's arrested me. They're not the feds. They all either have a healthy fear of my family or have someone working for us in theirs.

It's amazing how the metal detector just happens to turn off before I walk through and turn right back on when I'm on the other side. So convenient. I walk up to the desk sergeant, and he looks less than thrilled to see me.

"I know, I know. The guy's a rookie and his TO was talking to someone else. Jameson couldn't tell the kid why a baby officer's first arrest shouldn't be someone who works for one of the families."

The families. Yup.

"That's a lesson his training officer should have taught him the first day out. Where's Mitchell?"

"Locked up where he belongs."

I spin to my left and glare at the barely out of diapers cop. I'm certain it feels like my eyes bore a hole into his soul. I've been told that before. Ron Jameson tries to pull his partner's arm to keep him from approaching. The kid's got some balls on him. I'm about to make them shrivel.

I look at his name on the little brass plate when he tries to get in my face. We'll see how he feels the first time he gets that jabbed into him. He won't have his vest on when it does. In the syndicate world, we call it a warm welcome. The cops call it initiation. The rookies call themselves little bitches when they try not to cry.

I whisper, so besides the rookie, only Ron and Sam Wilkes, the desk sergeant, can hear me.

"Thomson, I may have the red hair, but I'm the Big Bad

Wolf. You're about to find out how Little Red Riding Hood felt right before she got gobbled up. Back up."

"Make me."

"You don't want to do that. Come on. We have paperwork." Ron tries to rescue the kid, but it's way too late.

Sam has no success either. "Tommy, come on. You have other stuff to do."

"Tommy Thompson?" I sneer at him. "Or is Tommy your nickname because you still have your training wheels on?"

"You don't scare me, O'Rourke."

Now I grin. I watch him flinch. It's not the grin I give my family when we're having fun. It's not the grin I give Tiera when she makes me happy. It's the one I give men right before I kill them.

"I will."

The douche finally gets the message and takes a step back. I take a step forward. I know people have stopped what they're doing to watch. I still whisper.

"Are you running away from the Big Bad Wolf? Does Little Red Riding Hood want his TO to keep me from tearing him apart? I know your name now."

"You—you—can't do anything to me."

Now I laugh. There's no mirth in it, and at least a dozen cops know what it means. I might not kill him, but I'll own him.

"Consider this the one and only strike you get in this game. I *am not* in the mood to play ball. I'm supposed to be with my family right now. Your petty attempt to prove your dick's as big as everyone else's wasn't well-timed. I'd get out of my face while you still have one anyone recognizes."

I won't mention Tiera because it would only add to the danger.

I straighten to my full height—not that I slouch—and I lift my chin and press out my chest until my shoulder blades meet.

I'm twice his size, and he's just realized it. You can't miss I'm bigger than him, but he looks scrawny now.

"You better not have missed leg day because you need to run." I cross my arms. I get my suits tailored to allow me to move in them. I need the extra fabric, so I can cross my arms or put them on my waist without ripping them. They still strain over my biceps and back.

He gulps and nods. He barely twists in time for me not to ram into him when I move forward. I look down at him since I'm a good four inches taller as our shoulders brush. He can't meet my gaze.

"Good job, kiddo. You learn fast."

Ron nudges Thompson away, and I follow Sam to the cells. Mitchell's relief is obvious to me, even if most people wouldn't recognize it. He's close to my dad's age and can sell milk to a cow. I don't blame him for getting busted. I'm certain the Kutsenkos were looking for any of our scalpers at the show. I wonder if Laura and Christina know that while they and their children were enjoying a kids' musical show, their husbands— Maks and Bogdan—were using their attendance as an excuse to pursue one of our guys.

Mitchell happened to be the unlucky bastard working that event. I don't know if he even spotted the Kutsenkos. One of the bratva guards might have recognized Mitchell and told Maks and Bogdan. However it happened, I need to get Mitchell out, get home to Tiera, and fill Dillan in, so he can plan our retribution.

"Shay, I'm fucking glad to see you. That little shit thinks his balls have dropped and gave me this."

Mitchell points to a livid bruise on his ribs when he pulls up his shirt. It reminds me of the bruise Tiera got during the game. I don't have any arnica for Mitchell. Oh, well. It looks like a billy club did the damage. I pull out my phone and snap pics. Mitchell knows what to do, so he turns in each direction. He will have conveniently taken photos earlier today with a time stamp of some sort.

If this goes to trial, we'll have evidence of unnecessary roughness. If it doesn't go to trial, we'll have a sound argument for the precinct captain to keep his fucking mouth shut when we take care of Tommy boy. We make sure all our scalpers and fencers take pics before they go out in case we need them to compare later. Whether it's selling tickets illegally or selling knock-off or stolen goods, our guys are pros. These are guys who've been trained to do it since they were in middle school and pickpocketing tourists. They've grown into their positions.

"Did he say anything useful?"

"Nah. Read me my rights after taking me to the ground as though I was resisting. Plenty of people saw, and some were even taking videos."

"Were you by the street camera?"

"Of course."

He won't have turned his face toward it, and he's wearing all black. I'm certain he had a ball cap on, too. But he will have been visible, so I'll get the video from the city. We'll say someone leaked it to us. And by that I mean, the city's system to encrypt the security videos is shite compared to what my cousins can do. It's like the city gives it away to us. Info given to us by someone on the inside is a leak. Once Mair gets it into the newspaper, the TV news will pick it up. Then people will come forward with their videos.

Thompson can go to his union rep, but it won't do him any good where we're concerned. Bobby McLaughlin is like my fifth cousin and knows which side his bread is buttered. He's a great union rep for the cops—until we're in the picture. Then he rolls over just like we pay him to. The NYPD won't have any choice but to act since we'll stir up the public outcry if they don't. If we don't feel they adequately punish him, then we'll take care of it.

"Anything I need to know?"

"He got me to the ground, and I put my hands behind my head without him asking. He was shouting at me like I was fighting him, so that's what really drew people's attention. Once he got me on my feet, he kept shoving me until we walked past the Kutsenkos. Maks wasn't looking at me because he was corralling his twins and Bogdan's son with Laura and Christina, who's seriously pregnant right now. Bogdan saw me and winked. Fucking winked. I watched him slide his phone back into his pocket before picking up his little boy and wrapping his arm around Christina."

Pushed him toward the Kutsenkos? Is Thompson getting paid?

"Who spotted you?"

"I don't know. I think one of their guys. When we got here, dipshit hauled me into an interview room. Before Jameson could do anything, fuck face whips out his club. I take two to the ribs before I can point to the CCTV that's recording all of this. Jameson snatched the club from Thompson and put me in here. I don't know what happened after that, but Jameson definitely looked terrified when I told him I was calling Cormac. I knew you were in Trenton, so I didn't want to bother you."

"You did the right thing. Did you make the recording worth it?"

There's nothing private about a detainee with ties to a syndicate making a call to their leaders. They were definitely listening in and recording. I'll subpoena it if I must. For now, I'll blackmail the captain with it.

"Oh yeah. I detailed everything."

"Are you sure there's nothing I need to know? If I make an

arse out of myself defending you, you won't get a second chance."

"I know, Shay. No funny business. I swear."

I nod. "Hang on."

I head back to the desk sergeant who has paperwork already laid out on the counter for me.

"He's the ninth precinct's captain's nephew. Take it easy on him if you don't want more attention. He thinks he's the shit because of his connections. He hasn't learned that no one here is going to protect him from his bad choices. Teach him whatever lesson you want, but be discreet."

"That's fine. How long to run the paperwork?"

"I'll see if I can expedite it."

"Good idea."

I sweep my gaze over the police station, and it makes me think about what Tiera's facing. Someone in law enforcement could be involved. They could probably get their hands on the bug Tiera's stalker used. They'd also not worry about anyone in their department turning them over since he went after a lesser syndicate, and they all bleed blue until their family's at stake. A cop could have an over-inflated sense of security, which would be their hubris, since no one is safe from my family once they've crossed us.

I'll ask Finn to look into Mitchell's shite, but I'm going to ask Sean to do the digging. His ability to hack exceeds anyone else I know. If anyone can go down the rabbit hole to find out who's after Tiera, it's him. If this isn't a cop, then I'll have to start from scratch. My next best guess would be a fed. If it's someone in the private sector, they have connections.

I want to figure this shite out for Tiera's safety's sake, but also to discover who thinks they're so untouchable. Who knows what else this fucker is doing that Gareth doesn't know about?

I'm certain there's more. Is there more Gareth hasn't told us? Most likely.

I sweep my gaze around the open office space, taking in the officers I know. The ones we pay, the ones who wished we paid, and the ones like Thompson with a superiority complex. They're the ones who have also learned to stay out of arm's reach. They might like to posture like they're better than us, but they also know that landing on our radar isn't good for their health.

A few cast glances toward me, but most have returned to work, pretending to ignore the mobster in their midst. The mobster they know has a gun and is a far better shot than any of them. They might be good on the range, but I'm better in real life. And I don't get any pretty padding either. I have a bullet-proof vest I wear on some missions, but usually, gun fights don't come with invitations. They're rather impromptu by nature.

I can see Mitchell from where I stand, keeping one eye on him to ensure no one gets a couple last punches in. Sam comes back with the paperwork in order, and I watch the bars slide open. Mitchell doesn't strut, but he certainly isn't humble. He doesn't quite have platinum status hotel points at NYPD's finest detention centers, but he's creeping up there. He might get caught from time to time, but nothing sticks.

He meets Sam at one of the desks to sign his release papers. It shouldn't take long since I worked on getting the charges dropped while I was on my way here.

"O'Rourke."

I turn toward Ron who barely tilts his head enough for me to notice the signal. I follow him to a quieter corner that's still visible to some but is discreet in such a crowded space. It ensures no one can claim he's taking bribes at the station. He takes them somewhere else.

"You need to watch out for Thompson. He has aspirations of grandeur. He thinks he's on the path to Commissioner. He's trying to make a name for himself from the start. He doesn't get the only name he's going to make is one on a hit list. He's not targeting you any more than he is the other syndicates. He thinks he'll single-handedly clean up the city. A city that's had organized crime since the days when it was unorganized. He needs to watch *Gangs of New York* and get a history lesson. It should be mandatory viewing for all douches at the academy. Like a screening process. Anyway, he's going to keep causing trouble. I can only do so much since he's his uncle's favorite. Just watch out and remember he's connected."

"His uncle is Burke, right?"

"Yeah. The captain hasn't filled his nephew in."

"That he's as dirty as they come." Drew Burke has been taking bribes and kickbacks since before he went to the academy. His greed made him become a cop. He thought it was the easiest way to extort people without getting caught. He makes enough off his hustle to pay off or threaten away anyone who comes sniffing around to turn him in.

"Right? I'm trying with the kid, but he's stubborn. He could be a good cop if he got off his high horse before one of you drags him off."

"Who's he got his eye on next?"

"Diazes. He at least knows some of his limitations. He hasn't mentioned Enrique, but he wants Alejandro. He thinks he's senior enough to make a good impression on the brass but not so high that he can't reach."

"The Kutsenkos might be trained psychopaths, but the Diazes are by birth."

"You know that. I know that. Every cop in the city knows that except my dipshit trainee."

Enrique, the *jefe*, grew up in Colombia with time spent in America, getting an expensive education. Since Enrique has no kids, his nephew through his brother, Pablo, is the heir presumptive, just like Dillan was in my family. Pablo grew up in New Jersey, so he had as normal an upbringing as I did—it's all relative. He's their head enforcer. His soul is dead.

His cousins—fucking hell. *Tres J's*—Javier, Joaquin, and Jorge—didn't come to America until they were teenagers. They basically grew up like an undomesticated pack of mongrels on the streets of Bogota. They had more money than they knew what to do with, but no rules or consequences.

They are the quintessential poor little rich kids because Enrique's sister—their mom—couldn't keep up once her husband died in a deal gone as wrong as it could. She eventually gave up trying to tame them while keeping herself alive and unmarried. They came to America to give the boys a chance to learn how to be cartel leaders rather than learning on the streets with guns to their heads. Now they hold the guns.

But Alejandro. Double fucking hell. He grew up in Queens, but he's spent his adult life going back and forth to Bogota. He deals with Enrique's uncle who's still the *jefe* down there. No one's proven it, but the guy committed—commissioned—fratricide. He had Enrique's dad killed, so he could assume control. Enrique's never forgiven the guy, so he made his *tío* his bitch.

Alejandro makes sure *everyone* in Latin America knows Enrique is the *jefe de jefes*. Boss of bosses. We might run the Irish along the Eastern Seaboard and may be the oldest crime organization in America. The Italians might have dominated for generations before mine came along to knock them off their pedestal. And the bratva might be the newest syndicate and armed with paramilitary tactics. But Enrique Diaz runs a continent and a half. No one in Central America or South America wakes up each morning without thanking God that Enrique hasn't looked in their direction.

Alejandro is their chief strategist. He's their version of Dillan. He doesn't want to be *jefe*. He doesn't aspire to replace his cousin. He's happy to be the one to represent his uncle and remind pretty much everyone south of the US-Mexico border they live because he allows it. Enrique's given him carte blanche to take out anyone he doesn't like. He doesn't like anyone. The man drinks the blood of his enemies.

Thompson's going to run to us for protection.

I shrug my shoulders nonchalantly. "Thompson's going to learn fast what happens when he goes near Alejandro. I recommend you give him some space, or you'll wind up skinned alive too." I'm not exaggerating.

"I'm four fucking years from my pension. If that shitbag gets me killed..." Ron's expression hardens as he looks toward Thompson, who's chatting with some other young cops.

"Do what you have to, or we will."

Ron nods. It wouldn't be the first time he's trained a rookie for real. Most catch on. A few don't and meet untimely on-the-job deaths. We'll take care of it for our own sake, but we'll let Enrique know they owe us a favor.

"Does Thompson have connections anywhere else?"

"You mean other precincts?"

"In general."

"Not that I know of. Just his uncle."

"Okay."

Along with Tiera's phone, I'm going to ask Sean to look into Thompson. Finn could do it, but if anything comes up, I want Sean to follow it to Earth's core if he has to. I want to know everything from his first cavity to the last time he shat.

Maybe I'm seeing shadows where there are none. But what if he's connected to someone in Trenton or knows someone who knows about Tiera? How can I not look into him?

Mitchell and I walk out to the town car waiting for us. My driver, Joey, grins at Mitchell.

"Fucking Slick Rick in the skin. Have a pleasant stay?"

Mitchell flicks off his best friend before laughing. He gets in the town car on his side while I slide in on mine. I just need to drop him off.

The door's barely closed before Joey drops the privacy glass. He glances at Mitchell in the rearview mirror before he meets my gaze for an instant as he pulls away from the curb.

"Shay, are you involved with a woman named Tiernan?"

"Why?"

"I heard two cops say your name and hers as they walked by. I didn't catch everything, but one of them said something about a friend in the Trenton Fire Department who knows her. It sounded like there's a warrant for her. Apparently, she was involved in some cover up while she was a fire inspector. The guy who was listening mentioned you and that he didn't want to be the one arresting her."

"Anything else?"

"No. They kept walking, so I couldn't hear anything. If they wouldn't have seen my reflection in the door, I would have followed them. But I know they saw me in the car when they walked past. They'd have noticed if I got out."

"Thanks."

Joey raises the privacy glass, and it leaves Mitchell and me in silence. The latter keeps quiet until we get to the subway a couple blocks away. He declined my offer to take him home. He said he had some errands to run before he saw his wife. Flowers and a box of chocolates.

I pull up the group chat.

ME

I need you at my place ASAP. I'll be there in 45. It just keeps getting worse. I'm taking Tiera there as soon as I get to her.

My brother's response is immediate.

CORMAC

Dad called. I was already on the way.

ME

WTF happened???

CORMAC

Nothing for sure but Eli told Dad someone tried to get into her building's back gate but didn't have a fob. A woman recognized the guy but it felt off to Eli. We were going to take her to your place.

DILLAN

Mair's already at Uncle Ronan and Aunt Breda's place and Finn's taking Nikki and Ally over there now. Sean and Shane are with me. Do you want us to pick up food on the way? We were going to grab something anyhow.

ME

Sure but make it fast.

SEAN

I'll call Paul's and have pizzas ready by the time we get there.

Finn owns a few restaurants, and Paul's Place is one of them. If they're in Brooklyn, they must have been collecting on some overdue loan payments. Assuming no real traffic, a stop to get the pizza and a drive to East Harlem should have them there around the same time as I get Tiera there.

ME

No fecking anchovies Shane. I don't need my place stinking like a fecking wharf.

SHANE

Fine but only for Tiernan's sake.

I sit back and try not to feel restless or panicked. But I do.

Chapter Twenty-One

Tiera

"Tiernan?"

I step out of my office when Kieran calls out to me. He gestures me over and holds out his phone.

"Do you know this man?"

There's a side view of a guy at the back gate to my building. It's pretty clear, so I can tell what he looks like. I shake my head.

"I don't think so. Why?"

"Our guy saw him trying to get into the gate without a fob. He took a photo right before someone talked to the guy and let him in. Cormac's on his way. We're going to Seamus's. Get whatever you need. We're leaving in five minutes. As soon as Cor comes up."

I stare at Kieran's phone for a moment before I nod.

"It doesn't mean he's a credible threat. But it is concerning, considering what's going on. We're just using caution. My son will lose his mind if he finds out we didn't take you somewhere else."

"And it's safe for me to go out there?"

Right after Seamus left, Kieran went through my entire condo with a fine-tooth comb. He checked everything. Baseboards, carpet edges, cabinets, drawers, light switches and fixtures, mirrors, tables, and chairs. Anywhere a camera or listening device could possibly fit. While he was searching the living room, I dashed to my bedroom to grab my vibrator and shoved it in my purse. He'd already searched my bag. He found nothing.

"That's why Cormac's coming. Two more of our men will come up, and the four of us will escort you out."

They'll surround me. Human shields. I hate thinking anyone has to be that for me, but it won't be the first time I've had guards. I just hate the idea it's my boyfriend's dad and brother. I don't want to be the reason anyone dies, especially not them. It makes me want to cover my belly. But Kieran will misunderstand, and I don't want anyone doubting what's going on between Seamus and me. Questioning why he's with me.

"Let me get some stuff."

Fuck. Seamus told me to get stuff for five days. That's different from having enough to keep me occupied for today. I know Seamus is thirty-two, but what will his dad think when he realizes I intend to spend the night? Will that be an issue in his family?

I hurry to my bedroom and grab an overnight bag. I head to my underwear drawer and pull out a couple bras. I glance at my panties and smile. Should I pack a couple just to get a rise out of Seamus? I swallow my laugh at my own pun. I grab two.

I move to my closet and pull things out, barely noticing whether the items go together. Then I head to the bathroom and round up my toiletries. It only takes me a few minutes.

When I come out of the bathroom, I hear two men's voices. I know they're speaking Gaelic, but I don't understand any of it. I'm hesitant to interrupt, and I'm embarrassed about the bag. Seamus and I are both in our thirties, and I've been married. But it's still awkward in front of his dad. His brother is okay, so I don't cringe when I spy Cormac.

I have no opportunity to say anything because when the door bursts open, I'm ready to run. But I recognize Seamus as he makes a beeline for me. He pulls me against him. He's not breathing hard. His heart isn't racing. He doesn't even feel tense around me. But he's not happy. When he kisses me, I know an overnight bag in front of his father is the least of my concerns with modesty. I drop the bag and wrap my arms around him. He presses me against his chest but looks over his shoulder at his father and brother.

"*Chuir mé glaoch ar Eli ag an am céanna a bhí Liam ag labhairt isteach ina chluas. Lean Liam an fear tar éis do Eli téacs a chur chuige. Thóg an fear an staighre go dtí an díon agus d'fhéach sé thart ar feadh cúig nóiméad ansin tháinig sé síos go dtí an urlár. Bhreathnaigh Liam air ag seiceáil amach gach doras. Ansin chuaigh sé síos an staighre arís agus d'imigh.*" I called Eli at the same time Liam was speaking into his earpiece. Liam followed the guy after Eli texted him. The guy took the stairs to the roof and looked around for five minutes, then came down to this floor. Liam watched him check out every door. Then he went down the stairs again and left.

I don't know what Seamus is saying, but Cormac's and Kieran's expressions show their dismay. I lean away and tilt my head back to look up at Seamus. He shifts his focus to me.

"You packed?"

"Yeah. Your dad said we were leaving."

"We are. Can you show me that file you were working on earlier?"

I don't know what he means, but I nod. He takes my hand before I lead him to my office. He closes the door quietly before wrapping his arms around me from behind. I lean back against his solid chest, but it soon isn't enough for either of us. I turn in his embrace, and I slide my hands up his chest to cup his neck before tunneling them into his hair. It's like silk. It's softer than mine.

"Daddy, I'm okay. I didn't know what was going on until your dad said I needed to get some stuff together. Cormac arrived while I was packing. Neither of them appeared upset."

"The roof could crumble around us, and they wouldn't appear upset if they want to keep you from panicking. Did you see a photo of the guy?"

"Only his profile."

Seamus pulls his phone from his back pocket and unlocks it. He taps his texts, and I see the second one down is from Makayla. It's unread from yesterday. He's had plenty of time to look at it. He knows I can see it. Is it because he has nothing to hide? Or is it to make me jealous?

"*Cailín*, I've had more important things on my mind than her. If you want to read the message you can, but I'm not interested. I don't think I need to block her or anything, but I will if I need to."

"What counts as needing to?"

"She says anything about us being together again. I'm not interested."

He's so matter of fact as he taps the top text thread. He scrolls back a few lines until a photo appears. He taps it, so it's full screen. I think I'm going to be sick.

"Tiera?"

I can only nod. He looks at the desk chair but thinks twice about it. Tears prick the back of my eyes as he opens the door. I don't want to go out there. He scoops me up, and I have a moment of self-consciousness before I remember he said he could carry Cormac. His brother may not weigh a ton more than me, but he's still got twenty pounds on me.

I close my eyes and rest my head against his chest. He says nothing, but I know he shakes his head at his dad and brother before he takes me upstairs to my room. He elbows the door closed before walking to the bed. He sits on it with me on his lap.

"If I didn't know Aaron died in the car next to me, I'd swear that was him. If I hadn't seen his body, been at the funeral, I'd swear it was him."

I take the phone from Seamus's hand, pulling it away from where it pressed against my ass. I enlarge the photo and breathe easier. Zoomed in, I can tell who it is.

"That's Aaron's cousin, Jude." Judas?

"He was snooping around here. Judas?"

"I just thought the same thing. I don't know why he'd be here. I haven't seen him in three years. Not since the funeral. I'd only left the hospital the day before. Aaron's parents delayed the funeral because I wasn't well enough to make any plans. They wanted me to be there because they knew it was important to me. We buried—they're together."

I squeeze my eyes shut and inhale deeply.

"He and Aaron weren't close or anything. Jude grew up in Kansas City, Kansas. We met at the wedding and the funeral. Otherwise, we got Christmas cards his wife probably sent."

"What does he do?"

"He's a high school guidance counselor. I can't think of any reason for him to be here. His and Aaron's moms are sisters, but Jude's family still lives in Kansas City. Their shared grandparents are dead and have been for a decade. It makes no sense to me."

"Is it the photo, or do they look that much alike in real life?"

"The photo makes them look more similar, but it's clear they're related if you knew Aaron. Daddy, why would he be here? He didn't come to my door."

I didn't plan to call Seamus that, but I feel inordinately vulnerable right now and need his reassurance.

"I don't know why, but my cousin will investigate."

"Do you think it's a coincidence that he was here to visit someone else, and I live here?"

He hesitates to answer before he shakes his head. "One of our men followed him up the stairs to the roof. He looked around for five minutes before coming back down to check all the doors."

"He never saw someone following him?"

"No one sees them unless they want to be seen."

I live in a duplex condo. They're not typical in New York, but I was thrilled to find the two-story condo. It's not a loft but a proper two floors with three bedrooms. I have the feeling of a house without all the maintenance. But right now, I'm wishing I had a single-family structure like I once did with an alarm system for the entire place, including the back gate. Clearly, my good Samaritan neighbors trust anyone. I wish I had a place without other people living truly on top of me.

"Can we go right now?" I'm scared.

"Yes."

He's ready to help me up, but I'm not ready to let go. My fear outweighs my wish to leave and never come back if there's been someone poking around my home. Again. Knowing there's nothing here right now that's recording us tempts me to insist we don't go outside.

"Little one, my dad, Cormac, and I will be with you. One of the men we trust most, Joey, is also here. He's guarded my cousin Finn's wife plenty of times. He's good at what he does."

I doubt I want to know exactly what he does. I nod, but I

still don't get up. I have to talk myself into it while Seamus rubs my back. With a fortifying breath, I rise. He follows me and hugs me again. With a kiss on the forehead because he understands I need affection and courage right now, I head to the door. We don't make it to the landing before my front door practically explodes. It flies open with an enforcer following it. The police-style battering ram weighs about twenty-five pounds, but a strong enough person can pack far more power into it with momentum.

Gunshots follow immediately. I can't see who's shooting. Seamus wraps his arm around my waist and hauls me off my feet as he draws his gun from behind him. He uses his broader body to shield me as he pushes me into my bedroom.

"Lock this door, then go in the bathroom and lock that door. Get in the shower. Now."

He leaves me inside the door, and I scramble to lock it. He speaks through it once he knows I've secured it.

"Stay there unless it's me, Cormac, or Da. No one else. I don't care what they say. Only the three of us."

"Yes, Daddy." The words tumble from my lips, but I don't know what I'm saying. I just tell myself it won't be long before one of the three men comes to get me. I bolt to the bathroom, locking that door too. I crouch in the tub with the shower curtain pulled. I can still hear the gunfire. I wonder what my neighbors must think. Maybe they're all at work, so no one hears. Maybe they'll think I'm watching a noisy action movie.

Furniture crashes, and I hear feet running but no voices. There are still gunshots. Wouldn't pros use silencers? Or is that just in movies? Hell, if I know. I never asked Aaron about that kind of shit.

Someone's banging on my bedroom door. I wait for a voice to call out to me. My name. Anything.

Nothing.

Just more pounding. It sounds like they're about to break it down like they did my front one. I don't know who it is. Police? Would they open fire without warning? Or did Cormac and Kieran start shooting first? Is it whoever's been stalking me? Another syndicate or gang that found out where three head mob members were and thought this place was unsecure? Where are the men Seamus said Dillan stationed around here?

I hear my bedroom door give way. I don't move. I can't hear myself breathe. I pray over and over that Seamus is alive. If they made it up here, then these invaders made it past my boyfriend and his family. Oh, God. Are they dead because of me?

"Tiernan Furey, this is the NYPD. We have a warrant for your arrest and extradition to New Jersey. Come out with your hands where we can see them."

Not a fucking chance in hell. I don't know who that is. I don't know what're lies and truths. I'm not admitting I'm in here. If the guy wants to slip a warrant under the door, then he can go for it. But I'm not acknowledging him. Asking to see it just confirms where I am.

"Ms. Furey, open the door. You have ten seconds to comply, or we will enter the bathroom."

I think about what I can reach to use as a weapon. I ease the shower curtain open and stretch as far as I can to open the cabinet beneath the sink. I grab the bottle of spray disinfectant. I hear the doorknob jiggle. I grab the second bottle. I thought of Seamus as a cowboy gunslinger when we were at Gareth's, and he had the two handguns.

Holy fucking shit. That was this morning.

Now I'm the gunslinger. I almost want to try twirling the spray bottles over my fingers.

"Ms. Furey, this is your last warning."

The guy pounds on the door three more times before it flies open. He kicked it. I sweep my gaze over him and the men behind him. They're in police uniforms, but I see the patch on the arm. It looks like NYPD, but it's not. There's not an easy way to describe what's wrong since the design is correct, but it's just off. I've spent a lot of years looking at the emblem. I know when it's fake.

He approaches, and like a caricature of someone from the Wild Wild West, I wield my spray bottle, shooting him straight in the eyes. He bellows and staggers back. The next man pushes forward, dodging away from where I just aimed. He didn't notice the bottle in my other hand. I aim for his open mouth as he's about to say something. He splutters, then curses. He reaches for me, but I spray him in the eyes too. He puts his hand up and shields himself, but not until after some of the liquid meets his face.

A third guy points his gun at me. My disinfectant is no match for bullets. I'm not ready to back down, but neither am I going to antagonize the man who can put a bullet through my head. I don't put either bottle down. I don't even lower them. I just don't pull the trigger. I watch him approach as the first two men rub their eyes and cough.

"Ms. Furey, that wasn't wise. Drop the bottles, then step out of the bathtub. Keep your hands where I can see them."

"Where are the O'Rourkes?"

"Dead."

That wasn't the right answer to give if he wants me to cooperate. Even if it's the truth, it won't make me come any easier. They'll be dragging me out before I leave Seamus behind. Whether or not he's alive doesn't matter.

"Who are you?"

"NYPD."

"No, you're not. Who are you?"

"You don't need to worry about that."

"Then who's your employer?"

He grins, and it turns my blood to ice.

"You don't need to worry about that either."

"His dick is so small he has to send men to do his work for him."

I'm testing him. There's a flash of something in his eyes that makes me wonder if his employer—he's a mercenary for sure—is a woman. If it's a woman, then this is about vengeance. Makayla comes to mind since I saw her name in Seamus's texts. She's been around for three years, but I've only known Seamus three months. Hillary comes to mind since she was pissed about Aaron and me, but she's married with three kids now. She loves her husband and hasn't shown any interest in me since she met the guy. Could that have been for show? I mean, she could be happy with her life and still hate me. Gretchen? We don't like each other, but we haven't argued in years.

What woman could I have pissed off that much?

What man could I have pissed off that much?

I have no idea, and I've been thinking about it ever since I finished my letter of resignation. I've wracked my brain to come up with anyone who'd loathe me so much that they'd spend three years extorting Gareth to get to me. I even wondered if it was Aaron from the grave. Did he hire someone to carry this out posthumously?

I don't have answers to any of these questions, and I'm unlikely to until I meet whoever is behind this. I haven't ruled out the O'Briens' rivals either. The northern New Jersey Italians haven't been that strong in a decade. The Mancinellis moved in when a bunch of the Stiglionos went away. It was a bone of contention that the Stiglionos ever rose to power since they're from Italy's Matera region and not Sicily.

Maybe it would have been fine, but they called themselves *Cosa Nostra*. "Our thing" is only for Sicilian Mafia, so the Mancinellis took offense. They systematically got Stiglionos put away until they could move in without much fuss. I played a part in that. Darren wanted to weaken the Stiglionos, so he helped the Mancinellis.

He wanted to take over a contraband cigarette ring, and he had some men he wanted gone. He opened the door for the Mancinellis, thinking they'd do the dirty work and take the fall for it. He made me plant evidence that condemned half a dozen Mancinellis. They'd committed murder, then arson, and Darren was supposed to say thank you to Salvatore Mancinelli. Instead, he made sure I slipped into the crime scene at night and moved things around to prove it wasn't a gas leak. He gave me DNA evidence to leave at the scene that tied the fire to the New York *Cosa Nostra*.

Have the Mancinellis been getting revenge all these years? Would they have that kind of patience? For sure. But I thought the difference between them, and the Stiglionos and Darren was they don't target women. I don't know much about them beyond their reputations. I didn't want to know more. I wanted in and out. It was bad enough Darren made me do shit like that.

I refused once, and he drained my bank accounts. He left me with one penny in my checking and one in my savings. It was a snub worse than if there'd been nothing left. Gareth convinced him to give the money back. He warned his dad if I had no money to trace, and no means to pay my bills, there was nothing stopping me from taking money under the table from someone else. That money could have come from me selling secrets.

As though he had ESP, he came knocking again. I thought about refusing a second time. It was when I found out I was pregnant, and Aaron wanted me guarded better. Aaron knew what Darren forced me to do, and he was scared someone would think a pregnant woman was the perfect weak target. I was—for Darren.

He had men follow me out of the station house one night. I was working a desk job since going on calls was too dangerous. I ended my shift while Aaron was fighting a fire and there was next to no one at the station house. I walked out to my car and noticed three men in the shadows. I had my mace and my keys in my hands. I was walking across a long parking lot, and I sensed the men getting closer.

They tried to encircle me a few feet from my car, but I set off my car alarm. I ran in the opposite direction—fucking painful since my ligaments were tight around my belly—and got back into the station house. One of Aaron's friends found me panting and doubled-over. He guessed men were out there, but he was unaffiliated. I tried to make him stay inside, but he went to check. No one was out there, but he refused to let me leave until Aaron got back and could take me home.

All of this whizzes through my mind at warp speed as the guy takes yet another step forward. I scream as loud as I can. I keep screaming as the man reaches for me. There's nothing I can do once he has his hand around my throat. Definitely not police procedure. Definitely nothing like when Seamus holds me in place. When he puts his other hand on my jaw, I still. I don't want my neck snapped.

"Good, little girl."

How the fuck does he know about that? Seamus has never called me that where anyone could hear him. He's never been to my place before.

The town car today.

It must have been bugged. Or did the driver have the intercom on? Someone betrayed Seamus and the O'Rourkes, and now they've got me.

Chapter Twenty-Two

Seamus

Motherfucking son of a goddamn bitch. What the fuck just happened to me?

I roll over, trying to figure out where I am and remember what just happened. I turn my head to the left and find my brother lying in a puddle of his own blood and immediately my mind goes to the worst possibility.

My gaze sweeps around the room because I need to find my father. But when it lands on Da, he's lying there with his eyes closed, too. I try my best to push up onto my side to sit up eventually, but I groan instead.

"Seamus?"

"Yeah, Da. What happened?"

"I think we were ambushed." My dad's ironic sense of humor is not what I want right now. I want to know what the hell happened and where Tiera is. What if she's... No.

"Tiera?... Tiera?... Tiera!... *Cailín*!... Tiera!"

Over and over, I scream, but there's no response. I look to

307

my brother yet again, but he hasn't stirred despite all the noise I make.

"Da, we have to get to Cormac."

I came round face up. I do my best to roll onto my side, then onto my stomach. I manage to push myself up to a crawling position and make my way to him. I'm unsteady on my hands and knees as I reach out and shake his shoulder.

"Cor, Cor. I need you to wake up. Cor, where's Tiera?"

My brother doesn't respond, not even a groan. I check his pulse. It's still there, steady as it always is, but he won't wake. I look over his body to see where he's bleeding. The wound's not visible, but he's breathing heavily now that I've tried to wake him. There's blood coming from the back of Cormac's shoulder, and there is a nasty circle through his clothes. I try to pull up his shirt, but I can't reach without my own wounded shoulder screaming with pain because I can't balance.

My dad has a nasty gash on his forehead, but that's all I can see. He's moving faster than I am. He comes to squat next to me and rips open the back of Cormac's shirt. When he does, we see what we expected. The bullet is still in there. We're going to need our family doc to pull it out. If I were in better condition and had the right supplies, I would do it too, but this isn't the time or the place to play doctor.

"Da, we need Meridith."

"I know."

I assess the deep gash on my dad's head. That seems to be the only thing wrong with him, but I need to make sure.

"Da, are you hurt anywhere else?"

"No."

My dad rests his hand on my shoulder as I force myself to squat on my haunches so I can better assess Cormac. We're seven months apart because I came two months early. He says he never remembers a time without me. How could he? He was still an infant when I was born. Sean and Shane may be the twins, but Cor and I may as well be.

We don't have the exact synchronicity Shane and Sean do, which is uncanny even after knowing them their entire lives. But Cormac and I are close. We don't necessarily know when the other gets injured, and we don't necessarily feel each other's pain, but I do today. It's as though the bullet ripped through my other shoulder.

"You look almost as bad as Cormac. Sit down."

I practically collapse rather than lower my arse to the floor. I look toward the stairs leading to Tiera's bedroom as I push back my left cuff and raise my wrist. I don't feel my phone in my back pocket, and I'm sure they took Da's and Cormac's too.

"We have our watches. I can still see yours underneath your sleeve. I have mine, and Cormac has his."

"Push your alert, and I'll do the same for mine. Then I'll do Cormac's."

I watch my father pull his watch down his wrist until he can see the side. All our watches have a distinctive, bigger dial on the side. It's really a button that, if we push, sends out an alert to everyone in our family that we're in distress. It's the smaller dial that sets the time. I press mine, and I watch my dad do his own, then my brother's.

My mind's a jumble now that I'm sure my father and brother are still breathing. Where's my girlfriend? Where's the only woman I have ever loved? The only woman I will ever love. I planned to tell her that when we had dinner together. But obviously, that all went to shite.

I didn't know for sure until this morning when I needed to protect her. Yes, need. Not want, not should, but need to protect her. Nothing was more important to me than making sure Tiera got out of Gareth's house unharmed. Now I have no idea where she is or who has her. I remember parts of what happened. Men burst in here, and I didn't even get a good look at them as I ran down the stairs to help my father and brother once the intruders started shooting.

I was barely halfway to the bottom step before searing pain ripped through my thigh. The pain that I know all too well. It wasn't the first time I've felt it, and I doubt it will ever be the last until I'm put in the ground. Blessedly, I know this was just a graze. Before I could do much more, pain tore through my left shoulder when I slammed into the wall to avoid getting shot again. Fortunately, my gun was in my right hand. Even though I could shoot ambidextrous, it meant I didn't drop the weapon.

I know I squeezed out several rounds, and I hit at least one guy before I went down from a guy pistol whipping the back of my head. But there're no bodies here but that of my dad, my brother, and me. Where did they go? Who were they? And where did they take Tiera?

Anger boils inside me. It's instantly turning to rage. Actually, it's already rage. I want nothing more than to find the people who did this to my brother, to my father, and who took Tiera. But I have to remain calm despite how difficult it is. If I lose my shite, then I'll be no good to anybody. I have to think logically in order to rescue Tiera. If I don't, will I have a chance to tell her I love her?

I know most people would think this is lust. Most people would say it's infatuation. People would think I'm ridiculous to believe it's love after a couple months, but I'm not. I know how it goes. I've heard the stories about my parents. I've heard the stories about my aunts and uncles. I've watched my cousins fall in love with their soulmates.

I know who Tiera is to me.

She might not be ready to feel the same way I do. Even though I know she didn't have a good marriage, I still fear she loves her dead husband and that she can't give me her whole heart like I want to give her mine. Even if that's the case, I will live with it because life with her is so much better than life without. I worried if I could handle living with a ghost in our relationship. I will if it's the difference between having a future with Tiera or not. But to have that life, I have to find her.

My rage continues to boil until it threatens to spill over. And I remind myself over and over that'll be counterproductive. It will get us nowhere.

"I need a shirt. I need to stop Cor's bleeding. I need something to press against the wound."

When I shake myself out of my trance and start thinking about what my brother needs, I notice my father is already pulling his shirt off. He's about four steps ahead of me, and that makes me feel guilty for not focusing on what's right before me, that I'm letting someone else come ahead of my brother. I've never done that before, but this is different.

Tiera is different. Tiera is the one who comes first for me. My family will always be a millimeter behind. Nothing has ever been more important to me than family, and nothing ever will be. Tiera is part of my family now. I don't know how long it will take to make that official. I pray it happens. But for now—as far as I'm concerned—she's more than just my girlfriend. She's my forever.

"Seamus, I'm well enough to go look for Tiera. Let me go upstairs and make sure she's not still up there."

"Thanks, Da."

I hate that I'm still too weak to do it myself, but my head's ringing enough for me to want to vomit if I move. I don't want to think someone took her, but I also don't want to think the reason she can't respond while still up there is because she's dead. God help me if that's the case. I refuse to even remotely consider she is. If I let myself think that, I'll shrivel into a ball and be worthless to everyone. If I think that, I'll picture her being tortured by the sick fuck who peels faces off.

I don't know that I'll ever recover. Whoever did this shouldn't have touched my family. They will pay for the rest of their very—*very*—short life.

I watched Da grab the banister as he hauls himself up the stairs. He's moving far slower than I've ever seen him except for when he's been close to death. That's an experience I've never been fond of, and it's happened more than once. I know the pain I've felt watching him get hurt is exponentially less than the pain he feels when it's one of his sons. I can't imagine how he feels right now with my big brother still unconscious. He's doing what he has to because it's what he was trained to do. I also think he needs a few minutes alone, so I don't question whether he should climb stairs when his head's still bleeding.

It makes me think again about a future with Tiera. If we have a baby girl, her gender would protect her. A daughter might be called a princess, but that's not how it goes in syndicates. That's what people outside our world call them. There's nothing spoiled about the women in my family. Or even those in the other syndicates. They're as tough as nails, for lack of a better way to say it. Tiera is one of those. She might not be a daughter, or sister, or niece, or even a cousin of a mob boss. But she has been around it her entire life.

If we have a son—a little boy—then what happens to him? I know Dillan, Finn, and Sean wonder the same thing if they have a son. I'm certain Maks and Bogdan Kutsenko wonder that, too. So far, Niko has only had a little girl, but Ana's pregnant again just like Bogdan's wife, Christina. None of the other bratva couples have children. I'm sure Luca Mancinelli is grateful he's only had a daughter with his wife. But I suspect Maria might be pregnant. What then? What would Matteo do if he has a little boy?

What would I do?

We've been mob for four generations on one side of my family and three on the other. There was no getting out for my grandparents. There's no getting out for my parents. There's no getting out for me. None of us can walk away because it would make us greater targets. That means it's inevitable my son would become a mobster too.

Even if Dillan and our family were to relent and relinquish our position, any family who took over from us would invariably seek revenge. It would be punishment for what we've done to subjugate those who've tested us. They would track us and kill us to ensure we can never return. Whoever assumes the position would need to prove they belong at the top. That only makes us a greater target if we don't have our men to support us. Our men would see us as nothing but traitors if we walked away since they can't.

But I would do it if there were even remotely a chance. I would do it to keep any son Tiera and I have from becoming mobsters. It would protect Tiera and any of our daughters from ever becoming potential targets.

It should protect them, but to be honest, being female is no longer a guarantee of safety. And we have no one to blame but members of our own community. That's the problem. Women were off limits for generations. Then Uncle Donovan and Declan fucked it all up. Shite bags that they were, they got women involved. Now, any woman is a target.

I don't want to think about that because inevitably, it makes me think about Colleen. And if I think about Colleen, I'll picture what happened to her. If I picture what happened to her, I'll think of what might have happened to Tiera. And right now, that's the last thing I need. I'm forcing my mind not to picture the exact same thing happening to Tiera. My mind keeps trying to imagine her being tortured. It feels like I've spent a lifetime compartmentalizing my thoughts and emotions. I need to do that now. I need to be the man I hate to find the woman I love. I need to be a mobster.

God, this is actually taking my dad a long arse time to get back down here. I can't wait any longer. I force myself to stand, but then my dad appears on the landing.

"Stop, Seamus. I'm here. I'm coming. She's not up here." He hurries down the stairs, moving on steadier feet than before. "I've looked everywhere. I can see where she put up a struggle because the shower curtain's ripped, and there are disinfectant spray bottles on the ground. I don't know if she used them to defend herself or whether they used them to control her."

"I'd prefer to think that first part. Could she have sprayed their faces?"

"There are more sets of handprints that don't match each other on the walls and mirror, but none are the right size to be hers. It tells me she fought back, but they outnumbered her."

Da gets to the bottom of the steps, and we stare at each other. He said aloud what we already know. But we don't have the finality of him finding her body. I want to believe she walked out on her own and wasn't carried out because she's dead. They took the bodies of their own men we killed. I know Cormac killed two, and my dad got one. I'm sure I got at least one.

They came with a squad of men. They knew Tiera wasn't alone. They knew at least my dad, if not Cormac and I, were here.

Was this all planned? Or was it a coincidence?

Did they think they needed nine men to pull one woman out of her home?

If they believed it was only Da and Tiera, did they think they needed that many for a man and a woman?

Did they do it to eliminate a third of my family?

Did they know I was here?

Did they wait until they saw all three of us here?

I don't know. I sure as fuck want to find out.

My dad and I sit in silence, watching Cormac's shallow breathing, knowing it's going to take time for my family to get here. They know we're not at my place, so they'll have to track us to Tiera's condo. I don't know if they'll come together as one because they were already at my place, or if they will come in their own vehicles. They'll know it's not a coincidence that all three of our signals are going off. Not being able to reach any of us by phone means the situation truly is dire.

I shake Cormac again, and this time he groans. But he still doesn't wake, and he's still losing blood. Da eases him onto his side, so I can examine his injury. When I peel away my dad's shirt he wadded up and put beneath Cormac's injured shoulder—they fucking shot him in the back—the blood isn't coming out as fast as I feared. There's nothing we can do but wait until the others arrive.

It feels like hours pass, and I keep an eye on my watch. Forty-five minutes from when I first pressed the alert. It's only a moment after I check my watch for at least the thirtieth time that my family bursts through the door with guns ready to shoot anybody or anything in sight. Dillan's the first through the door. He never leads from behind. He'll never send anybody out to do a job he isn't willing to do himself.

Finn is right behind him because they always pair together, and Finn's his second-in-command. They're the only ones without a brother to pair with. Dillan's never had brothers, and Finn's brothers came as a matching set. It's meant Dillan and Finn have always been together. They're also older than the rest of us by a couple years, so they started training before us. Sean and Shane enter the condo with their backs toward me and with their guns raised, ready to shoot anyone who approaches from behind.

Once all four of them are inside, they rush to put their guns back in their holsters and run toward us. Sean drops onto his knees as he goes to examine Cormac. He and Shane both trained as paramedics while they were in college. They keep their certifications up to date. But it's been a long time since either of them has had to use their training on a gunshot wound in the field. I hate that it's on my big brother.

Dillan looks around before he looks at me. "What the fuck happened here?"

"I don't know why they came or where they went, but they took Tiera. They broke in while I was upstairs with her."

"Cormac and I were here. We don't know who it was. There were no distinguishing marks on them except for some fake NYPD badges on their arms. They didn't look like anybody we would recognize. They didn't speak at all. Not even a word. Not even a hint. They clearly knew who was here and what they came for. They'd already decided who would go for Tiernan and who would stay behind."

I don't remember any of what my dad just said. None of it sounds familiar, but I know he wouldn't make any of that up. I still can't remember whether or not they spoke. Whether or not they made any hand signals. That makes me feel even more incompetent and incapable because I didn't notice the things my dad did.

Sean turns to me and holds out his phone so I can see the contact on the screen. I hear it ringing. He's calling our doctor. I look at Shane.

"Can we move him? Can we get him home?"

"We should wait for Meridith to get here. He isn't bleeding that much, but he's already lost a lot of blood. If we move him, it could make the wound worse. I don't think we should risk doing that. If Meridith says it's okay, then we will. But I think she's going to need to stitch him up first. At the very least, he needs an IV."

I have to accept what Shane tells me. I know he's not exaggerating. I know it's the truth. And I can't put my needs above my brother's. Even if it means it takes more time to find Tiera. It's pure agony as I listen to Sean talk to our retired British Navy physician. She's a surgeon and has been patching us up for as long as I can remember. She came on board just before my grandfather died, so I was still a teenager. She's patched up my dad and my uncles too many times. If she's good enough for them, she sure as hell is good enough for me.

While we wait, we can still think about what we can do. I look at the others and consider our options.

"Shane, give me your phone. I need to call Tiera's dad and see if he knows anything that's happening."

Shane pulls the phone from his pocket. As he hands it to me, he wonders aloud what I already have. "Do you think he knows? If her kidnappers called him or Gareth, would he tell you about it?"

I shrug and tilt my head slightly to the right, and it hurts like a motherfucker. How I forgot I took a blow the head is beyond me. How I'm still thinking straight is beyond me. I think it's sheer nerves and fear that's doing it. Like how those mothers can lift cars to protect their children. I feel like I could do that to protect Tiera. She's what matters most. I don't need to remind myself of that. But my mind won't stop repeating that over and over and over.

I shake my head and wince. Shane misunderstands and frowns, but I do it to clear my mind. I need to focus again. Fortunately, I already know Brant's number by heart just like I do Gareth's.

Chapter Twenty-Three

Tiera

My fucking head hurts like a bitch. Someone rung my bell like it's church on Sunday. I can't—and don't want to—open my eyes. The effort is too much, and I fear any light shining into them. Instead, I listen...to silence. I sense nothing around me. There's no one moving or talking. Even the air is silent. I have no sense of where I am.

I fought with all I had to keep the men from taking me. I clawed, I scratched, I bit, I kicked, and I punched. I practically ripped the shower rod from the wall as I tugged on it to keep the third man through the door from snatching me off my feet. When he picked me up, I kicked him in the balls. He dropped me, and I smashed my head against the lip of the tub's side. I want to reach back and see if I have the goose egg I suspect.

The shower curtain came down with me as I fell. The first guy through the door—the one I sprayed directly in the eyes—grabbed a hand full of my hair and wouldn't let go. I got the shower curtain over his face and rolled all my weight onto him, pinning him face down as I tried to smother him. Even as the second man—the one I sprayed in the mouth and nose—yanked at the back of my shirt, I wouldn't let go. I just squeezed my thighs around the ribs of the guy I straddled. Thank God for all those hours of running. My legs are far stronger than the cellulite would make you think.

But it wasn't enough. I didn't know there were two more men waiting in my bedroom. It took four of them to haul me out, kicking and screaming. The one I tried to suffocate at least had the decency to pass out, so I felt like I accomplished something in my own defense. My success lasted a heartbeat. One man zip-tied my wrists behind me.

That wasn't enough to stop me from kicking backwards, landing blows against his shins. Another soccer move, using my heel to drive backwards. All I got for my efforts was the man grabbing my pussy and warning me they'd all have turns if I didn't stop. I threw my head backwards and cracked him in the nose. I pretty sure he bled on my shoulder.

After that, things moved faster than I could keep up with. The barrel of a gun pressed against the base of my skull and nudged me forward. They tried to rush me down the stairs, but I stumbled twice, and it was enough to convince them they had to let me move slower unless they wanted a captive with a snapped neck. But I was three stairs from the bottom when I recognized Seamus. I leapt down the last ones, nearly skidding in blood that belonged to an intruder. My captors didn't expect me to move so fast, so I got to my boyfriend's side and dropped to my knees.

One guy said I was where I belonged—on my knees and ready to suck them off. Vulgar fucker. The only person who gets to tell me something like that is Seamus, and he'd only do it while we're roleplaying. He'd never speak to me that way if we weren't being intimate. They tried to pull me back onto my feet, but I thrashed harder than I had in the bathroom.

I didn't want to leave Seamus's side, and I sure as hell wouldn't go with a speck of willingness. Even with the gun back at the top of my spine, I still refused to leave. That's when things went black. One of them pistol whipped me, the side crashing into my temple and making me crumple.

That's where my head hurts the most right now and is causing the throbbing pain that forces me to keep my eyes closed. I feel dried blood on my cheek. I'm lying on my side with my injured side up. My wrists are no longer bound. None of me is bound.

They either believe I'm going nowhere and have no chance of escape, or they want me to try and fail. Either way, I'm their hostage. But I won't be forever. Either they'll kill me, or Seamus will come for me. I spotted the wound in his thigh where a bullet ripped his pants and grazed his leg. He was paler than usual, but not so much that I feared he was on death's doorstep. I saw his chest rise and fall, and he groaned when I called his name. I think me saying his name over and over was rousing him, but I didn't get a chance to say it more than three times. I don't know that it was enough.

Cormac's shoulder seemed far worse from the blood beneath him. I don't know if the bullet passed through or lodged in there, but it didn't appear to hit a major artery. His blood didn't geyser, and he didn't have the pallor of someone about to die. I've seen burn victims just before they pass away. I've seen smoke inhalation victims just before they breathe their last. I know what imminent death looks like, and Cormac's coloring was still too ruddy. But he might be by now.

Seamus had no noticeable wounds besides the grazed thigh. Something invisible caused him to remain unconscious. What if he wasn't able to activate his tracker? I'm certain he has one. I wish I did. I'm certain he will insist upon it before I can even ask. I refuse to consider the possibility I won't reunite with him. Fate owes me a fucking happily ever after. I kissed my frog. Now I want my prince. It's not that I believe I deserve happiness. I don't know that I can ever believe that's a natural right.

It just doesn't happen to enough people in this world for me to believe it's a condition everyone is meant to not only experience but be in a permanent state of. But having even another five minutes with Seamus would make me happy. I want a lifetime, though. I've already lost so fucking much. Do I deserve to lose even more?

What did I do to earn a place in hell on Earth? I know I've broken the law far too many times to ever claim I'm the mob's innocent victim. I could have turned myself in. I could have turned over Gareth, Keith, and Vince. But what would have been the cost to my parents if I had? Far too much. Far more than I'm willing to pay.

So, I gave in each time Darren or Gareth came knocking. They manipulated the fuck out of me in the beginning. Then they didn't have to try very hard. I gave in before there was anything for me to argue. I rolled over like the dumb bitch Vince called me more than once.

That's something Seamus can never find out about. He'd lose his ever-loving mind. It's bad enough he vaguely knows the things said to me. But to know that was a specific insult hurled at me too many times to count would make Seamus unstoppable. I know I couldn't. Not with my words or with my body. I don't think anyone—including Cormac or his dad who are as big as him—could once he decided retribution would be the best way to protect me.

My head hurts from my thoughts bouncing from one thing to another. I need to open my eyes just a crack. I need to get oriented. The eye closer to the ground opens a slit, but my other one doesn't want to. It's not swollen shut or anything. I'm just not that awake yet. Wherever I am is pitch black. I can't see an inch in front of me.

I force both eyes open and try to adjust to the darkness. I refuse to panic, so I keep my breathing measured. I've had panic attacks since the accident. I know what they feel like when they're coming on, and I know how to prevent them. I go through my breathing routine, and I feel my heart slowing.

I'm not afraid of anything jumping out at me, though I'm not thrilled at the prospect that something might crawl on me. But I'm afraid that I'm so disoriented I have no idea if it's day or night. I don't know how long I was unconscious. Was it an hour? A few hours? A day?

I scan the walls where I think they likely meet the ceiling. I see no red dots representing a camera. If they can't see me on screen, can they tell I'm awake with an infrared, heat seeking device? If I move around, will they know I'm awake? If I stand and tried to find the end of the room, will they watch me like some red and orange alien? What if this is my only chance to explore my surroundings? They could come back at any moment, and I'll be none the wiser about where they're holding me. If I know how much space is around me and any doors or windows, I might plan a successful jail break.

I push up on my elbow and wait. Do they care what I'm doing? Are they waiting to pounce until I'm in an even weaker position? Are they laughing at my expense because Seamus is already dead, and they enjoy seeing a woman pine for him?

The thought that Seamus is dead rips such a searing pain through my chest it steals my breath. Why the fuck does it have to take something like this to confirm my feelings for him? I've known all along that I'm in love with him, but it's beyond question now. I've been in love before, so I recognize the emotions. This is everything I remember, yet so much more intense. It might tempt me to think it's infatuation instead, but there's a calmness that comes with it.

Don't get me wrong. I feel the excitement of new love—the eagerness to see him, the missing him when he's not around, the joy when he is, the deep need to know he's happy and that I'm part of that. At the same time, I feel the contentedness of having been with the right man for as long as I can remember. It took me years with Aaron to get to this point, and even then, it wasn't a sensation that enveloped me like a cocoon that would help me emerge into the person I'm meant to be.

I don't *need* Seamus because I can't handle life. I *want* Seamus because I choose to have him be part of my life, and he makes it easier to be the person I'm meant to be. I thought I needed Aaron because he was the key to happiness. I learned fast that I couldn't rely on him for that. I understand more about the situation he was forced into and that his intentions were good—though I don't know if they were born of love or duty to his wife—but I wouldn't have lost my faith in him as a husband if he'd clued me in even a little.

There was no way Seamus could hide who and what he is, and I've known from the beginning the type of man I'm involved with. I don't feel the bait and switch I did with Aaron. The biggest difference between them is Seamus wants to let me in while Aaron shut me out. Seamus will keep far more secrets from me and tell me way more lies than Aaron ever did, but he doesn't lie about his lies.

My mind wanders because I have nothing else to do in the dark. Wherever it's headed, it leads back to the simple fact I love Seamus.

I sit up and wait for something to happen. I don't let myself do more than that for seven minutes. I count. It's an unpredictable amount of time in case someone's watching me. I stand, and a wave of dizziness washes over me. I know there's a wall behind me, so I reach back to steady myself. When I don't feel like I'll hurl, I put my hands out in front of me and turn to my left. I shuffle my feet, so I step on nothing and will feel anything I might trip over.

I'm not reaching another wall as quickly as I assumed I would. Maybe the space isn't that wide, but it's long. I keep going until my fingers bump into a man's bare chest. I recoil, but nothing else happens. I'm standing close enough that now I know someone's there, I should be able to sense their presence. I get nothing. I lift my arms again, allowing my fingers to skim over the person in front of me.

Fuck. Fuck. Holy fuck.

The skin is cold. Not like he's been outside in winter cold. The been-in-the-fridge-for-too-long cold. I slide my hands up until I reach his shoulders. I gasp and unadulterated terror seizes me.

There's no head.

"I've been waiting to see how long it would take you to explore."

I freeze—terrible pun all things considered since there's a corpse in front of me. I don't know the voice, but it's coming from in front of me. I'm giving nothing away. I can't see who it is, but they know where I am. They know I found this body. The only thing that matters is that I know it's not Seamus. I already know what it's like to have him beneath my fingertips.

"Are we playing the silent game?" I don't appreciate the mocking tone, but they aren't wrong.

Since I doubt I'm going anywhere anytime soon, I'm in no hurry. I sense they'll get frustrated with me before I'm willing to give in to them.

"Come now, *Tiernan*. Ignoring me won't endear you to me. Play along, and I won't torture you. Make this boring, and I'll have no reason to keep you alive."

If this is who's stalked me for the past three years, then I don't doubt their willingness to physically torture me after the emotional and mental fuckery they've inflicted.

I want to keep them talking because something might give away how I know this person. I don't recognize the voice. It's not anyone I know. It's not Aaron's cousin or Gareth. It's not Keith or Vince. It's not Hillary or Gretchen. It's not that bitch Stella, though I never considered it might be. I'm just naming people I don't get along with.

I swallow my aversion and slide my hands down the corpse's right arm until I get to the top of the man's forearm. I feel the scar. I know who it is.

Vince.

I lean to my right, my hand outstretched, to see if there's anyone else there. I do the same to my left.

"It's just you, me, and Vince. I know you recognize the scar. Aren't you wondering how he's still standing if he doesn't have a head?"

I am, but I suspect there's a meat hook sunk into his back to keep him upright. I don't want to reach around to find out.

"Still as stubborn as you've always been. You refused to give up when you were six and couldn't master those drills your coach gave you. You spent hours in your backyard practicing. You refused to give up when you were failing chemistry in tenth grade. You convinced the fire chief to pay you to clean the station house, so you could pay for a tutor without anyone knowing. You refused to stay in New Jersey when Aaron asked you not to go to Chicago. You did what you wanted and loved having him follow you like your little bitch."

None of that is wrong, though the last bit is distorted. It made me feel loved when Aaron offered to give up everything he had at home to follow me to Chicago for two years. We hadn't been dating long, but we wanted a future together. We were already in love. I think that desire to have found the one and to have the chance to settle down rather than be alone drove him to offer and for me to accept since we'd only been dating a few months.

I'd already applied to grad school when I met him. I knew what I wanted professionally, and I'd already spent so much time and energy working toward it. I didn't want to let it go. Aaron realized that and made it easier, so we wouldn't have a long-distance relationship to juggle along with work for him and school for me.

"Remembering the good old days, *Tiernan?*"

The mocking tone is back, but I want this person to keep talking. They're giving things away. They've known me most of my life if they knew about the soccer drills. They had connections in my local volunteer fire department if they knew about me cleaning to pay for tutoring. I didn't admit the truth about why I worked there to anyone but the fire chief. Everyone else thought I was doing it to save money to buy Christmas presents.

"You're wondering how I know all this, *Tiernan.*"

My captor stresses my name each time. It's filled with disdain.

"You were awfully quick to abandon your married name and go back to your maiden name. You were always an ice princess. Cold and aloof. The last name might have suited you, but the first name—you've been a disappointment since you were born. Your parents wanted a boy. Instead, they got you."

That refrain's gotten old over the years. I believed it for a long time once I knew it was a man's name. But that wasn't why my parents gave it to me. I tune that out like I did when Vince used to say the same thing.

"Vince used to tell you that, didn't he? You're remembering that, aren't you?"

Fucking mind reader now?

Heat explodes across the back of my left ribs as an electrical current jolts through me. It's so unexpected, I can't stifle my scream. It burns enough to make me sink to my knees. A matching blast of pain bursts through my right shoulder.

What the ever-loving fuck was that?

"You seem to need a little prodding to answer my questions. You're as fat as a heifer, so a cattle prod should do the trick."

So, we've escalated to physical torture. I was warned.

The pain steals my breath, so even if I wanted to answer, I can't. I was so focused on the person in front of me I never sensed someone behind me. The moment I feel the tip brush against my right ass cheek, I spin away, twisting and reaching. My hands encircle the rod, so I yank as hard as I can, throwing my weight backward. I nearly go flying when I rip the cattle prod from its wielder's hands. I swing it like a baseball bat, aiming for where I think someone is.

I contact something hard, and the person yelps. I do it again three more times until I hear something hit the ground. A string of curses tells me where they are. My hands have already found the trigger button, so I shove the zapping part of it forward. When it makes contact, I press the button.

"The fucking bitch just electrocuted me."

I press it forward and activate it again. The bellow of pain is satisfying since I recognize this voice. I move it around like I'm poking coals in a fireplace, triggering it to release its surge of electricity wherever it touches. I miss sometimes, but other times I succeed. I keep going until massive hands grasp my upper arms and tug me backwards. I tried to swing the prod like a club back over my shoulder, but the hands tighten like manacles.

"Fuck you, Keith." It's the first time I speak since waking.

He's not the one to respond. My tormenter's voice is beside my ear.

"Luck's run out, my little ice princess. You refused to die despite my best effort to kill all three of you in that car. I'm going to try harder this time."

Darren?

Chapter Twenty-Four

Seamus

"Brant, someone took Tiera."

I don't bother with pleasantries. I don't know if he deserves any, and I don't have the patience to offer any. Meridith just cleared me from having a concussion. She's already tended to Cormac's shoulder, which she did first, then the graze on my leg and the gash on my dad's forehead.

"What the fuck happened? Where's my daughter, O'Rourke?"

There's shock, anger, and fear in his tone. I hate to say "good," but it reassures me he isn't part of this.

"We were at her place. Nine men broke in and overpowered my dad, Cormac, and me. We killed a few, but not before they shot Cormac and me. Two of them went for my dad. It took both of them to control him enough to slam his head against Tiera's coffee table and knock him out. One pistol whipped me from behind."

I found out that's how my dad got the cut on his forehead that wound up needing a row of stitches.

"You're talking, and you said they knocked Kieran out. What about your brother?"

I appreciate he has the decency to ask.

"They shot him in the shoulder. He bled a lot, leaving him unconscious."

"So, you're all alive. Three mighty O'Rourkes couldn't protect my little girl."

I hear the last two words. They don't mean the same thing as they do when I say them, but it produces another wave of rage deep in my gut. I want *my* little girl back. My *cailín*.

Brant isn't done. "You insisted you could protect her better. She's not under your care for a day, and someone's taken her. Who the fuck touched her?"

"If I knew, I wouldn't have called you. I'd be on my way to get her. Tell me the fucking truth. How much of this shite did you really know about?"

"You motherfucker. You still think I let someone go after my daughter for three years and did nothing about it. She hid the truth about how bad things were. No one clued me in that there was an outsider involved. I didn't know shit."

"You stayed behind after we left. Does Gareth know more than he admitted?"

"I don't think so. But I believe Vince and Keith do. I don't have a solid reason, but I have a feeling I can't shake."

"I want all three of them."

"You can play your torture games later. My only priority is finding my daughter."

"No shite. But we have no idea where to start if we don't talk to those three. I'm sending Shane to get them. You better be on that plane when we set off. If you don't come willingly, I'll fucking drag you. Until I know where Tiera is, I hold everyone affiliated with the O'Briens responsible. Even I can admit my limitations. Nine to three in an ambush didn't leave me or my dad and brother much chance to overpower them. They burst in shooting."

"Where was Tiera during all this?"

"Locked in her bathroom. They shot at me and grazed my thigh. When they shot at me again, I slammed into a wall, then someone took the butt of their pistol to the base of my skull. It knocked me out. They broke into the bathroom and took her while all three of us were unconscious."

"You got shot at twice protecting her?"

"I'd look like a fucking piece of Swiss cheese before I voluntarily let them take my woman."

That sounds prehistoric. It sounds misogynistic. It sounds patriarchal. It sounds fucking true. She is mine, and someone dared touch her. Now I'm going to kill them.

"How're you getting the three of them and me to you in New York? You said a plane."

"Shane's flying us down."

Cormac flies helicopters, and Shane flies planes. We have expensive pastimes. An IV and stitches brought my brother back around, and he's listening to this conversation along with everyone else. But he's in no condition to go anywhere.

I was about to call Brant when Meridith arrived. She got to work immediately, and with Sean and Shane's help, Cormac had an IV going while she stitched him up. He came to thrashing and snarling like a bear. It took Dillan and Finn to hold him down while our dad talked to him enough to calm him down. Once he opened his eyes and saw Da and me, he was as docile as a lamb.

"How long till you're here?"

"Forty-five minutes."

It's a twenty-minute flight, but we have to get to the private airport where Shane keeps his planes." Yes, more than one. He had *just* a glider, VP-12 two-seater, and a biplane for years. He now has a Cessna that fits ten. A pilot, copilot, and eight passengers. He says he got it for when we have short-distance missions like this when our larger jet takes too long to fuel and get off the ground. I think he got it partly to do something nice for his brothers and our cousin.

A couple weeks ago, the three couples decided to go on a triple date to Hyannis in Massachusetts. But it got cancelled because Shane, Cormac, and I had to make an impromptu trip down to Miami to deal with a shipment—one of the times I disappeared and couldn't give Tiera specifics. We had to take the jet. Shane bought the plane, so we have a second way for people to get around now that our family's growing.

"I'll be ready when you get here."

"Meet me at Gareth's."

"Fine. I'm calling him now."

I hang up with Brant and dial Gareth's number on Dillan's phone. I didn't need the memorized numbers since my cousin already has them stored in his phone. Unlike most people these days, we all have at least two dozen numbers in our heads. Sometimes it's because we need to call them, but a lot of times, it's so we recognize them when we're tapping phones or coercing people to use them.

"You piece of shite. Where's my girlfriend?"

"Seamus?"

"Where the fuck is my girlfriend?"

"Tiernan?"

"Fucking hell, Gareth. Where the fuck is Tiera?"

"I—I—Goddamn it. Would you fucking watch what you're fucking doing? Sorry, Aidan's stitching me up and has hands like fucking bowling balls."

"Stitching you up?"

"Yeah. Vince, Keith, and I were in one of my SUVs when we were hit head on. Men swarmed the vehicle and pulled us out. One fucker stabbed me in the left pec. When the knife wouldn't go deep, he slashed me with it. They took—Mother-fucker! I told you to fucking watch what you're fucking doing."

I'm trying to be patient, but I'm being sorely tested.

"Gareth, what happened?"

"I'm fucking getting to it. They took Vince but left me for dead."

"Keith?"

"That piece of motherfucking shit face cum dumpster asshole walked away with them."

"He's in on this? Whoever's been after Tiera—he's part of it?"

"It looked that way. I was half-conscious, but Vince went kicking and screaming. He didn't stop fighting until they knocked him out and shoved him in their own SUV. They escorted Keith to the vehicle, but he put up no fight. He had guns pointed at him, but it didn't look like anyone planned to shoot him. It looked like it was more for show."

"Is he the mastermind?"

Gareth snorts. "That shitwad couldn't lead his own ass to a crapper without holding its hand. He's a follower and always has been. He set me up."

"Did you recognize anyone?"

"No. They wore ski masks and said nothing. I watched them pile into a few cars, but I passed out before I saw them drive away."

"Where were you?"

"On our way to our place."

Our place. That never means someone's comfy home. It means where we take care of shite. If Gareth doesn't prove useful, he'll be going to our place. The abandoned railway station in the Bronx that hasn't been in use in over a decade. The city's forgotten about it except for once or twice a year when a random inspector comes out to do a cursory look. They never examine it closely, so they don't notice the hidden door that's easy to miss unless you know where to look.

Down in our subterranean lair, we have next to no contact with the outside world. Our phones are off, and we only keep a satellite phone for emergencies. We take nothing of value in with us since we burn everything before we leave. We cover our shoes with booties since those are harder to replace than our suits. We go through thousands of dollars of clothing each year, but a good pair of shoes is hard to replace. None of us wear jewelry except for the married men who all have rings. They take those off and put them in the safe before getting to work.

Everyone thinks they know where our place is. The other syndicates in New York thought it was a vacant storefront in Queens for a long time. Now they think it's some storage unit there. It's not. For starters, Queens is too obvious since we're all from there. The bratva, *Cosa Nostra*, and Cartel might have theirs in that borough, but we picked the Bronx because it's the least likely. We like them having no clue where our place is when we know exactly where all of theirs are. We know where Gareth's is too.

"Is there anything you remember about them? Cologne? Eye color? Height?" I need some type of clue to piece all of this together.

The men who attacked us didn't wear any hats or masks to disguise themselves. They thought we were dead. I thought about it while I watched Meridith, Sean, and Shane work on Cormac. They didn't care that my dad, Cor, and I knew they were mercenaries, but they wanted to trick Tiera into believing they were the police. They assumed she'd go with them either out of fear or familiarity since she's worked alongside law enforcement for nearly two decades.

"They had on fake police uniforms. It made no sense when they wore balaclavas, too. The badges would have passed for authentic to anyone who doesn't know what to look for. All the stitching was slightly off."

"We saw the same thing. I'm certain Tiera spotted it too, and that's why she put up such a fight."

"She fought them? Is she all right? Did you find her blood anywhere?"

Gareth's rapid-fire questions might almost make me think he genuinely cares. But then I remember why we're in this mess, and my blood turns to ice.

"Be ready when we get there, Gareth. I don't care what shape you're in, I'll drag your arse out."

He hesitates, then thinks better of whatever he was going to say. "Fine."

We hang up, and I look down at Cormac. His head is resting in my lap as he stretches across the second row in one of our black SUVs. We look so fucking much alike. It's as though I'm staring at myself, having an out of body experience. He's not unconscious anymore.

"Shay, I can feel you watching me. It's creepy as feck."

"Sorry that I don't want to ignore you and let you die."

He tries to laugh and groans, his good arm going around his middle.

"Always so melodramatic. You love me too much to allow me to die. Besides, Mom would skelp you alive if you didn't come home bitching about how I'm the more popular one."

Trust my brother's sarcasm to not have drained out of him along with the blood. I suppose mine hasn't either. He knows it's a distraction from my antsiness, which I'm sure he's felt since I'd had to stop myself from jiggling my knee up and down.

"Shay, we're going to find her. I promise."

I hope he's right. I've always known I was the little brother even if we couldn't be much closer in age short of being real twins. He's seven months older than me, but I used to look up to him when we were really young. That was before I realized we were the same size and could do the same things because we've pretty much been developmentally at the same stage our entire lives. I was lucky as fuck that being a preemie by nearly nine weeks didn't cause me any lasting health issues. Nowadays, I give him shite for being the older brother but not being stronger or faster than me. But this is one time I pray he's right. The one time I want my big brother to know more than I do.

"You know I'm coming with you, right? I'll be the one Mom's skelping if your pretty face comes back with even a scratch."

I stare down at my idiot brother. "The feck you are. You were unconscious until ten minutes ago. You nearly bled to death."

"There's that melodramatic side again. You should have done theatre in high school. I was napping. I needed to get my strength back. I'm not staying behind, Seamus."

Our expressions match. Mulishness we inherited from the very woman who scares the shite out of us. We jest—sorta. Our mom and aunts are beautiful middle-aged women who laugh a lot and smell like flowers. They're also the most competitive rugby players I have ever met. They will take you out at the kneecaps, then help you up.

Before Tiera, no one could make the world right again like my mom. I know the other guys feel the same way about their moms, even if it's morphed a bit for the married guys. But heaven help us when our moms are mad at us. I'd rather go ten rounds in the ring with golden glove boxer Maksim Kutsenko.

"You've lost your fecking mind. Da, tell him he's not going."

I look over my shoulder at our dad, who's texting someone.

"He can come as long as he stays with the plane." Our dad's only half paying attention.

"Da, no!" Cormac doesn't agree. Shocking.

"Would you like me to send you home?" This time, Da looks up.

I can see his expression, but Cormac can't. I widen my eyes, warning Cormac to stay quiet. He doesn't take the hint. He grabs the back of the seat and the side, pushing himself to sit up. He goes puce.

"I am not letting my brother go without me. We've never been on missions without each other. It doesn't start today. I'm not having it."

I swallow my smile since he sounds like we did when we were five, and everyone discovered our tempers matched our hair. I look at Da, and he cocks an eyebrow. I pinch Cor's right ribs, but he shifts away. He's about to give Sean a run for his money as the stubbornest in the family.

"You are not leaving me behind."

Da shakes his head and goes back to texting. That only pisses Cormac off more.

"Can't you pay attention for two minutes? I'm going."

"I'm busy getting your uncles to round up my gear and meet us at the airport."

"What?" Six voices say the same word at the same time.

"Da, you can't go either. You have a mild concussion." I shake my head.

"Would you like me to send your cousins to find your girl-friend? Don't argue."

I scowl, but I wisely turn away from my dad before he can

see. I have more sense than Cormac. I'm thirty-fucking-two years old, and I still take orders from my dad. I know that'll never change, but he really would bar me from going if he thought I was a danger to myself or the others. He'll let Cormac go, and none of us will disagree. But we'll all insist my brother waits at the plane. He'll have a conniption, but it's the only compromise any of us will make. I'm certain Cor knows that.

If Da's getting Uncle Ronan and Uncle Tate involved, he believes we need them. They don't go on missions that often anymore, but they can. They're still in as good shape as any of my generation are. They have more experience than us, so we still listen to their advice. We all follow their lead when they're with us. Even Dillan, who's our boss, follows behind his dad and uncles. If Da's getting his brothers, he wants to make sure no one walks away but us. He's also doing it so Tiera and I and the rest of the world know she's an O'Rourke now. She's as good as his daughter, and he'll burn the entire fucking world down to protect his kids.

I look back at him and nod. He offers me a tight smile, but he reaches out and covers my hand where it's resting on the seat back to keep it from bumping Cormac. He gives it a squeeze, and I have a moment of certainty that everything will be all right just like he said. I keep looking forward, wondering where the fuck my *cailín* is. I learned from the best. There won't even be ashes left of whoever did this.

Finn drove us to Dillan's house to grab our gear and let the airport know to get Shane's plane ready. While we were on the road—and I bickered with my dad and brother—Sean was combing through whatever it is he finds when he's piecing together someone's life history. He's sitting at Dillan's dining room table with his laptop and portable trifold monitors. No one's disturbing him while he works, but the rest of us are discussing what the mission will look like. Cormac's finally gotten his way, and Da and I relented that he could come without further argument. He admitted he wasn't up to anything more than waiting by the vehicle once we get wherever we're going. It's actually the most important job. If anything happens to our vehicles, and we have no way of leaving, it's usually a pretty sure death sentence.

I put my foot down when they turned the tables and tried to tell me I couldn't lead this mission, that I should hang back too because of my head and thigh. The fuck I am. I looked at every married man in the room—so everyone except Cormac and Shane—and asked them if they planned to hang back when it's their wife's turn to get rescued. None of them appreciated me insinuating something would happen to the women they love. I raised my eyebrows as if to say, "See? Try to stop me."

"You won't believe this shite."

We all turn to Sean as he looks up from his computer.

"Guess who's on the O'Brien payroll."

"I'm not in the mood to guess. Hurry up and spit it out." I'm not in the mood for anything but revenge and holding Tiera.

"Sam Wilkes. The fucker's double-dipping. He's been leaking info to Gareth for months. He's the one who dispatched the police to swoop up Mitchell. Gareth wants to pin us on the NYPD's radar and to cost us money to get them to lay off. Money Wilkes will invariably snag, then split between O'Briens and himself."

"Does he have anything to do with whoever's been bugging Tiera's place, work, and car? He'd have access to the high-end surveillance equipment."

"He's the shite to someone, but I don't know that it's connected. I don't recognize the name."

I walk over to peer over Sean's shoulder. He points to a name, and I want to throw something. Motherfucker. His death is going to be slow and excruciating. It might be the worst torture I've ever committed. My pulse throbs in my ears.

"I need a moment."

I ignore everyone else and head out Dillan's French doors to the backyard. I pace for a moment while I breathe.

You can't lose your shite. You can't lose your shite. If you lose your fucking shite, you can't think straight. You need to get to Tiera. Calm your arse down.

I talk to myself, trying to push back the rage. It's no use. I walk over to the rocks around a rose bush and pick one up. I hurl it as far as I can, as hard as I can. It whizzes through the air and sails halfway down a long backyard. I throw two more before I spend the urge to crush something. I head back inside to eight faces watching me. My uncles met us here, their go bags and my dad's waiting by the door. Clothes, money, passports, and weapons. We can travel light.

"He's someone from Tiera's past that's taken advantage of her at her most vulnerable. He's betrayed her for years. She trusted her wellbeing to him, and he's been abusing her all along, and she never knew it."

At their confused expressions, I grit my teeth. I don't want to reveal anything about Tiera's private life. I try to devise a way to hint at it without actually giving anything away. The longer I look at everyone the more it dawns on them without me having to say.

I don't want to know about my parents or aunts and uncles, but I know all the men in my generation have similar proclivities. I've heard some of the wives call their husbands Daddy, and I suspect it's for the same reason Tiera does. I know for a fact none of them are Daddy Doms, and only Sean, Cormac, and I have had long-term subs.

The others—including my dad and uncles—ew—nod their understanding. At least I don't have to say it.

"What's his address, Sean?"

He rattles off a place in Astoria that's a half an hour from Forest Hills on a good day, assuming there isn't too much traffic.

"Are you certain about Wilkes's involvement?"

"Yeah. I traced the money, calls, and texts. They all lead to this guy."

"I want Wilkes at the station." I look at Dillan when I speak.

He nods and pulls out his phone. He'll make sure Sam Wilkes is strung up naked and afraid until I get around to dealing with him. I want to know more from Sean.

"What about this fuck wad? Is he the one extorting Gareth?"

"It looks like it. But I don't know why. He's good at covering his tracks. There are only a few things linking them together, and it's vague at best. But I'm certain there's a connection."

"Then that's where we go first."

No one questions it. Instead, we suit up in our black tactical gear. Our moms, Ally, Nikki, and Mair were hanging out in the family room while we met in the dining room. Even with Dillan's spacious study, it still gets tight with all nine of us in there. We each take up a lot of space. The dining room is like our board room when our dads are here too.

I watch my parents say goodbye. I've always thought it was sweet, but now I have a pang of jealousy that's only amplified when I watch Aunt Siobhan and Uncle Tate, Aunt Saoirse and Uncle Ronan, Dillan and Mair, Finn and Ally, and Sean and Nikki. I don't want to leave Tiera behind to go off to do God knows what. But I want to know I have her to come home to.

Sabine Barclay

"Soon, cousin."

I turn to look at Shane. He offers me an understanding smile and nod. I return it before walking to my parents. My mom wraps her arms around Cormac and me as best she can. I feel Cormac sigh the same as I do when our arms go around each other too. My dad is behind us, making a sandwich with my brother and me in the middle. I know my cousins are getting the same from their parents. We try to never leave on missions without this moment as a family. We all know how easily it could be our last.

Husbands and wives exchange one last hug and kiss before we pile into an SUV Shane drives. I look out the front passenger window as we wind our way through Queens. I shoot off texts to Brant and Gareth, telling them we have a person of interest we need to check out before we fly down there. We could be cat burglars for how quietly we creep up the stairs to the fourth floor. Sean slides a camera beneath the door, which isn't easy since there's a rug right inside. He looks at the image on this wrist display. He holds it out for us to see.

The living room and kitchen are empty. We spotted the shit bag's car in the garage as we sneaked in. But that doesn't guarantee he's home. He's more likely to use public transportation than drive. I pull out my lock picking set and jiggle the tools until the bolt turns. I slide the packet into my cargo pants' pocket. With our weapons at the ready, I ease the door open. We pour into the condo. Cormac's downstairs with the SUV, so I'm paired with my dad. I point toward what I'm sure is the main bedroom.

When we get to the door, I hear a woman moan. Fucking hell. I press my earpiece, barely whispering when I let the others know.

"*Titim ar ais. Níl sé ina aonar.*" Fall back. He's not alone.

"Sir."

344

I freeze. I know that voice.

"That's a good little slut."

My gaze darts to my dad who glances at the door before moving away. He turns a corner, staying close enough to cover me, but he won't be able to see in when I kick the door open. I'm certain he can still hear Tiera.

My mind feels fuzzy. My vision tunnels to black like I'm about to pass out, but I feel more alert than I ever have. What the fuck is she doing in there?

I kick the door open and freeze.

Zack Montgomery spins around, his hand still on his dick. He takes me in. Black cargo pants. Black shirt. Black gloves. Black beanie. Black rifle. His mouth hangs open as he lets go of his dick, which wilts as he stands buck arse naked while a video of him with Tiera plays on a big screen TV between two windows. He's jacking off to the woman he terrorized and stalked for three years.

"Why?"

He grins at me as though I'm not pointing a high-powered, high-caliber gun at him. I raise it to a shooting position, and he gets real serious, real fast.

"Because it was entertaining."

I wait for more, but he offers nothing else. As I stare at him, I realize he's serious. He did all this because he could.

"Why Tiernan?"

"Because she amused me with how desperate she was for someone—anyone—to care about her. To make her feel worth living. I had that power. I knew when I pushed her away, she'd fall into despair. When I drew her closer, I knew I could make her do anything. I held her life in my hand because I could."

Sick and twisted bastard.

"Why the O'Briens?"

"Darren owed me money. He sold her to me in a way. He

had her followed and knew she joined a BDSM club. He told me how desperate she was and that I could have her to do what I wanted in exchange for paying down his debt. You killed him before he finished paying me off. He owed a lot. When I went to collect, Gareth refused. It pissed me off. I knew he cared about Tiernan like a sister. I made him dance to my tune by threatening her."

"He knew all along it was you?"

"No. Darren knew who I was. I remained anonymous to Gareth. It was far more intimidating and persuasive."

"You did all of this to fuck with a widow? You accepted her in place of cash?"

"Yes. I mean, you've fucked her. Watch her on the screen. She loves it rough. I might not have liked how flabby she got, but that was a small price for the way she begged. The way her tongue felt wrapped around—"

I can't listen to any more. I aim my gun at his junk and squeeze the trigger. I've shot guys there before. I know exactly where to aim to penetrate—poor pun intended—the dick and balls.

"Where is she?"

His grin is nothing short of malevolent despite the incredible pain he must be in. He's taunting me. I shoot the right side of his pelvis. He reacts as though nothing's happened.

"Was Tiera a top sometimes? Or do you have your own Domme?"

Surprise flashes in his eyes before he sneers at me.

"That weak bitch is too pathetic to ever command anyone. She can barely keep her shit together to put one foot in front of the other. She lives because I let her. I gave her the confidence to keep going just like I could yank her chain and make her want to end it all."

"You sick fuck."

If I didn't still need to find her, I would end it right now. I can't stand looking at the sado-masochist. He enjoys receiving pain as much as he enjoys doling it out. He probably has a Domme since he's obviously used to extreme pain.

"You're nowhere near as good as you think you are. You shouldn't have walked away without checking that the job was done. You might have singed your eyebrows, but you wouldn't be searching for your fuck bunny if you had."

What the hell—No. No.

"That was fast. You know who. But you don't know where."

As though on cue, my phone buzzes in my pocket. I'd ignore it if there were no chance it could be Tiera calling for help. I slide the phone from my pocket. Right now? That fucker? I push it back into my pocket.

"What? Not your little girl—your *cailín*—calling to beg you to rescue her pitiful fat ass."

My phone buzzes again as I put another bullet into him. This time the left side of his pelvis. None of these three wounds will kill him immediately, but they should immobilize him, even if he revels in this kind of twisted pain. I tap the preview

ALEJANDRO

We know where she is. Darren

I can't see the rest. I unlock the screen and tap the app.

ALEJANDRO

We know where she is. Darren has her. We're on our way.

I killed the arsehole... At least, I believed I did. He has to be dead. He couldn't have survived the bullet I put in him or how I disposed of his body. Or rather how I thought I disposed of his body. That's what Zack alluded to a moment ago. I'm still holding Zack at gunpoint when I tap on Alejandro's contact.

Yes, we have each other on speed dial. All four families have each other on speed dial. For many of us, we got those numbers from each other when we were kids and still played little league sports together. That's how fucked-up this life is. Alejandro used to be on my t-ball team, then my baseball team all the way through middle school. We played travel ball. We liked each other for the most part most of the time as kids. Though he never forgave me for allegedly breaking his Hot Wheel. That was his shitbag cousin Juan, who's already dead.

We'd all play sports together on the weekends, and our dads had to play nice with each other. They were the snack parents alongside our parents. Monday rolled around, and they were plotting how to kill each other. It went on that way all the way through high school. We were friends until we each turned twelve and started carrying knives. The truces ended when we were each fourteen and started getting in fights with one another away from school and athletics. It was war once we were each sixteen and started going on missions.

Why should I believe him?

Why shouldn't I?

I can't risk him telling me the truth and me ignoring it out of spite. If it's a trap, I'll finally kill the motherfucker. If it isn't, I might buy him a new fucking Hot Wheel.

I hit the call button, and it doesn't even ring.

"Shay, Darren has her. She's at the old mill outside Elizabeth."

Shite. Elizabeth's an hour from the city. Lord only knows what they've done to her in the time it's taken to get our shite together. At least, it's closer than Trenton.

"How do you know?"

"Because until today, it was useful knowing Darren was

still alive. He crossed a line a long time ago that we didn't know existed. He called me today. He bragged about having Tiernan and about selling her. He knew about the shit that happened with Maria and thought we'd be into it."

Maria Mancinelli was kidnapped in Miami and almost sex trafficked by a Cuban. All the families helped each other because Misha Kutsenko's sister-in-law was also a victim. Maria is neutral ground like Colleen was until Declan—Maria is the kindest soul alive. She's nothing like her shitbag family. She was kind to all of us when we were growing up. She doesn't like any of us now, but she's the only one who's still polite.

The Diazes role in saving her was playing along with their Cuban contact to find out where she was. Apparently, Darren doesn't know the Diazes killed the fucker.

"What the fuck are you doing about this? Why are you already on your way and just now telling me?"

"Because I had a meeting with him before we found out he had your girlfriend. We were already on the road when Darren called to tell me to bring more money."

"Tell me the rest later. Send me the address. What do you know about Zack Montgomery?"

I haven't taken my eyes off the motherfucker since I tapped the call button. I watched fear enter his eyes when he realized who I was talking to.

"You know him?"

"He's part of Tiera's past. He's been stalking her for three years."

"Kill him."

"I don't take orders from you. Besides, he's already dead." Okay. Good as dead.

"He tried to seduce my aunt just last week. He heard she was a wealthy widow and targeted her. He wanted her to sign over her entire inheritance—from my grandfather and my uncle

Sabine Barclay

—but she refused and went to *Tío Enrique* straight away. He threatened her two days ago, so my uncle stepped in. He just ordered *Tres J's* to pick him up tonight. They were going to take him to our place. If you've already done the work for us, I suppose I can thank you."

"You can, but you haven't."

"I will when you will. Thank me for saving your girlfriend, then I'll thank you for helping my aunt."

"Arsehole. If I helped your aunt like you claim, your gratitude shouldn't be conditional. I'll be sure to tell her the next time I see her at a reception."

"Should I mark a date on the calendar for your wedding?"

"Pish off. Do you want the body?"

I grin at Zack. He's heard the entire conversation since I've had it on speaker. Wisely, he's remained silent.

"Nah. We don't have time. We'll leave you Darren and Keith."

"Keith?" It shouldn't surprise me. It doesn't. It just pisses me off even more.

"He's been Darren and Zack's go-between. He's always been the bitch in the relationship."

"Get Tiera out of there, and I'll let you have the biotech company in Pennsylvania you want."

"Gee. *Gracias.*"

"If you—"

"Done."

"Let me know when she's safe."

"Will do."

I hang up and toss my phone on the bed. I stalk forward until my rifle's muzzle jabs into Zack's chest. I pull the trigger. I don't wait for him to hit the ground. I put a bullet between the eyes as he drops in front of me. I'll never walk away again without making sure the man is dead.

350

Chapter Twenty-Five

Tiera

I'm Catholic and a pretty good one—mostly. I squeeze my eyes shut about the "thou shalt not steal" one. So, as the product of a great Catholic school education, I can't believe Darren's been resurrected to stand before me. He is *not* the one I expected to come again.

"Shocked to see I'm not dead?"

"Regretful is more like it."

Blind rage rises from the tips of my toes, shooting a burning heat far more intense than the fucking cow prod. It engulfs me, urging me to lash out. Only a single synapse in my brain says, "don't do it yet."

If I attack him, I'll kill him before he can tell me why. If I attack him, I won't live long enough to learn why.

"Did your boyfriend tell you he was the one to pull the trigger? No? Pity you won't be the one to tell him he failed. If he gets to you before the bears or bobcats do, he'll see how it's really done."

I didn't know Seamus was the one to shoot Darren. He never hinted, and I never dreamed of asking. I suspected an O'Rourke murdered him, but the perpetrator left no evidence. The only reason I believed it was them was because Gareth suddenly became indebted to them in a way Darren had never been.

Gareth ordered me to examine the remnants of the car explosion to determine what caused it. I couldn't find it. Whoever'd set it was a pro. The coroner found a hole in the skull of the charred remains, but someone had knocked out all the teeth, so no dental records would identify him.

"You're wondering how I did it."

A light snaps on, and I blink as my eyes adjust. I'm on my feet again with someone holding my arms back. I don't think it's Keith since I got him with the cattle prod more times than he got me. I smelled his burning hair and skin. It made me retch, but it was the smell of a small victory.

I feel bile burn the back of my throat as I stare at Darren's nearly unrecognizable face. The burns on both sides of it and his neck are macabre. I dart my gaze to his hands. They're no better. How the hell did he survive short of being the devil himself?

"Do you know who pulled me out just in the nick of time?"

If he says Gareth, I'll murder them both with my bare hands.

"Your dad. In all fairness—before you lose your shit on your poor old dad—he thinks I'm dead. I should have been. He only pulled me out so he could put Jimmy Patricks's body in there for me. He knew there couldn't be a record that the O'Rourkes succeeded in murdering me. He got Jimmy in place and out of the way right before the second explosion. If he'd been a foot closer, he'd have died instead of me."

Darren laughs. It stretches his already grotesque face into something that looks like Harvey Dent—Two Face—from *Batman*. The movie version with Aaron Eckhardt—fuck—the irony—the pathos—of that. My Aaron is dead, and Darren survived. It ignites my rage all over again.

"Don't you want to know how I survived?" He can't stand that I won't ask.

Darren's too narcissistic to believe anyone isn't interested in him when he's the center of the story. I want to know like I need my next breath. But I refuse to give him the satisfaction of asking. He'll volunteer an explanation if I wait long enough. He can't help himself. He likes nothing more than to talk about himself.

"I don't care if you think to wait me out, Tiernan. I prefer the sound of my own voice to yours any day."

I stare but don't move. I think he wants to snarl, but he can't pull his lips back that far. I'm goading him rather than the other way around, and it's driving him nuts.

"Your dad called Vince and Keith to come and get my body. He knew I was alive, but he was certain I wouldn't last the time it took for them to get to me. He'd wrapped me in a blanket and rolled me around to put out the fire that was burning my skin from my bones."

A fiberglass fire blanket. They can extinguish small fires. I gave my parents three sets each one year for Christmas. Since they're highly heat resistant, they're often used by wildfire firefighters to protect themselves when the wind changes, and the flames blow over them. It would have put out the flames of hell that licked at Darren's heels. My dad's going to regret what he did for the rest of his life. But he did what he was supposed to: save his mob boss before all else.

"Vince and Keith were nearby since they were supposed to

be at the meeting too, but I'd suspected the O'Rourkes were going to attempt my assassination."

Assassination makes him sound far more important than he is. Murder would be more fitting. If only Seamus had succeeded.

"They got me to Mikey, who got me into a private hospital without any questions. Amazing what money and Vince could do. Seamus put a bullet through my head, and God's benevolent mercy healed me."

I want to smash him in the face. He's never believed in anything but himself. He never went to church, not even to make a show of support to families at baptisms, weddings, and funerals. He couldn't be bothered. He waited around for people to kiss the ring. He's mocking my faith.

"I spent nearly a year recovering. Once the bullet was out and the skin grafts were complete, it was a matter of waiting and plotting."

Darren died—supposedly, I guess—not long after Aaron. Gareth, Vince, and Keith made it sound like the harassment started before the car bomb, then escalated almost immediately. Did it take a year? Was Keith carrying out Darren's orders and doing the dirty work? Vince clearly crossed Darren since he lost his head for it.

The timelines never seem to match up whenever I think about them. Gareth said things started before his dad died. But what did? I wouldn't know since no one fucking told me. Darren orchestrated the car accident, but was that because someone was already extorting him? Did Aaron or I piss him off, so he made sure someone picked up his mantle after we thought he died?

"Don't think so hard, *cailín*. It'll hurt your pretty little head."

My place was bugged. Or maybe my car. Or I don't know where because I can't remember all the places Seamus has called me that. I thought only outside and in my home. But Kieran searched it. Did someone go in and collect them while Seamus and I were in Trenton? Was his car bugged?

"You don't like it when I call you Seamus's pet name for you. What else was it he called you? His slut. His whore. Sounds about right. You let Keith only fuck you from behind because that was the only way he could get it up with you. You wanted it so much you never questioned it. You begged Aaron to fuck you when he still wanted Hillary. What man wouldn't take a woman who threw herself at him? I guess you were a better lay since he kept coming back. You could only get your Dom's dick up when he practically beat you to get hard. But I can't fathom why a man like Seamus O'Rourke, who's been fucking a woman who looks like a supermodel, walked away from the perfect little submissive for a sow like you."

How does he know anything about my Dom? Darren was around when I was with Keith and Aaron. He's clearly around for Seamus. Who fed him information about—

"The penny just dropped, didn't it?"

The betrayal I feel threatens to snap my resolve. Zack used everything I ever confided against me. I never invited him into my home, and he never rode in my car. I don't know how he got into either of them, but he worked for Darren. He approached me one night at the club I'd just joined. I'd figured out what was missing after reading that book *The Red Drifter of the Sea*. The relationship—a realistic version of the erotic fantasy—was what I wanted. But I didn't want it to be romantic. I didn't want to risk giving my heart to anyone else. How repulsed was Zack to have to keep fucking me as I gained weight? He did it because it was a job. That's all I was. Man-whore.

"Why reveal yourself now?" It's the first question I've asked.

"Because the timing's right. Someone wants to fuck with the O'Rourkes even more than I do. Alex!"

A swarthy man I don't recognize walks in. He's drop dead gorgeous. Like too good to be true. Like he makes Armani models look like schlubs pulled off the street. Like so hot you can't look away because it draws you like you're craning your neck to see a car wreck. He's got the too perfect look Finn has.

He does nothing for me. He's not rugged like Cormac. He's definitely built, but he doesn't have the bulky build that makes me feel shielded from the world. There isn't enough muscle for me to run my hands over, finding more dips and ripples each time he flexes. He doesn't make my panties—if I wore them—wet like Seamus has since the moment I saw his back.

"Alejandro, fuck nut. We aren't friends."

The man snaps at Darren, and I watch my tormentor—co-tormentor—swallow. Menacing with a soulless aura radiates from the man as he prowls past Darren and comes to stand before me. He looks over my shoulder at whoever is restraining me and lifts his chin. The hands release me immediately.

"Tiernan, I'm Alejandro Diaz."

He has the audacity to stick his hand out to shake mine. I don't look at it, and I don't offer mine. My gaze locks with his, and I refuse to blink until I can't stand it. It's a second after he blinks first. He grins, his white teeth looking like they belong on a toothpaste commercial.

"I get why Seamus wants you. Spunky."

He grows serious as soon as the last sound is out. He surveys me like he's buying a racehorse. I half expect him to peel my lips back and examine my gums. He wraps his hand in my hair and tugs until my head snaps back. He runs the back of his fingers along my neck before he leans in to whisper. His accent is the distinct Spanish speaking New Yorker.

"You are going to make me a lot of money, *señorita*."

"You plan to ransom me to Seamus?"

"Eventually. Not before I sell you to someone else first."

There's something in his tone. It's like he doesn't quite believe himself. But maybe it's all to fuck with me, and he should win an Oscar. I don't know. I don't want to know. I want out.

"You want World War Three."

"Such a cliché, *chica*. I know this'll start a war with the O'Rourkes. That's exactly what I want. I also want the money a man's already promised me for you."

A man? Who the fuck wants to buy me?

"I didn't know your family were sex traffickers. Does your uncle know what you're doing?"

Enrique Diaz is the head of the Colombian Cartel in New York. He's also one of the most powerful men in the world. I've heard of him, but I know little about him. I just know nothing comes in or out of Latin America without his permission.

"My uncle trusts me to do whatever's needed to make our family more money."

"And selling women is one of them?"

"Selling you is one of them."

"Why me?"

"Because you're who Seamus wants."

"Did he steal your favorite toy or something when you were in preschool?"

"He did actually. He took my favorite Hot Wheels, but that's not why I took you. I got back at him by wrecking his Mercedes Maybach the day after he got it. I took you from him just so he knows I can. Just so all the O'Rourkes know I can."

Alejandro turns toward Darren and gestures him over. The

gleam in Darren's eyes tells me he expects a fat payout. Alejandro practically rolls his eyes in disgust.

"*Javier, llévala al auto.*" Take her to the car.

Another man steps into the light. He looks remarkably like Alejandro. They share the same features, but his aren't quite as perfectly symmetrical as Alejandro's. He's still shockingly good looking. But arrogance oozes from him, and it's off putting to an extreme. He grabs my arm, but his hold is surprisingly gentle. When I look at him, his gaze warns me to remain silent.

I realized while we talked the men who kidnapped me brought me to an abandoned grain factory. The air was stale, and I recognized the machinery. The thing that's like a massive funnel that drops grain onto a conveyor belt gave it away. Javier guides me to the door. We're just about to step outside when I hear Alejandro call out.

"*¡Ándele!*"

Two men who could be twins—actually triplets to Javier—enter with rifles. There are silencers on them, but I see the muzzle flash since the light was on but dim. They shoot men I never noticed. Keith tries to run, but one man puts a bullet through the back of his knee. Darren's frozen in place with Alejandro's gun between his eyes. I watch as five men drop. They're the ones with the fake NYPD uniforms on.

"We need to go."

Javier's accent is different from Alejandro's. He's not a native English speaker. His Spanish accent is too thick. That scares me even more since he really is a Colombian sex slaver. I fight against him. I don't want to leave. I don't know where I'm going next. I refuse to go with him any easier than I did the men who came into my home. I don't let his gentleness fool me after the blood bath I just witnessed.

"Tiernan, Seamus is looking for you. We've arranged a meetup. We have to go."

I writhe against him. "I don't believe you."

"I know, and I don't blame you. But you need to trust my brothers and me. My cousin put on a show to get you away from Darren. He and my brothers are going to stay until Seamus can get here and decide what to do. He needs to know you're safe first."

"You're lying."

"Don't struggle. If I leave a bruise on you because you fought me, Seamus will castrate me. I have plans tonight."

"He'll kill you."

"He's tried, but I refuse to give him the satisfaction. Seriously, Tiernan. Stop fighting me. I'm stronger than you. You will go where I want. I don't want to hurt you to do it.

I keep resisting, so he scoops me over his shoulder. He's the same size as his cousin and brothers, so he's by no means a small man. But he's not the same as Seamus and Cormac. He's more like a normal sized mobster. My guess is the same size as Seamus's cousins. It shocks me how easily he lifts me since he doesn't strike me as a man as strong as Seamus. I guess he is.

"I will spank you if you kick me one more time."

"You wouldn't dare. If you really take me to Seamus, I'll tell him you touched me inappropriately."

I can't believe I'm saying that. It sounds fucking ridiculous. It is fucking ridiculous. I refuse to give up my struggle. I won't go any more willingly with him than I did the other men who took me. They forced me to walk past Seamus, then they put a sack over my head. I couldn't see anything until the light came on in the factory.

I realize Javier's told me Seamus is alive. Alejandro did too. I can't remember what Darren said, but maybe he gave that away as well. I knew he couldn't be dead. I refused to believe he was. I'm certain I would have known in my marrow if he was dead. God, does he think I am? Does he think he's trying to recover my body rather than rescue me?

"Primo, cuidado. Silba y araña como un puma." Cousin, watch out. She hisses and scratches like a puma.

Javier chuckles as we approach a man who is Seamus's size. He's burly like Seamus, but where Seamus is fair, this man is even more olive skinned than Alejandro and Javier. Cousin? Is this man Alejandro's brother? They look as much alike as Javier did Alejandro.

"Ms. Furey—" Another Spanish New York accent. "—Seamus will be here soon. Don't make us lock you in the vehicle. We can't leave the key in there to keep the air conditioning on. It will get hot fast."

"If you want to lock me in there like a dog, you'll find out fast just how big a bitch I am."

The new guy has the audacity to laugh aloud. I feel Javier's shoulders shake with his silent mirth. I pull my left foot back and swing it into his junk as he lowers me. He drops me, and I tumble backwards. The unnamed man catches me, and his hold is as gentle as Javier's was when he first grabbed my arm.

"She's not going to give Seamus a chance to castrate me. I think she broke my *huevos*."

Eggs... He means nuts. Balls. Gonads. My aim is excellent.

"Ms. Furey, I'm Pablo Diaz. I'm *el tigre*. I know your father is in the mob. Do you know what that means?"

"The tiger. You must be pretty high up."

"I am. I'm my *tío's* heir. My men call me *el patron*. My official position is *el secretario*. The only person more senior to me is my uncle who's *jefe de jefes*. Boss of bosses."

"I know who he is. I can't believe he'd sanction you selling me to Seamus or anyone else."

"Ms. Furey, no one is selling you. My cousin said that to

make Darren hand you over. I'm certain whatever he said made your skin crawl. He's very believable."

"If that's the case, he's a psychopath."

Javier and Pablo laugh again. I see nothing funny about any of this. Pablo shakes his head, but he's still smiling when he responds.

"*Señorita*, we laugh because the O'Rourkes say the same thing about him. About all of us. They are the pot calling the kettle black."

"*Pablo, tenemos que áarnos prisa.*" We need to hurry up.

"*Yo hablo español.*" I speak Spanish.

"Then you understand we need to leave and get to a meeting point. Seamus won't want you to see—"

Javier has no chance to finish when an SUV that must seat eight pulls up. I don't know if they didn't see us or what, but O'Rourkes spill out of every door. I recognize Seamus immediately. I struggle against Javier and try to call out to Seamus. But Javier's hand goes over my mouth, and his arm is a steel bar around my middle.

"You missed your chance to leave. You can't distract him. There are more men than you saw. You're about to see what I'm certain Seamus prayed you never would."

Javier tries to turn me toward him, but I won't budge. Pablo steps in and tries to help. My foot kicks out and lands against the outside of Pablo's ankle. He pulls it back, and I take advantage of his momentary shift in balance. I throw my weight sideways as best I can while pushing against Javier's waist. I break his hold and swing my right fist, striking Pablo's throat since I can't reach higher. My elbow goes to Javier's nose.

Neither of them expects me to be as fast as I am. Nor do they expect me to be as agile as I weave away from them. It probably looks like I'm chasing an imaginary soccer ball. I'm nearly to the O'Rourkes vehicle—which I intend to lock myself into—when I hear the howls of pain. The muted sounds of gunshots reach my ears, and the ping of bullets hitting metal reverberates in the surrounding air.

I freeze with a clear view into the building. The O'Rourkes look like something in an action movie. They move with synchronicity that comes from hours of practice. They look like they're in the military as they work their way through the massive open factory.

I practically jump out of my skin when another hand covers my mouth. I try to scream.

"It's me. Cormac. Don't move, Tiernan. He'll see the motion and get distracted."

I sink against Cormac in relief. At least until I hear his grunt of pain. I try to pull away, worried I'm hurting him. But he pins me against him. His body feels the same as Seamus's, yet it feels nothing like his brother. They're built the same, but just like none of the handsome Colombians do anything for me, neither does Cormac. I just want to get to Seamus.

I can't tell who's Finn, Shane, Sean, Dillan, or the other three men since they all wear beanies to cover their red hair. From a distance, they look like the same man but seven of him. I think one is Kieran, so my guess is the other two are his brothers.

"My dad and uncles are in there. Don't distract them either. I want my entire family to come home tonight."

Cormac confirms my suspicions. I turn my head at movement to my right. Alejandro and two other men sprint toward us. I look to my left and see Pablo and Javier approaching slowly. When Alejandro and the other two are near the open door through which I'm watching Seamus and his family, they creep closer. No one wants to distract the men inside.

It feels like it takes forever, but it must have only been a few minutes before O'Rourkes and O'Briens—I suppose men loyal to Darren—stop shooting each other. Seamus pulls his beanie off and walks toward Darren, who's kneeling in front of one of Seamus's cousins. I'm unprepared for Seamus to pull a knife and stab Darren through the eye. I cringe, but don't turn away. Seamus pulls it out as the men outside with me try to shield my view.

"Let me see." Cormac's hand muffles my demand. It tightens over my mouth, so that I can't open wide enough to bite him. He's prepared.

I go still, hoping they believe I've finally given up. They don't. None of them move out of my way.

"Don't look, Tiernan. He wouldn't want you to see this. Please. He won't forgive himself if he finds out you saw that. This isn't the man he wants you to see when you look at him."

I shake my head, trying to get my mouth free. I headbutt Cormac, throwing my head back into his nose. It loosens his hold on my mouth.

"You don't decide that for me. I want to see him kill Darren. I want to know the bastard is finally dead. I want to know Seamus finished what he started. I want to watch Keith suffer for everything he did to me. I'm certain he's the one who fucked with my husband's car and killed him and our baby. I have a right to see."

I try harder than ever to get free. That rage I tamped down earlier to let Darren spew his truth consumes me now. I fight harder than I thought I could. It does me no good because Cormac doesn't let go, and now Pablo stands directly in front of me.

"Move the fuck out of my way. I have a right to watch the men who destroyed my life have theirs taken from them. It's my right."

I keep repeating the last sentence.

To subdue me without hurting me, Pablo shifts, and I can

see past him. I can see Seamus again. I watch as his knife slices off the little that's left of Darren's left ear. He says something, but I can't hear. Darren remains quiet. It's the wrong response because Seamus puts a gun to Darren's ribs. Blood explodes from the wound. Darren lurches sideways as he screams.

He hits the floor still screaming. Seamus kicks him in the belly. When Darren doubles over, Seamus's boot lands in his chest, pushing Darren onto his back. Seamus pounces, one knee pressing into Darren's chest as his fist rains down on Darren's face until there's surely nothing left of it. I watch, mesmerized, as Seamus lifts Darren's head and slams it into the floor over and over and over. Blood spreads out beneath Darren's body, coating Seamus's knee that's on the ground. He takes his knife to Darren's throat before putting a bullet straight between his eyes. Seamus stands and puts one through Darren's heart for good measure.

"Tiernan, don't watch any more. Seamus is going to be beside himself to know you saw that. Please. This isn't about you. It's about my brother. Please."

I hear Cormac's beseeching tone. I want to watch what happens to Keith, but I know he's right. I know this is going to upset Seamus to the point he might walk away rather than let me be near the man he is right now. That's the last thing I want. I nod and turn on my own.

I glance up and see the damage I did to Cormac's nose. I wince since it's clearly broken. My hands cover my mouth and nose as my eyes widen when I take in the blood on his face and collar, then the sling his arm should be in. He looks like he's going to pass out.

"Fuck. I'm going to kill his brother." I mutter more than anything else as I reach behind Cormac and try to open the SUV door.

"I'm not going to die yet. It would take attention away from Seamus's reunion with you, and he'll kill me for that."

Cormac offers me a lopsided smile. What the fuck? He's cracking jokes.

I turn my head when one of the Colombians I haven't met speaks up. His accent is as thick as Javier's.

"We laugh, or we cry. It's not very macho to cry in front of our men. We save the tears for when we're alone."

I twist to see who spoke. It's about the most profound thing I've ever heard. My gaze darts back to where Seamus is now working Keith over. I whip my head back around and reach for the car door again. I get it open a crack.

"Cormac, sit down. Seamus won't forgive me if I kill you. I'm so sorry. I didn't notice how wounded you are. How were you able to hold on to me?"

"Because no one means more to my brother than you. I'll do anything to protect you just like I would him. I used to ask my parents if we could trade Seamus for a sister. I get to keep a pretty cool brother and get an even better sister."

I stare up at him, and I must look like a beached fish. I'm in an alternative universe. I have to be. I'm fucking Dorothy in the Land of Oz. It's all a dream. The Colombians helping the Irish. Mobster and Cartel members cracking jokes while my boyfriend goes Vlad the Impaler on my stalkers. I seriously doubt this is how any O'Brien mission goes. I might be the one who needs to sit down.

"Tiera!"

I'd know that voice in a coma. The men move apart before I throw punches. I burst into a sprint as Seamus half runs, half hobbles toward me. He wraps his arms around me and lifts me off my feet, so my mouth is level with his. The rest of the world vanishes as we kiss. We can't stop. It's as though we both fear the other will disappear if we let go. We flick our tongues at each other before I suck his into my mouth. I feel how hard he is against my pussy. I want nothing more than to strip him and fuck him now that I know I'm going to live, and he survived a gun fight.

When we pull apart, I run my fingers through his hair. I notice the lump on the back of his skull as our foreheads press together. I open my mouth to demand he put me down when I realize it was what knocked him out.

"*Cailín*, I'm going to spank your arse raw for watching."

Chapter Twenty-Six

Seamus

"Yes, Daddy. Do whatever you want as long as you don't let go."

"I won't, little one. You're free of them. All of them."

"Zack—"

"I know. We'll talk about it later, but he can never hurt you again."

"Did you do to him what—"

"Tiera, you shouldn't have seen that. I never wanted you to know—"

"Seamus, please tell me you did the same thing to Zack. I want him to have suffered. It would have taken a lot. He likes pain."

Now that the adrenaline's wearing off, I'm feeling every bit of agony I ignored. I close my eyes and swallow down the bile that's burning my throat.

"Seamus, oh, my God. You need to sit down. What the fuck

am I doing? What the fuck are you doing? You're ready to pass out. Fuck me."

"I will in a bit, *mo stóirín*. I just need to rest for little."

Uncle Tate and Uncle Ronan see how I sway and rush over. I let them hold me up as I talk to Tiera.

"He's dead." A black tunnel seems to close around me and not from hyper-focus. "He suffered, but there wasn't time to make it what you just saw. I'm sorry."

Things go black, but it felt like only a minute passed. When I wake, there are smelling salts under my nose. I recoil, having always loathed their scent, which is exactly why they work. Tiera's crying, and her face is ashen. I reach for her, and she takes my hand.

"I'm sorry, little one."

"Don't apologize, Daddy." Her lips are beside my ear, so no one else hears her. Her words are only for me.

"I didn't mean to scare you, and I'm sorry I didn't give you what you needed."

"I needed Zack, Darren, and Keith dead, so they can never come near me. I don't care how it happened. They can't hurt either of us."

"I'm sorry I failed to protect you. I've promised so many times to always—"

"Stop, Seamus." She snaps at me, and it surprises us both. She gentles her tone. "You did *not* fail me. Don't say that. We live in a fucked-up world where we need bodyguards because this sort of shit happens. If there weren't credible threats, then no one would need protection. There were at least nine of them. I know you and Cormac and your dad killed at least four or five. There were four who came for me upstairs. No matter your training, they outnumbered you. You weren't in a great defensive position, and they had more weapons than you. Don't blame yourself. I don't. All that matters to me is that you survived. I knew you'd come for me."

"Tiera, I wish I could offer you a better life."

"You either need a shit ton more pain meds, or you're already on a shit ton if you can't see you are my better life. I've had plenty of time to think about us and how I feel. I know there's no one else I'll ever want. How could I? You're the most handsome, intelligent, kind, sexy man alive."

"Even more than Alejandro?" I know what people with a pulse and any sexual appetite think about him.

"He's too pretty."

I hoot with laughter, but fuck if that doesn't hurt. I turn my head from where I'm now sitting up in the back of the SUV.

"Alejo! Did you hear that? My girlfriend thinks you're too pretty." Tiera swats at me. "I didn't even tell her I've been saying that since we were ten, and you cried because I bruised your cheek when I punched you. You thought Emily Melvick wouldn't think you were cute enough to have a crush on. Turns out, you weren't. She had a crush on me."

"I might be pretty, but my woman doesn't fight better than me."

"You don't have a woman."

I watch Alejandro shrug. "I'd still pick Tiernan over you in a fight. You're the one who punches like a girl."

I furrow my brow, and Tiera blushes until her cheeks are fuchsia.

"What did you do?"

"Your girlfriend's head is as hard as yours. She broke my nose." Cormac steps into sight, and he has cotton orange wedges up each nostril. His eyes are already blackening.

"Cormac! I'm so, so sorry. I—"

Tiera bursts into tears. I glower at my brother as I wrap my arms around her.

369

"Shh, *cailín*. He probably deserved it."

That didn't help because she cries harder. I jerk my head, and Cormac steps away. He'll make sure no one from our family interrupts. The Diazes are already getting in their cars, so I'm not worried about them seeing me with Tiera. I push myself all the way back in our SUV's trunk until my back hits the third row.

"Come here, Tiera." I hold out my arms.

She looks around before she climbs into the back with me. She leans against me, but she's careful not to put any weight on me. I don't like it. I pull her until she's half draped over me, and my hand can reach her arse. Life is good.

"What's the matter? We're both safe.

"I was horrible when they wouldn't let me see what you were doing. I deserved to see. I kicked and scratched and punched. They wouldn't move so I could see some of what you did to Darren."

My blood runs cold. When I looked out of the building and spotted her, she was much closer to the door than I expected. But with the men surrounding her, all of them at least half a foot taller than her, I assumed she hadn't seen anything. That she'd tried but couldn't.

"I told you I would spank you for watching. You better tell me just what you saw."

She retreats and doesn't want to look at me when she sits up. I capture her hand before she can scoot away. I tug, but not too rough. She shakes her head. I sit up straighter and inch myself over until we're hip-to-hip.

"Cormac said you'd be upset. I should have listened. I broke his nose because I wanted to see, and I didn't like him telling me no. What kind of person am I?"

"One who's had a lot taken from her. To see those who did it punished might have restored some of the power you lost. To

370

not see it felt as unjust as the loss itself. I get why, Tiera. But I hate you saw me like that. I never wanted that. I never want you to look at me and see the monster I can be. I don't—"

"Wait. Seamus, do you think that's what I see, or I will see? That I'll think you're a monster for protecting me? That you're a monster because you never want those men to come near me again? That's not what I see at all. I'm grateful that you did what you did. That you're capable of doing it. I wanted revenge, but I was in no position to get it. I've known all along what you're trained to do, and it's never made me want to walk away. I'm not surprised by what you did. You do it because you have to. I *wanted* to do it. I *wanted* you to do it. What kind of person does that make me? How fucked-up am I? Do you want to be with a sociopath?"

I tilt my head down to kiss her temple. I see the bruise from where she either got hurt struggling against Cormac or when the men took her. I'm careful not to press too hard.

"You are not a sociopath, T. You aren't broken or damaged. You're hurt and still scared. How could you not be? If you can accept me for what you saw, then I will count myself fortunate. I don't want you any different from how you are now. I'm certain I told you that before."

"And I'm certain I said the same thing in response. Shay, I want us to go home and have a lot more than those five days."

"We're going to, baby girl. And not just because I need to convalesce. The outside world belongs outside. It's just the two of us."

I know that won't last, and I'll be lucky if I get an entire day, but I can dream. I have to deal with Brant and Gareth. I haven't forgotten about either of them. I just didn't include Brant once I discovered Sam and Zack were involved. It was bad enough what my dad heard. I didn't want her dad there, too. It'll mortify her when she finds out my dad might have thought she was having sex, and we could hear her. It would horrify her if her dad did.

"Daddy, we both know it won't happen. I said I want that. I didn't ask if we could have it. I know better than that. This isn't over. I'm certain you called my dad, and he's got to be tearing Gareth to shreds right now. You need to learn whether Gareth truly was ignorant. Can we go to your place for tonight once my parents know I'm safe?"

"Of course. Whatever you want."

"Will you hold me for a couple more minutes? I know we have to go."

"No one is going to rush us."

She nestles against me again, and my hand slides up and down her back three times before I cup her arse. I still haven't fucked my future wife there. It probably won't be tonight since I might pass out the next time I stand up. But I'm sure as fuck going to watch her come.

"*Dadeee!*" She hisses the word.

"What?"

"Are you thinking about us having sex?" She's so quiet I can barely hear her.

"I'm thinking about making you come on my face."

"Oh, my God. Seamus, shh. Someone's going to hear you. It's bad enough it'll only take one glance to know you've been thinking about someone."

"Not someone. You. I'm thinking about you. Nobody gets me hard but you."

"Nobody gets me wet but you."

"Not even Alejandro?" Where the fuck did that come from? I did not mean to say that out loud.

Tiera rolls fully onto her side and pushes up on her hand. She cups my jaw and leans in to press a tender kiss that makes me feel like an idiot for asking.

"It's like walking onto a movie set with New York's syndicates. It should be mathematically impossible that every man from the ruling families is hot. Like those odds are steeper than anything in Vegas. I'm not blind, nor am I going to pretend to be. The other men are attractive, and Alejandro is hotter than most. But there is only one man who makes me wet. One man who makes my pussy ache. One man whose cock I want pressed against my tongue. One man I want to feel inside me, whose cum I want inside me. I only want you, Seamus. No one comes close to how attractive you are to me. Let someone else fall for Alejandro. I couldn't give two shits who. I'm too busy wanting you to care about anyone else."

"Did you know you're a sweet, sweet woman?" I grin like a fool.

"Do you remember the pain pills your dad gave you when you came round?"

"No."

"I think they just kicked in."

"In that case, I'm invincible. I think I'll tell everyone to fuck off, so I can fuck my girlfriend."

"*Dadeee!*"

"I love making you say that, that way."

We hear a loud throat clearing, and Tiera ducks her head against my chest. I wrap my arm around her shoulders and give her a squeeze. Can't we have one private conversation?

"What Finn?"

"We need to get going. Brant's been chewing Dillan and your dad out for the last ten minutes. They muted it and have been talking about dinner while he rants. Tiernan really needs to call him, and we need to head out."

"Shit." Tiera tries to scramble out of the back of the SUV, and I'm tugging her wrist again.

"Finn, bring us the phone." I cup Tiera's ear after I sit up with a groan. "I've heard his wife, Ally, call him Daddy when she thought no one could hear. I've heard him call her *cailín*. You're the only one I've called that, but I suppose I got the idea from him, Dillan, and Sean. I'm pretty positive their marriages are like our dynamic. He won't tell anyone."

She nods, but she's blushing again. She's gorgeous.

Finn pokes his head around the open door long enough to hand the phone to Tiernan. She takes it off mute.

"Dad, it's me. Dad. Dad, listen. It's me. I'm okay."

I listen to Tiera speak to her father for five minutes. It takes that long for him to calm down and to stop threatening my life. He's rightfully pissed I didn't let him come. Tiera lets him vent his spleen. But when she's had enough, she lets Brant know.

"Dad, if this had happened when Aaron was alive, he would have deferred to you. You would have been the man to decide how to protect me. I told you at Gareth's what I'm telling you now. Seamus decides. I love you and I don't trust you any less than I always have, but Seamus is who I need and who I trust the most. When it comes to my safety and the family we hope to have one day, you must let Seamus decide."

"Are you pregnant, Tiernan?"

"No. I'm not married or even engaged. But everyone knows that when an O'Rourke lets a woman into his life, he won't let go."

No truer words have ever been spoken.

"Dad, we have to go. Seamus and Cormac are both injured. I don't know how they're running on fumes, but they are. They both got shot protecting me. Seamus is looking flushed, and he's sweating."

I want to think she's saying that to get her dad off the phone, but I realize she isn't wrong. I don't feel so well all of a sudden.

It's been two days of sweating my arse off and feeling like death. Apparently, I shouldn't have sweat into my leg wound, and I shouldn't have rested on my knee to whale on someone's face. So much for it just being a graze. I got it infected. But I don't regret it. Darren is dead, and so is Keith. They can never come near Tiera again. Zack can never fuck with her mentally or emotionally ever again. I'll take feeling like shite warmed over to know I protected her in the future even if I failed her the other day.

She's been by my side since the moment I passed out in the SUV. I don't remember how I got home. Plane? Car? Pegasus? She was holding my hand each time I came to. I just needed to know she was still safe. Then I was out of it again. We're at my place, and I woke once to her arguing with Dillan about getting some rest. I caught something about how he should go home to his wife and hide behind her because Tiera was going to knock him out if he tried to make her leave again.

"*Cailín?*" I'm pretty sure I mumbled that several times because each time I did, I remember it feeling like someone kissed my forehead. I hope I didn't embarrass her by saying it in front of my family.

"Yes, Daddy. I'm here."

We must be alone.

"Will you get into bed with me?"

"I don't think that's a good idea, Seamus. I don't want to jostle you. You're supposed to remain immobilized as much as you can."

"And I think the only thing I need right now is to feel my future wife in our bed."

Shite.

I sense Tiera doesn't move. The room is completely still. I force my eyes open, and I see her staring at me. Did I imagine everything? Wasn't she here? Was it guilt that made her stay?

"Daddy, what did you just say?"

"I said my future wife should be in bed with me." I feel sick, and it isn't the fever I had.

She perches on the edge of the bed, careful not to touch me. "How drugged up do you feel?"

"Tiera, I'm not fevered. Check me. I'm not drugged up. I'm completely lucid for the first time in days."

I watch her lean forward to grab the thermometer from the bedside table. Her shirt gapes open, and I have a view down it.

"You have the finest pair of tits ever made." I look toward the door and see it's shut. "Take your shirt off. Now."

She looks down at me like she intends to ignore me and grabs the thermometer. I take it from her and toss it onto the far side of the bed.

"Don't make me repeat myself, little girl."

"Seamus, this really isn't—"

"Take it off before I rip it off." I try to move my left arm, but it doesn't cooperate. It's sorer than I expect after slamming it into the wall, then using it to eviscerate Darren's head. Some of the command is gone when I'm too weak to lift even my hand. I tug her forward and bite the front before yanking with the other hand.

"Okay, okay." She whips it over her head. Her push-up bra is completely unnecessary. I know how magnificent they are.

"No more bras either. When I want to suck your tits, I'll do it. I want nothing in my way. Fuck, Tiera. I'm hard."

"I see that."

She looks down the bed at my groin. The sheet's pushed up over my obvious arousal. She unclasps her bra and leans forward. She offers her tits to me, and I groan. My good hand squeezes her right one until she moans. She reaches across me to balance as she brings them to my mouth. I latch on and bite. Hard.

"Daddy." It's a breathy sigh that makes my cock twitch.

I switch and play with her other nipple. I flick it over and over, sucking every so often. I can tell she's just as aroused and needs to get off.

"Straddle my thigh, *cailín*."

"That's too much. You aren't supposed to move around."

"I'm not supposed to move my other leg. I can hold my future wife's arse as she grinds on my thigh until she gets off. Do it, or you'll turn around for a spanking. I still owe you at least one."

"You still want to punish me?"

"Yes. Tiera, what you saw—I don't like that you watched me do that. But it wasn't safe to be there. You ran toward an open door anyone could have shot through. God forbid we hadn't won, those men would have seen you and gone after you. You wouldn't have stood a chance to get away. I know no one—especially not my brother—wanted to manhandle you to restrain you. You could have gotten hurt. I told you your safety was the one thing I would never budge on, so I will punish you."

"Can I punish you for not taking care of yourself and doing too much? Can I punish you for going into the situation where you might not have been able to defend yourself? Can I punish you for overexerting yourself so much you've been unconscious for two days? Can I punish you for scaring me that you were going to die?"

Tears well in her eyes, and I hate I caused them.

"Come here, little one. Straddle my leg like I told you, but put your head on my chest."

I hold my good arm out to her. She does what I say when I

gentle my tone. My hand grasps her arse and pushes her to ride my thigh.

"Shh, baby girl. I'm sorry I scared you. You're right about all of that. I'm used to being accountable to my family, but they're in the same boat I am. I'm not used to having someone waiting for me at home who isn't used to this."

"I don't think I'll ever get used to it."

"You will because it's unavoidable. You just won't like it." I guide her to keep rubbing her clit on my thigh. "I fecked up because of pride. But I also fecked up because I love you. I'd do it all over again and a thousand more times if it meant getting rid of a threat to you. Yes, someone else could have taken care of them, but I needed to know I could. That I did. I needed to know I protected you like I promised after I failed earlier."

"I told you that you didn't fail. I wish I could have told you before you thought you needed to prove anything. Seamus, I love you, too. I know I'm safe with you. God forbid something like this ever happens again, let your family deal with it. It doesn't mean you didn't protect me. Just the opposite. Allowing your family to help means there's nothing you wouldn't do to keep me safe. I need you to live, Daddy. I want a life with you. I don't want to wait to become something in the future. I want us to be a couple now. I want—fuck, Seamus. I need more. I need you. I ache for you, Daddy—I want to spend time with you like a normal couple getting to know each other. I—uh—fuck I want to feel you inside me. I need you inside me, or I need to ride your leg harder. I ache so much. Help me."

I love how she tried to stay focused. I didn't tell her to grind on me to keep us from talking or to distract her. I wanted to soothe her by getting her off gently.

"Lock the door, *mo stóirín.*" My little darling. I enjoy calling her things no one else does. I want her to know how special she is to me.

She moans with frustration, but she does as she's told. She dashes across the room and turns the lock. She hurries back to me, her tits bouncing. I might come just from that.

"Take your pants off."

She peels them down, and I glower.

"What the feck are those?"

"Panties."

"And why are you wearing them?"

"Because I'm still more used to having them on than not."

"You thought I'd still be out of it today, and you wouldn't get caught. You're adding a long tally to your spanking. Take those fecking things off. You will give me all of them. I will get rid of them. Straddle my face."

She climbs onto the bed, but she's ready to turn away from me.

"I didn't say you were going to suck me off. You're going to hold on to the headboard and ride my tongue first."

"Yes, Daddy."

The way she whispers those two words...

They make me want to wrap my hand around my cock and squeeze. She positions herself, and I encircle my arm around her hips and pull her down to my tongue. I lick her cunt before sucking on her clit. I release her hips and land my hand across her arse with a loud spank. She moans as the force sinks her clit deeper into my mouth. I spank her again after she pulls back. It drives her forward again. I slide my tongue inside before the third one. I keep going, alternating licking and sucking, the spanks getting progressively harder until she's panting. I pull my mouth away, her juices coating my lips.

"Turn around and fuck my cock with your cunt."

She does as I command without hesitation. She leans forward, bracing her hands on my shin, then the bed. It pushes her hips back to me and shows me the place I still haven't fucked. Her arse taunts me. I alternate spanking each side as she rocks her hips. I know this position won't give her the friction she needs against her clit. It gives me a glorious view, though.

"Do you know how much I love looking at you from the back? As much as I love looking at you from the front. I want to lick and touch and kiss every inch of you, Tiera. I want to enjoy every bit of you because you drive me out of my mind with lust. But I always want to lick and touch and kiss every inch of you because there isn't a part of you inside or out that I don't love. And it's possessive as feck too. I want to know there's no other man in this world that has what I do. That every bit of you is mine to worship."

I run my hand up her back as far as I can reach. I trail my fingertips along her spine until I get to her arse. My thumb presses against the hole, the tip slipping in.

"You still haven't fucked me there, Daddy. I can't truly belong to you until you've marked me inside there, too. Until you've been inside me and shot your cum into me. Seamus, I've worn plugs before, but no man's ever been inside my ass. I'm an anal virgin. I need you to claim that because it's the only thing I can give you that I've never given anyone else."

"Turn around." I demand it, and she's quick to obey. "Lean forward."

When she does, I fist her hair rougher than I ever have before. I intend it to hurt—not harm—hurt. She pants while she keeps riding me, and I don't stop her. I keep my voice low. It's not only I don't want anyone hearing me having sex with my girlfriend. I don't want anyone to hear the most intimate things we say.

"You might be my little anal virgin now, but you're going to be my whore soon enough. You're going to beg Daddy to fuck your arse because that's what whores do."

"Yes, Daddy. I'll be your slut. You can fuck my cunt until I'm too sore to take any more. Then you can fuck my ass until I'm begging you to stop, but I don't safe word because I really don't want to stop. Not truly. I want to look in the mirror and see bruises you left from holding onto me."

"I'll mark you however I want." I tug her hair hard. "Look at me." She does as best she can. "You belong to me. I own every part of you to do whatever the fuck I want. Do you want to stop me?"

"No, Daddy."

"Good because you can't."

I watch her like a hawk to make sure our dirty talk doesn't go too far. I don't want to scare her or make her think I'm threatening her. Despite how it must hurt, she leans to whisper in my ear. I let go of her hair, fearful I will harm her with pain she doesn't enjoy.

"Daddy, stop worrying. We're roleplaying, and I know that. But I know there's also an element of truth to the last part. I know I'm not your sub, but I want to submit to your kind of possessiveness. I can be who I need to be and want to be because of it. I am yours, Seamus, but that's because I know you're mine just as much."

"I am, T. I've always been meant to be yours. You have all of me. Heart, mind, and body. You're part of my soul."

"You're part of mine too."

"*Tá mé chun tú a phósadh.*"

Chapter Twenty-Seven

Tiera

It's been six weeks since the gunfight at the O.K. Corral. It took Seamus nearly three weeks to fully heal. The man was like a puppy straining on his leash. When Meridith—a woman who's gentle but delightfully terrifying to Seamus—finally cleared him to work out again, he took that to mean vigorous sex with me. He kept us locked away in his place for ten days—twice what he promised me. We went for walks and the park to kick the soccer ball around, so he didn't truly keep us isolated. I know there were men from his family somewhere nearby. I didn't see them, but I know he wouldn't have let us go out into the open without them. We had those ten days to ourselves. No one called him about work. They didn't text either.

He deleted a text from Makayla without reading it. I saw it come in, and I saw he hadn't read the last one. He blocked her. I thought it was unnecessary, but he said he wasn't interested in anything she had to say since he'd already explained he'd met someone and that they were over.

I've been ignoring Gareth's calls, and so has Seamus. He resorted to calling Dillan, but Dillan refused to speak to him if Seamus wouldn't. The last of it is all coming out right now. Gareth just called. I hesitated, but I answered.

"Tiernan, I can't tell you how I figured out where Dad lived the whole time he was alive, but I did. I just spent six hours there tearing it apart. Like ripping up the flooring, putting holes through the drywall. I found a lock box with documents and email printouts."

"Seamus isn't here. He should hear all of this too."

"I spoke to him a few hours ago. He said I should call you."

Seamus and I agreed yesterday I would speak to Gareth because we suspected he learned shit. I told Seamus I would be fine to hear whatever it is without him, but I would prefer if he heard it straight from Gareth too. I'd meant together, but this will have to do.

"What'd you find out?"

"The real reason Keith wanted to break you and Aaron up is because Aaron discovered he and Dad were embezzling from our widows fund."

How fucking cliché and trite is that?

I'm only slightly surprised. I listen as Gareth continues.

"When Aaron threatened to take you and disappear, Dad took him seriously. He decided Aaron was a credible threat that needed to go away. That's when he started tapping the house phone and bugging your place. He started sending the photos and videos to me to make it look like someone from the outside was stalking you. Tiernan, I really hate this part the most. I'm so sorry. He'd originally told me that he thought the calls before the accident were from some guy in Chicago trying to pressure us. The emails I found make it look like he thought he'd laid the foundation for the car accident by making this guy out to be some stalker who flipped out because you were having another man's—your husband's—baby."

"Except I didn't die."

My rage surges back, and I want to throw something.

"Around that time, he took a loan from Zack to repay what he embezzled. It was a shit ton of money, Tiernan, because he'd been doing it for nearly twenty years. He had to do it because Aaron did more than say you'd disappear. He went to the feds. But the investigation died when everyone thought Dad died. The O'Rourkes discovered Keith was laundering money. That's what you walked in on and heard when you came in the house that day you showed up with Seamus."

It wouldn't surprise me if Sean dug into Zack's accounts and history and learned the money Keith laundered was what came from the fund and Zack's loan.

"Your dad wanted to keep me too emotionally battered to do much more than eat, sleep, go to work."

And fuck Zack. Seamus told me Zack got involved after I became a widow because Darren sold me to him to repay a debt. We didn't know what kind of debt, but I guess we do now. Darren and Zack arranged for Zack to meet me at the BDSM club I joined after Aaron died. Darren kept the threats going, and Zack got off on that, so he added to it. The torture shit Zack sent Gareth came from somewhere on the dark web.

The men who went to clean up what was left of Zack searched the place. They found a dozen thumb drives with hours of Zack and me having sex. He recorded almost every time we were together. I skimmed them to make sure nothing valuable was on them. Seamus was beside himself and tried to stop me. I suggested he do it then. I think he threw up a little in his mouth. No one besides Seamus and I know exactly what's on them, but it wouldn't surprise me if the others guessed.

"Tiernan, I'm still working on it, but I still don't know why Dad murdered Vince."

That's been hard on my dad because, even though he didn't like Vince, he was still my dad's baby brother.

"Is that everything?"

"For now, at least. I wish I could tell you everything, but I don't know it yet. I gotta let you go because I need to call Seamus back about something else."

I don't want to know what that something else is, but I guess I'm sorta glad I spoke to Gareth. I don't know whether I'll keep ignoring his calls or not. I have mixed feelings about that.

"All right. Bye."

"Bye."

I've answered when my mom or dad called every day. Seamus urged me to, and I'm glad I did. Their panic subsided after the first two days. Then it pissed them off that I refused to see them, even though I explained we weren't seeing anyone. By the end of the first week, they'd relented and even spoke to Seamus during the calls. The last time I talked to them, they admitted they could tell how different things were between Seamus and me from how they were before and after I married Aaron.

But there's still something lingering. He hasn't told me anything specific, but I sense things remain unresolved.

I received a pretty bouquet from the Diazes that made him scowl darker than I've ever seen anyone scowl—and that's saying something because I've seen many of Seamus's different expressions and moods. The card was simple, but it still annoyed him.

We're glad you're safe. We know you're too good for him, but love is blind.

I suppose that would annoy me too.

"Tiera?"

386

"In the laundry room."

Seamus has been out all day. He said he had to meet with Dillan, but he didn't say how long he'd be. It's been like five hours. It tempted me to call him, but I told myself it was a normal workday for him, and that couples survived for centuries with no need to talk to each other throughout the day. Just because I don't have a job right now doesn't mean he doesn't have work.

"Stay where you are. Do not come out. I'm serious. Close the door and stay in there until I come and get you."

"What's wrong?"

"Tiera, don't argue. Do as I say."

"Okay."

I turn to reach for the door to shut it, but I have a slight view of the front door. I close the laundry door and turn to lean against it. Holy fuck. He's covered in blood, and I don't know what else. I inhale through my nose and exhale through my mouth. If he were injured, he wouldn't sound as strong. With that much blood, he wouldn't be upright. He wouldn't hide it from me because he knows he can't. It's someone else's blood. Relief and fear alternate pulsing through me.

I put my ear to the door, but I can't hear anything. I keep listening, and at least two minutes go by before I hear the shower turn on. He told me to stay in here because he didn't want me to see him like that. I know what it means. He warned me. Something was out of the O'Rourkes' control. It didn't happen like they planned. They couldn't take care of it at their place. It means Seamus could have died. That makes my heart race.

It was bad enough seeing his wound after Meredith stitched it. Seeing it and truly accepting it came from being shot made me vomit so hard Seamus panicked. He pounded on the bathroom door until I thought he was going to knock it down. I told him I was fine, but he didn't believe me until he was hugging me. He trembled the entire time. He was more upset that he'd upset me than I was about the understanding fully sinking in.

I joked that if he couldn't handle me puking over that, then he'd be a mess when I have morning sickness. He looked like he might faint. The man needs control. He needs to know the people he loves are safe and that he can protect them. A loss of control equates to failure for him and an imminent threat. He's not wrong. At least, not about the threat part. I hate that anything makes him feel like a failure.

"T?"

I hear him call to me through the door. He didn't say open it.

"Stay in there a little longer, please. I'm stepping out, but I'm just going to be in the hallway. I'll be back in a moment, then you can come out."

"Okay."

He sounds a million times calmer than he did when he came in. He's back in control. I sigh and rest my head against the door.

"*Cailín?*"

"Can I come out?"

"Yes."

I ease the door open. He's in a t-shirt and track pants. His hair is wet, but otherwise, he looks like he does when we're hanging out at home. I walk straight to him and wrap my arms around me.

"I'm sorry about that. I didn't mean to be so rude."

"Daddy, I think I need you to tie me to the bed and edge me however you want."

He was semi hard as soon as I hugged him. Now he's got a

fucking iron pipe pressing against me. Just the idea of fucking me gets him this hard every time.

"Damn, Tiera. I have to meet with the others. They'll be here in a couple minutes. They're going to know I want to fuck my girlfriend the moment they walk in."

"Then I think you better give me a quick hard fuck, so you don't wind up with blue balls."

"How altruistic of you."

"I live to serve." I wink at him before grinding my pussy against his hard on.

He hefts me over his shoulder and carries me to the couch. I'm still not used to any man being able to do that since my body changed. He does it whenever he wants—which is often just because he can. The first time he did it after recovering from his injury, I assumed he was teasing me at Finn's. He whispered I was taking too long to finish talking to Ally, and he had a backseat in a town car begging to be fucked on. I backed myself into a wall before he could get hold of me. Everyone else thought I was joking. Seamus understood. He told Cormac to come outside with us.

"Pull your skirt up and open those pretty thighs for me."

Seamus's leg healed with barely a scar. It looked like it was a slight nick, not a bullet grazing him. When Cormac walked over to us by the town car, Seamus put me on my feet and hunkered down like a football lineman. Before Cormac or I knew what was happening, his older brother was over his shoulder, swearing at him because Cormac claimed he'd eaten too much to be fecking around. Seamus ignored him and walked to the end of the driveway and back before walking up and down the four steps to the front door. He put his brother down and cracked a joke about how it couldn't have been that uncomfortable since his middle was getting soft from too many of their mom's brownies. Cormac's in as good shape as Seamus.

Cormac headed back inside, and Seamus gave me a look that told me to get in the car without a word. I think Joey must have taken us up to Connecticut and back down to Jersey before getting us home. It was definitely a scenic tour because it shouldn't have taken that long, but it gave Seamus a chance to prove he really would lick and kiss every part of me. I haven't said a thing about him carrying me since.

"Put your feet on the arm of the sofa, little girl. Knees all the way out."

I obey as he pulls his pants down. He strokes himself and grins. He knows I love watching him do that sometimes, but not this time. If this is supposed to be a quickie, I want him inside me now. He taps the head of his cock against my cunt, then trails it between my pussy lips until it's gleaming with my sticky wetness. He does it slowly, so I'm unprepared for how hard he thrusts into me. I moan and squeeze my eyes shut for a moment.

"You're so tight, T. I won't last."

"Then don't. I don't want you to."

"I'm not getting off before you. Rub your clit."

I do as he says, but he knows I won't get off. I can't concentrate on what I'm doing while I feel him inside me. It's too distracting. He knows when he's fucking me or making love to me—we like it gentle and vanilla as much as we do rough and kinky—only he can get me off.

He scoops me up, and I wrap my legs around him as he perches on the armrest, supporting me as I tilt my hips to the right angle.

"That feels amazing, Shay. Don't stop...Please, don't stop... I'm close... I'm so close...I need to come. Keep going."

"Come on my cock. Then I'm going to fill you with my cum. You're going into our bedroom and getting onto the bed naked. Do not touch yourself. Watch TV. Read a book. Occupy yourself until I come in once the guys are gone. I'm going to watch your pussy push my cum out to know you obeyed."

"Yes, Daddy."

He thrusts three more times, and we both get off. We're kissing and holding each other when the doorbell rings. I guess the guys used to walk in and out of one another's places without thinking about it. But now, they announce themselves when they arrive at a couple's place. I'm glad; otherwise, they would have seen us in a compromising position more than once.

He gives me a kiss and a swat on the ass as I hurry to the bedroom. I walk around to his side of the bed to grab the remote. I'm about to take my clothes off, but I don't get a chance.

"Tiera, can you come out here, please?"

My brow furrows as I toss the remote on the bed. I head down the hallway to the living room. It surprises me to see my dad and Gareth there along with the other O'Rourke men. I walk to Seamus's side and look up at him. His expression is grim, but he tilts his head ever so slightly toward my dad. It's not permission so much as reassurance.

"Hi, Dad." I wrap my arms around him, and he gives me a tight squeeze.

"Hi, nugget."

I hold on for another moment, but then I pull back and shoot him a smile. I let go and walk to Seamus's side. He slides his hand into mine before we take seats in the living room. It's obvious Seamus is used to having his entire family over because there's a massive sectional along with armchairs. When we're out here, we usually cuddle on the chaise part, or I sit on his lap in a reclining armchair. We take spots on the extended part of the chaise, facing everyone else.

I study the group, and no one looks happy to be there. I look up at Seamus again and keep my voice down, not that I think everyone else can't hear us.

"Does this have to do with earlier on?"

"Yes." His tone isn't gruff, but it's clipped.

My gaze darts to Gareth, then my dad. They looked no more pleased than any of the other men.

"What happened?"

I'm still looking up at Seamus, so I watch him jerk his chin toward Gareth. I swipe my gaze to him and immediately grow suspicious.

"Tiernan, I got a call this morning. It was obviously a recording since Zack's dead, and it didn't respond to what I said, but it was his voice. It differed from the other calls I've gotten. It mentioned Seamus. The voice told me I needed to break you up by making it look like Seamus went back to his previous arrangement and didn't tell you. If I didn't, he'd record Cormac somehow and send it to you. If I failed, he'd wipe out your bank accounts and sell off all your investments. He knew everything about you, so he knew you're frugal. He knew you have a nest egg."

I do, and I haven't kept that a secret from Seamus. I told him I had enough to live on until I find another job. He didn't argue with me, but he also doesn't let me pay for anything but my mortgage, utilities I don't really use anymore because I've essentially moved in with him, and my student loans. Anything else, he covers.

We talked money, and I've never met anyone with as much as he has. He could probably buy a small country and feed the entire population for five years. I will never earn as much as he does. And it was all from legal ventures. I have no idea how much he has from—other stuff.

Seamus wraps his arm around my hips and rests his hand

on it. My dad and Gareth don't miss the gesture. I lean into him.

"Who made the call?"

"You won't like it." Gareth looks like he wants to sink into his spot on the sofa.

"No sh—Of course I won't like someone threatening me." I catch myself in front of my dad.

Seamus pulls out his phone and taps a contact.

Motherfucker.

Seamus makes the call and puts it on speaker.

"What do you want, *pinche care chimba.*"

I don't know that one. Cormac leans to whisper to me. "Fucking vagina for a face or there abouts."

"Watch your mouth, or I'll wash it out for you. Tiera can hear you."

There's a long silence. I glance at Seamus, but he's looking at the phone. Isn't anyone going to say something?

"Why'd you do it?" There. I gave in and spoke first.

My question is met with more silence.

"You're something of a Catholic, aren't you?" It's rhetorical so I don't expect an answer. "I'm one too. I didn't have to memorize huge chunks of the Bible in school, but I remember some verses. The Gospel according to Matthew. It goes something like you've heard of an eye for an eye and a tooth for a tooth. But if a man strikes you on one cheek, you turn it and offer them the other. If he strikes that one, then you give him your cloak. Do you remember that one? I know Seamus said you went to Sunday School together. There's this other one from Romans. I don't remember the exact words, but the gist is I do not do the good I want, but the evil I don't want is what I keep doing. Does that one sound familiar?"

I still don't think I'm going to get an answer, and I don't.

Who knows who else might be listening on the other end? I don't give a flying fuck.

"Because I can't help but do evil, I just can't seem to live by turning the other cheek. I've spent three years tampering with evidence to make fires look like they started themselves. Sometimes I make it look like something else started it, just so I can hide who did it. Sometimes they look like the building owner set it for the insurance claim. I didn't do the good I wanted even though I knew the things I did were evil. But I feared what would happen if I didn't. I couldn't bear what did when I refused."

I let what I just admitted sink in.

"Since I can't help it, I can't be expected to turn the other cheek. I seriously suggest you get an extra fire policy on everything you own. The things the rest of the world knows about and the things I will dig up because I have the time to do it. To understand how to put out a fire, you have to know how it starts. How it thinks. You have to know the ways it will outsmart you. Do you know those things?"

The silence is predictable and stupid at this point.

"I do. I will burn all your shit down, Alejandro. I will burn everything that belongs to your family. Everything I think might belong to you. I will burn all the things you want. You fucked me over, and now you'll take it up the ass like a big boy. Fuck you."

I'm practically shaking with how pissed I am. I don't know if he's known about me for years or a few weeks. I don't know if he's been a part of this from the start or just since we met. But he saved me just to fuck with me by being my rescuer. He kept me alive to torment me.

Seamus speaks up. "Do you know what the name Furey means? Icy or cold in Irish. Tiera might sound heated right now, but I promise you, there will be nothing in her veins but ice when she goes after you. I won't stop her either. You wanted to suck a woman into this, now you're going to deal with the consequences."

My dad moves to sit next to me, and Cormac takes his spot. He puts his hand out, and Seamus hands over the phone.

"This is Brant Furey, Tiernan's father. I have some questions of my own. Do you know what Brant means? It means firebrand or sword. I'm both fire and ice. I'm an enforcer who can make a weapon out of just about anything. I'm paid to cause as much trouble as I end."

My dad pauses, but I think it's for dramatic effect.

"Her mother's name is Orla. Do you know what that means? Golden princess. People have said Tiernan's mother and I gave her a man's name because we'd wished we'd had a son. We wished for a boy or a girl as long as our baby was healthy. Do you know what Tiernan means? It's little lord. My daughter comes from a golden princess who fell in love with a man made of fire and ice. When she was born, she struggled to breathe, and it made her skin colder than normal. But once she did, she commanded the room with a single cry. So, my daughter has been the little lord of ice since the moment she came into this world. But she has every bit of my fire in her."

My dad gives mirthless chuckle, and it makes the hair stand up on my arm. This is the enforcer, not the man who cuddled me when a dog terrified me.

"She was destined for what she does. When she tells you she'll burn you to the ground, you better believe she will. Just like she commanded that delivery room, she understands fire, and it follows her commands. Do not underestimate my daughter ever again. I am not who you should fear. The O'Rourkes aren't who you should fear. It's my daughter because she's Tiernan Furey, the ice princess."

I've heard that story before, and it's never meant as much as it does now. I don't think I've ever heard my father so proud of me, and he's always been my champion. I took Aaron's last name when we married, and I debated whether to keep it. But I reverted to my maiden name because my parents chose my first name for its significance.

I look at Seamus. The O'Rourkes were once a powerful clan that ruled what is now County Leitrim. I looked it up. It's said the name comes from an Old Norse word for king. The clan's motto is "victory." I rather like the sound of Tiernan O'Rourke. I think it fits.

Seamus takes the phone from my dad and speaks to whomever is there. The call hasn't ended, but no one's said anything after the original greeting.

"Alejo, I know you're still there. I can hear you panting in fear. Whatever twisted shite you thought to cause once you realized how much Tiernan means to me is going to cost you. I won't stop her. I'll hand her the match. I have never trusted you, but you fooled my future wife into thinking she could trust you. I don't like that. You know I've come close to killing you more times than you've come close to killing me. You know the only reason I can't is because of your uncle. Enrique, I'm sure you can hear this. It was one thing when Alejandro and *Tres J's* fecked with me, but they brought my woman into it. Not only won't I stop her from whatever she's plotting—and believe me, from her expression right now—it's going to cost you. A lot. I will have my pound of flesh. You know that from how your morning started."

Was that why Seamus came home and needed a chance to get cleaned up and calm down?

"Seamus, you haven't scared me a single day of your life. You don't scare me now. Ramble your threats, little boy. I've been in this world nearly twice as long as you. There is so much more I can do that I've been holding back. I've let you and my nephews squabble over the years because you can sort your own petty shit out. But come near my nephews for real, and you will have a widow before you marry her."

"Are you threatening Seamus?" I speak up. I assume I'm listening to Enrique.

"I wouldn't get involved, Ms. Furey."

"Your *pinche gurrupleta sobrinos* got me involved by supposedly saving me just to turn around and extort my future husband. They used me as bait. Rather than threatening Seamus, I suggest you get a hold of your family. From the outside looking in, you don't seem to have control of them. They're doing what they want despite your position because you can't stop them. That's usually called a mutiny. I can be fair if nothing else. You and all your nephews apologize to me. Whatever deal you have going on—no, I don't need nor want to know the specifics—that's worth at least five million goes to the O'Rourkes. And you promise your family keeps all the women in this family off limits. Do that, and I won't torch your quaint and crumbling empire."

It's going to take me a while to get past the fury—the real kind, not what Americans think my name is—but I can offer an olive branch first. I'll follow through on my promises, but I don't want this powder keg to explode until Seamus's family is in place to benefit.

"Ms. Furey, I pray one day Seamus realizes what a remarkable woman he's found and how lucky he is you've even looked in his direction. I've looked up your past because it's inevitable you're going to be an O'Rourke soon. I don't doubt anything you've said. I will not give your soon-to-be in-laws a penny, but I will agree to the rest."

I've been watching Seamus, and he nods.

"I accept on the condition that I reserve the right to retract my peace offering since your nephews wished to cost me something worth more than five million dollars. They wanted to take Seamus from me. Fuck around with me, Enrique, and I'll make sure your family's in the building when I torch it."

I'm a sick and twisted fuck because I mean it. The need to protect Seamus and our relationship is pathological. I'm certain the Diazes believe I'm posturing and full of shit. They're probably laughing at my expense because they believe I sound ridiculous. Let them. I won't do anything until I'm properly provoked. But I won't back down.

"Enrique, you and your fecking despicable nephews—Tiera's right about that—owe my future wife an apology. I haven't heard it yet."

One by one, I hear Enrique, Pablo, Alejandro, and the three brothers I learned are called *Tres Js* apologize.

"I accept. Have a good day, Enrique. It doesn't look like it'll get too hot."

I sit back and exhale. I haven't looked at anyone but Seamus since my dad handed the phone back to him. I expect to see shock, disdain, or mockery when I look at the other men. Gareth looks like he'll bolt the moment he can. But the O'Rourke men are grinning and elbowing each other. My brow furrows.

Finn laughs but keeps his voice down. "Anastasia Kutsenko scares the shite out of Salvatore Mancinelli. No one knows exactly what she did to defend herself when a rival bratva kidnapped her, but it was violent to a degree most of us won't go to. She had to do it because his nephews caused her kidnapping. He keeps a healthy distance from her. You are Enrique's Ana. He's going to stay at least ten arm's lengths from you."

Dillan shakes his head but is still grinning. "I thought my wife reminded me a lot of my sister because she doesn't back down for shite and neither did Colleen. But God help us all. You'll be the new ringleader, just like Colleen was. She got us in trouble with a pretty smile on her face. When Seamus and Cormac somehow always got away with whatever the rest of us didn't, Colleen doled out her own kind of justice to make sure they were punished, just like we were. Seamus won't get away with shite. About time."

Seamus holds up the phone to block my dad from seeing his other hand. We all know he's flicking his cousins off. He looks back at the phone.

"Enrique, make no mistake. I've neither forgiven nor forgotten. Stay away from the O'Rourke women, or I'll tell Laura."

"Who?" I lean past my dad to ask Cormac.

"Laura Kutsenko grew up next door to Pablo. They used to be super close, and she used to think of him like an uncle. She won't speak to him after some stuff that's happened. She doesn't care about anything going on that isn't bratva, but she doesn't tolerate any woman being the Diazes' target. She's made it very clear she will be Enrique's judge, jury, and likely executioner. She'll find out about this, eventually. He'll have to face her, and that's a punishment of its own."

"I think I'll like Laura." Even if we can never be friends.

Seamus hangs up the call and looks around. I'm certain he still needs to talk to his family, but the men stand before I can. They're quick to say bye, and my dad leans over to hug me. Before I know it, I'm alone with Seamus.

"Are you angry I butted in? Did I sound completely crazy?"

He says nothing, but he leans back as he takes my hand. He covers his dick with it, and he's as hard as he was just before he fucked me against the very sofa we're sitting on.

"I'm beginning to think you being hard has nothing to do with me, and everything with you just breathing."

"Oh, it's all because of you. You just breathing is enough to turn me on. I love you fierce. Come here and let me show you."

He taps his lap, and I straddle him. He stands, and I clutch his shoulders. He'd never let me go, but it always feels like it for a moment. He carries me into the bedroom and straight to the bed.

"I'm going to make love to you, *cailín*. I'm going to take my time and worship all of you. You're strong, resilient, confident even when you don't think you are, brave, and caring. When we're done—and that may not be for a month or two—I'm taking you to the jeweler to pick out your engagement ring."

"Are you proposing to me?"

"Not yet. I need the ring first."

His grin is so boyish and cute. He might have a baby face, and he might have been shy when we met, but he's all man as he makes love to me.

Saint or sinner—I don't know. But Seamus O'Rourke is the greatest blessing I've ever had.

Epilogue

Seamus

I'm glad Tiera and I decided on this vacation. We needed it individually, and it's been good for us as a couple. She's always wanted to come to the Azores, so I gassed up the jet and off we flew to the secluded—they are in the middle of the Atlantic, after all—islands to hike and lay out on the beach. I glance over at her and reach out my hand to rest it on her thigh before I close my eyes.

We have a private bungalow that opens out to the beach we're on. We have a pool too. So far, we've had sex in the pool, on the beach—not to be repeated because it leaves your arse itching for hours—and in the ocean. I haven't convinced her to swim naked in the pool, but I got her to toss her bathing suit far enough onto the beach not to wash away.

I can't blame her for the pool part since my brother and cousins are here, too. She actually asked if Cormac and Shane could come. She felt badly about the married guys, but the wives assured her they expected their husbands to go. She's more relaxed than she would be if we hadn't brought my family along as security.

I sat next to her on the sofa while she picked out bathing suits online. I begged her to get a particular bikini that's pretty much dental floss. I used my fingers, my tongue, my dick. Anything I could think of to convince her. She relented after the fourth orgasm. I haven't pressed her to wear it since we've gotten here. She's more comfortable in a one piece, so that's what she wears most of the time. But we've slipped out to the beach just after dusk three times, and she's worn it then.

The first time, I came humiliatingly fast. Like so fast, I just looked down in shock and betrayal at my cock. She wrapped her hand around it as we stood on the sand after I watched her walk ahead of me—that was not an accident. She didn't even stroke me once, and I was done. The second time, I at least fingered her first and got her off because the moment I was inside her, I came. The third time, we didn't even make it out of the bedroom before I had her bent over the bed, fucking her arse.

That reminded us of the first time we were together. She brought that dress with her, and she wore it out to dinner the first night here. Unfortunately for the dress, Tiera needs to find a seamstress to mend it. I got a little excited when we got back from dinner and might have ripped a few seams open. I wince thinking about that since she said she loved that dress.

"Daddy, are you thinking about us having sex?"

I open my eyes and shield them against the sun. "Why do you ask?"

She points to where it's obvious I have been. But that tends to happen whenever I think about my girlfriend. I squeeze her thigh and tug it toward me as we recline on side-by-side loungers. I roll onto my side, and I know she's trying not to stare at the scar on my thigh. It still bothers her, but she never says anything. As much as she hates me thinking I'm a failure for what happened that day, I hate her thinking she caused it.

I push up onto my elbow and lean across her and give her a searing kiss. Her hands roam over my back and shoulders until I want to slip inside her. My relatives nearby be damned.

"Fecking hell, Tiera. I'm going to embarrass myself again, and this time my brother and cousins are going to know about it. Stop being sexy as sin."

She giggles, and I love hearing it. She says she hasn't laughed as much as she has in the past seven months since she can't remember when. She still thinks I'm joking and shakes her head.

"Haven't you realized yet, *cailín*, I'm not prone to exaggeration?"

She snorts her laughter. She trails a hand from my neck down my chest, along my belly to my board shorts' waistband. She tugs at the drawstring. She pulls the front away from me and peers down my shorts and licks her lips. Does she even realize she did that? I truly don't think she does.

"We can both see I'm not exaggerating when I say you're a colossus." Her other hand glides down my back.

"You touching me isn't helping."

She lets go, and the elastic snaps against my skin. She draws her hands in and tucks them under her chin playfully. She tries for an innocent expression, but it's pure seductress instead.

I stand and slide my arms underneath her. I carry her back to our bedroom and set her down gently.

"Put a shirt on and pair of shorts. We're going for a walk before I maul you."

"I don't mind if you maul me. I rather like it."

"Clothes, Tiera."

When she turns to the closet to grab something to wear, I marvel at how lucky I am. I've found someone who understands me on an intuitive level. She knows what I need and when I need it. She knows when I need a partner, an equal I can talk to about things going on. She knows when I'm struggling to feel like I have any control in this fucked-up world we exist in. She submits and lets me feel like life isn't spinning me in a dryer. She makes me laugh with a silly side I never suspected—a side she thought died three years ago.

"Okay. I'm ready for a walk." She doesn't sound ready. She sounds annoyed.

"Come here, *mo stóinín*."

I hold out my hand, and we go back out through the French doors in our bedroom. We head to the beach, and I guide us in a direction we haven't been before. We chat about the new job she's starting in two weeks when we get home. She's going to be a reliability engineer for the NYFD. It's a dip in salary, but it'll allow her to continue to use her education in applied mathematics and her knowledge of fire sciences.

She knows no one in my family will ever ask her to get involved in our off the books businesses. She offered because she couldn't imagine not after all the years the O'Briens took advantage of her. She cried with relief when I practically yelled at her to never suggest she get involved in anything that could get her arrested or hurt.

"Do you want to stop up ahead? I think the view'll be nice." I point to a spot about a hundred yards from us. The view—the landscape not Tiera—is nice everywhere on these islands.

"What's that in the sand?" She squints as we approach. "Is that a mini soccer pitch? Did someone draw goal boxes?"

She glances up at me and is about to look back when she halts. She tilts her head to look at me. She studies my expression before she keeps walking. There's a soccer ball waiting in the center. She walks to it, but I let go of her hand and jog to the far goal.

"Seamus?"

"Let's see how you do with me as keeper." I stand in the goal box I scrambled to draw when she was in the shower this morning. I told her I needed to check with the guys about our dinner reservation. I did, but I also dragged Cormac here to help me get this ready.

She shakes her head and shrugs. She slips her foot under the ball and kicks it up to bump it higher with her knee. She uses her chest to push it forward before dribbling it toward me. She takes ten steps before she stops. She picks up the ball and turns it over until she can read the writing.

For the longest time, my only goal was to survive. Now my goal is to make you happy until my last breath. An bpósfaidh tú mé?

She walks toward me, carrying the ball. She's staring at it, clearly trying to sound out the part she doesn't understand. She stops when she nearly bumps into me. My hands go around the back of her thighs as the ball drops from her hands.

"Seamus?"

"*Is breá liom tú, cailín. An bpósfaidh tú mé?*"

I open the ring box in my hand, but she appears too surprised seeing me down on one knee. I watch her swallow.

"I only understood one word. What does the rest mean?"

"I love you, little girl. Will you marry me?"

She nods vigorously.

"I need to hear it, T."

"Yes! Yes! All the yeses!" She sinks to her knees and nearly knocks me over with her enthusiastic hug. "Daddy, I love you."

Her kiss makes life worth living. Knowing I'll come home to that for the rest of my life is like a prayer come true. Knowing we'll have a family together one day is what hope is made of. Knowing she's said yes makes me feel like more of a man than any fight I've won, any punishment I've doled out.

I gave up thinking redemption is possible for a man like me. I sin without repentance because there is no choice besides life or death. Mine, my family's, and now Tiera's. But Tiera's granted me three miracles—she's shown me I can be loved, I can love, and I can be more than a mobster. Surely, that makes her a saint.

When Shane responds to a security alarm about a trespasser on his construction site, he never imagines he'll find a woman ready to go toe-to-toe with him on everything. He soon discovers she's one secret layered upon another. They're more alike than either wants to admit. Discover Shane and Ella's story in *Mob Bride.*

Before you go, would you like a *free extra epilogue* with a steamy public scene days before the wedding?

Subscribe to my newsletter and get this gift from me to you.

Get a bonus epilogue

Enjoy this free bonus epilogue with a scene from *Mob Saint* where Seamus and Tiera have a not so private steamy moment after a soccer game.

Check out this extra sexy scene with Seamus and Tiera. Get your Copy here.

Don't miss the next installment

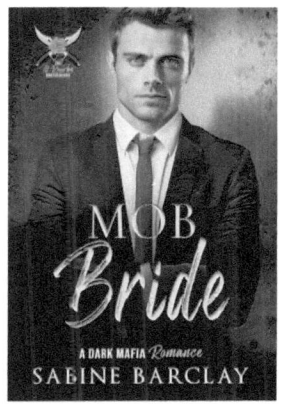

Family comes before all else.

I'll do anything to protect them.

I just didn't expect to need her to do it.

But she's mine now.

She makes me happy.

She understands me.

I'll go the ends of the Earth to make her just as happy.

Get in the way of that, and you'll wish you hadn't.

Meet Shane and Ella

Thank you for reading Mob Saint

Sabine Barclay, a nom de plume also writing Historical Romance as Celeste Barclay, lives near the Southern California coast with her husband and sons. She loves her days at the beach soaking up way too much sun, a good Netflix binge, and a strong hot chai. Her heroines are independent women who can defend themselves but love their Alpha heroes who want nothing more than to protect their soulmates in her Mafia Romances. She's Gen Y/Oregon Trail and loves creating engrossing contemporary romances that will make your toes curl and your granny blush.

Subscribe to Sabine's bimonthly newsletter to receive exclusive insider perks.

www.sabinebarclay.com

Join the fun and get exclusive insider giveaways, sneak peeks, and new release announcements in
Sabine Barclay's Facebook Dubious Dames Group

Do you also enjoy steamy Historical Romance? Discover Sabine's books written as Celeste Barclay.

The O'Rourke Brotherhood

Mob Boss
BOOK ONE SNEAK PEEK

DILLAN

I hate meetings like this. I don't need to wear pants from some shitty off-the-rack suit that are too tight to *try* to make my dick look bigger. I'm secure in my cock size, and I don't need to show how big my balls are for people to know I run this part of the city. I loathe strip clubs too. I'm past the point where naked women make my jimmy do jumping jacks. I can appreciate a hot bod and gymnast level strength, but it does nothing for me. These douchebags? They're practically ready to come in those cheap arse pants. Why am I here? I keep asking myself that. Seamus and Shane are doing just fine with these negotiations. I'm just here to look good. I'm the muscle today. Or rather my name and my position. Who the fuck thought— way, way back in the day —that giving the mob hierarchy nautical names was a good idea? Fucking Skipper. This isn't motherfucking Gilli-

413

gan's Island. None of these numb nuts are the Professor, even if they think they're fucking Mr. Howell.

But who is that? If this is *Gilligan's Island*, then she's Mary Ann.

I glance at Seamus, but he's focused on the Albanian he's trying not to lose his shite at. Shane smirks at me when I dart my gaze to him. I cock an eyebrow as the waitress walks over. She's definitely not a dancer. She has too many clothes on. But you can barely call the pieces of thread she's wearing clothes. She's got on a bikini top that's barely more than pasties, and the skirt she's wearing would make my Catholic grandmother do somersaults in her grave.

It's the standard uniform for this place, but somehow it doesn't look right on her. Not because she doesn't have a banging body because she does. Not because she's a butter face— but-her-face —as in great bod, not so great face. She's beautiful in a super understated way. That's part of what makes her look out of place. She has next to no makeup on. I think those are even her real eyelashes. The natural beauty is drawing way too much attention.

"'Scuse me."

She tries to step around Zef Hoxha, the *kyre* of the Albanian mafia here in New York. When he reaches out to grab her wrist, I'm out of my seat with my hand around his. He never gets a chance to touch her because my hold is so tight he can't bend his fingers. I keep squeezing until it must feel like I'll snap the bones.

"No touching."

Zef drops his arm as much as my hold allows. I let go and stare at him before I tilt my head toward the waitress. I narrow my eyes, and he knows what I expect.

"I apologize, miss."

"That's all right, sir. Here's your drink."

She's polite as she hands him his glass. Unfortunately, to put down the rest, she has to bend forward, giving everyone a view of her glorious cleavage. Tits and arse are what sell here, and she has them in spades. I'm certain it's why my cousin hired her. If I sit down, everyone will know I'm just as guilty as these fuck nuts because she's made my dick do something that hasn't happened in a strip club since I was like twenty-three. I'm now thirty-three.

Mob Boss
Mob Star
Mob Princess
Mob Saint
Mob Bride
Mob Knight

Do you also enjoy steamy Historical Romance? Discover Sabine's books written as Celeste Barclay.

The Ivankov Brotherhood

Bratva Darling
BOOK ONE SNEAK PEEK

LAURA

As I sit across from the four Kutsenko brothers, I press my lips together to keep from drooling. No four men should be so strikingly handsome. Not all from the same family, anyway. I fight a valiant battle against letting my gaze drift toward the eldest, Maksim, whose ice-blue eyes bore into me. After years of negotiating billion-dollar investment contracts while facing countless ruthless businessmen, I've learned to keep my expression studiously blank. But it's a true struggle today. Instead, I focus my attention on the squirrelly lawyer sitting across the conference table. While he's disingenuous with each comment, he's a good negotiator. But I'm better. How cliché am I?

While I feel Maksim watching me, I focus on Dmitry Yakovitch as he continues to argue the merits of the venture capitalist company I represent, RK Capital Group, merging with

Kutsenko Partners. What he means is the merits of Kutsenko Partners acquiring RK Capital Group, then stripping it and making it another money-laundering shell corporation. While most people in New York have little awareness of the Russian mafia, I do. The Kutsenko brothers' names appear on no titles or deeds anywhere in New York City, but it wasn't difficult to determine which shell companies likely belong to them. Their assumption that I'm unfamiliar with them is proving beneficial to me as they continue to whisper amongst themselves in Russian. I think they may even believe they're convincing me that they don't speak much English.

The senior partners of RK Capital Group know who I'm negotiating with, though they may not know I'm aware of these Russians' more nefarious operations. They've given me the go-ahead to agree to a merger with an eventual acquisition, but only for the right price. A price to the tune of twenty billion dollars. Considering an investment firm like Goldman Sachs is worth nearly one-hundred-and-twenty billion dollars, my clients' asking price appears reasonable.

"Mr. Yakovitch, I shall stop you now." I raise my left hand, pen caught between my index and middle fingers. When I have his attention, I lean back in my chair and casually twirl the pen over my index finger and thumb. "Fifty billion is my clients' asking price. You know that. Your clients know that. RK doesn't oppose the merger. What they oppose is the insulting offer you've made. It's nearly noon, and I'm hungry, Mr. Yakovitch. I have a delicious ham sandwich waiting for me. I even have three chocolate chip cookies waiting for me. If we aren't going to make any progress, I shall let you go, so I can move onto my eagerly anticipated lunch."

I cant my head just enough for me to appear as though my gaze rests solely on the opposing attorney's face, but I can see each

Kutsenko brothers' reaction. My face battles yet again against showing my emotions as I fight not to smirk. Their muted but surprised expressions confirm what I already know.

"Please tell your clients to make a reasonable counteroffer, or I will conclude this meeting and enjoy my ham sandwich and cookies."

Dmitry glares at me before turning to Maksim and his three brothers. In rapid Russian, he doesn't interpret my suggestion. Oh no. There's no need for that. I can't catch every word because his voice is too low. But I catch something along the lines of "The bitch refuses to budge. What now? A fucking ham sandwich. More like a stick up her ass."

Maksim swivels his chair to look at his brothers. In Russian, he says, "Fifty billion is ridiculous. She's not so stupid or naïve not to know that. My guess is they'll settle for twenty billion. We offer fifteen."

"That's barely better than what we already offered," Aleksei, the second-oldest brother, argues. "She'll be eating the fucking sandwich and dipping her cookies in milk before we walk out the door. We need the buildings."

"We offer twenty, Maks," Bogdan, the youngest, insists.

As I watch the brothers discuss, their voices barely lowered, I pull my lunch sack from the black leather satchel by my feet and set it beside my laptop. It's a ridiculously pink floral bag with an embroidered monogram, the L and D overlapping. It's an empty prop, but they don't know that. I watch as five sets of eyes narrow. I offer a smile that would appear innocent in any setting other than this meeting. It's patronizing, and I know it.

Bratva Sweetheart
Bratva Treasure
Bratva Beauty

419

Sabine Barclay

Bratva Angel
Bratva Jewel

Do you also enjoy steamy Historical Romance? Discover
Sabine's books written as Celeste Barclay.

The Mancinelli Brotherhood

Mafia Heir
BOOK ONE SNEAK PEEK

LUCA

This asshole is pissing me off. We've been going around in circles for five minutes, and the longer we stand out here, the greater the likelihood someone will spot us. I have a sixth sense about these things. It's why I'm still alive at the ripe old age of thirty-one.

"Espinoza, enough already. Either sell to us or don't, but we set the price. Your tequila is good, but it isn't nectar from the gods."

I'm watching Carlos Espinoza, some lackey for the Mexican Culiacán Cartel, try to maneuver me into paying more than the agreed upon price. I know it's so he can skim off the top.

"It's as close as you're going to get. You've upped the order, so the price per case goes up."

My uncle, Salvatore Mancinelli, is the New York don. He negotiated this deal, and I warned him it was a bad idea. But what do I know as his underboss and heir? I'm not backing down.

"Haven't you ever heard of a bulk discount? The more I order the better the price should be. No one else around here is buying from you. You know we're your only choice in three out of five boroughs. You aren't going to the Bronx because you won't get more than pennies there. You aren't going to Queens because you don't want to run into the Colombians. You aren't going to Manhattan because then you face the bratva along with us. And what are you going to do in Staten Island? Sell to us anyway? We control Staten Island and Brooklyn when it comes to liquor stores, so take the money and go."

"Luca, there are plenty of liquor stores in Brooklyn that aren't owned by Italians. I'll go there."

We aren't friends. He's patronizing me by using my first name. Fuck him and the horse he rode in on. I have other solutions for this shit.

"And I'll just take what I want from them for free. That's not a half bad idea. The deal's over. Take your shit with the worm in it and go."

"Motherfucking racist. Not all tequila has a worm in it."

"You're selling Mezcal. It's known for the fucking worm. I wouldn't start calling me names, you *penche hijo de puta.*"

Fucking son of a bitch.

He has twenty-five crates of stolen tequila that he's trying to offload because he knows he can't sell it at his own liquor store.

"What did you call me?"

Carlos takes what he thinks is a menacing step forward, and his two bodyguards do the same. Not smart. Neither of my two bodyguards nor I react, but the three men in each of my cars open their doors. They won't do more than that. It's just a reminder that the Culiacán can try, but the *Cosa Nostra* still run New York City.

"This is the third and final time I say this. Sell or leave."
Every head turns toward the liquor store's back door as it opens.
A gorgeous blonde steps out, and I wish I had the time to
appreciate her beauty, but she's about to die. Carlos and his
men draw their guns and pivot toward her. My men pull their
weapons too, but we keep them pointed at the Mexicans. The
woman stands like a deer in the headlights for a second before
ducking behind the industrial garbage dumpster like a frightened rabbit. Three shots hit the metal almost at the same
moment. That's all it takes for my men and me. The two bodyguards standing with me aim for a guard each, and I set my
sights on Carlos. We squeeze our triggers, and the men fall.
Screeching tires tell me Carlos's driver takes off. I hear more
gunshots as at least one soldier in my cars tries to shoot the
escaping vehicle. Glass shatters, but the sedan keeps going. I
hear more tires squeal as one of my SUVs takes off and chases
the guy. I holster my gun and wave my men to do the same.
I inch forward toward the trash can, but I see the shadow shift.
The woman bolts from the other side. She's still the frightened
rabbit, but I'm the fox pursuing her. She's fast, I'll give her that.
But she has to be at least a foot shorter than me. My legs are a
lot longer and cover a lot more ground with each stride.
She weaves among the cars, most likely believing it's harder to
hit a moving object. She isn't wrong, but I have no intention of
shooting her. I push myself harder and pounce as she darts out
and tries to cross the last stretch of parking lot to reach a better
lit area near a bus stop. I lunge.
"Stop running, *piccolina*. I won't hurt you."
I wrap my arms around her and pull her back against my chest,
but I'm quick to spin her around and put space between us as I
grasp her arms. Of course, she fights me.
"If I wanted you dead, I would have shot at you, too."
"It doesn't mean you won't kill me after."

423

She's breathless as she continues to struggle. I almost let go to take a step back, insulted at what she implied. But I can't blame her. If I were a woman, I'd be terrified of the same thing.

"I'm not going to rape you. I'm going to talk to you."

"Talk? You are not a man who talks if you just killed a guy."

"To keep him and his men from killing you. I told you, if I wanted you dead, I would have shot at you too. And I wouldn't have missed."

She stops struggling against me, but her eyes continue to dart from one place to another, trying to find somewhere to flee. I know I can keep her in place with only one hand, so I release her left arm. I still have a firm hold on her right one, but I haven't held it nearly as tightly as I could.

"I'm Luca. I know you figured out you interrupted something you shouldn't have. Did that man know who you are?"

"Yes."

"What about his driver? Would he know you?"

"Yes."

"Do you have a name?"

"Yes."

"*Piccolina*, we won't get very far if yes is all you can say. Are you willing to answer me with more than one word?"

"No."

I knew that was coming, and I grin. I can't help it. I wasn't wrong about her being gorgeous, but I doubt she wants to know that's what I think. At least, not if I want her to know I won't assault her.

"Fine. I have more than twenty questions I can ask that you can answer with one word. Do you work at the store?"

"Sometimes."

Ah, an improvement.

"Did Carlos know you were still working?"

"No."

"Do you have a car, or do you take the subway or bus?"

She raises her chin and remains silent. Smart but counterproductive.

"The subway or the bus will get you killed. You're too easy to find and follow. Do you have a car?"

"Yes."

"Can you stay with someone instead of going home?"

She refuses to answer.

"If that man knew you and you sometimes work in the store, then he knew where you live. If he found that out, so will someone in his cartel."

"I know. Let me go. The longer I stand here, the more likely someone is to come back for me."

"No one will touch you while I'm here."

"Arrogant. If he shot at me, he would have shot at you."

"And he would have died, anyway. What's your name?"

"Jane."

"Look, I know you won't get in one of my cars and let me drive you somewhere. In most cases, I would say that's a smart move. But you did nothing wrong tonight except for leave work at the wrong time. I know that, and you know that. But the Culiacán won't see it that way, *piccolina*."

She freezes for no more than five seconds before she trembles so much that I can see it. I don't know what drives me next, but it's the same instinct that's made me call her little girl three times. I pull her to my chest and tuck her head against it. I stroke her hair down to her shoulders, rubbing my hand up and down her back. This is the most inopportune moment to notice she isn't wearing a bra. I will my body not to react.

"What does that mean?"

Her voice is barely more than a whisper, but I know what she's asking.

"It means little girl."

"I should be insulted, but the way you say it..."

"It has nothing to do with your height. I know you're not a child."

God, do I know she's not. She feels amazing. Her tits are soft as they press against me, and I can see she has the most delectable ass. I'd love nothing more than to cup it and squeeze until she goes up on her toes and begs for me to wrap her legs around my waist and fuck her. For fuck's sake. Stop, you disgusting asshole. That is not what you need to be thinking about.

"Why didn't you shoot me? Whatever you were talking about, if it was with a Cartel member, then it wasn't completely legal. Carlos didn't want me alive to talk about seeing you together. Why are you letting me live?"

"I told you. You did nothing wrong but try to leave work. He should have checked the building before starting the meeting. That was on him. The only thing I take issue with is you leaving by yourself and walking into a dimly lit parking lot. I suspect you do that often, and that's too dangerous. Jane Doe, I don't hurt women."

Mafia Sinner
Mafia Beauty
Mafia Angel
Mafia Redeemer
Mafia Star

Do you also enjoy steamy Historical Romance? Discover Sabine's books written as Celeste Barclay.